Peng

JILLAROO

Rachael Treasure was born in Hobart in 1968 and now lives on a sheep farm in Tasmania with her husband John, her daughter Rosie, and a menagerie of farm animals including working dogs from their Castleburn kelpie and border collie stud. Rachael and John spend part of each year helping John's family with their High Country cattle operations on the Dargo High Plains in Victoria.

Rachael began her working life as a jillaroo before attending Orange Agricultural College in New South Wales. She has a BA (Communication) from Charles Sturt University, Bathurst, and was a rural journalist before becoming a full-time fiction writer. Her first TV script, *Albert's Chook Tractor,* was made into a drama for SBS TV. Her second, bestselling novel, *The Stockmen*, was published by Penguin in 2004.

Futher information about the author may be found at www.rachaeltreasure.com

JILLAROO

RACHAEL TREASURE

Penguin Books

PENGUIN BOOKS

Published by the Penguin Group
Penguin Group (Australia)
250 Camberwell Road, Camberwell, Victoria 3124, Australia
(a division of Pearson Australia Group Pty Ltd)
Penguin Group (USA) Inc.
375 Hudson Street, New York, New York 10014, USA
Penguin Group (Canada)
90 Eglinton Avenue East, Suite 700, Toronto, ON M4P 2Y3, Canada
(a division of Pearson Penguin Canada Inc.)
Penguin Books Ltd
80 Strand, London WC2R 0RL, England
Penguin Ireland
25 St Stephen's Green, Dublin 2, Ireland
(a division of Penguin Books Ltd)
Penguin Books India Pvt Ltd
11 Community Centre, Panchsheel Park, New Delhi – 110 017, India
Penguin Group (NZ)
Cnr Airborne and Rosedale Roads, Albany, Auckland, New Zealand
(a division of Pearson New Zealand Ltd)
Penguin Books (South Africa) (Pty) Ltd
24 Sturdee Avenue, Rosebank, Johannesburg 2196, South Africa

Penguin Books Ltd, Registered Offices: 80 Strand, London, WC2R 0RL, England

First published by Penguin Books Australia 2002
This edition published by Penguin Group (Australia),
a division of Pearson Australia Group Pty Ltd, 2005

3 5 7 9 10 8 6 4

Copyright © Rachael Treasure 2002

The moral right of the author has been asserted

Design by Cathy Larsen © Penguin Group (Australia)
Thank you to our cover models Rachel Parsons and Chris Stoney
Typeset in 10/14 Sabon by Post Pre-press Group, Brisbane, Queensland
Printed and bound in Australia by McPherson's Printing Group, Maryborough, Victoria

National Library of Australia
Cataloguing-in-Publication data:

Treasure, Rachael.
Jillaroo.

ISBN 014 3004085.

1. Family – Victoria – Fiction. 2. Family farms – Victoria – Fiction.
3. Man-woman relationships – Victoria – Fiction. I. Title.

A823.4

This project has been assisted by the Tasmanian Writers' Centre and the Australia Council,
the Federal Government's peak arts funding and advisory body.

www.penguin.com.au

For my husband John, who made this book happen,
and for my dearly departed Dougall dog.

PART ONE

CHAPTER 1

Rebecca Saunders whistled to her dog.

'Mossy, go way back.'

In the glow of morning sunlight the little kelpie, light on her feet, seemed to float out around the mob of sheep in the holding paddock. All that could be heard was her chain jingling around her neck as she cantered and crouched on the dusty ground. The sheep huddled and turned their heads towards Mossy's motionless red and tan form. Bec turned to open the gate, knowing Mossy would bring the mob steadily into the yards. Unclipping the chain, she dragged the gate's creaking rusted frame across the dust and whistled Mossy to stalk towards the sheep. Rebecca watched the sea of ewes move slowly towards her, with the ram in their midst. He held his head high with his lip curled up. His horns spiralled pompously around his face like a barrister's wig. Bec frowned at him. His scrotum really bothered her. It had been on her mind most of the night.

She remembered her withered, wiry grandfather holding out his hands with his bony fingers curved around the air.

'Two full beer cans,' he had said. 'Two full beer cans. That's what they're s'posed to feel like.' Her grandfather had lifted the weighty scrotum of one of his rams and jiggled the hefty sack in the palms of his hands.

'Here, girl, have a feel.'

So, how come, Bec thought to herself this morning, the ram which her father just paid $2000 for had one full beer can and one minibar bottle of gin for a scrotum? She shook her head as she closed the gate. If only her father had listened to her.

Walking briskly to the yards she wondered if she could persuade him to take the ram back. She pictured the tweed-coated stud ram breeder with the grey hairs growing wildly from the tip of his nose and lobes of his ears. She couldn't believe the man still spoke with a voice from the Mother Country.

'Yars, he's a fine upstanding sire,' the breeder had said as if chatting to the Queen. He'd folded his arms across his belly and jutted out his chin. 'Covered magnificently to the points, with a noble head.'

'Wanker,' she said out loud to the image in her head. If only they could take the dud ram back and spend the money on a performance-tested ram, one that was guaranteed to make an impact on the flock. But Rebecca knew her dad would never agree.

As she swung the splintery wooden gate open into

the largest yard, she heard an outburst of barking and the rush of hooves raising dust.

'Bloody oath, Dad.' Bec shook her head, sighed and rolled her eyes.

Her father, Harry Saunders, was slipping through the wire fence yelling as he went, 'Mate, Spot, Mardy . . . *come behind*! Get back in *behind*! *You dogs*! Mardy! Come here! Get out of that!'

His crew of motley dogs were working in a pack, singling out a sheep and chasing it to the fence, biting as they went. Little Mossy was doing her best to keep the mob together while the other dogs zoned in close to the sheep, causing chaos.

'Geez Dad. Are you sure you need all those mongrel dogs? I almost had them yarded.' She put up her hands to shade her eyes from the sun and squinted at the circling mob. 'Useless!'

Her father, red in the face, was holding Mardy by the collar. The young pup's eyes were fixed on the sheep and his tongue lolled to the side of his mouth as he panted. So keen to work, Mardy was oblivious to the fact he was being choked.

'Don't you start, girl,' her father warned, pointing a finger at her. To prove her point Bec whistled gently and called softly, 'Mossy, come here to me.' Mossy turned one ear towards Bec, glanced at her, then trotted to her side. Rebecca turned her back to her father. She knew he hated the fact that her dogs worked so well for her, but at the same time she felt sadness for his untrained dogs.

'Yard the friggin' sheep yourself then,' she said under her breath.

'What did you say, girl? What did you say to me?'

Ignoring him, she marched off to sort out the tangle of tubes and drench-guns, which lay in a pile on the floor of the shearing shed's grinding room.

A while later her father's large silhouette appeared in the doorway of the shed. His shadow spread across worn and weary floorboards.

'You know we really don't need you in the yards today, Bec,' the shape said. He moved into the dimly lit shed. 'Your brothers will be down after they've fixed the pump. They can do the drenching and I'll shift the stock.' He wouldn't look at his daughter's face.

'But Dad, I told you, I've finished school . . . I'm home to work. For good.' Rebecca heaved a twenty-litre drench drum onto the grinding room bench with a thud.

'Bec, you know there's not enough room for all three kids on the place. We've had this discussion before. No daughter of mine is going to make a so-called career out of farming. There's no future in it.'

'But farming's good enough for your sons?' Bec turned to look at him and stood with her hands on her hips.

Harry took off his sweat-stained hat and ran his fingers through his greying hair.

'That's different Bec. The boys don't know anything else . . . It's what they were raised to do . . . The boys are capable of making a go of it here.'

'And I'm *not*?' Bec moved to meet his eyes.

6

'It's for your own good, Rebecca.' Looking away from her, he turned his attention to the drench-gun on the bench. 'Your best bet is to go do a teaching or nursing course, then you can marry a nice farmer who isn't up to his neck in debt or paying his way out of a bloody divorce and . . . then you can . . .'

'Bulldust Dad!' exploded Bec. 'Listen to you! Do you know how bloody sexist you sound? I was born here and I'm staying here . . . I have just as much right to the farm as Mick and Tom.'

She threw down the cluster of tubes which were entwined around an empty drench pack. 'There's no way I'm going to become a nurse or a teacher so I can marry some conservative sexist pig who expects me to bake scones all day and join the CWA with his mum. Stuff that . . . and stuff what you think.'

'Don't you dare talk to me like that, girl.' Harry had his back to her and Bec could see his shoulders tense in anger as he pretended to adjust the dose on the drench-gun. Knowing she was pushing him, she moved closer.

'Dad. I'm not doing what you say. I'm not doing teaching. Or frigging nursing. How can you be so . . . so . . . bloody pigheaded. Chrissake, Dad! Mum's a *vet* for crying out loud. You know all about career women who live on farms . . . and the way they have to race about to please their husbands and families and then juggle their workload. Just because you couldn't handle Mum having a brain . . . and a life, don't take it out on me!'

7

'Leave your mother out of this!' He turned to face his daughter. 'If you hadn't stuffed around so much with your dog training and horses and worked harder at school you could've got into vet science Rebecca. It's your own fault.'

'But I never wanted to be a vet! All I've ever wanted was to come home here to Waters Meeting and get this farm running how it should be.'

'What's that s'posed to mean?' Harry slammed the drench-gun down on the oily wooden bench. 'Are you saying I don't run the place properly?'

'Anyone can see this farm's run in the dark ages. Mick and Tom are too afraid to ask you to look at the books. You're always threatening to kick them off the place if they don't toe the line. You don't know half the things they'd say to you if they had the guts . . . like the fact that the new-beaut ram you've bought is a dud. They're scared of you. The same way you were scared of Grandad.'

At the mention of her grandad, Rebecca saw a muscle in her father's jaw flinch. She knew she should walk away now and go up to the house. But she continued.

'We're going down the gurgler, Dad, because you won't let go. So now I'm telling you. I'm not going to do teaching or nursing. I've enrolled in agricultural college next year and I'm going to get a degree in business and then come home and sort this mess out. I need a year's practical experience as a jillaroo before I go, which I'll do here and now, on this place.'

'Like hell you will.' Her father stood to his full

height and took a step towards her, towering over her and pointing a large finger in her face.

'Let me tell you, Little Miss High and Mighty – you won't be doing work experience here for your useless snobby uni course. Either you respect and obey my wishes or you pack your swag up now, take your precious well-bred dogs with you and get off this property. And then you won't be coming back to this part of the river so long as I'm alive on it.'

In disbelief, tears began to well up in Bec's eyes, but her father just dug deeper.

'Your brothers will be glad to see the back end of you. Miss Self-Righteous. I never wanted another child. I told your mother no, it will be hard enough to carve up this block for two boys, let alone a third child . . . let alone a girl. Now get out of my sight.'

Rebecca felt her bottom lip begin to quiver, so she bit it, trying to keep the hurt inside. Since the day she was born she had been her grandfather's girl – never her father's. From before she could remember, Grandad had rugged her up and sat her high in the saddle in front of him. They had ridden, she and he, up into the mountains looking for strays. He always muttered along the way, about the world around her, about the animals and the trees and how to find a beast and how to work a dog. She never remembered her father being there, or teaching her how to crutch a sheep or rope a calf or even boil a billy. The more love and attention her grandfather gave Rebecca, the more Harry withdrew from her. Over the years, the anger of the two men grew and the silence sizzled between them. It spilled over to Harry's wife, Frankie, and then to his daughter.

In the shearing shed, standing before her father, Rebecca couldn't take it any longer. The words came in an angry burst and her face contorted with grief as she shouted at him. The rest of the shed blurred around her and she raged at his face.

'No wonder Mum left you! You can't see it, can you – you're going to lose the lot!'

'Shut your self-important little mouth and get out of my sight. You'll be off the place by lunchtime or I'll shoot all of your wretched dogs. I've had it with you.' She felt his fingertips press angrily into the flesh of her shoulders as he shoved her towards the doorway. Shocked by the violence of his touch, she half stumbled down the steps. She looked up at her father and wanted to shout at him, but no sound came. Mossy trotted to Rebecca's side and whined. Rebecca looked into her father's unblinking eyes. There was cold in them. Even hate. She knew he meant it. Their frequent clashes since she was a child meant she had turned to the mountains, the soil, the plants and that beautiful river for happiness and strength. Deep down she knew her father resented her because she had a passion and a connection with the land that he never seemed to grasp even after years of farming. She became absorbed in the world of her dogs. She trained them, loved them, talked to them, studied them. She peered deep into their brown eyes and reached their souls. Her dogs were a way of escaping her father's seething undercurrent of anger and his inability to show her love.

Now that her mother, Frankie, wasn't here to place a calming hand on her father's shoulder, she knew she had to go. She turned from his eyes and ran away from the shed. Mossy trotted after her and leapt up to lick at her hands in an offer of comfort.

Bec was almost wailing as she threw clothes into a worn rucksack in her bedroom. The sobs jarred and caught in her throat. She ran down the stairs and out of the darkness of the house. Bundling her bags and swag into the back of her old Subaru ute, she motioned for her three dogs to jump in the back. They looked at her with worried eyes as she clipped each one onto the short chains. Shaking hands turned the key in the ignition. Her sobs turned to strangled screams of anger and she pounded the dashboard with her fists as she drove. She'd been at school when her mother had packed up and gone. She wondered if her mother had sobbed and wailed, or just calmly driven off with her proud head held high. Through a film of dust on the rear-vision mirror, Bec saw her father standing with his fists clenched by his side at the door of the shearing shed.

In the paddock next to the driveway her black mare tossed her head and galloped along the fence line beside the Subaru. When the ute shuddered over the grid, the mare propped at the last minute and skidded to a halt just inches from the splintery strainer post.

From the road along the hillside, Rebecca couldn't bear to look at the sleepy green valley below. It tore her heart out to leave her river. Waters Meeting. Her place.

Harry had watched his daughter as she jogged away from him towards the large stone house on the rise. Her light-footed dog had danced at her heels, looking up at her. How many times had he seen her swipe away the tears like that? He could still see her as an angry red-faced child screaming at him after he had said no.

No, she couldn't come mustering on the High Plains. No, he wouldn't drive her to a dog trial. No he just wouldn't. No. When Harry said no, she would run to her grandfather who said yes. The feelings of guilt flooded Harry. Guilt over only half loving his family and his farm. He had always been too busy for Bec. He had spent his days brooding in the machinery shed. Lingering around the homestead to avoid his father. Driving the tractor for hours sowing a crop, not dreaming of the rich green shoots which might come with rain, dreaming instead of being some place else, of being an engineer or an architect, even a pilot. Not here, trapped on the farm, living under the same roof as his father.

Never had he heard a kind word or any praise from his old man. They were cattlemen. They were farmers. Nothing was said. As a young man, when Harry pushed the cattle too hard and they came tonguing into the yard with saliva stringing from the sides of their mouths and steam rising from their backs, Harry's father turned his back in disgust. The natural stock-manship that could never be learned had skipped a generation. It wasn't in Harry. His father made him feel he was an outsider in his own home, but he had nowhere else to go. Harry was the only son and his pre-determined role in life was to take on the farm. It was just the way it was.

Harry had watched Rebecca slam the house gate and stomp through the leafy green garden. She'd marched onto the verandah and disappeared inside the old house. Squinting, he had looked for her in her room on the second storey, then closed his eyes and sighed. What was it about his daughter that made him so angry? Why couldn't he give her a chance?

Suddenly he heard his dogs bark excitedly outside and he remembered the ewes in the yard. Harry rushed through the shed and out into the glaring sun.

'Friggin' dogs.'

Like well-fed wolves the dogs toyed with the sheep simply for the sport of it. They worked the sheep back and forth until they were tight on the rail. Some of the weaker ones were down, smothered by the weighty push of the mob. Standing on his hind legs, Mardy mounted a sheep which was jammed against the rail. He gripped his white paws around its hips and thrust his puppyish pelvis towards it. His eyes glazed over with pleasure and his pink tongue dangled.

As Harry came near, the older dogs dispersed, slinking through rails and out of sight. Young Mardy continued to thrust at the sheep.

'Git out of it. Ya dirty mongrel!' Grabbing a fistful of fur and puppy skin, Harry yanked the dog away from the sheep. The pup grovelled at Harry's feet, wagging his tail frantically and widdling all over himself and Harry's boots. Harry stooped and picked up Mardy by the scruff of his neck. He slammed the pup's body into the ground so hard that his yelp was more like a strangled cry as the air was forced from his lungs.

'Git out of that!' he yelled and shook the dog again before tossing him over the yard fence like a split log on a wood heap. Mardy rolled twice in the dust, found his feet, then cowered and scampered away under the shadowy shearing shed, tail jammed up to his belly.

Harry had still been shaking mad when he'd returned to the experting room to set the drench-guns up for the day. The white liquid had sped along the clear plastic pipe as he'd squeezed the nozzle of the gun. He'd set a higher dose as the ewes were looking heavy. Trying to ignore the fact his hands were shaking, he'd slung the drench pack over his back and just then heard the engine of Rebecca's ute fire and turn over with a grumble. He'd glanced towards the entrance of the shed where the bright sun lay in a square on the wooden boards. Dumping the pack he'd moved to the doorway to look for the ute. All her dogs were on. Her swag too. The little white vehicle had buzzed over the house paddock grid and sped past where he was standing. As she'd fleeted by, Harry had seen her profile. Her jaw clenched tight, her pretty mouth twisted with anguish. Rebecca hadn't even slowed at the second grid as she roared down the road with a trail of dust flying up into the air.

She was leaving. She was really going. He didn't think she would. Like his wife Frankie, he didn't think she would. They were both such bright sparks, mother and daughter, both so full of laughter and ready for fun. They always had a joke to fill in the angry gaps Harry created in the huge broody homestead. Frankie and Bec had all the words. It was Frankie who always did the talking for her boys. Like an interpreter she would bridge the gap between Harry and Mick and Tom. On the day she left she ranted to him about his lack of love, and all the while, trapped in Harry's mind, were words which would not come out. He'd wanted to say, 'Don't go, Frankie.' He'd wanted to talk it through. He loved her. He would sell up for her. But the words wouldn't come. The words never came. He just stood still and watched his wife drive away. On a grey Monday morning, she simply drove away and left him there. With the kids and the farm and the huge gaping hole that was his life. And of course, with the silence that remained.

His fists clenched by his side, Harry's body began to shake in slow waves. A hoarse expulsion of air from his lungs turned into shuddering sobs. He put a big hand to the splintery doorframe to steady himself and covered his eyes as if to ease the shame. The shame of hurting Rebecca so much. The shame of crushing his sons. He was losing his family. Losing his land. He slowly walked down the rickety shearing shed steps and sat on the bottom one with his head in his hands. From under the dark grating he saw two frightened brown eyes staring out at him. Gently he whispered, 'Here pup. Come here Mardy. I'm sorry mate.'

Mick and Tom sped towards the yards on the muddied four-wheel bike. From over Mick's shoulder Tom could see his father halfway down the race, jammed thigh-deep in sheep. Mick parked the bike in the shade of a twisted old red gum and waited for Tom to get off the back. Tom could tell from the way his father handled the sheep that he was in a stinker of a mood.

Head bowed, Tom walked towards the end of the race and bent to grab the plastic straps of a drench pack.

'Getting through them, Dad?'

'I'd be getting through them a lot faster if you two had got here sooner.' Harry pushed the metal nozzle into the mouth of the sheep and gave it a shot of drench. Its teeth rattled against the gun as Harry roughly withdrew it and shuffled forward to reach for the muzzle of another ewe. He wouldn't look at his son, but Tom had seen. He was too afraid to ask why his dad's eyes were red and his face drawn and grey. He wanted to say, 'What's the matter, Dad?' But you never said things like that to Harry. Tom could talk to him about the weather, or the river, or the price of wool and beef, but never feelings. Not with Harry.

Tom slung the backpack onto his broad shoulders and went to the drafting gate end of the race to make a start on the ewes. It was hard to believe his father had been crying. It shocked Tom.

Mick leaned against the rail, arms folded across his broad chest, not noticing his father's mood. Mick had modelled himself on his father. He used his height and size to make his presence felt, not his words.

'Where's Bec? She could muster the next mob while I get started on the cultivating,' Mick said.

'She won't be mustering today. Now get going. We'll be through these by the time you get the next lot in.'

Mick shrugged off his father's gruffness and ambled towards the bike. Tom clenched his jaw. She's been fighting with Dad again, Tom thought. Typical.

Tom had to wait until after lunch to look for his sister. In the kitchen he pushed the dry crust into his mouth and stood up to leave. He looked over to his father and Mick.

Mick was slouched at the massive wooden table which stood in the centre of the room. An old-fashioned cedar clock ticked loudly from a high mantlepiece behind him. The pendulum swung behind golden rushes painted on glass. Mick bit noisily into a carrot and chewed slowly as his eyes scanned the classified ads in the machinery section of the newspaper.

Harry didn't spend much time in the kitchen since Frankie had left for the city. He used to sit where Mick was sitting now. Instead, Harry spent his lunchtimes in the glass sunroom which had been added to one end of the kitchen. Frankie had insisted it be built to let some light into the old house. She'd demanded it when they were first married and it had at last been built when the children were in primary school and after Harry's mother had died. The room was made of glass set in steel frames, with a large sliding door opening out into the leafy old garden. Over the years grapevines and wisteria had covered the structure, bringing the view of twisted green climbers, grapes and drooping purple flowers into the house.

Tom looked at his father in there now. He remembered when he was a child sitting in a patch of sun in the brand-new room. He was home from school, sick with the chicken pox. Frankie had spread out big sheets of butcher's paper and crayons onto the slate floor.

'There you go, Tom. Have a go at these. You could find your calling. You never know.' When Frankie came back in and saw the swirling colours of fish, an ocean garden and a castle under the sea, tears came to her eyes and she put her hand to her mouth.

As a child Tom had always wondered why his drawings made his mother cry. Later, when he was much older, he realised that she was stunned by his artistic talent and at the same time devastated that his future would be determined by his father.

That day, when Harry had screwed up his son's drawings and shoved them in the woodstove, was the day Frankie had begun to loathe her husband's need to dominate his children. It was the day she'd realised he would repeat the pattern of fatherhood that he had learned. It had filled her with a quiet, endless fear.

Harry now lay back on a cane couch beneath the leafy ceiling. Rural newspapers, letters, bills and torn envelopes were scattered around him. A china plate covered in crumbs and a browning apple core sat next to a half-full mug of tea on the slate floor. His feet, clad in rough woollen socks, were crossed at the ankles, his brown arms folded over his slim stomach. An *Australian Farm Journal* magazine covered his face as he dozed.

Tom stared at his silent brother and father. Peas in a pod. Since Frankie had left, the task of cleaning up the kitchen had fallen on Rebecca and Tom. Mick always seemed to worm his way out of anything to do with housework or stock work. But Bec and Tom liked it like that. They gave each other comfort. But sometimes in the dark, in his room, Tom pulled angrily at his hair. He wanted his mother back. He felt guilt over Rebecca. He leant on her to mother him. Some nights he cried for his mother, on other nights the anger towards her raged inside. Voices in his head. Angry, wailing voices.

In the sunny kitchen, Tom sunk his teeth deep in the white flesh of an apple and shut the kitchen door behind him. He needed to find Rebecca.

The concrete on the back step felt cool through his jeans as he sat and pulled his boots on. The ginger cat smudged its stripes against Tom's back.

'There are two places to find her when she's cracked it like this,' he said to the cat.

'Come on, Ginge. Let's go find her.' He set off down the path. The cat sat and watched him walk through the garden gate and down an embankment towards the river.

He expected to find her at the river, throwing sticks to her dogs. He visualised her small frame and long blonde wavy hair stuffed under a cap. He saw her in his mind standing there with a vague smile, tossing sticks into the slow-moving water. But this afternoon she wasn't on the riverbank.

He walked to the side of the house. A clump of peppertrees shaded a line of hollow logs. He remembered the fight Rebecca had had with their father over the kennels. She hadn't wanted to put her dogs in the run with Harry's pack of barking crossbred and inbred dogs. She'd wanted her dogs nearer the house so she could teach them to be quiet. Her father had said no and called her a dog snob, but she'd moved her dogs there anyway. At night Tom would sometimes hear her open her bedroom doors and step barefoot onto the verandah to speak gently to her three dogs.

This afternoon at the kennels none of Bec's kelpies danced on the end of their chains or whipped up clouds of dust with their tails. The chains lay in the dirt and a wind blew up and whispered in the dark pines which shut out the sun. Tom looked up at the house to the second-storey verandah and pictured his sister

20

leaning with her elbows on the white wooden rails, her long hair blowing gently in the breeze. Without her dogs here, Tom knew she was gone. He could feel she had left Waters Meeting. It was the same cold feeling he'd had when his mother had gone. He jogged to the house and opened the heavy front door, tearing cobwebs away as the door swung open.

In the musty dark of the jumbled office Tom quickly dialled his mother's number. He glanced at the office door while he waited for an answer. If his dad caught him using the phone in the middle of the day to speak long-distance to his mother, he'd hit the roof. At last he heard his mother's efficient but friendly voice on the answering machine.

'Hi, you've called Dr Frankie Saunders, leave your name and number and I'll get back to you. If it's an animal emergency please call our North Road surgery on 87 34592 . . .'

Tom waited for the beep.

'Mum. Tom here. I think Dad and Bec have had another fight again. This time she's taken all her dogs. She's probably headed to your place so when she gets there tonight, give me a call. Thanks Mum. Bye.'

Tom hung up and went back to the kitchen to take some chops out of the freezer for tea. Mick and Harry were still in the same position as when he'd left them. They said nothing and didn't look up when he came into the room. Despite the glaringly bright day outside, Tom felt the darkness of the house wrap around him. It covered his shoulders and pressed down on the back of his neck. He shut the kitchen door quietly and climbed the stairs in the hallway.

On his bed, Tom curled up and hugged his legs to his chest. 'Stop it,' he told himself sternly.

CHAPTER 2

The dogs in the back swayed and bumped against each other as the ute swept around a corner. The back wheels slid for a second on corrugated gravel and then regained their grip. Rebecca clasped her hands tighter around the steering wheel, her knuckles white.

'Bastard!' She thumped the dusty dash. Tiny particles flew into the air and hovered in the sunshine. Her head hurt from the anger. The initial tears, fear and panic had evolved into rage. Rage against her father. Against the divorce. Against his bloody arrogance. She wiped her face and nose with the sleeve of her old work shirt. Couldn't he see that she'd only ever wanted to be at Waters Meeting?

Her grandfather had recognised she was not only intensely interested in the farm but was also smart about farming. Savvy. He could see she had a head for business as she sat by him when he tallied the books. And in the paddock she had an incredible understanding

23

of the sciences that went with nature. Every week she read the rural newspapers, and she devoured farm journals and stock magazines. And she always asked a stream of questions about everything.

Then there was her 'gift'. Her grandfather called it that. She had a natural affinity with animals. A talent to move a mob of sheep or a herd of cattle quietly and confidently. Dogs looked her in the eye and responded to her every command. Horses settled under her weight and pushed themselves for her when she asked them to work harder. She was gentle with cattle and sheep and understood their pecking orders and natural movements. As soon as she could ride, Rebecca couldn't get enough stock work. At ten years of age she'd happily sit in the saddle from dusk till dawn. She loved to listen to her grandfather talk about each beast – the merits of eye pigmentation in Hereford cattle, the genetic traits most likely to be carried down the lines, like white faces, or horns.

Her father, on the other hand, gained pleasure from cogs, rivets, pistons, hydraulics, nuts and bolts. He avoided stock work and volunteered for all the machinery jobs about the farm. He was a 'shed man'. A 'tool man'. A 'diesel dick' as the men in the pub would say. Harry's father neither admired nor respected this fact about his son. Rebecca knew that. And right from the start Mick was like his father. As a young boy he tinkered endlessly in the shed. Bec remembered him with a spanner in his small hand, standing above the lawnmower with its insides spread across the ground.

'What's Dad gunna say?' she'd said to her older brother as she kicked at the wheel of the mower.

'Shut up, dick brain,' Mick had said and smeared grease down her cheek. Sometimes when they were kids, Mick made Bec so mad her cheeks would flush red and she would jump on him from behind and pummel him with small closed fists. Tom would always come to Bec's side and try to calm her and drag her away from Mick.

But the one thing that they all shared was their love for the river. It seemed to bond the whole family together at times. In flood. In drought. In the good times. The long summer days of swimming. It held them together. A long watery thread running through all their souls.

Bec longed for the river now. She slowed the vehicle and pulled off the gravel road onto a grassy bank. She kicked open the creaking door of her ute and got out to unclip the dogs.

'Hop off,' she said, as all three kelpies launched themselves from the tray. Bec squeezed between the brown rusted wire of the sagging old fence. On the steep bank her Blundstone boots slipped and gripped on dry gum leaves. The dogs bounded ahead, sniffing, squatting and sneezing. Mossy stood and examined the air with an upturned nose while Dags and Stubby clattered and crashed in the nearby scrub. Rebecca was making her way to the river. Her river. The river that carried her name and on days like this, she thought, her soul.

The Rebecca River was in surprisingly good health

for an Australian river. Its clean free-flowing waters slipped over golden-brown boulders and past enormous rivergums. On its steeper banks young grey-blue wattles and dusty green ti-trees dipped their leaves into its coolness.

The Saunders' homestead overlooked the Rebecca River's source, where two headwaters carved their way around a massive craggy mountain range. The Rebecca River opened up onto the rich river flats of Waters Meeting. There, the red and white hides of Herefords could be seen through open bush on the hillside, and prime lambs and merinos dotted black-soil river flats which sprouted green most of the year. But a few kilometres on, the mountains closed in again. The sheer rocks forced the river's water to darken and race through steep gorges. Above Waters Meeting the reliable rain on the mountains gave birth to the river and controlled its many moods.

One thing her father had right about farm management was the river. He loved it. The mountains isolated their property from other farming communities so weeds along the river's banks were easier to control and eradicate than further downstream. Every year, armed with backpacks sloshing with spray, Bec, Tom and Mick were sent on search and destroy missions for blackberries.

Bec would cry out to the hills, 'Who ya gonna call?' Her brothers, leaping to her side with spray nozzles in hand, answered in unison, 'Berry-busters!' On long summer days Bec could hear Harry's chainsaw ringing in the hills as he cleared the willows which had once choked the Rebecca River's sandy banks.

Now, through the thick heat of the bush, Rebecca could hear the river gushing and rushing over smooth boulders. Rain had flushed the river fresh so she could smell its sweetness as she neared it. The dogs splashed into its coolness and swum with their ears flattened and their mouths pulled back as if smiling. Sitting on a rock, Rebecca tilted her head to one side and smiled sadly at them.

'Not a worry in the world for you fellas . . .' Mossy flopped her tail in a wet wag, acknowledging Bec's voice. Stubby, a little black kelpie with tan eyebrow markings and tan paws, the most comical of her dogs, cantered out of the waters to her and shook silvery droplets from her short coat. Silver river beads landed in Rebecca's hair and smattered on her shirt.

'Piss off, Stubby!' She smiled at the dog and flicked her hand in the air. The dog bounded away into the water, tail wagging.

As the dogs rolled and romped on the riverbank Rebecca's eyes again filled with tears. Salty drops falling into the fresh shallow pools which lapped at the rocks. She thought of home, upstream. She had seen hate in her father's eyes this morning. The tears flowed as she thought of her horse, Ink Jet. Maybe she could've hitched the float and taken her. She kicked the toe of her boot on the river stones. It was all so impossible. Her tear-smeared cheeks itched so she rubbed her face with her hands and pushed back the strands of hair which had escaped from her ponytail. Gazing into the cool green river water she peeled the papery bark from a stick.

Her mind wandered back to the past when she lived at home. Before she was sent to boarding school. Before her mum left.

In Bec's eyes, Frankie had been a legend. Up and clattering around the big old homestead by five-thirty. Wood for the stove. Lunch for the kids and Dad. Dinner for that night in the freezer wrapped in Gladwrap and labelled 'Tonight's tea – just heat'. She'd get the three kids to the school bus by seven-thirty, then she'd be off to work for the day. Pulling calves, bleeding sheep to test for Johne's disease, cutting the nuts out of cats.

Some nights her mum stayed in town with friends so she could go preg-testing early in the next valley. Or she'd arrive home in the dark, long after the chooks had roosted and the dogs had retreated to the warmth of their hollow logs. Frankie would bustle through the door in splattered overalls surrounded by a waft of cold air and the smell of cow dung. Her auburn hair awry in a halo of waves, her cheeks flushed a lovely pink. But within minutes of her busy entrance, the silent anger and resentment from her husband would drain the pink from her cheeks and she'd brush her hair flat and get on with the washing up. Rebecca now knew her father's seething mood had been over an affair that had never existed.

Sometimes in the high-ceilinged hall Bec would hear the low growl of her father and the gentle pleading of her mother's voice. She only caught glimpses, but even as a child she sensed what her mother felt. He'd wanted a country bride but had married a vet. He'd wanted farming in the grand sense but the wool prices had fallen, the beef prices plummeted and the yards and fences slumped further into the soil each year. His silent sulks when Frankie left for work turned into a seething mute rage that was taken out on the animals he ran for his livelihood. Harry's veins bulged in his neck when a cow went down on her knees in the crush; electric jiggers stung and stung her until her deep bellows echoed in the hills. Sheep blocked in the race eventually staggered through the drafting gate with bloodied noses, tottering, punch-drunk. Harry's ribby dogs felt the bones of his knuckles slam into their sides. As his bank balance fell, so did his love. Hope could be seen in his sons, but blame was laid on the females in the family. Rebecca felt it. She felt his hate and blame grow.

She remembered the day he said it. He was standing by the wood stove peeling an orange with his sleeves rolled up. 'We've enrolled you at the Ladies' College.'

'Stuff that for a joke,' she'd said and felt her ear burn hot with the cuff from his huge hand. The smell of orange lingered in the strands of her hair.

The day she left for boarding school she'd stood before her brothers.

'Seeya, shortarse,' Mick, her eldest brother, had teased. He'd bunched up his big fist and jovially punched her on the arm.

'Hope you come home a loidy!'

Tom, who was only eleven months older than Rebecca, hung his head and shoved his hands deep into the pockets of his baggy jeans. She ruffled his sandy hair until he looked at her. His eyes were solemn and brown. Bec thought they looked like collie-dog eyes. Quiet and gentle. He gave her an awkward hug and simply said, 'Seeya, sis.'

Tom had wanted Bec to go to the local high school with him. He was shy. The teachers labelled him 'arty', but as the other boys began to sense Tom's differences, he soon learned to hide his talents. In primary school Rebecca had always stood up for him. Defended him against Mick's taunts and the punches from the other boys.

'Don't worry, Tommy,' freckle-faced Rebecca had said, 'I'll punch them in the guts. Then they won't come near you.' In the tiny country school, Rebecca and Tom had shared classes. She'd sat next to him and scowled at the bigger boys.

When Tom finished primary school their father had demanded both boys stay nearby to work on the farm, so they went to the local high school on the bus.

Now she was being sent away to boarding school Bec carried with her a quiet ache that came from the prospect of being separated from Tom. In the sandpit and in the river, or in the dark attic at night, the two shared dreams together. Whispering stories about Waters Meeting. Dreams about the farm and the animals that they might one day have when they grew up. Tom always followed Bec's lead. Without her he'd sink into a quietness. Bec knew he'd suffer as much as she would while the school term stretched endlessly on.

From the car, Bec had watched her brothers' shapes grow smaller and smaller in the distance as they stood and waved outside the front of the house.

'Why didn't you stand up for me, Mum? Why didn't you tell Dad I shouldn't go? Why?'

Her mother just shook her head.

'We can't afford it anyway, Mum . . . I know it. Why the hell didn't you stand up for me?'

'I can't at the moment, Rebecca. I just can't at the moment. You'll understand one day.' Her mother had stared straight ahead at the road, bolt upright as if a glance at her daughter would cause her whole soul to crack.

Bec had wanted to scream, 'Why did you marry him in the first place? Why?' but instead she'd looked out of the car window and watched the rush of gumleaves as they drove away from Waters Meeting.

The three dogs now came to lie by Bec's side on the grassy patches by the river. They stretched out flat, the sun drying their coats, Stubby on her back with paws spread out in the air.

'You ol' tart, Stubs.' Bec scratched the dog's belly which was swollen with pups.

'Oh what to do, what to do?'

She knew she could travel south to the city where she had boarded and where her mother now worked. Four hundred ks south and she could be there by dinnertime. Her mother might be home from the surgery by then. Frankie would open the door of her flat smelling of perfume and hibbataine disinfectant. Rebecca pictured her mother's smile of greeting yet she'd feel the stiffness of her mother's hug. Rebecca knew Frankie would be thinking, 'What's she done now?', while rolling her eyes as they hugged. Frankie would fuss over what to do with the dogs because, like she'd said before, all the surgery kennels would be needed for clients. Bec would feel as though she was getting in the way of Frankie's busy city life. But she'd turned up there before like that, when it'd all got too much with her father. And Frankie had fitted her in.

On the riverbank Rebecca looked into the brown eyes of Mossy and sighed. It would be so easy to head south to her mother's.

'Bugger it, Mossy, let's head north.'

When Frankie Saunders dumped her shopping down at the front door of her flat she was thinking about anal glands. The groceries she had bought from the twenty-four-hour Coles sunk down in the bags which sighed and rustled on the floor. As Frankie scrabbled in her handbag for her keys, she thought back two weeks ago to the consultation with a border collie–corgi cross. It had been one of the worst cases of blocked anal glands she'd seen in a dog for some time. She'd been in such a hurry to get the awful job over with that she'd only noticed the presence of the dog's handsome owner when he was about to leave.

The man, Peter Maybury, had smiley blue eyes which were surrounded by lines of laughter. He was a little overweight but nice, in a big, soft sort of way.

'Bring him back in next week, Peter, if you could, and we'll express his glands again for you.' As she looked into his eyes and handed him the receipt their hands touched. Frankie felt a tingle run through her and she smiled back at him.

When he brought his dog, Henbury, in again, Peter lifted him carefully from the slippery surgery floor onto the table.

'There you go, Henners, it's all right.' He stroked the dog firmly and slowly as Henbury stood on the stainless steel bench on his wonky feathery legs. Frankie asked all the standard questions and then started to gently pry a little. She liked this man.

'He's a touch overweight. Does he get plenty of walks?'

'I walk him every evening,' Peter said.

'There's no one else who has time to take him in the morning?'

'No! No. Divorced.' Peter shrugged.

'Ahh,' said Frankie. 'You'll have to cut back his food intake then.'

'It'll be tough. I love cooking and he's so convincing when he looks up at me with those hungry eyes. You know that look.' Peter tried to replicate a hungry look.

Frankie smiled and snapped on a glove. 'It's all right, boy. It'll be over before you know it.' She frowned as she inserted a curved finger. 'The left gland is fine, the right is a bit full again . . . but I think the problem's under control.'

With her ungloved hand Frankie gave the dog a piece of dried liver and held his muzzle up so he looked into her eyes.

'Tell your dad, no gourmet meals from now on, okay?'

After he'd lifted Henbury onto the floor Peter went to take Frankie's hand and said, 'Thank you so very much, Dr Saunders. He looks much more comfortable now.'

'Oh!' She smiled and snapped off the surgical glove quickly before Peter shook her hand.

'Call me Frankie,' she gushed, smiling, and then blushing. The soft warm skin of his hand felt so comforting. She was used to the crackling dry roughness of farmers' hands.

In the reception area she put a line through the pencilled-in words in the appointment book, 'Henbury Maybury – Anal Gland'.

'That'll be thirty-six dollars, thank you.'

As she opened the till, Charlotte bustled in from the street, hitching up her stockings beneath her nurse's uniform.

'Sorry I'm a bit late, Frankie – long line at the bank . . . You head off to lunch. I'll handle this.'

'Lunch!' said Peter. 'Now there's a good idea! Shall we, you know, we might as well, eat together.'

'Why not,' said Frankie, and Charlotte smirked.

Out in the bright sunlit street with the hum and

roar of traffic rolling past, the two virtual strangers sat at an outdoor table of a café not far from the surgery. Henbury, tied to a pole nearby, settled himself down on the pavement. He placed his white paws neatly together as if surveying his nails, and occasionally twisted around to lick at his feathery bottom.

Peter brought up the topic of his divorce first and pulled mock-horror faces at the 'custody battle' over Henbury.

'It was worse than the kids!' He laughed with his eyes and then waved the issue away with his hand. 'They had all begun university by then and had no need for me, the struggling teacher.'

Frankie found herself telling him about Harry and leaving Waters Meeting and her children.

'I worry about Tom so much. He was always the sensitive one. He's the middle child, yet to me he feels like the baby of the family. It's him I have the most anxiety about since the break-up.'

Peter smiled gently at her and nodded, but said nothing, urging her on with his eyes. She felt safe with this man, so she took a sip of her coffee and continued.

'Michael will be okay in life, he's just like his father,' she said dryly. 'But Rebecca, ahh Rebecca, I worry about her every day. She's a wild one. She was always running amok at boarding school. She has the brains to do anything she chooses but she wouldn't stay with me here in the city after school finished last year. Had to go back to the farm. Back to the river. She's dog and stock mad.' Frankie fingered the thin paper tubes

35

of sugar which stood in a glass before her, and Peter smiled understandingly.

'It's hard, isn't it,' said Peter, 'carrying that guilt.'

'Yes,' Frankie said.

They had written their after-hours number on the soft paper serviettes which tore if they pressed too hard with the pen. Each had laughed when they shook hands goodbye. Frankie had watched Peter and Henbury walk away down the street. There had been a spring in Peter's step that hadn't been there before.

Now, entering her flat, the first thing she looked for was the red light flashing on the answering machine.

Had Peter called? It was after nine p.m. A diabetic cat admitted at five had held her up. He'd had plenty of time to call. Frankie threw her keys on the bench and went back to the doorway to retrieve her groceries. She pressed the play button on her way past to the kitchen area.

As she bent to put the milk away in the small fridge she heard Tom's voice and paused, listening before she shut the fridge door.

She looked up at the clock on the wall. Sighing, she made her way to the phone to call her son back and tell him there was no sign of Bec here. To calm herself she said out loud in the stale air of her small flat, 'Bec has done this sort of thing before.'

Rebecca had always been a feisty girl, but after the separation she had gone completely off the rails. Mrs Snell, the boarding school headmistress, would be on the phone at six a.m., complaining in her nasal best-of-British voice.

'Saunders? Dr Frankie Saunders? Your daughter ran orf from the boarding school yet again last night. She's back with us now though. We can't have this, you know. We shall have to take disciplinary action of some sort. We can't have her run the risk of a pregnancy or worse. It would bring down the school's name. She's influencing the other gals too, I might add. Of course we do take into consideration, Rebecca's . . . errr, family situation, but something must be done. Family breakdowns are so disruptive to children. Would you be so kind as to pop into the school before you go to the surgery this morning? Shall we say eight o'clock? Sharp? Good. See you then.'

It was after another little episode with the school, when Bec smuggled three year-eleven boys into her dorm, that Mrs Snell finally said, 'Take her away.' She was allowed to attend as a daygirl, but Bec hated being crammed in the flat with her mother. Worst of all she missed her dogs.

Sometimes after walking home from work, Frankie found the carport empty, her car gone. Rebecca would've skipped school and driven the three-hour trip to see her dogs, even if it meant incurring the wrath of her father at the other end of the journey. Tom often covered for her. He'd only been out of the local school himself for a bit over a year. It was Tom who fed and exercised her dogs while she was away at school. It was Tom who hid the car down the drive and smuggled food to Bec as she slept in a swag in the hayloft so her father wouldn't send her back to the city.

Tom will be so worried about her, Frankie thought as she dialled the number for Waters Meeting. Her daughter certainly hadn't been here in the flat today.

She heard Harry's voice on the other end of the phone. He'd obviously been sleeping so his 'Hello?' was a gruff one.

'Harry, it's me. I'm looking for Bec. Tom seems to think she's taken off with her dogs. What have you done to her?'

Harry's silence on the other end of the phone filled Frankie with fear and panic. Whenever Bec pulled a stunt like this Frankie couldn't help but whip herself with negative thoughts. That she was a bad mother. That it was her fault. That she put her career before her kids. Then the anger would rise towards Harry. If only he'd talked more. Been more of an emotional support.

'For Chrissakes, don't you care about your daughter?' Her outburst was met with silence. Typical, she thought.

'You know how she drives when she's mad. She could be dead in a ditch somewhere, in a car accident. She's young and attractive. She could be picked up by a rapist! Have you been out to look for her?

'She'll be right,' was all Harry said.

'She'll be right? No she won't be right. God knows . . . she's not "right"! She could be anywhere! You're the one who drove her away, Harry. It's up to you to go and find her! For godsakes, take some responsibility for your children!'

'You're a fine one to talk,' Harry said quietly.

Tears of anger welled in Frankie's eyes as she

slammed down the phone. She felt the guilt and the anger rush in. Then, as she sat on the couch, she felt fear. Fear for her daughter. She carried the feeling with her, in her gut, throughout the night. Her daughter was capable of anything. But then again, she thought as she rolled over in the tangle of sheets in her bed, her daughter was capable full stop. She could look after herself. It was on this thought that she drifted off to sleep to dream of her little girl splashing in the river and laughing. When the waters rose and roared and swept her daughter away, Frankie woke with a start to the electronic scream of the alarm clock.

Frankie stumbled into the surgery that morning with dark circles under her eyes and her hair brushed back and clipped crookedly at the nape of her neck. As she scanned through the appointment book her mind failed to register any of the words. Rebecca was the only concern which ran around in her head. The fear had subsided to a quiet anger towards her daughter. How often had she disrupted her work schedule? How many times had Rebecca stolen her concentration when she had important surgery to do? Frankie felt the tension in her shoulders. It was like a knife twisting in her neck.

By midmorning, when Charlotte knocked on the tearoom door to tell her a Peter Maybury was on the phone, Frankie had barely drawn a breath.

'Coffee tomorrow?' he asked in a light chirpy voice.

'Yes. Fine.' Her answer was dull and flat. She hesitated and nearly asked Peter if she should call the police, but instead hung up quickly. She decided to head home first to check for a message on the machine.

In the flat, the red light flashed. She pressed play on the machine and sank into the couch when she heard Rebecca's cheery voice. 'Hi Mum, it's Bec. Well that'd be obvious to you, cause you're my mum an' all. Anyway, I'm calling from a phone box. I'm on my way north. Dags, Stubby and Moss send their love, don't you guys?'

Frankie smiled as she heard the chorus of dogs bark in the crackly background of the message. Bec must've given them the hand signal to 'speak up'.

'This time Dad and I have had a doozey of a fight! It was a humdinger. Don't reckon I'll be back there for a while. The ol' bastard. He doesn't want me there.'

Frankie heard her daughter's voice crack.

'Anyway, I'll phone you, Mum, when I get to wherever I'm going. Love you.' And the line went dead.

Frankie's hands began to shake and her eyes stared ahead. She sat on the couch, put her quivering hand to her mouth and began to cry.

It was all such a mess. Such a terrible mess.

CHAPTER 3

Bec reached for the hot spongy chips in the paper cup between her legs. The high-pitched chug of her Subaru engine was drowned out by the tinny sounding cassette which played full bore in the dusty tape player.

Tom and Bec had fixed the player to the underside of the dash with rusted bolts just after she had got her licence, and they had laughed together when Tom bent a stubby top in half and used it as a fuse.

John Cougar's distorted voice screaming 'Hurt so good' thumped through the speakers in the doors. The white line dotted and ran past the whirring tyres and Bec sang as she chewed, checking the dogs occasionally in the rear-vision mirror. The song reminded her of Sal, her friend from boarding school. Sally had just started university at a campus a couple of hours east of the town Bec had just sped through.

She'd be in a tiny bricked-in dorm room somewhere, hungover or pissed, perhaps with her slim limbs slung over some bloke she'd picked up from orientation-week bar night. Or she'd be stooped over a desk with her long fine nose in a book on agricultural economics, a small furrow between her tidy arching eyebrows.

Bec smiled as she pictured her best mate. The first time she saw Sally, she had been in her school uniform, leaning against a brick wall and chewing slowly on an apple. Tall and slim, Sally had looked good even in the dull greys of their drab uniform. Bec had looked down at her own rumpled shirt and ill-fitting blazer and had begun to walk by, thinking this girl was too sophisticated to be her friend.

'Want a bite?' Sally had asked.

'Not with your slobber on it,' Bec had said and they had both laughed. It had been the start of a hilarious friendship – they were two girls who didn't ever quite fit into the chattering group of 'young ladies' who went to the school. At first it was their dry sense of humour which linked them, but soon their friendship ran deep and they shared nearly every thought and concern that came with being teenage girls immersed in their confining, hypocritical, private school culture.

To pass the time during lunch hours Sally often imitated her father, a doctor. Even after twenty-five years in Australia his Oxbridge accent was so strong and he still insisted on having proper afternoon tea each weekday.

'You got a D for chemistry, my gal. Splendid!' Sally would imitate as she gesticulated wildly and jutted out her chin. 'That's a vast improvement on last year, my petal!'

Dr Carter always used words such as 'petal', 'blossom' and 'pumpkin' when he talked, but his most common phrase was, 'my dear'.

'More tea, my dear?' he would say to Bec as she sat on the edge of the chintz lounge in the Carters' weekend house. A smile would pass between the two girls as Dr Carter handed Bec a floral teacup with a gold-edged trim and offered her a HobNob biscuit.

Dr Carter was in such contrast to her own father that Bec often caught herself staring at him, watching his every move as though he was an alien. Mrs Carter was equally fascinating as she tiptoed about the garden with her hands sheathed in flowery gardening gloves, a cane basket hanging in the crook of her arm.

'Geez,' Bec said to Sally as she watched Mrs Carter from the window. 'She reminds me of Mrs Bucket off the ABC.'

Sally rolled her eyes as she bit her nails.

'Come on, let's find the key to the grog cabinet and we can get stuck into Mum's gin before she comes in,' she said with a wink.

Bec often spent weekends with the Carters. When Dr Carter wasn't at his surgery, they ran a small hobby farm near the city. Rebecca always stared incredulously at the tidy fences, neat American-style barns and the potholeless gravel driveway that was lined with white agapanthas.

'Crikey Sal, look how many droppers your dad's got

on that fence . . . and he's used ring-lock wire! It must've cost him a fortune! What's he planning on putting in the paddock? Elephants?'

'Alpacas,' Sally said dryly. Bec could sense her friend was embarrassed by her father's yuppy style of farming.

'I suppose he's planning on an olive grove and a vineyard too,' Bec said.

'No.' Sal folded her arms. 'Truffles.' She sighed.

It was no wonder Sally had ended up at university doing an agricultural economics degree so she could become a rural financial counsellor. She had researched a zillion potential farm enterprises for her father and had done all the costings and quotes for him. But mostly it was the rugged mountains and rich river flats of Waters Meeting that had lured Sally into a career in rural business. She had loved escaping to the Saunders' farm during the long stretch of summer holidays. And it was Bec who had taught Sally all about the type of farming that went on in the region. Sally would be devastated to hear Bec had left Waters Meeting for good.

Bec shoved the last of her chips into her mouth, wiped her hands on her jeans and threw the paper cup onto the floor of the ute. She considered calling in to see her, but Rebecca knew if she did, Sally, with her level-headed approach to life, would talk her into turning round and going back. She decided to phone Sal later to tell her about the fight with her father. By tonight she'd be several hundred kilometres away and there would be no turning back.

The first night on the side of the road, Bec slept restlessly in her swag. She'd unrolled it in the back of the ute, with the tailgate down and the tarp over her in case it rained. She told herself the shivers running down her body were from cold, not fear. Her dogs lay curled up in little hollows they'd dug in the dirt under the ute where Bec had tied them. She knew they would watch for her and listen in the night and she knew the sound of each bark and what each dog meant to tell her.

In the next three days Rebecca headed north, then west, stopping only at roadhouses to get food and fuel. Sometimes she pulled up near tufty-grassed public parks or cool shaded riversides to give her dogs a run or a swim. Then early one morning, after her bank account had dwindled to fifty bucks, she pulled into a sale yard which was bustling with men and stock.

Trucks were backing up to loading ramps and stock agents in blue shirts with company logos and canvas chaps jogged up and down laneways hurrying sheep as they went. With her best yard dog, Dags, at her heels, Rebecca made her way down the rows of sheep pens until she came to the loading ramps.

A truck driver in navy King Gee pants was lifting up big old wethers which jammed and propped at the truck's gateway. He swore under his breath at the sheep and again called to his dog, who stood under the ramp in the shade, panting heavily. Another man, wearing a stock agent's uniform, stood beside the truck and poked at the sheep with a short piece of black poly-pipe. The buttons on his blue shirt strained and stretched against his belly. His pants hung low on his hips and seemed to threaten to fall down altogether, if not for a leather belt which was stretched tight below his gut. His ruddy face shone with sweat even though the sun had not yet warmed up the day.

'Need some help?' Bec called as she put one hand on the top of an iron post and leapt over a mesh fence. The agent frowned at her, pushed his hat back and scratched his head. Bec knew what he was thinking. Young. Female. She ignored his narrow eyes and stern mouth.

'Your dog looks a bit knocked up,' Bec said lightly. She nodded at the truckie's little black dog which let out little squeaky barks as it panted in a feeble attempt to move the stock from where it stood in the shade.

'Mine's fresh and he won't bite stock 'less you tell him to.' Bec stooped slightly to touch Dags's ear. The potbellied agent took one look at the well-muscled black and tan kelpie and muttered, 'If he does bite and draw blood, you're paying for it, so I hope you've got some cash on you.'

'Well. Actually I don't,' said Bec, 'I'm flat broke, unemployed and homeless . . . but at least I know my dog won't bite.' Bec smiled a dazzling half-sarcastic smile at the man and said quietly, 'Dags. Here. Hop up in here.'

The dog leapt over the metal race which was clad with iron sides and landed deftly on the backs of the sheep.

'Speak up there,' called Bec, and Dags let out a deep

bark, his tail wagging fast and low between his back legs. With a series of whistles Bec sent her dog up the ramp into the bottom deck of the truck. The sheep bustled out and flowed like a river in flood into the laneway.

The truckie and the agent looked at one another and Bec was sure she saw the agent wink.

'Backs all right,' said the truckie as he nodded towards Dags who seemed to be surfing along on the backs of recently shorn wethers.

'Not bad,' said the agent. Turning to Bec he said, 'Where'dya get 'im?'

'I bred him. I've got a litter of pups by him on the way,' said Bec as she nodded towards Stubby, who sat prick-eared in the back of her ute.

'Be good to see how they turn out. Rodney Phelps is my name anyway,' said the agent and held out his hand.

'This here's Darren Barnett, one of our local carriers.'

'Rebecca Saunders.' She shook hands with them both.

'Where'd you blow in from?' Darren asked as he slid the heavy door of the truck shut.

'Oh, down south,' she waved a hand vaguely. 'I'm looking for work if you know anyone who's got any.'

'You off a farm?' asked Rodney.

'Yes.'

'Not many of the stations round here take jillaroos, but I can ask around for you, love.' Rodney reached for a blue notebook in his top pocket, then turned his back and began to walk away.

'Can I help you out some more?' Rebecca asked quickly. 'Before the sale starts?' Bec tried to contain the urgency in her voice. She thought Dags's performance would easily convince them she'd make a good stockman, but the men weren't coming round. Darren and Rodney again looked at one another and the truckie shrugged.

Rodney looked down at Dags. He muttered through a thin mouth, 'The sale starts at nine. You can shift them sheep into that back pen with the tree in it.'

Bec nodded gratefully at him and whistled Dags, who cleared the fence by a foot, and they headed off to yard the sheep.

'I'll need a count on 'em though,' shouted Rodney after her. 'You can count sheep, can't you?'

Bec turned, smiled, nodded and began to jog in the direction of the sheep. She knew, thanks to Dags, she had a chance. A chance of finding a job and a new start.

As the sun rose higher and sweat formed on her brow, more and more buyers, sellers and 'tyre-kickers' trickled into the yards. Some leaned on the fences and yarned with each other. Others clanked the chains from gates and entered pens to press fat farming fingers onto the backs of the sheep. Old men with sagging skin and weeping red eyes bent over the wool sheep and opened up their fleeces with a deft touch. They peered at the whiteness, pretending to themselves and to others that they could see the neat tiny crimp in the wool's staple. The blue-shirt clad agents milled here and there, talking purposefully on mobile phones or jotting down pen numbers.

Soon Rodney was up on the catwalk above the pens with his pencillers beside him, clipboards in hand. He called out 'Sale-O! Sale-O!' and the men in the pens moved forward and crowded at the rail, forming a huddle of hats. The sheep beneath Rodney jumped and pushed away from his voice, their muzzles resting on each other's backs, jammed in a corner. Soft yellow eyes shaded by white eyelashes watched the buyers crowd round.

The first pen of sheep had blocky-tipped wool. The surface of their fleeces opened up in tiny cracks like dry mud around a dying puddle. Some of the sheep leapt up in the push, while others sniffed at the concrete surface beneath their hooves. Rodney yelled out the vendor terms in a string of words, as all of the men here had heard them a hundred times before. The sale soon eased into a pacy momentum with Rodney whacking his cane on metal railing, declaring, 'Sold!' above each pen.

Bec moved with the flow of the men in hats and felt their eyes on her. Eyes roving over her face and over her breasts beneath the red T-shirt she wore. She pulled her hat down lower and tried to guess the price each pen would bring.

As she looked up at the tubby form of Rodney auctioning against a backdrop of blue sky, a wry smile formed in the corner of her mouth. He had the habit of adjusting the contents of his undies before moving to the next pen and beginning the next bid. It happened each and every time. A quick flick of the hand on denim. Bec wondered if the local buyers noticed. No one seemed to care. He must've been around the auctioning game so long, the buyers had ceased to notice or joke about it. Rodney was good at his job, running on nervous energy. His fingers twitched by his side as he called out the bids.

'What am I bid for this lovely pen of ewes? Straight off-shears and in good nick too. I'll start at $20, $20, what am I bid? Fifteen, fifteen.'

The spotter by his side, eyes moving back and forth over the crowd cried out, 'Yes!' and held his notebook in the air pointing to a buyer on the fence. A nod at the back from a man in a straw hat moved the bid along until Rodney banged his cane down at $40.

'Sold! V. C. and G. Goodman, Sandhurst,' he said to the penciller. The crowd shuffled on to the next pen, taking Bec with it.

After the first row of stock sold, the trucks began backing up again to cart the sheep away. Bec heard their engines fire and rumble so she whistled to Dags who lay under a shady tree, dozing and snapping at flies. He bounced to attention at her whistle and they went off to the truck race in search of more work.

When she brightly asked each truckie if they knew of any work, they all shook their heads and her heart and hopes began to sink.

As the sale moved on, from where she worked at the loading ramps Bec noticed the voice of the auctioneer had changed. Rodney was taking a break and they were giving a younger auctioneer a turn. From up high on the loading ramp Bec looked out across the crowd. Rodney was talking to a short man and they were looking in her direction. She quickly whistled up Dags and he efficiently padded his way over the backs of the sheep. The confident dog put in a strategic bark here and there and had the sheep filing onto the rattly double-decker semi in no time.

Bec rolled the heavy door of the truck shut and dropped in the pins. When she turned she noticed the short man walking towards her.

'Good dog you got there . . .' he called to her.

Bec looked up from under the brim of her hat to see the short silvery-haired man leaning on the fence. Like Rodney, a belt below his belly strung up pants which sagged around his legs.

'Trained and bred him myself. We're looking for work if you know anybody.'

'We?' asked the man looking around for a young man.

Bec laughed at herself and smiled at the man. 'We as in just me. Just me and my three dogs.'

'Ah I see. Well, we don't normally employ females. We don't have separate quarters.'

'Separate quarters? Oh don't get me wrong. I'm used to roughing it and I was raised with two brothers, so if you think that'll stop me doing my job properly . . .'

The man held up his hands to silence her.

'I've no doubt you'll cope. Rodney's had a word in

my ear. It's no wonder he's the best agent around, he can talk me into anything. We've advertised for a jackeroo but haven't found anyone suitable, so the quarters are empty for the time being. We can put you on a two-month trial. But if there's a whiff of trouble with the men, you'll be off the place.'

'Which place would that be?' said Bec, trying to steer the conversation back on track.

'I'm Alastair Gibson. Manager of Blue Plains Station. 'Bout thirty k out. I'm not there full-time. I run it from the city, but the headstockman, Bob, and his wife Marg are good people. They'll look out for you and sort you out with the things you'll need to know.'

'Thanks Mr Gibson. I'm Bec. Rebecca Saunders.' She reached a dusty hand across the rail.

'Nice to meet you, Rebecca. Come and see me at the bar after and I'll fill you in on what we do.'

'Righto then,' she said and watched him swagger off towards the crowd clustering below the agents.

'What is it about blokes wearing their pants halfway down their bum?' she muttered to Dags who panted by her side, his big mouth stretched in a wide kelpie smile.

By the end of the sale, as the sun sunk below the peppertrees and the cockatoos cried out from the power-lines, Bec had a cold beer in hand and a job as a jillaroo on Blue Plains Station. It was part of a chain of proper-ties owned by Australian Rural Company, better known by the workers as AR. Blue Plains was 160 000 acres of mostly downs country, which historically ran merino sheep. In more recent years the company had diversified, introducing minimum tillage grain cropping and eight hundred head of breeder cows. Alastair said the season had been good for the past few years so stock numbers had been lifted and 30 000 sheep now grazed the flat plains and crackling yellow wheat stubble. He leaned against the side of the agent's ute and swigged on his beer.

'You could be just the girl for the job of preparing the rams for show season. They've been downsizing the showing, so we've done away with our full stud crew. But the company policy has been to support a few key shows. We'll be needing someone when the season gets underway.'

While Bec was a bit wary of stuffy sheep shows and the tweed-coat cronies they attracted, she nodded keenly at Alastair's words. She thought back to the infertile stud ram her dad had bought and the hairy, up-himself man who'd bred it.

'Sure!' she smiled. 'Great, Mr Gibson. That'd be great!' Bec knew they often ran sheepdog trials at the sheep and wool shows. It could mean she might be able to give her dogs a run in the trials when she wasn't handling the rams.

She raised the stubby in Rodney and Alastair's direction. 'Thanks for the shout and thanks for the job.'

'Looks like you owe me one of your pups when they're born,' Rodney winked.

'Looks like I do,' Bec said as she clinked her stubby against his. Then they all drank. Ice-cold liquid ran down her throat. It was the best beer Rebecca had tasted yet.

CHAPTER 4

Tom pushed the door of the pub open and Mick strode into the throng of people. From behind the bar a pot-gutted man threw up his hands.

'Woo-hoo! The Saunders boys are in town! Look out girls!'

The steady volume of the crowd dropped a little as heads turned to see. From the corner of the pub a group of girls leaned forward and whispered excitedly to each other behind cupped hands. Their eyes ran over Mick. He was much taller than Tom. He held his shoulders square and his head high. Stubble lined his strong jaw and his blue eyes glinted beneath dark lashes as he glanced about the pub, his gaze remaining on the table of young female drinkers. He continued on to the bar through the crowd.

The girls' eyes followed the shorter brother. He too was handsome. But there was something less confident about him. An aloofness in his large brown eyes.

Despite that, they were the best-looking boys in the bar.

As the Saunders brothers made their way through the crowd, some of the local lads let out a cheer and some slapped Mick on the shoulder or held out their hands to him. Tom followed quietly behind.

'Dirty Weatherby! How would you be?' said Mick as he rolled up his shirt sleeves and leaned his strong arms on the bar. Mick pulled his wallet from the back pocket of his jeans while Tom sat on the barstool he always sat on during their Friday night drinking sessions.

'The usual, thanks Dirty,' said Mick pulling out a $20 note.

As Dirty pressed a glass up to the pourer on the Bundaberg Rum bottle he called over his shoulder. 'Any word from your little sister?'

'Nope. None. She could be anywhere,' said Mick.

'What's your dad doing about it?'

'Not much he can do,' Mick shrugged.

'Well, tell 'im she's safe and sound, no thanks to him.' Dirty pulled down a postcard which had been stuck on the brown tiles that lined the bar. He slid it towards them. 'This came last week.' He walked away shaking his head.

Tom grabbed at the card. It was a photo of a large saggy-skinned Brahman bull. He turned it over and noticed the northern postmark. Mick read Rebecca's writing over Tom's shoulder – about the drive north, about the dogs and the promise of a new job out west.

'Geez! She's gone way up the woop woop!' said Mick.

She'd written a p.s. Tom turned the card sideways and squinted to read it. His full lips closed in a thin line. A muscle tensed in his jaw as he read the tiny writing.

'If you see Tom and Mick, give them my love and tell them I'll send them my new address when I've settled in.'

Tom downed his rum and sat a $5 note on the sodden bar mat.

'Hiiiii!' He heard a girl's high-pitched voice behind him. He turned to see Angela Carmichael standing there in a crop-top, looking up at Mick.

'G'day, Ang,' said Mick, flashing a charming smile.

'Mick.' She kissed him on the cheek just above the dimple she particularly adored. She turned to Tom.

'Hi.'

'G'day,' said Tom as he sipped his rum and coke.

She stepped aside for a moment to let her friend near.

'Mick. I'd like you to meet a friend of mine. This is Trudy Gilmore. She's just started as teacher at the school.' Angela pushed Trudy in front of Mick.

He took her slim pale hand and kissed it lightly, looking into her eyes and then winking. She smiled a smile that Mick had learned to recognise in women. He watched as she tucked her straight hair behind rather sticky-out ears.

'Hello, Michael,' she said.

Tom turned back towards the bar. Friday night had

got underway pretty much as usual, except this time Rebecca wasn't here to keep him company.

From the edge of the darkness Tom looked back at the lights of the Dingo Trapper Hotel as he pissed unsteadily in a bush. It was a sunken old pub tucked in a sharp meandering bend carved by the Rebecca River. Mick liked to call it the Fur Trapper – over the years he'd picked up most of the local girls there. When a local girl wasn't about, he'd set his targets on the back-packers who occasionally wandered in during boozy, beer-hazed nights. Big-boned Swedish girls or smooth-skinned English girls, all wanting a large serve of Aussie male. Mick played the part so well.

Tom saw Mick dancing now with the skinny girl. They were framed by the window and a patch of light shone into the darkness on the grass outside. Tom watched her hair flying and her mouth smiling as she spun in Mick's arms. This teacher, this girl, thought Tom, seemed different to the others. She had an agenda. Tom sighed, zipped up his fly and walked back into the pub.

A Garth Brooks song blared from the glowing juke-box and the floor shook. Mick and Trudy were dancing close, pelvis to pelvis. Mick stooped now and then to kiss her on the neck.

Tom sat back on his barstool and stacked up his change again into a neat pile.

'She's too skinny for him, that one,' said Dirty,

nodding towards Trudy. 'That country your old man's got is rough . . . if your brother's looking for a wife to take on that kind of country, he wants a good strong woman who can fence and fornicate. Not a skinny piece like that.'

He plonked another rum and coke in front of Tom and sifted through the coins.

'What about you, Tommy boy? Where's your woman?'

Tom turned to watch Mick lean over Trudy on the pock-marked pool table. She let out squeals of delight as the other girls watched jealously.

'Oh she's about, Dirty. She's about.'

But Dirty had already moved away to serve someone else at the other end of the bar.

Tom looked into the dark pool of his drink. He was hooked on Sally Carter. Rebecca's friend. As if he'd tell Dirty that.

As a teenager he'd hunted around Bec's room for a letter, a borrowed jumper. Something. Something of Sal's. After she'd stayed weekends at Waters Meeting, Tom had searched the sheets of the spare bed for strands of her shining straight hair. He had lain his cheek against the pillow she'd slept on and felt the erection stirring in his jeans. 'Sicko,' he'd chided himself.

In the hallways of the old house, Tom had tiptoed. Lurking near doorways. Eavesdropping. Trying to hear if Sally mentioned him. A few times he'd heard her say his name, but it was always attached to another word, like Shy Tom. Little Tom. Quiet Tom. Once she'd said 'cute little Tom' and his heart had skipped a beat, but then it had sunk again when she ignored him at the family dinner table and flirted with Mick.

He drained the remainder of his rum with a quick flick back of his head. Screwed-up Tom, he thought and slammed the glass on the bar. He hated the fact that he still dreamed of the quick kiss she had placed on his seventeen-year-old lips in the musty dark of the hay shed. He hated how stuck he felt.

'Rum on ice this time, thanks Dirty,' Tom said.

'Getting serious, are we?' Dirty scooped up the glass.

From out of the crowd Mick and Trudy, arm in arm, stumbled up to Tom. When Trudy saw Tom's blank face she pulled away from Mick. She straightened the pale pink collar of her shirt, pulling it up. Then she smoothed down her neatly bobbed hair and fiddled with a silver fob chain around her neck.

'Having a good night?' she yelled over the crowd.

'Great.'

'Tommo mate.' Mick slapped a hand on his shoulder and leaned towards his brother's ear. 'I'm in. She's asked me to stay at her place tonight. Reckon you can come and pick me up in the morning.'

Mick winked and was gone.

PART TWO

CHAPTER 5

Rebecca wasn't the kind of girl who usually had time to paint her nails, or would even bother. But she had the feeling tonight would be special. The dancing glossy nails seemed to belong to another person as she wrapped her hand around the metal handle of the bucket. Still-warm sheep guts slushed inside. A white cockatoo screeched from the sun-struck gum. The tree's gnarled old limbs hung tiredly over the creaking tin roof of the killing shed. Squinting into afternoon sunlight, Rebecca looked up at the bird before summoning her strength. The pig bucket was always extremely heavy when it was filled to the brim. She strained as she lifted it onto the front of the four-wheeler bike. The guts wobbled jelly-like inside and made little sucking noises. Her dad's voice came into her head, 'Don't burst your pooper lifting that, Rebecca.' She tried to banish the thought of him. It had been ten months since she'd seen him. And here she was on Blue Plains, getting eighty bucks a day and tucker.

She remembered the day she first drove into the station. Despite the heat, goosebumps covered her arms as her Subaru bumped over the wide grid and she looked up at the white glossy sign that read, 'Blue Plains – AR Co'. As she drove along the drive, she studied the pastures, the fences and the stock-watering systems, noting the windmills and huge concrete tanks.

'I bet I'll have to go on water patrols and climb one of those bloody things,' she said to herself.

As she drove over a rise, to the east she saw a D-6 bulldozer labouring up the side of a huge mound of dirt in a distant paddock. Black smoke puffed from its stack. She found out later that Stumpy was the driver. In the machinery shed during her first tour of the property's many buildings and houses, she had shaken Stumpy's hand firmly and quickly discovered the reason for his nickname. After ten months she was sure she'd heard every far-fetched story about how he lost his fingers. But Stumpy still insisted on telling her a different tale as he held a rollie between the two remaining fingers and puffed smoke from his cracked lips.

The machinery guys were okay to work with, Rebecca thought. She had enjoyed their company when they were burning off stubble. Stumpy was there with the dozer to carve out a firebreak. He was so proud of his machine, and Rebecca had learned a lot from him. He treated her as though she was part of the team. But there was one machinery bloke she had to be careful of.

If the stockmen had a breakdown with the four-wheel drives they would call on long, lean and very alcoholic Jimbo. She'd learned to avoid Jimbo. He was a leering, oily mechanic who took time out from under vehicles to stare openly at Rebecca's breasts, and he'd attempt to flirt with her at every chance he got. She'd been tempted to mention it to Alastair Gibson when he next flew in from the city, but she decided it was all part of the job. So long as Jimbo didn't touch her, she'd put up with his innuendo.

Bec had been glad to discover the head stockman, Bob Griffith, was a decent man. It was hard to tell his age. Bec guessed about early forties, but he could've been in his late thirties. There were laughter creases around his eyes and on the sides of his mouth. His face was so brown it made his blue eyes stand out. He had large square hands and never wore any colour other than varying shades of brown. Brown boots, tan belt, brown Wranglers and a beige checked shirt. He said very little, and sometimes when droving a large mob of cattle Bec was sure Bob must think she was a mind-reader.

At first Bob had been furious with Alastair for sending him a female worker, but when the first week came to a close he had knocked on the door of the quarters with a cold beer. His wife Marg stood behind him holding a basketful of biscuits and cake. At the table of the jackeroo's quarters, Marg sat quietly as Bob began to ask Rebecca questions about how she had learned to ride so well.

'You can try Rosie next week,' he had said, swigging

on a beer and shaking his head at his wife's offer of a biscuit. 'She's pure quarter horse. A bit shy about the head, and only a youngster, but she'll turn a beast on a twenty-cent piece. Have you got a horse of your own at home?'

Bec smiled as she thought of her mare. 'Yes.'

'Are you going to bring her up here one day?' Bob could tell from her reaction not to ask any more questions about 'home'. He quickly changed the subject. 'And those terrific pups of yours. What bloodlines are you on?'

Marg had sat in silence as Bob and Bec chattered on until all the beer and biscuits were gone.

It wasn't until weeks later that Marg had come on her own to the quarters to see Rebecca. She had settled herself down at the table and talked and talked.

'I thought you were one of those dreamers from down south. You know the sort. They turn up thinking they can do the job, their heads filled with romantic ideas about what it's like out here. There are some girls just looking for men . . . you know the sort.'

Bec nodded and listened, relieved that Marg was at last opening up to her.

'But I can see you're so caught up in your dogs and horses that you don't even turn your head at the blokes. And from what Bob said, you're handy in the yards. He told me how quick you were on the head-bale when you were tagging those young weaners. And that you didn't cry when that crazy old Brahman cow kicked you through the rails. Bob's pretty impressed.' Marg

66

smiled warmly at her as she ran her fingers through her short curly hair.

'Can I get you a rum and coke?' Bec had asked.

Marg had said, 'Yes,' and Bob had found the two of them three hours later, laughing hysterically and waltzing to Tom Jones' songs. After that Rebecca had a fuzzy recollection of spilling out to both of them all the events that had happened at Waters Meeting and about her anger towards her father. Bob and Marg had been so caring and sympathetic. They'd decided she had needed cheering up. So much so, Bob'd declared that another bottle of rum would do the trick. It hadn't been long before Elvis was belting out from the CD player and the small party of three were dancing round the room.

Yep, things have turned out okay, Bec thought as she swung a leg over the four-wheeler and stretched out a red-nailed finger to press the start button on the bike. The sound of the engine firing and revving was good. She'd done the kill as quickly as possible, within reason. Bob always went crook if she took too much selvedge off with the skin. But the carcasses didn't look too bad, all tidy pink and hung up in the meat shed.

Bec's nails looked so out of place on the handlebars and throttle of the bike that it made her smile as she bounced over the dusty red track. They reminded her of the cover of a Jackie Collins novel, not that she'd ever bothered to read one. The only books that lay scattered by her bed were kelpie training manuals and the Department of Agriculture's guide to building better sheep yards.

She felt the warm wind on her face. The sun was so liquid golden it spread like treacle across the white dry grass. In the ten months on Blue Plains she'd learned to love the flat open country. At first she'd missed home and the hug of the mountains on the skyline, but out here the sky was so huge. Every sunset was a masterpiece on a massive canvas. Extravagant, bold golds and pinks hung for a moment in the air and then were gone.

What this grand western country didn't have, though, was the rich black soils of Waters Meeting, nor the constant shussh of the river. Bec had first swum in the Rebecca River before she was born, in the warm waters of her mother's womb. Her mother bobbing on her back with her rounded belly pointed to the sky. Water rippling through outstretched fingers as insects skitted by, hovering over a mirror of deep green. But there was no river out here, just bores and windmills and concrete troughs which sprouted tufts of green grass at their bases where the valves dripped. She tried to keep a check on her thoughts of home.

The pigs were milling around from the sound of the bike. As usual Miss Oink was at the gate first, squealing a greeting as her piglets charged around the back of the pen. The collection of now-tame feral pigs shrieked and bustled, waiting for the bucket of offal to be thrown into the pen. She lifted the lid of the rusted forty-four-gallon drum and scooped out grain with an old Milo tin into the trough. The pigs raced to the trough, bunting each other out of the way, except for Miss Oink who always took prime position.

'And now for dessert,' said Bec, as she lifted the heavy bucket over the fence and tossed the sheep guts onto the ground. Forgetting the grain, the pigs ran to rip, fight, chomp and chew at the offal.

'Manners, please!' Bec said as she swung a leg over the bike. She again thought of her father. He would be horrified to know Bec had been feeding offal to pigs, but as Bec had learned, rules and regulations didn't really apply out here. She loved the wildness of the place and the people who insisted on pushing the boundaries.

Revving the bike, Rebecca headed back past the machinery shed to the dogs which were housed in concrete-based kennels surrounded by high mesh wire. Stubby, Dags and Mossy and her pup wagged their tails frantically and whined in excitement, jumping and clawing at the wire. Bec turned on the hose, refilled the old drench-drums with water and scooped out brown dog biscuits from an old tin garbage can into the array of dog dishes. Some were made of old hub caps, others from retired and rusted plough discs. She said a silent prayer for her dogs, hoping Bob would remember to feed them and give them water while she was away. She ached at leaving her dogs but there was no way she could take them with her this weekend to the Dust-raisers B&S ball. Slipping her hand through the wire cage she scratched behind Stubby's silky ear. Next to her, Mouse, the last of Stubby's six pups, jumped up and down.

'Calm down, Mouse.'

Rebecca's dogs had become quite a talking point in

the district. She'd had no trouble selling Mossy's pups for good money, but she'd hung on to Mouse, her favourite in the litter, to train her up and sell her for bigger money as a started dog.

'Like my nails, Mouse?' Bec smiled into the rich brown eyes of the dog. 'Na, didn't think you did. Now you be a good girl while I'm away.'

She started the bike and rode towards the jackeroos' quarters. The B&S ball tonight would be a blast.

'Yeah baby, yeah!' she cried as she gave the bike some extra throttle and threw out some dust in a perfect fishtail.

The screen door on the verandah slammed behind her and Rebecca kicked off her boots. In the kitchen Dave, the jackeroo who now shared the quarters with her, was at the sink. He stood in holey footy socks and was sloshing red cordial into a beer glass which they'd stolen from the pub. He turned the tap, filled the glass and then held it up to the light.

'Errrk! Plenty of wrigglers.' As he gulped loudly his Adam's apple danced up and down in his throat.

When Rebecca had first arrived at Blue Plains, she'd pictured herself bunking down in the quarters with a tall, dark, excessively muscled jackeroo with wonderful culinary skills, domestic awareness and an array of conversation topics. Instead she got Dave. Red-haired, freckled, skinny and with the largest repertoire of blonde jokes Rebecca had ever thought possible.

Dave shuffled to the kitchen table. He smothered tomato sauce onto a slice of white bread and shoved it into his mouth.

'When are we heading off?' he asked, still chewing.

'As soon as we're ready,' Rebecca said, swigging on a glass of water. The day had been hot.

'You're keen to get a bit, judging by those nails,' Dave said, reaching for another slice of bread. 'You planning on breaking the drought tonight.'

'Na . . . I'm just aiming to get on the fizz with my friends. My best mate Sal might be coming up from uni for the weekend.'

'She is! Is she a looker?'

'A stunner. A bit flat-chested and nonblonde for you, though, Dave-shmave.'

'Oh I'm not fussed!'

'No, I realised that after you picked up the publican's wife . . . and that woman with the prickly chin.'

'That's all crap,' said Dave, waving a butter knife at her.

'Tis not!'

'Tis so! She didn't have a prickly chin . . . just hairy legs.'

'Awwwh! Gross me out! I'm going to get frocked-up!' She walked out of the room.

In the shower the red dust on Bec's face turned to tiny rivulets of brown which trickled over the curves of her body. Bubbles of shampoo ran down her back. Her arms and shoulders were golden brown from wearing singlets in the sun. As she scrubbed her scalp she noticed the lean muscles in her upper arms rise to a defined shape. The work on Blue Plains was hard. Harder than home where her dad had breathed down her neck all day and sent her away from the yards and sheds. In the short time she had been here she had learned so much, not least of all about her own stamina. She was expected to do everything Dave did. From lifting heavy mineral lick-blocks for the sheep onto the ute, to banging steel droppers into the rocky ground.

The skin had cracked on her fingers so tiny webs of dirt remained even after she'd scrubbed them. Calluses formed on her palms, and she picked at them absent-mindedly.

Her firm muscles and strength, the curves on her small frame and long curls of straw-coloured hair drew men's eyes to her. Bec, oblivious to this, treated all men like her brothers. She looked up at them openly with her big blue eyes and unknowingly melted hearts.

As she stretched out the foreign-looking nails to the bottle of conditioner Bec began her best Rod Stewart parody of 'Do Ya Think I'm Sexy?' She watched the red nails slide over her soapy skin and smiled.

Later Rebecca stood in the kitchen in her short red dress. Dave looked up and gave a low wolf whistle.

'Cheers, buddy,' she said as she cracked open a beer, raised it to him and drank. She leaned against the fridge, which was covered with every B&S and rural pub sticker imaginable. It stood as the legacy of those jackeroos who had gone before them. Hundreds of dollars spent on hard nights of drinking.

'Suppose we'd better get to and collect another sticker for this little baby.' Rebecca patted the fridge.

'You bet,' said Dave.

Through red dust they lugged swags, bags and eskys and threw them under the tarp of the Subaru ute which was parked beneath a peppertree. Turning the ignition key the cassette player came to life and Shania Twain blared from the speakers.

Using his stubby as a microphone, Dave sung along. Rebecca looked over to him and smiled. She would miss all this. Her enrolment at Tabledowns University had come through. The crisp letter signifying the beginning of another phase of her life had arrived last month in the drum which served as a mailbox.

Tonight the white forty-four stood alone by the grid as the sun sunk lower towards the flat horizon of Blue Plains Station. She thought about stopping to peer into its dark and rusted interior, but she knew Bob had picked up the twice-weekly mail yesterday.

To Bec the mailbox was a lifeline with Waters Meeting. Some days she found small, roughly sealed envelopes from Tom. She tried to find more information within the looped ink about the farm and its future. But Tom skimmed the surface, writing only of rain and harvests and of shearings and crutchings. There was virtually no mention of Harry in the letters, though Tom often wrote about Mick's girlfriend,

73

Trudy. How she'd tried to cook them a roast in the temperamental wood stove, or taken it upon herself to iron and fold his undies, or how she just generally annoyed the crap out of him. Tom often speculated why Mick had given up his womanising since he met Trudy. Why he had chosen her. Tom surmised she was so efficient at getting her own way that it was easiest for Mick to go along with her rather than endure her pouting, silent moods.

Rebecca read between the lines and knew Mick needed someone stronger than himself, and it sounded like Trudy was stronger, in her own way. Rebecca believed Mick wanted the comfort of someone who bossed him, organised him and, most of all, mothered him.

After reading Tom's letters she'd fold them, put them back in the envelope and place them neatly in a shoebox. The box was filling fast. Not so much with Tom's letters, but mostly with letters from her mother. Frankie wrote in big messy scrawls as she rushed here and there about the city. She'd mentioned a man named Peter a few times in her disjointed letters and Rebecca could tell that Peter was at long last a welcome distraction from her mother's obsession with her veterinary work. Even though she loved to receive letters from her family, on mail days Rebecca was filled with a sense of unease. She knew why, but found it hard to admit it to herself. She was always hoping for a letter from her father. One that said, 'Come back.'

Dave's voice snapped her out of her daydreams.

'Wanna get a dim sim from the roadhouse?' he asked.

'Yeah sure. And a square bear from the pub!' she said with a smile. They sped along a blue-grey road as the sun lit the land and turned it golden.

It was almost midnight but Rebecca had no idea of the time, nor did she care. Leaning on her Subaru she slipped off her black shoes and threw them into the tray of her ute. Rummaging in her bag she found some red football socks and her work boots.

'Ahhh! That's better.' She stomped on the ground, pushing her heel into her boot.

A small distance away by the fence line, a scruffy-haired lad stood enjoying a lengthy piss.

'Hurry up, Johnno,' Rebecca called to him. He burped and farted as he zipped up the fly of his dinner suit trousers.

'Must get more rum,' he slurred and slung an arm about her neck. They set off across the bare paddock on Wilmot Station, stumbling on rocks and kicking piles of dried sheep pellets. Laughing. Flirting.

Ahead of them the shearing shed shook with loud music. The lights splayed out, illuminating the fringes of the party scene. People were dotted about amidst stockyards, portaloos, refrigerated trucks and food marquees.

Behind them the sky was ink black with an icing-sugar sprinkling of stars. Bec looked up at it as Johnno swung her round and put his wet rum lips to her mouth. She tilted her head back and held her plastic blue cup in her hand, enjoying the sensation of his tongue inside her mouth. He smelt of sweat and grog. He leaned a little too firmly on her and they both swayed backwards and laughed. Her eyes shone and a broad smile glowed on her face.

'What was your name again?' he asked her.

As they climbed the steep ramp of the shed and walked onto the grating, Rebecca was filled with a buzz of excitement. The crowd was thick. Boozey blokes in dinner suits sloshed rum. Girls in coloured dresses laughed and screamed, their hair hanging in sticky strands, wet with rum and coke.

A red-faced fat boy ran forward. Rebecca saw him squeeze a container of food dye into his mouth and swig on a yellow plastic cupful of beer. He ran at Johnno, grabbed him by the arms and spat smatterings of red dye over Johnno's face.

'Arnie! You dirt-bag!' and Johnno was off pursuing his attacker through the crowd.

'When the food dye comes out, you know the party's really started,' came a voice from behind her.

It was Sally, her fingers spread around four plastic cups of rum.

'Good lordie-mama, Sal, you look smashed!'

'Not used to so much grog,' Sally slurred.

'Crap! From what I gather from your letters you've been drinking and doing naughty things with boys all the time!'

'Na! Not since I failed a subject in first semester. I've really pulled my finger out. No grog. Minimal boys. And dedication to the pursuit of excellence!'

'Well I'm so bloody glad you're not pursuing excellence now. Thanks for coming up to see me. It's so good to see my bestest buddy.'

'Well it has been nearly a year! And since I'm only here for the weekend, we'd better get on with it,' said Sally as she handed Rebecca two cups of rum. With a cup in each hand above their heads they bullied their way through the rowdy drinkers. In the thick of the crowd Rebecca felt the cold splash of rum across her face and chest. It soaked into her dress and trickled down her cleavage. Her hair formed in ringlets around her face, some sticking in sugary strands to her skin. She quickly gulped down a rum, tossed the cup away and wiped her face with the back of her hand.

When she looked back at Sally she laughed out loud. Sally's bare shoulders were smattered with blue food dye and her face was dotted with reds and yellows.

'The bastards got me,' Sally laughed.

Despite the smatterings of dye, Sally still managed to look good. Her tall slim figure in a black dress stood out in the crowd. Her short hair slicked back highlighted her long slim neck. As she stood there, wiping beer and dye from her eyes, a boy bit her on the neck.

'Ahh!' Sally screamed and batted him away. He danced off into the crowd.

'Shall we?' Sally yelled to Rebecca.

They moved into the sea of jumping, sweating bodies dancing maniacally beneath bright lights in front of a band.

Blokes in black trousers, stained white shirts and an assortment of wayward-looking bow ties swung Bec and Sally about roughly.

The long-haired drummer thumped on his gleaming black and silver drum kit as the guitarists pounded out a Lee Kernaghan number.

Beneath flashing coloured lights, Bec let out a 'woo-eeeEEE' of excitement and felt the thump of the drums inside her body. Guitars twanged, harmonicas sung and the vocalist 'Hey-uped' in true country style. When the chorus came the dancers slung their arms around each other's waists and turned their heads to the rafters and corrugated-iron roof, singing till their throats hurt:

We're all members of the Outback Club.
She don't back down and she don't give up.
She's living in the land she loves.
Born and raised she's a member of the
*   Outback Club.*

In the haze of alcohol, Bec was certain Lee Kernaghan had written the song just for her. She sung along as hard as she could.

She rides the boundary fences with the blokes.
She's a match for any man alive when she
*   works a mob . . .*

The next thing Bec knew, Johnno's lips were on hers and his tongue was sliding into her mouth. She felt the weight of his body against hers. His dark hair

78

fell across his blue eyes which shone wickedly in the lights.

Then, in an instant he was gone again. Whisked away by his mates. Drunk and unconcerned, Rebecca continued to dance with Sally in front of the fleshy brick wall of security staff. A line of men with blank faces, low brows and arms folded across their chests.

Crouching down in the crowd on a slippery floor awash with rum, sheep shit and plastic cups, Bec and Sal decided to tie a bouncer's shoelaces together. They had just about succeeded when Dave arrived, jumping up and down like a Masai warrior. He yelled at the band.

'Play some Barnsey! Khe Sanh! Play Khe Saaaanh! Chisel! Play some Chisel ya bastards!'

He turned to Sally and Bec and said, 'Haven't picked up yet?' Rebecca rolled her eyes and waggled her head in the direction of the shearing board.

Johnno was up there with Arnie, the fat boy. Arnie was leaning over Johnno, pretending he was on the long blow in a mock demonstration of shearing. His imaginary handpiece jiggered in his hand as he finished taking the wool from Johnno's tail. With two hands on Johnno's buttocks Arnie pushed Johno-the-imaginary-ram headfirst down the count-out pen slide which dropped away underneath the shed. He disappeared with a clatter down the chute, his Red Wing boots and dinner-suit-clad legs the last thing seen by the crowd of onlookers.

Rebecca decided to search for him beneath the shed. She was feeling pumped. She wanted to taste him again. Whoever he was. She left Sal and Dave on the crowded dance floor.

At the wide sliding door at the top of the shed's ramp she felt the cool night air on her skin. The ramp, normally used to funnel the sheep up into the shed, had become an area for impromptu stunt work. There was a crowd of guys out on the slatted surface holding onto a shopping trolley. Their eyes looked up towards the edge of the roof above the ramp.

'Carn Basil! Do it! Come on!' they shouted collectively from the top of the ramp.

Following the boys' eyes Bec looked up and saw in a halo of light against the night sky a naked young man. He was wearing a red plastic bucket on his head and standing on top of the guttering. The light cast shadows over his tall, muscled frame. He flexed a few comical muscleman poses to build the drama of his stunt. If Sal had been there, Bec thought, she would've said out loud, 'He's got a big wanger!' But Bec tried not to look at the white dangling penis which was framed by a deep shadow of hair. Instead she cast her eyes over his shoulders and strong arms, in particular his huge hands and square jaw. She licked her lips and felt a tingle of desire run through her. He had a damn good body.

'Jump Basil, jump!' The boys began to grunt like gorillas. 'Ooogh, Ooogh Ooogh!'

The young man took a slight run-up on the creaking corrugated-iron roof, launched himself into the air and landed with a clatter in the shopping trolley. The silver metal trolley leapt to life like a startled horse and scuttered down the ramp until its wheels hit the slats of wood which were nailed across the ramp. It flipped and lay on its side, wheels still spinning. The stunt man sprawled at Rebecca's feet. For a moment he was still. Then he looked up at her.

His bucket helmet was skewed to the side. In the spotlight his eyes shone. Startling green eyes with a fringe of long dark lashes.

'Shopping trolleys are very, very unforgiving,' he slurred. He dropped his bucket-enclosed head on the ground with a clunk and pretended to pass out.

Bec smiled down at him as his mates clustered around cheering, laughing, clapping and whooping. They grabbed him by his arms and stood him up. He wobbled a bit, leaned left and then took a staggering step to the right as he nearly toppled down the ramp. With a broad brown hand and a flash of gritted white teeth he flicked the metal handle of the bucket from under his chin and swiped the bucket off his head to reveal short-cropped black hair. Tossing the bucket on the ground, he flung out his arms to push his friends back.

'Excuse me, men, I have business to attend to,' he slurred. He made his way towards Bec.

'I think I love you.' His green eyes twinkled. The cluster of boys whooped again and slapped him on his bare-skinned back.

'Charlie Lewis,' he said holding out his hand. 'Better known as Basil round these parts.' Rebecca took his hand in hers and shook it firmly, her eyes smiling into his.

'Rebecca Saunders,' she replied.

'Ooops!' he said and quickly cupped both hands over his pubic area. 'Forgot I was starkers!' He crouched down and grinned up at her. Suddenly Charlie's mates converged on him, picked him up and carried him off down the ramp into the yards and away into the night. Laughing, Rebecca watched them go.

As the rainbow of lights flashed from inside the shed Rebecca felt desire run thickly through her. She smiled to herself excitedly. She had just met Charlie Lewis. And he was gorgeous.

The sun, creeping above the trees, lit up silver threads of spiderwebs in the grass. Hungover B&S party-goers stirred in their swags as they lay on the ground or in the backs of utes.

Rebecca was awake but lay with her eyes closed listening to the thump of music coming from the speakers of a ute parked further along the row. They were playing 'Thank God I'm a Country Boy'. She groaned and wiped a hand across her mouth. She was thirsty.

Opening her eyes she watched the diehard drinkers stumbling around the bonfire which had long ago lost its red roaring glory. From behind the tyres of her ute she saw the green hump of Dave's swag which was rolled out near the bullbar.

'Hey Dave . . .'

'Mmmm?'

'I feel like crap.'

'Mmmm,' said Dave. He pulled back the canvas of his swag and propped himself up on one elbow, eyes squinting, carroty hair sticking up.

'Geez. You *look* like crap,' Rebecca said. There was a rustling movement and from inside Dave's swag the face of a dark-haired girl emerged.

'Morning,' said Bec. She remembered the girl from last night. What was her name? Annabelle? She'd been on Dave's tail for most of the evening. She must've caught him.

'Mmmm. Feel sick,' said Annabelle, before slumping down again.

A little while later a loud cheer and the rev of an engine woke them again. A yellow Holden ute circled wildly in an area of bare paddock. Hitched onto the back was a portaloo. Its door swung open and shut as the ute spun around and around. Glimpses of a boy, pants around his ankles, clinging to the sides, could be seen as the ute stirred up dust with fat spinning tyres.

B&S committee members in striped rugby jumpers ran onto the area waving their arms, trying to stop the driver. As the vehicle slowed, the tubby toilet-goer leapt from the loo, tumbled in the dust with his trousers still down and in one smooth motion rolled to his feet taking a good-natured, bare-bottomed bow.

From their swags Rebecca, Dave and Annabelle applauded and whistled along with the other party-goers who were emerging from their swags to sit on the backs of their utes.

'Looks like the party's starting again,' said Bec. 'Better crack open a breakfast beer.'

Dave drove Rebecca's ute in the line of B&S traffic along the dusty road. Annabelle sat on her ample bottom in the passenger seat while Sally and Bec sprawled in the back, their feet propped up on an esky. The B&S was shifting camp and everyone was headed for the recovery site on the riverbank.

'So what happened to you last night?' asked Rebecca.

'Mmmm! Where do I start? I'll give you a clue.' Sally waved her hands in the air as if drumming.

'Oh God! Not the drummer! You cracked onto the drummer!'

'Mmm . . . those arm muscles!' Sally took a swig from her stubby.

'What about you?'

'Oh. I lost Johnno. He was just a beer-goggle thing. I dipped out last night, mind you, I did meet the most drop-dead gorgeous guy with the *best* body and nicest baggage you've ever laid eyes on.'

'Really! Who?'

At that moment a Hilux ute pulled out from the line of traffic and drove with two wheels on an embankment past them. On the back, amidst a crowd of boys, Charlie Lewis raised his beer in the air when he saw Rebecca.

'I think I'm in love with you!' he called out to her as they drove past.

'Him,' said Bec to Sally.

On the river's edge they sat in clusters. Drinking, skylarking, dancing to the band which played from the back of a truck. Sally's eyes wandered over to the drummer quite often and she'd sigh a little and smile. Rebecca was lying on her back looking through the golden shine of a Bundy bottle. She rolled onto her stomach and poured the rum into plastic cups, mixed it with warm flat coke and then handed one to Sally. Sally lay down next to her friend and they clipped the cups together and drank.

'Heard from your dad?' Sally asked.

'God, don't bring him up now while I'm enjoying my square bear!'

'Bec. You've gotta deal with this family crap at some stage. We're learning all about succession planning strategies at uni. You need to communicate with your dad.' Sally pulled her sunglasses down her nose and looked into her friend's drunken blue eyes.

'Dad's stuffed. So's the farm and Tom's dropping his bundle. The whole thing is rooted.' Bec ran a dirty hand through a tangle of blonde hair and bit the rim of the cup.

'That good, huh?' There was silence between them as Sally unsteadily poured another drink.

'I miss home, Sal,' said Bec as tears welled up. She began to cry silently. 'Bloody Dad. What am I doing, Sal? I just want to go home. Home to Waters Meeting and my river. I miss my horse . . . the animals, everything.'

85

Sal threw an arm over Bec's shoulders and rested her forehead on Bec's.

'Buggered if I know what you can do, Bec.'

'Buggered if I know either.'

There was a pause.

'Hang it, Sal! Let's just get hammered.'

'Um Bec, we're already hammered, and is that solving anything?'

'Mmmm.' Bec began to blow bubbles in her cup, then tossed the liquid into her throat, rolled onto her back and let out an 'Eerrrrgh.'

Sal did the same, 'Errrrrggh!' Then they 'Errrrr-gggghed' some more and let out some snorts, just for the drunken sake of it.

Suddenly Rebecca and Sally felt hands around their wrists and ankles. Dave, Johnno, Arnie and a short weedy boy were lifting them to the river. At the river's edge Rebecca felt herself swinging, then the hands let go and she was in the air. She landed and cool water splashed about her.

When she stood up she found she was in waist-deep water. She pushed her hair off her face. The boys splashed in after her, some calling, 'Wet T-shirt! Wet T-shirt!'

Rebecca looked down at her breasts, revealed beneath the wet fabric clinging to her body. She dived into the murky waters of the river and swum under-water to the centre of the swimming hole. As she trod water she saw Charlie Lewis on the riverbank. He was slumped on a purple inflatable couch with a rum bottle tucked under his arm. His mates fell about him, pulling the rum from him and picking him up couch and all. With a cheer they tipped him into the muddy shallows of the river.

When he surfaced and saw her treading water in the centre of the river he swum over. As he neared her she saw his eyes. So green. Long dark lashes wet with river water.

'Howdy dudey,' said Bec.

'Why Miss Rebecca, I do declare. We meet again,' he said, offering a wobbly handshake as he trod water overzealously. She was surprised he could remember her name after last night's drunken shopping trolley introduction. She felt the shimmers of Charlie's finger-tips stirring the water as he paddled near her.

'Shall we swim upstream or downstream?' he said with a flirty glance.

'I like it up,' said Bec, pushing off the murky bottom with the very tips of her toes and breaststroking against the gentle current.

A large log which had fallen long ago provided a wet lovers' seat for them as they sat and looked into each other's eyes. Both shivered a little. Charlie stared at her and brushed strands of hair tenderly from her face.

'Have I got a booger or something?' said Bec, rubbing her nose self-consciously with her hands.

Charlie laughed a little and took her hand away from her face. 'Nope. Your nose looks perfect to me.'

Water lapped just below Charlie's nipples and even

though he shivered, his hand felt warm holding hers. Bec waited for him to kiss her. She almost held her breath, amazed at how much she craved this man. She studied him. The perfection of him. Tanned skin, square jaw tinged with dark stubble, full lips and those eyes.

As he ran his hand up her arm and over her shoulders, her mind was awash with questions. Like where was he from? Did he like dogs, or ice cream or cricket? Why was she so attracted to him? Did he feel it too? Was it just the rum?

Instead, she said nothing. She just let his lips touch lightly on hers and soon she was swimming. Swimming in the warmest rum-kiss which melted her heart. Even though she was drunk, it wasn't like Johnno's kiss had been. This river kiss. This Charlie kiss. This everything kiss. Their hands ran over each other and their breath quickened with desire. She felt the skin of his legs touch hers and he pressed his broad chest against her body. Lust.

Suddenly someone screamed and Bec's eyes flashed open.

'Floater!' someone yelled.

A bloke on the riverbank was running up and down waving his arms and yelling, 'Yobbo's done a floater! Clear the water! Clear the water!'

'What?' said Bec.

'Ahhh!' said Charlie. 'Yobbo's laid an underwater cable and it's floating downstream! Yirk! Let's get out of here.' They swum downstream laughing and drunk again with pleasure and the warmth of rum in their bellies.

She felt his distance, though, when he neared his mates. He slipped away from her in the water, trying to hide his self-consciousness.

'I'll catch you later,' she said coolly and then walked out of the river, trying to look as Bo Derrick as possible, even though she was smeared with mud and river weed stuck to her skin like leaches.

Later she danced in front of the band, dodging tussocks and stomping on dust with the other drunks. Sal was at the front of the crowd in the hot afternoon sun, flashing her little pert breasts every now and then to the band.

While they danced Bec yelled breathlessly at Sal. 'The kiss of my life! It was the kiss of my life! And it was interrupted by a *floating poo*!'

'*What*?' shouted Sal over the music. Bec shrugged and danced harder. Life was like that.

CHAPTER 6

Rebecca heard the shearer's machine pull out of gear and the scrabble of hooves finding their footing. Automatically she moved on the cue of the sound. She picked the fleece up in one smooth action and threw it. The white fleece floated through the air and spread across the slatted wool table. She grabbed a broom and swept the locks away before Barney dragged out his next wether.

For Rebecca, rouseabouting was like a dance. She knew the steps off by heart, almost without thinking. It was a dance she had learned as a child when she worked beside her grandfather during Waters Meeting shearings. Right from the beginning she loved the smell of the fleeces as they fell away from the sheep. She would stand, watching, mesmerised by the movement of the shearers. The men in the team, all regulars, encouraged Rebecca in the shed. They let her finish the last few blows of the sheep just before smoko so that by the time she was sixteen years old she could shear a sheep in less than four minutes. Her grandfather showed her how he classed the wool, running the long white staples of fibre through his thumb and forefingers and testing it for strength with a flick of his middle finger. Rebecca would help him stack the AAA fleeces in a high white mountain in the bins. Shearing only ran for two weeks at Waters Meeting, but Rebecca loved every day of it.

At Blue Plains they were on their third mob and two weeks into shearing, with still several weeks to go. Already she was looking forward to the cut-out party. Alastair was flying in for it from the AR head office in the city, with a promised bottle of rum for Dave and a bottle of Baileys for Rebecca. For her, Alastair was a true mentor. She hung on his every word when he forecast the economic future of each agricultural industry or the gossip on property takeovers. He was in touch with agricultural trends across the globe and was able to translate that information into management decisions about the enterprises on each of the AR properties. Rebecca looked up to him, and she knew Alastair saw potential in her. She was the company's youngest employee, but Alastair made it clear she was one of their best. He often liked to recount the story of how he 'found' Rebecca in the stockyards with her dogs. But he neglected to remember that he had promised her work with the stud rams. While Rebecca loved the labouring work on Blue Plains, she longed to become more involved with the stud work, to study genetics and try to piece together a pattern of the types of fleeces that came from each sheep.

Lately, however, on the board in the shed, her mind had been a mile away from wool. As she sifted and sorted fleeces Rebecca dreamed of the river kiss. She relived each moment, except for the bit about the floater. Since the B&S, she'd asked after Charlie. His B&S persona, 'Basil', had legendary status. He was from down the south-west somewhere. 'A diesel dick' someone had called him, and a 'crop king'. Rebecca knew that sort of farm boy – the sort who loved tractors, seeders, cultivators, trucks, grain bins, dozers and anything else made of metal. Happy to spend day and night on a tractor lumbering up and down in straight rows or be swallowed up by machinery sheds for whole days at a time to tinker with motors or invent things. Diesel dicks were the sorts of guys who would watch and wait anxiously after harvest time for rain to come so they could get started with the next round of ploughing and sowing. Rebecca smiled as she thought of Charlie, up there in a big John Deere. Naked.

She shook the thought out of her head and stepped quickly forwards, scooping up the belly wool and hastily removing the pizzle stains; then she binned the wool like a basketballer and began to sweep the locks under the table, smiling at Neville the woolclasser as she went. She loved rouseing. It was like nonstop aerobics for four two-hour sessions every day. Never once did she lean on a broom. The shearers noticed this and liked her for it. As for 'doughey Dave', he endured endless teasing from the shearers, or in their terms he copped a 'piz-zling'. They called him doughey because he was as slow as dough to rise. He took his time on the board, especially when he stooped to pick up a fleece.

'Sheep-O!' cried out Reg as he dragged the last hefty wether from the pen. As the wether slumped between his legs, Reg hitched up his blue pants, wiped his face on his towel, then bent and pulled the cord of his shearing machine. He reached for his handpiece and began to shear. When the shearers called out 'Sheep-O' Bec always beat Dave to it. She whistled Dags and he bounded to the back pens.

'Push up. Push up,' she urged and Dags surfed the sheep into the pens. She had learned to read how the stock ran in the shed. If she timed it right she could get them all in at once with a little push and shove on the gate. But if she mistimed it the lead sheep propped and butted and stayed put. One by one she'd have to turn their faces and half throw them in the direction, using the gate to stop them from running back. She knew she couldn't be off the board too long either, because Dave couldn't cope when two fleeces came off at once.

But with Dags there, she could do the job in no time. Even Stubby's pup, Mouse, was showing promise in the shed and a lot of force. A shearer had put in an offer for $500, but Bec wouldn't budge until she had more than double that. Mouse was worth it.

Rebecca tried not to watch the clock as run after run slid by, but this afternoon she couldn't help it. There was only five minutes to go until afternoon smoko. Katie the cook would soon bustle in with a big basketful of sandwiches and sausage rolls wrapped in tinfoil. Dave had already turned on the urn and its steam rose and fogged the window, making the bright sunny day outside seem misty and grey.

When smoko came, the silence was wonderful. Each whirring Sunbeam ground to a halt as the shearers reached for oil cans, cutters, towels and smokes. When each man settled down to a cup of tea, all that could be heard was the sound of hooves on grating as the sheep milled about slowly in the shed. While AR managers were pretty strict in most of their sheds on their other holdings, they were yet to revamp the clips' quality control at Blue Plains. The bureaucrats hadn't made it out this far, so smoking was still allowed in the shed and they ate smoko on low wooden benches near the wool bins. Bec liked it that old-fashioned casual way, but knew the industry had to change. At Waters Meeting, she'd tried to talk her dad into controlling wool contamination and building a lunch room, but her suggestions had been met with a simple but final, 'Bull,' which in her father's language meant he didn't want to know anything more about it.

Here at Blue Plains, this was the last shearing before the shed was revamped. It would probably be Bec's last shearing here too as her course began in a matter of months. She decided to make the most of it by giving the shearers a laugh. She begged Dave not to eat the egg sandwiches.

'It causes an adverse reaction in the nether regions,'

she explained, desperate and wide-eyed, 'which is somewhat painful and distressing to live with!'

Dave let out a rip-roaring fart which reverberated on the lanolin-darkened floorboards on which he sat.

'Point taken,' said Barney who ripped the sandwich out of Dave's hand and threw it over the catching pen doors onto the grating. Barney then threw his sweat-covered towel over Dave's head.

'Oy!' protested Dave from beneath his striped headdress.

The shearers went on to talk sport and weather with Bob, while Bec talked dogs with Barney. Dave just sat and chewed slowly.

Annabelle was coming over tonight, Friday night, so Bec had offered to cook them a roast. She'd have to run at knock-off time if she was to get the dogs fed and the roast in the oven on time.

The thangs you do for lerve, she thought. Other people's lerve.

She was just putting the heavy pan into the greasy oven when the screen door shrieked that someone had come onto the verandah. It was an out-of-breath Bob.

'Phone for you,' he puffed.

The workmen's phone, which was a payphone, was for some reason installed in the corner of the skillion shed which housed the motorbikes. It was a bugger chatting to people on cold nights, and not very private when the machinery blokes lined up to use the phone. As a result Bec hardly ever rang anyone.

The receiver dangled off the hook and Bec frowned, wondering who it would be.

Her 'Hello' was tentative.

'Sis!'

'Mick! What the flock are you ringing for?' It was the first time she'd heard from him in months. She'd only ever heard news of Mick through Tom or her mum. She immediately panicked. 'What's wrong?'

'Nothing's wrong, you dork. I just rang to say I'm getting married.'

'Married! Holy moley. I mean that's great! To Tur . . . I mean, Trudy?'

'Yeah! Here. She's just here, I'll put her on.' Bec began to protest but Mick was gone and she could hear a sugary, 'Hi Becky.'

'Errr. Ahh. G'day. How's it going? Nice to meet you over the phone. Um. Congratulations I guess! That's great news.' Bec pulled a 'spaz' face at herself and shoved her hand deep in the pocket of her sheep-manure stained jeans.

'I insisted that Mikey rang you. He's been putting off phoning you for ages – I can never get him out of that machinery shed. And he hates talking on the phone. You know him.'

'Yep. So . . . have you set a date for the wedding?'

'Oh. February 14. St Valentine's day.'

'Mmm. Good choice.'

'You'll come, won't you, Rebecca? You have to

come. I'd like to meet you. I think for Tom's sake you should. He misses you . . . mind you, not that he'd say so to me . . . Anyway, we'd better fly. We've organised drinks at the hall tonight.' Bec heard Trudy cup her hand over the phone as she called out, 'Michael, come and say goodbye to your sister!' Then her voice was back, clear and bubbly in Bec's ear.

'He's waving.'

Bec heard Mick's voice in the background: 'See ya, bucket arse.' She heard Trudy chastise him as she put down the phone. Drinks at the hall? Not at the pub? Something was wrong, thought Bec, as she jogged back over to the jackeroos' quarters. Mick hated being called Michael. Yet he seemed happy enough. All through their childhood he rarely spoke to Rebecca. Just bossed her, or teased her. He had always been distant. He was the eldest son – the one in line for most of the farm. So it was always Mick who was taken in the ute by their father. It was Mick who was first to drive the new trac- tor, or went to town with Harry with a load of hay in the truck.

Oh well, thought Bec, it was nice of them to ring, and so long as Trudy made him happy, it was fine by her. But then Rebecca thought of Tom's letters. She remembered him writing that Trudy didn't really understand what it was like to be a farmer's wife and how, no matter what the season, you lived cash-poor. Oh God, she thought, and a vision flashed in her head of an imaginary Trudy wearing a fur coat and dia- monds. It had happened before – entire farms and fortunes had been whittled away by gold-digging wives. Nice homestead and garden, shame about the pastures and stock, thought Bec dryly. Why was Mick marrying her? Surely he could see? All of a sudden the thought of what lay ahead for Waters Meeting filled Rebecca with dread.

Instead of jogging back to the quarters, she turned and ran towards the dog pens. She needed to talk to Mossy and find a little bit of comfort in her dogs. As she ran, Rebecca didn't even notice the massive orange sky behind her as the sun sunk beautifully beneath the plains.

CHAPTER 7

Charlie Lewis dropped his dusty canvas bag on the floor of his bedroom and fell face first onto the bed.

'Charlie?' came his mother's voice. 'Is that you dear?'

All Charlie could do was groan. The roof of his mouth felt rough and his whole body ached. He shut his eyes tightly and swallowed down the nausea. Mrs Lewis put her head around the door.

'Your father's been having a fit all morning. All weekend actually . . . Oh you haven't done that to your hair . . . again!' Charlie didn't move. He lay like a dead body on the bed. Mrs Lewis sighed and bustled into the room. She proceeded to unzip his bag.

'Have you got any washing?'

'Leave it, Mum.' Charlie's gravelly voice was muffled by the mattress.

'You might as well take off those disgusting clothes while I'm doing a load. You look worse than the last time when you came back from that B&S party.'

Charlie rolled over and looked down at his clothes. All the buttons were ripped off his blue shirt and his jeans were grimy with dust and splotchy with spilled rum and coke. Splatters of tomato sauce had stained them in strange coloured blobs. God, he groaned, the sauce fight . . . they'd been kicked out of the pub for that. He let his head fall back on the bed.

'I just don't know what you get up to when you go to town with your friends, Charlie, but I'm certain I don't want to know.'

With that, Mrs Lewis began tugging at her son's football socks, which wouldn't have bothered him that much normally, except for the fact they were still on his feet and he was certain he'd sprained his ankle.

'Alright!' he said angrily and he sat up, batting her hands away from him. He began to peel the stinking clothes from his body, handing each item to his stern-faced mother until he stood in only a pair of blue checked boxer shorts.

'I'll radio your father and tell him you're home.'

'No, Mum. Just give me an hour or so.'

Mrs Lewis shook her head and hurried angrily out of the room with an armful of Charlie's filthy clothes.

'Thanks Mum,' he said as he again lay down on the bed. Mrs Lewis didn't hear him. An instant later as he heard the pipes clunk and the washing machine begin to fill, Mrs Lewis called out, 'And have a shower before you get on that bed again.' Charlie pulled a face before sliding in between the cool sheets. God, he thought, his old man was going to tear strips off him. He thought back to Friday night when he had kissed his mother goodbye and nodded to his father.

'I'll be back to service the vehicles by Saturday afternoon,' he'd said and his father had eyed him over his newspaper saying, 'Don't be late.' And then Charlie had left, leaving a waft of shampoo and soap in the air. His mother had ironed his shirt to within an inch of its life, and as he drove in the ute towards the pub he'd rolled his sleeves up roughly over his tanned arms and tried to loosen the starchy collar.

In the bed, Charlie rolled onto his stomach and groaned again. How did that happen? He'd left on Friday night, and now it was Monday morning. It was those bloody cotton blokes. They'd finished their module building and harvest work and were having a real blow-out. Charlie had got caught up in the celebrations. Friday night at the pub had rolled on into Saturday morning. He'd emerged from his swag, staggered to his ute and had been about to drive away when he'd discovered someone had taken his keys. No amount of farting on blokes' heads or nipple-cripples could extract the information as to who the culprit was. Charlie just gave up. He sauntered in through the creaking screen door of the general store and charmed the somewhat tubby and stringy-haired Janine into microwaving him a pie and heating up the oil so he could have some chips for breakfast. By the time the keys were recovered Charlie was again too drunk to drive. At least too drunk to drive home. Instead the collection of wayward-looking lads took themselves down to the irrigation channel where they lolled against eskies and told jokes. By midafternoon, Charlie had forgotten the promises to his father and Boof had brought his windsurfer along!

'Surf's up!' cried Charlie, standing in just his shorts. He licked his finger and held it in the air. Not a single breath of wind. He ran for his ute and revved it up onto the straight bank of the channel, then tossed Boof a rope. They were off, speeding along the bank, the ungainly surfer clinging for dear life to the windsurfer as the ute raced along the channel.

Lying on his bed, Charlie moved his shoulder and remembered the bad stack he'd had when Boof let the rope go slack.

'What an idiot,' he said to himself.

Stiff, sore and sunburnt, the lads had limped their way into the pub on Saturday night after Charlie's ute had run out of fuel by the channel. In a blur of pool games and dancing by the jukebox, Charlie remembered buying an old alcoholic drinks all night and repeatedly telling him, 'Madadsgunnakillme.'

Sunday morning was spent vomiting and sleeping in his swag out the back of the pub by the cardboard boxes and crates. He remembered some ribby old dog coming up and pissing on his swag. He remembered Rog kicking him with the toe of his boot, saying his mother had phoned the hotel looking for him – again.

In the store Janine was in no mood for the now foul-smelling Charlie, so the lads decided breakfast beers were the go. By the time the Sunday Session kicked on at the pub, Charlie had lost his boots and the boys had shaved his head again. In the pub, a band had been put on for the afternoon. Charlie cringed as he remembered dancing with a group of lads. All with their pants down around their ankles. They had drowned out the duo who chorused 'Welcome to the Hotel California'. Instead the boys gave their best rendition of 'Up there Cazaly'. Charlie cringed again as he remembered joining a group of tourists at their table. As he ate their chips he chatted to them about a staggering array of subjects, including illegal immigration and the merits of the new variety of Dixon's wheat. His mates egged him on as he began to insert chips in his ears and nostrils. That's when the sauce fight began, and that's when Rog, the massive-gutted publican, had hurled the boys outside.

It was Rog who, at dawn on Monday, had handed Charlie a fuel drum and pushed him in the direction of his ute.

'Go home to your folks,' Rog had said tiredly, and he'd watched Charlie stagger away.

Charlie's eyes flashed open as the covers of the bed were roughly pulled back.

He felt his father's huge hands grip into his flesh and close agonisingly on his sore shoulder.

'Get out of bed.' His father shook him a little and started to pull his son up from where he lay.

'Dad!' He could see his father's furious eyes close to his face and smell his breath. It smelt of instant coffee.

'Get dressed and get out to the machinery shed now!'

In the shed Charlie nursed his pounding head in his hands while his father lectured him.

'Your mother was worried sick. If it wasn't for Roger at the hotel, she'd have called the police by Saturday night and told them you were at the bottom of a ditch somewhere in the wreck of your ute. She was hysterical.'

'I'm sor–'

'Don't you give me that bulldust. Pull yourself together, son. Take a bit of pride in yourself! And get to work.' He thrust a plastic container of motor oil into Charlie's hands, got into his ute and revved away down the dusty road.

Charlie kicked the tyre of the tractor. The words had been on the tip of his tongue . . . he wished he'd said it. He wished he could tell his father to get stuffed. He pictured himself standing tall in front of his large father. 'Bugger you, Dad,' Super-Charlie yelled. 'You never give me any time off! Never! You and Mum treat me like I'm a little kid! Well I'm not taking it any more, Dad!'

Charlie began shadow-boxing in the machinery shed, his boots dancing in the dust, his teeth clenched. 'Take this . . . and this . . . and this!' But soon his head pounded too much so he squatted next to a tyre.

'Must be still pissed,' he slurred to himself. He thought about the last time he'd been on such a huge bender. It was months ago. At that B&S ball, the time he met Rebecca Saunders.

'Stunner,' he said out loud and proceeded to lift the dipstick from the tractor.

CHAPTER 8

At first he seemed awkward in Frankie Saunders's flat. He filled up too much space in the tiny living room as he wandered about with his hands clasped behind his back, stooping to peer at family pictures. He tried hard not to look at the ex-husband too long, but he wanted to seem interested in the three smiling children and the array of dogs.

'What would you like to drink, Peter?' came Frankie's voice from the kitchen. After she uttered the words, she quickly turned her back to him to fuss at the kitchen bench. She was nervous too, and the high-pitch strain in her voice showed it.

'Oh. Ahhh . . . Wine is fine.'

'Um. Wine? Oh. Ahhh. Wine.'

'If you don't have any, water's good.'

'How about beer?'

Frankie remembered she'd bought a sad-looking six pack of VB cans for her solitary grand final celebration in front of the television months ago. The cans were still in the back of her dwarf-like fridge, clustered together by plastic rings and taking up far too much room. She remembered she'd eaten one savaloy, watched the kick-off and gone to bed, without drinking the beer, to cry over grand finals of years gone by. Her children clustered together in her mind. Rebecca and the boys dressed in team colours, jostling with each other on the lounge room floor. Streamers framed the TV which throbbed and buzzed with a volume turned too high. She tried to remember a few of the homemade chants which didn't quite rhyme. When she thought more about football, she couldn't help but think of Harry and the vacant look on his face when he watched it.

Sometimes when she looked at him propped in the chair with his feet up on an old milking stool, she would swear he was about to dribble and imagined herself cupping her hands beneath his chin. Other times she felt like slapping him hard across each cheek and shaking him while screaming, 'Notice me!' But she never did, she simply shut herself off and hoped someone would call with an emergency calving or a poisoned dog.

After the marriage was over, Frankie tried to figure out what had gone wrong or, she wryly thought, what had gone right. She had always been a scientist, with a passion for her job. Frankie tried to remember when Harry had stopped talking to her. Stopped showing his love for her. But she could never pin the time down. She came to realise he had always been silent and broody. At first she had found in him an undeniable sexual power. He was a man's man – not at all like the academics she had dated in her uni days. Her friends had often asked her why she stayed so long, and her answer had always been, 'For the children.' But she knew deep down that she had never really been there for the children. She lived for her work. She lived for her science, and the more it took her away from the family and that huge cold house, the more complete she felt. Nowadays she used her science and her work to fill up the gaping hole created by her guilt.

In the kitchen she tensed her muscles a little and sighed. From where he stood in the living room, Peter looked at her kindly.

'I'm not really a beer drinker, but I'll give it a go. I usually only drink it on Australia Day or during football grand finals.'

'Oh,' laughed Frankie and she bent to move aside the wilting vegetables and drag out the six pack. She held them up to him, 'Not exactly boutique beer. How about I share one with you?'

It was half an hour before their dinner reservation at an Italian restaurant two blocks away. Frankie wished she had a dog or a cat, so they could focus their attention and conversation on its markings or its habits, but the flat was neat and cold. Perhaps she could talk about Henbury's anal-gland problem, but they had almost exhausted that topic and the dog had been well in its nether regions now for months.

'Have a seat,' she said, and her hand swept towards the couch like a hostess on 'Sale of the Century.'

The leather couch let out a farting noise as Peter sat. He tried to shift his weight again so the noise would repeat itself and Frankie would know it wasn't an actual fart, but the couch lay silent.

Peter perched himself on the edge of the couch and pointed to the family photo on the television.

'You have a handsome brood.'

'Yes.'

'Your daughter is a very attractive young lady.'

'She's a wild child. God knows what she's up to on that sheep station.'

'If she's anything like her mother, she'll be fine.' Peter looked into Frankie's eyes and he sucked in a breath as if he'd made up his mind about something.

Oh please God, don't let him kiss me yet, thought Frankie.

But Peter said, 'I know this is difficult for us both. We've both come through marriage break-ups, but I just wanted you to know that there's no pressure. We're both so nervous! Let's just be friends and see where the friendship takes us. Okay?' He searched her eyes for a reaction. 'Okay?' he urged.

'Sure,' said Frankie. 'Here's to friendship,' and as she raised her glass and chinked it against his, she thought, 'Damn!' After all, it had been almost four years.

In the dim light of the noisy Italian restaurant, Frankie and Peter laughed at the jovial fat-faced musician who lurked around the tables twanging on his instrument. They wrestled with dangling forkfuls of fettuccine, trying to put it in their mouths without dribbling sauce down their chins. On their second bottle of lambrusco Frankie almost mentioned that the fettuccine, in this dim light, looked remarkably like tapeworm, but she thought better of it. Peter, she thought, was very 'city'. It wasn't until Peter held up the fettuccine and said, 'Does this remind you of your work?' that she laughed louder than she had in years. Peter went on to explain he specialised in teaching sciences and his favourite subject was biology.

'We have several species of worm on display in our lab. I'll have to give you a tour one day soon.'

'That would be fabulous,' said Frankie sincerely.

'Perhaps we could do a deal with your surgery to provide animal parts for experiments in our lab,' Peter joked. All at once Frankie felt warmed by the wine and by Peter's eyes. Oh God, she thought, he loves science! She felt a tingle run through her.

After a raucous display from the musician and some hilarious dancing, Frankie and Peter settled back into their restaurant chairs. Soon their fingers entwined on the tabletop and the candlelight glimmered in their eyes.

'How about a quiet port before we tackle the road home?' Peter asked.

'Lovely.'

Outside the air was chilly. Peter linked his arm with Frankie's and walked close to her on the way home. They chattered drunkenly and laughed loudly in the empty street. At the entrance to the flat Frankie decided to check the mail. The little silver postbox-key slipped and scratched on the surface as they both giggled into their hands.

'I can't find the hole,' said Frankie.

'Are you sure you've got the right box?' Peter looked into her eyes and they both spluttered and wheezed at the innuendo.

'Here. Let me try,' and Peter eventually turned the lock and reached for the mail. He flipped through the envelopes. 'Bill, bill, bill . . . ahhhh,' he waggled an envelope in the air, 'this one looks interesting.'

Frankie saw the light from the street lamp glitter on the golden-edged envelope. She frowned.

'Here,' Peter handed it to her.

The large envelope was white and heavy, and the extravagant, swirly gold writing made her name, Dr Frances Saunders, seem so incredibly pompous. Her finger slipped beneath the golden seal and a chocolate heart wrapped in golden foil fell to the ground. Peter stooped to pick it up, his eyes on Frankie's puzzled face as she unfolded the crisp paper.

'Wedding? My son? Oh my God. My son is getting married.'

'Why, that's great,' said Peter enthusiastically.

'No. You don't understand. They didn't even ring me. I didn't even know. I don't even know the girl. I've never laid eyes on her. Oh my God.' She raised her hand to her mouth. Peter gently put an arm around her and ushered her into the unit building and inside the lift.

While she sat on the couch he placed a steaming cup of tea in her hands and sat down beside her, oblivious to the squelchy fart sounds the couch made. Frankie stared at the steam as tears welled up in her eyes.

'I'm sorry, Peter. I'm sorry. It's just such a shock. You know. He's my eldest boy. You know, Michael – Mick. He blames me. He thinks I should be home with his father. That's why he didn't ring.'

'Hey, hey, hey. It's okay. It's okay.' He took the cup from her hand and placed it on the coffee table. Then he took her in his arms. He wrapped his hand around the back of her head as she buried her face into his chest.

'Don't worry,' said Peter as he reached for the wedding invitation which lay on the coffee table, 'It says here, Dr Frances Saunders and partner. If you like, I mean, if you think it will help, I can come with you. I don't actually have to go to the wedding if you don't want. We could, you know, travel up as friends. Make it a bit of a holiday. I'll just come along for the ride.'

She wasn't sure if it was to shut Peter up or to show gratitude for his gentleness, but Frankie tilted her face up to his and placed her lips on his mouth.

CHAPTER 9

Tom sat back in his saddle and swore under his breath while he watched his father yank the ute into reverse.

'Get your useless dog out of the way,' bellowed Harry as he backed the ute quickly to the area where the sheep were breaking out of the mob.

Tom hated stock work with his father. Five of his father's dogs trotted wide of the mob in a group, too afraid to do any real work, yet too afraid to not work. Bessie, the little dog Rebecca had bred for Tom, hesitated at Harry's threatening voice but stood her ground on the other side of the mob looking and waiting for Tom's command. The gate was still a few hundred yards away and Harry was trying to drive the sheep along the fence with the ute and his dogs. Too much pressure and the sheep would break and run south up a steep hill. Those that weren't trying to bust out of the mob were knotting themselves up in circles and spinning in a huge whirling pool while Harry tooted the horn and 'haaa'ed'.

Tom shifted his weight in the saddle so that Hank, his stretchy chestnut, moved forward, ears flickering back and forwards at the commotion. Tom licked the dust from his lips and whistled Bessie in, so that she cantered in a wide arc around the mob and fell in behind Hank's hooves.

Ever since they were little Bec and Tom had watched stock-flow with their grandad. He'd even set up lessons for them in the yard. He'd pull a raddle out of his pocket and grab one of the five sheep which stood huddled in the corner and mark big slashes of red crayon on its nose. Then he'd pick out two other sheep and mark them with a blue raddle. His dancing collie dogs drove the five sheep to him as he walked in long-legged steps around the yard. Once marked, the movement of the stock was obvious to Bec and Tom as Grandad pointed out the flow pattern.

'See! See!' Grandad said. 'That red raddled fella there, he's your lead sheep. He's the one you look for when you move a mob . . . There'll be him and a few of his mates actin' as leaders . . . They'll take them blue followin' fellas through any gate you choose, if you can spot 'em and get your dogs to work 'em right.'

Tom frowned at his father's form in the ute. Grandad may have set time aside to teach his grand-children stockmanship, but he never got close enough to his son to influence him. Tom remembered what it was like, sitting at the big table in the kitchen as the clock ticked above them. Grandfather at the head and Harry seated down the other end. There was always tension at the table. Grandad would say things like, 'Tom, tell your father you can come with me tomorrow to the hut' or 'Tom, tell your father the Holden is due for a service.' He said it even when Harry was sitting right there in front of him. He used his grandchildren to speak to his own son. No wonder we're all so screwed up, thought Tom bitterly as he watched his father now.

After their grandfather died, Tom and Bec took on a lot of the stock work in their school holidays. Tom could almost see Harry seethe with envy when they brought a mob in. There was no yelling, no revving of utes, no flogging of dogs. The sheep seemed to drift along as Tom and Bec rode slowly nearby, their horses on a loose rein. They talked easily between themselves, Bec rambling excitedly about stock-breeding programs they could try or new crops they could sow.

'As *if*,' they'd chorus. They'd look at each other and laugh, both trying to survive the constraints of their father. Bec's dogs so far had been their only victory in changing how things were run on the farm.

Her kelpies had such refined instincts that they naturally brought the sheep towards her. Tom and Rebecca simply rode towards the front and flank of a mob along the fence and the dogs did the rest, herding the sheep forwards. If the mob broke out to run too fast, Bessie instinctively cast to the front of the mob to gently block them. She hovered a long way off so the lead sheep weren't spun around in circles. Then she would glance from the stock to Tom, waiting for her next command.

That's what Bessie had been doing today, but Harry just didn't get it. He was so different from Grandad. As Tom grew older, he saw more of Harry in his brother Mick. Mick rarely did any of the stock work now. He preferred to tinker in the machinery shed, servicing vehicles and ordering spare parts out of dog-eared oil-stained manuals. That was of course before Trudy came on the scene. Now he'd sometimes head off for long weekends away to visit Trudy's parents. Each time he returned, he was more and more distant. Now that they had ended their Friday night ritual at Dirty's pub, Tom barely spoke to Mick. Sometimes they'd have a chat about the farm, but Mick would only occasionally talk about his relationship with Trudy.

'You gotta grow up sometime,' Mick said. 'She's a good sort, once you get to know her.' When Tom's face remained blank, Mick ploughed on. 'She cooks me good tucker and besides, her old man's loaded.' Mick had been joking at the time, but Tom could tell there was an element of truth in it. Trudy was a devoted little rich girl, wanting to play the role of farmer's wife in a grand mansion.

Suddenly Hank pulled a little on the bit, turned his long head towards the road and pointed his ears forwards. Tom followed the gelding's gaze. It was Trudy. She was zipping down the hill in her red Laser, going far too fast and throwing out clouds of dust and tiny stones. When she drove past the mob she tooted the horn and waved from the window. Tom smiled to himself as the leaders in the mob propped and looked at the little red car which blared Celine Dion from its CD player. He pictured his dad in the ute cab, getting redder in the face and swearing. He'd say something like, 'Stupid bloody bitch,' and his veins would pop out on his neck.

She drove through the gate and then got out to close it.

'Leave it open!' yelled Harry from a few hundred metres away. Celine sung out over the paddocks – heartbroken again. Trudy put a hand to her ear and mimed a 'What?'

'Don't shut it! Don't – shut – it!' called Harry.

'Okay!' smiled a bouncing Trudy as she ran to shut the gate. Satisfied she'd done the right thing, she waved again, like someone departing on a world cruise, jumped into her Laser and roared off down towards the homestead.

'Bloody oath,' said Tom. There'd be a seething silence tonight at dinner, he just knew it.

By the time they'd opened the gate and finally got the spinning mob through and down the big hill to the river flats, the sun had sunk below a silent blue mountain. Hank knew his working day was almost done so he sung out a shuddering whinny to Rebecca's horse, which trotted up and down the home paddock fence calling out for her mate.

Every time Rebecca wrote to Tom or spoke to him on the phone she asked, 'How's Stinky?'

Frankie had saved the well-bred mare several years

ago. An old bloke down the valley had bred her on his place but couldn't afford the vet bills after the mare staked herself on a steel dropper. He was about to shoot her when Frankie showed up in her cluttered veterinary four-wheel drive and put a proposal to him. The old man had been drinking hard at the time but Frankie knew his watery eyes weren't from the grog. She treated the mare herself at great expense. And thanks to Rebecca's dedication in cleaning the oozing wound, the mare had survived. The deal was Rebecca could keep the horse, and the next foal she had, if she had one, would be sent back down the valley to the old man. She was registered as Australian stockhorse Beaufront Ink Jet. Of course, once under Rebecca's ownership, the name Ink Jet evolved into Stink Jet and then later Stinky. Rebecca's mother shook her head each time she heard Rebecca call her Stinky. It didn't do the mare justice. She was a tough little animal, stocky and solid with a nice temperament for a mare.

Tom watched her now as he led a de-saddled Hank to the gate. Stinky's well-formed muscles shone under her black coat in smooth hunks. The rich grass which grew on Waters Meeting river flats kept her in good condition – almost too good. She could be a bit pushy to ride. She arched her neck and sniffed at the impression the saddle blanket had left on Hank's sloping back.

'Hey beautiful,' said Tom gently as he stretched his hand out and laid it on her neck.

'Bec might be home to see you soon, girl. She might be coming home for the big "W". That'd be good, wouldn't it?' The mare's thick mane lay in tangled whirls against her neck. 'We'll have to clean you up a bit before she gets here, hey Stinker.'

On his way back to the little wooden saddle shed, which leaned like a lazy man against the old stone stable, he passed the workshop and glanced in.

There in the ute cab behind darkened glass sat Mick with an almost strangled expression of pleasure on his face. From where Tom walked he could see Trudy's legs behind the opened ute door and her head bobbing up and down over Mick's lap. Slowly Mick rolled his head forward and opened his eyes, eventually registering, with a sudden shock, that someone was watching. When he saw it was Tom, his face relaxed again and he winked.

Tom bowed his head, embarrassed, and hurried past to put his saddle away. He swore under his breath and then whistled up Bessie who was busy herding the chooks back to their pen for the evening.

Later in the warm kitchen, Tom looked at Trudy as she fluffed around the room as though she was in the running for the 1950s farm-wife of the year award. Scattered on the table were bridal magazines, their pages marked with yellow and pink sticky notes. The phone book lay open at F for Florists.

F for Flock off, thought Tom as he stared at her coldly.

Still, she prattled on. 'Of course my mum and dad can't understand *why* I would want a wedding in the bush. They can't even understand why I love the bush and want to live out here in the middle of woop woop. They want the reception at Dad's club in the city and the wedding in the church where they got married. They've offered to pay for everything, so I suppose I can't have it all my way. And it's not like Michael and I can afford it. Dad has picked out the MC already. He's a QC, you see. Don't you think that's funny, Tom, an MC who's a QC, UC?'

Tom knew Trudy was prattling on deliberately. He knew she put on an airhead act when it suited her. Tom likened it to his bitch, Bessie. She used similar tactics when she wanted to get away with something. He wondered if he should tell Trudy his theory now.

But before Tom could speak, Harry walked into the kitchen bringing with him the smell of cheap shampoo. He glanced at Trudy and sighed. Trudy stopped fluffing and fell silent. Harry picked up a copy of the *Rural Weekly* and walked through to the lounge room and its whispering wood heater, which had been brought to life earlier by Tom. He made a point of closing the door loudly.

'He's still mad at me over that gate thingy this afternoon,' whispered Trudy, leaning towards Tom as if confiding in him. She sighed and peered cautiously into the wood stove.

'But I'll get the hang of this place . . . and this family . . . soon,' she said through gritted teeth. Then she spoke again in her sugary voice, 'Tom, will you be a darling and call Michael, the meat loaf is nearly ready.'

'That'll be two meat loaves you've stuffed in your

mouth today then, Trudy,' said Tom as he ducked quickly out of the kitchen door. 'You won't fit into your wedding dress at the rate you're going.'

He left Trudy standing by the stove in chook-print oven mitts, her mouth open and her eyes wide.

'Bastards,' she said as she kicked the cat away.

CHAPTER 10

Rebecca, Dave and Annabelle were just putting their head-torches on and choosing their golf clubs when the screen door announced the late arrival of another potential player.

'What on earth are you up to? Or shouldn't I ask?' came the voice of Alastair Gibson. His presence in the jackeroo quarters stopped the would-be cane toad golfers in their tracks. The sight of him in the doorway was unusual. No. More than unusual. Neither Bec nor Dave had *ever* seen the manager in the building. Sure he'd come to the step on occasions, but never inside. He looked down at his boots and kicked them off, momentarily self-conscious.

'Flew in this morning with some international guests for the weekend. Bob's taken them to the pub for the evening. God help them. So I thought I'd drop in to see you.'

Rebecca cast her eye over the chaotic kitchen where

dirty plates, mugs and beer bottles lounged about on top of bare-breasted girls in Dave's filth magazines. The mess was spread as though a wind had blown it across the floor into the lounge room. It had become a ritual that Annabelle would come for dinner Friday nights, bonk Dave to *Rage* all Saturday morning, and then spend the afternoon cleaning up around his reclining form as he watched TV.

Bec often felt the guilt rise and would offer to help, gingerly scrubbing at the splatters in the toilet, but she drew the line at putting blue ducks in the loo and sitting mushroom-shaped stinky things on the cistern.

Now, with Alastair in their midst, she wished she had been just a little more houseproud.

'We're . . . err . . . um,' said Rebecca as she leaned the golf club against the chair.

'We're . . . er . . .' added Dave, 'going golfing. Except we're not using balls. Just cane toads.'

'Oh I see!' laughed Alastair. 'Suppose you're doing a good deed for the environment . . . It's amazing the little buggers have spread their way so far inland. This year's the first I've seen so many of them on Blue Plains. Do you mind if I postpone your match for just a few minutes. I wanted to talk to Rebecca.'

'Sure! No worries!' said Dave over-enthusiastically, looking around at Annabelle and Rebecca. His head torch, switched on, shone a beam of light wherever he looked, like an overzealous theatre spotlighter.

Rebecca dragged the elastic straps of her torch from

her head and coughed a little at Dave. 'Would you like a beer, Mr Gibson?' she asked.

'Please call me Alastair, and yes please, I would love a beer.'

'Um. Take a seat,' said Dave as he scooped up piles of newspapers from the couch and kicked cans and plastic coke bottles across the floor into the corner.

'Oh I won't be staying long. Just wanted to put a proposal to Rebecca.'

'Well, we'll get out of your hair.' Annabelle smiled brightly. 'Come on, Dave. Feel like a round?' She glanced at Dave and added almost too quickly, '. . . of golf.'

Taking up their clubs, the screen door wheezed and then coughed shut as they went out into the thick evening air.

Bec handed Alastair his stubby. 'I'd offer you a glass, but . . .' She motioned to the line-up of glasses on the sink. 'I can wash one for you if you like.'

'No. No. It's already in a glass,' said Alastair holding up his bottle with a smile as he sat at the kitchen table.

Bec took his lead and sat across from him, sipping on her cold beer and looking at him over the clutter of tomato sauce bottles, half-eaten bags of bread, Black and Gold soy sauce, Vegemite jars and small towers of plastic salt and pepper containers.

'Bob told me you handed in your resignation this afternoon.'

'Yes. That's right,' said Bec. 'I hope it wasn't taken

the wrong way. I love it here. I do. It's just my brother is getting married after Christmas, so I have to travel home that way anyway. Then I've enrolled at Tablelands University to do a business and farm management degree. It starts in March. I thought I'd give you plenty of notice by letting you know before Christmas.'

'Sure. Sure you have. It's just, you've been such a good employee. One of our best. Even though you're one of our youngest, you show a lot of initiative and the company can see you're an asset.'

The words fell like warm kisses onto Rebecca. Her life had been parched when it came to receiving praise from her father. Nothing she could do, no matter how hard she tried, had ever pleased him.

'When I first met you at the yards I promised you more to do with the ram shed and the showing side of the operation. I know that hasn't happened this year and you haven't been off the place. It's taken a while to talk Bob around into letting you youngsters have a go, but I think he's ready now and he can see you'd be a good thing for the showing of Blue Plains stud stock.'

Bec pulled at the label of her stubby so that it came away in a wet gluey patch. She stuck it back on and pulled it off again as she listened.

'We want you to take as much time off for your brother's wedding, but we also want you to come back, not as a jillaroo but as our stud promotions manager. There's a salary set aside to match that title . . . well almost, but it's a far cry better than what you're on. If you can defer your studies for at least another year, it'll give you the chance to save more and to learn more. I can't help notice that the local pub gets most of your and Dave's spare change.' He smiled kindly.

'So an extra year is all you're asking?'

'Yes.

Bec felt a tinge of sadness creep in. There was no way her father would put her in charge of a whole enterprise on the farm. She couldn't help wish she had a father like Alastair.

'Anyway Bec. I'll leave you to think about it. Let us know where you are by Christmas. I've asked head office to draw up a job description for you with details of salary and responsibilities. That should be through on Bob's email by Tuesday, so if you catch up with him after the weekend you can find out more.'

'Great. Thanks. I'll think about it, Alastair. That's very kind of you.'

Far off outside the window a 'Wooo-hooo!' could be heard.

'Dave must've hit a toad for a bogie,' said Alastair and Bec smiled. 'You're not going home for Christmas?'

'No.'

'Any family coming to visit?'

'Ahh. No.' Bec made a humble-smile face and shook her head self-consciously.

'Sorry to pry. I know things haven't improved with

your father over the months. Christmas is a good time to make amends, but if you're not ready, the invitation's there for you to come to the city to spend Christmas with my family.'

Rebecca smiled warmly. She'd never known a man his age to chat the way Alastair did. She liked him.

'Thanks, Mr Gibson. That's really nice of you, but I'd miss my dogs too much, and besides, Marg and Bob are planning a barbecue at the billabong, so I'll be right.'

'All right. So long as you promise me one thing.'

'What's that?'

'That you phone your family. Have a yack to your old man. I know if you were my daughter I'd want to hear from you.'

Rebecca looked at the ceiling and pursed her lips. 'Okay,' she said like a child. Then they both laughed.

When he'd finished his beer she thought he'd go, but instead he grabbed the golf club resting against the chair.

'Now,' he said, 'let's go golfing.'

Rebecca's mouth dropped.

'Okay!' she beamed. 'But you'll need these,' and she handed Alastair Gibson a pair of purple swirling wrapround reflector sunglasses, recently bought by Dave from the Price-Buster store in town.

'What on earth for? It's dark out there.'

'It's not just for looks,' teased Bec, 'and it's not just for the challenge of toad-hitting by torchlight. It's because their poison can spray you in the eye.'

As Alastair went to pull his boots on he muttered, 'This is not only sounding dangerous, but also ridiculous.'

'It's character building,' said Bec as the screen door banged a full stop on her sentence.

CHAPTER 11

The dogs on the back put their noses into the rush of heat and squinted their eyes in the wind. Inside the hot little cab, takeaway papers littered the floor and a drink bottle filled with water warmed between Rebecca's knees. Every now and then she splashed the water over her face and chest. The hot wind rushing through the opened window sucked the moisture from her singlet and left her a little cooler. Bec glanced at her right arm resting on the frame of the door. It was burning red, while her other arm was its usual honey-coloured brown. From the console she grabbed a tube of sunscreen and smeared a glob of white cream over her arm. She rubbed the remainder into her right leg, which was also catching the sun. She shifted a little, her back sticking hotly to the seat of the ute. She turned up the radio and tried to ignore the sweltering temperature.

The towns were getting bigger, more civilised, more standardised. McDonalds, KFC, neat all-the-same servos selling fatty all-the-same food. In one town Rebecca stopped at a large department store and wandered through racks of clothes, looking heartlessly for a dress for the wedding. She moved amongst the shoppers as though she wasn't there at all. She ran her brown fingers along the racks of pristine clothes while the shop assistant stared at her as if she were a shoplifter.

Bec had left her dogs on the back of her ute in the dark underground car park, and she worried about them. They were good-looking types – they could be stolen easily. Besides, she hated shopping. She turned to leave, but then caught a glimpse of herself in a mirror. Under the fluoro store lighting Rebecca looked at her reflection. A tanned, wind-blown girl wearing torn denim shorts. She frowned at herself. She looked different. She didn't know how, but something was definitely different about her.

Stuff it, she said to herself. She'd find something to wear in the next town. She rode the escalator down to the shopping centre's carpark and ran her hands over the ears of all her delighted bouncing dogs.

Hands shaking from gravel-road vibrations and nerves, Bec rang the bell at the Fur Trapper on the Saturday of the wedding. From the bar she heard Darren Weatherby call out, 'Hold your horses, won't be a minute.' Cigarette hanging from his mouth, he rounded the corner juggling empty cardboard boxes. When he saw Rebecca he dropped them at his feet in mock shock.

'Beccy Saunders, love!'

'Dirty!' She flung her arms about him and he planted a stubbly, smoky kiss on her cheek.

'Home for the weddin', are ya?'

'Yeah, thought I'd better do the right thing.'

'How is it up north? Been hearing a bit from Tom and your postcards. Said you'd been pig shooting, cane-toad golfing and wrestling wild bulls.'

'Yep. It's been great. Would rather be home on the farm, but that's the way of the snake up the gravelly path, ay Dirty.'

'Ahh! Hear you picked up that Northern "ay".'

Bec smiled and shrugged.

'Haven't seen your old man about much lately. He sends Mick into town to do his jobs.'

Rebecca looked around the pub. 'This place hasn't changed.'

'No,' said Dirty, also looking around. 'Worst luck.'

'Have you got a spare room for a night or two, Dirty? I'm not sure where I'm staying.' Bec could feel tears welling up.

'Ahh, love. We're fully booked with the weddin'. Got a heap up from the city, and all I've had are complaints. They keep asking if there's any "alternative" accommodation round here, something with private bathrooms. Been drivin' me nuts. We can find you a place for your swag, though, and you can use the shower. I suppose being dogwoman and all, you'll have all your dogs.' He glanced out the window, looking for her ute. 'You can tie 'em up out the back.'

'Thanks, Dirty. You're a legend.'

'We've missed you, girl. So has your brother Tom. Been in here drunk as a skunk most weekends.'

'Have you seen him this weekend?'

'He's out at your old man's getting groomed for groomsman. Trudy's at Angela Carmichael's getting her hair doova'd with the bridesmaids. They're going to the church straight from there. You should see St Matthew's . . . all the ladies are clucking around at the church doing the flowers and fussing and farting. Trudy's decided to have the reception at Waters Meeting.'

Rebecca felt a stab of shock as Dirty's commentary washed over her.

'They've done up the garden and 'parently hired a marquee and a jazz band from the city.'

Bec hadn't expected this. The invitation had said the hall. To return home now to some strange girl's wedding in her house, in her Waters Meeting house . . . She felt the hatred for her father rise in her heart, and nausea flooded over her.

'. . . for Chrissakes. A *jazz* band. I ask you, what's the world coming to!' continued Dirty. He stopped when he saw the strain on Bec's face.

'It's after eleven, isn't it, Dirty?'

'What? Oh.' He glanced at his watch. 'Just.'

'Is your bar open? Because I need a Scotch.'

'Bar's open any time for you, Bec. I'll make it a double, shall I?'

'Yep. Just a quick shot, then I'll settle my dogs in and get myself frocked up.'

He handed her the drink and she looked at the ice cubes suspended in yellowy-brown liquid. A lump rose in her throat. Large warm tears dropped onto the tufted, green and red bar mat and, as she moved the chinking drink, her tears splashed onto the ice.

'Hey Bec,' soothed Dirty, 'if you'd wanted water with your Scotch, girl, you should've asked.' He moved around the bar, took the glass from her and put his arm around her shoulders. She laughed a little and cried a lot all at the same time, and Dirty tried hard to brush away her embarrassment.

'They always say bar work involves 50 per cent drink pouring and 50 per cent counselling,' said Dirty to the top of Rebecca's bowed head. 'Between you and Tom, your dad's been providing me with a lot of business. I should send the rotten old bastard a bill.'

With that, he flicked on the jukebox and selected the saddest Dixie Chicks song he could find. 'If you're going to be miserable, you might as well do it properly and sink yourself low as you can, girl.'

The Dixie Chicks filled the empty pub with mournful twanging voices. Dirty handed Bec another Scotch and she looked up gratefully into his lined and kindly eyes. She could barely say thanks as the tears flooded again. The drink flowed into her empty stomach like a balm.

Frankie first saw her daughter standing outside the white weatherboard church. She was about to rush over to her, but something held her back. She watched Rebecca through the crowd and was shocked to realise that her daughter seemed like a stranger.

She looked different. Older. She wore her hair up and stood self-consciously in a sleeveless blue dress. Frankie concluded that Rebecca looked beautiful. Grown up.

Peter followed her gaze, nervously stroking down his tie. 'Rebecca?'

Frankie nodded.

'She's lovely.'

When Rebecca turned and saw her mother, she rushed over and hugged her warmly.

'Mum! Good to see you. You look great.'

'So do you! Look at that tan!'

'Outdoors lifestyle.'

They laughed and hugged again.

'Nervous?' Frankie asked.

'You bet.'

'Seen Dad yet?'

'No.'

Peter coughed.

'Oh! Sorry,' said Frankie to Peter. 'Rebecca, I'd like you to meet a friend of mine. Peter. Peter, this is my daughter. Rebecca.'

'Nice to meet you at long last,' said Bec, shaking his hand enthusiastically. 'You feature in Mum's letters a fair bit.'

'I do, do I?' Peter smiled at Frankie warmly.

Rebecca liked the look of him. There was a real

kindness about him and his eyes were so friendly. Just then the minister appeared at the arched doorway of the church and began to usher people inside.

'Mum, the man in the long frock is calling us to go have a yarn to God.' She nodded towards the minister.

'Oh, Rebecca!' Frankie rolled her eyes and smiled. 'I can see you haven't got any more respectful of the Church.' Then to Peter she said, 'My daughter has a problem with anything that requires conformity. Religion is one of them. And that man in the long dress is Father Peterson. He actually christened all my children and married me and . . . my . . . Harr . . . my ex-husband.'

The mention of Harry made Rebecca's stomach turn. The thought of him being here, inside that church, terrified her. This morning's whiskey had worn off and she'd begun to get a headache. Her mother took her by the arm and led her into the cool darkness of the church. Rebecca wondered if Frankie was offering her support or if it was the other way round.

Towards the altar, the old oak pews were crowded with people she mostly didn't know. The three of them shuffled and sidestepped along an empty pew at the back of the church. A few of the locals turned their heads towards them and made motions for them to sit further up in the pews reserved for family, but both Rebecca and her mother shook their heads, smiled and waved the attention away.

Rebecca could see her father sitting at the very front of the church. His hair was longer and lay in an untidy grey mat on his head. The pinstripes on his suit sloped downwards with the slump of his shoulders. His head was bowed towards his shoes.

In front of Harry sat Tom and Mick. Rebecca's heart leapt when she saw them. Even though the boys nervously fidgeted with ties and buttons they looked drop-dead gorgeous. Rebecca had forgotten how tall and handsome Mick was. His black hair shone and was freshly cut in a neat line across the back of his neck. He was clean-shaven and even his hands were no longer stained with oil. He looked magnificent. Then Rebecca studied Tom. His unruly sandy hair had been cut shorter and combed back. It suited him. His skin was the same golden honey colour as Rebecca's. He put a hand to his tie and adjusted it. He had beautiful hands, Rebecca thought. She wondered if he'd found a girl-friend. If one of Trudy's friends didn't set their targets on him tonight, Rebecca would be amazed. He was looking like a dish.

Just then a woman in a pink hat, her hair done in a bun of curls, fussed over the boys and smoothed down Tom's hair. Rebecca stared at her ample bottom sheathed in fuchsia silk, and her chunky legs which ran down to fat ankles and little feet that were crammed into pink strappy high-heeled shoes.

Frankie whispered to Bec, 'I think that's Trudy's mother.'

'The genetics do not look good,' Bec said out of the corner of her mouth and felt her mother's hand thump her gently on the thigh.

The woman at the organ began to press out groaning notes, which sounded like a cat in season. Then the bride made her entrance, swept along by her short, fat, balding father.

'The genetics are definitely not good,' Bec whispered again to her mother.

'Shhhh!'

'She's used a lot of mozzie net.'

'Shhhhh!'

Bec peered through swathes of white tulle trying to make out Trudy's face. She looked pretty, her face elf-like and her eyes shining with tears. Rebecca felt Frankie grab onto her arm and when she looked at her mother's face, it was contorted with emotion. Rebecca's self-defence of whiskey and clowning around fell away. She felt raw and alone.

As the booming voice of Father Peterson filled the church, mother and daughter wept silently, twisting tissues and dabbing eyes. When people glanced in their direction Rebecca and Frankie smiled back thinly. Rebecca sighed and looked at the backs of her brothers standing so square and still. She felt like a stranger to the men who stood in their wedding suits at the altar.

Coloured paper lanterns hung along the verandahs of the house. Bamboo torches burned around the freshly gravelled circular driveway and fairy lights glittered in gum trees. Possums skittered nervously in the branches and peered down at the crowd of people who stood about in clusters on the lawn. In the marquee on the homestead lawn, guests chinked wineglasses and laughed, draping themselves drunkenly over white plastic chairs.

In the corner, a sunken and drunk Harry slumped at his table and continued to throw glances at Frankie and Peter who sat with Rebecca.

At the long white bridal table Mick lolled with his groomsmen, like Romans at a feast. Trudy, in her perfect satin gown, flowed from table to table with a smile set firmly on her face.

'Thank you so much for coming,' she purred to Frankie.

'Well I wouldn't miss my own son's wedding, would I?' muttered Frankie into her wineglass.

Rebecca, hoping Trudy hadn't heard, jumped up from the table too quickly, knocking over a jug of beer.

'Oh! Whoops! I was just going to give you a wedding day hug.' As Frankie and Peter mopped up the spilled beer Bec and Trudy hugged awkwardly. She felt the bones of Trudy's shoulder blades beneath her bridal gown. When Trudy moved away to another table Rebecca grabbed for her glass of wine and threw back the tepid liquid.

Harry caught his daughter's eye and Rebecca deliberately turned her back on him. She watched couples dancing tamely to the jazz band. On the edge of the crowd was Tom with his shirt untucked and his hair regaining its normal wild state. He was straddling a white plastic chair, riding it rodeo-style. Tom spurred his chair and threw one hand in the air as if riding a rank bull. The chair leg snapped suddenly and he sprawled on the chipboard dance floor. Rebecca got up to help him, but Trudy's mother was already trotting over with her pink hat wobbling.

'Enough's enough,' she said through gritted teeth fixed into a smile. Her hand pinched his arm.

'We can't have you spoil Michael and Trudy's special day.'

'What's so shpechial about it?' said Tom to himself as he frowned and watched Trudy's mother's large backside wobble. He staggered over to an empty table and grabbed at a glass of red wine, then slung it back, draining it in one gulp.

'Having fun, Tom?'

'Ahhh! Bec! Let's drink to a match made in heaven!' He glanced over to Mick, who had a glossy taffeta-clad bridesmaid on his knee, and laughed.

'Come on! Let's make some merriment,' Rebecca said as she grabbed Tom's hand and together they dived under the white folds of linen that covered the long bridal table.

They crawled to where Mick sat with the drunken, giggling bridesmaid. Smiling wickedly, Rebecca ran her hand firmly up and down Mick's thigh.

'He's so stonkered he'll think it's the chick! He doesn't even know we're here,' Bec whispered. Tom pointed at the bridesmaid's legs.

'Go on!' said Bec grinning and nodding.

Tom stuck his hand roughly up the bridesmaid's dress. Thinking it was Mick, the curvy girl swathed in peacock-blue taffeta shrieked and fell backwards, trying to slap Mick as she went.

From under the table Bec and Tom wheezed with laughter as they saw Trudy's bridal shoes march towards Mick and the bridesmaid. In not so hushed whispers she told Michael to behave and Shelley to sober up.

Reaching for his hand, Trudy dragged Mick from his chair on to the dance floor and unleashed her determination to 'make her wedding day a success'. Still laughing, Bec reached out from beyond the drape of the tablecloth and grabbed a bottle of wine from the table. In their bridal cubbyhouse, both brother and sister prepared their glasses for a wobbly drunken toast.

'To Dick and Turdy!'

'To Dick and Turdy!' replied Tom as they chinked glasses.

'You've got red-wine lips,' slurred Bec as they sat cross-legged and hunched over, facing each other.

'So'veyou,' said Tom, waggling a wavering finger at her until she slapped it away. Both of them fell into silence as they wiped away the red wine crusts which lined their lips.

'Stuff it, Tom.'

'Yeah. Stuff it, Bec.' And they drank again.

'Stuff Dad,' said Tom.

'Yeah. Stuff him.' They sat in silence drinking.

'Stuff it, Rebecca . . . I'm in love with your friend,' blurted Tom.

'Who? Which friend?' asked Bec in mid-swig, eyebrows raised.

Tom shook his head, 'Na. Na. No one . . .'

'Come on, bro. Spit it out!'

'Sal. I love Sal. Sally Carter-Farter, she's delish. Trudy wouldn't ask her to the wedding.'

'Sally? Sally Carter? You love Sal? Oh my God, Tom.' Rebecca put a hand to her mouth to stifle her surprise. But Tom, you know what she's like . . . she's still going through her "try before you buy" phase with men. She's, well she's . . . very hard on men, Tom. Much as I love her, she's not for you. She'd screw you senseless then break your heart.'

Tom ran his hands through his hair and looked away, but she could still see the pain on his face.

'Just forget I said it.'

'Oh, Tom.' Bec gave him a hug. With her arms around him, she felt his whole drunken body crack and slump beneath her touch.

'Just come home, sis. Just come home. I can't stand it here without you. I can't stand it without Mum. I can't stand it with them. I can't.'

Rebecca held him at arms-length.

'Well leave! Come back to Blue Plains with me.'

'No.'

'Why not? Why not enrol in uni? Do fine art or something? You know you've got a gift. You could live with Mum in the city . . .'

'No,' sobbed Tom as he slapped her hands away from him. His face scrunched in pain. 'I'm never leaving here. I know it now. No matter where I went, he'd always be there . . . no matter what I did he'd spoil it.'

'Who?'

'You know who. Don't tell me you don't hear his voice in your head. Every day. Disapproving. I can't stand it. I can't.' He began to pull at his hair.

All Rebecca could do was hold the wide shoulders of her beautiful brother as he wept. She stroked his hair and said over and over, 'Shhhh. Shhhh. Shhhhh.'

Rebecca covered Tom's shoulders with a blanket, then put the ice-cream container at the edge of the bed. She leaned towards him and spoke as if talking to an elderly deaf person.

'If you feel sick, Tom, there's a bucket here. I've put it here for you, Tom. If you feel sick. Tom, a bucket.' There was no reply.

From the window she could see the shadows of people moving inside the marquee. Silhouettes dancing to the 'Chattanooga Choo Choo.'

She walked out of Tom's bedroom and into the hallway. Flowers on stands lined the walls. It had been years since she'd seen flowers in the house. She ran her hand along the cool wall. Rebecca jumped as a figure moved behind her.

She turned and it was Frankie. It was so strange to see her standing there in the house.

'Mum!'

'Don't tell your father. I've been having a sticky-beak. The house is certainly tidier than when I was here,' she said, 'but it's still dark and cold.' She shivered a little.

Rebecca felt like saying, 'No wonder it was messy, you were never home!' But she kept her thoughts to herself and said gently, 'Mum. It's Tom. He's not well.'

'Don't worry. He'll sleep it off. Remember that time after the annual sale when you were twelve and he was thirteen when you got hold of that case of champagne and –'

'No. That's not what I mean. He's not, you know, *well*.' Rebecca tapped her head with her forefinger.

'Bec, he's always been the sensitive one. You know that. He'll get through it. His moods pass.'

Rebecca grabbed her mother's arm. 'Mum, you need to talk to him. You need to face it.'

'Face what? He's my son. I know about his moods. They pass.' Rebecca stood dumbfounded by her mother's reaction. 'Is that all you ever do in life?' Rebecca said, suddenly angry and charged with emotion.

'What do you mean?'

'Run away. Run away from the hard parts in life – like your family.'

'Rebecca, this is not the time and place.'

'Oh, so when is a good time and place for you to face the fact that your son is being crushed by his father?'

Frankie's face twisted and tears came suddenly to her eyes. 'I can't deal with this now, Rebecca. It's hard enough coming back here . . . You don't understand what it's like.'

'No I don't, and I hope I never do,' Rebecca shouted. 'Why don't you go and find your new boyfriend and leave this mess for me to sort out, like usual?' She pushed past her mother and stomped down the hallway, instinctively walking into her old bedroom. She slammed the door shut and leaned her back against its heavy wooden surface, shutting her eyes to keep the sobs inside her. When she opened her eyes, shimmering light filled the room from the paper lanterns outside. It danced magically on the golden lettering of her show ribbons and lit up the tiny faces in the photo frames. She flicked the light switch and suddenly she was standing in front of her past. Her room. Her home.

Everything was how she had left it, except on her bed were boxes filled with wedding stationary and the same golden ribbons that had tied the white roses at the church. Trudy had been in her room. Rebecca clenched her jaw and moved over to the cupboard.

Inside, her hide-tanning and beer-brewing kits sat beneath her clothes, clothes which looked as if they belonged to a stranger.

She stood at her desk and leaned towards the photos on the pin board. A young Rebecca with pigtails smiled out at her. She was sitting on the front steps of the house with her brothers and her cousins. Reg, her old red dog, leaned on her leg and looked up at her. In another shot she was older. Hair flying out as she jumped a log on Ink Jet. Driving the Deutz during hay cutting. Standing on a lookout on a mountaintop, pulling a face. The same stupid face as Tom. Sitting behind candles with her mother at a dinner party in the big dining room. Hanging upside down from the side of a ute with her brothers, grubby and sick after a B&S.

Rebecca folded her arms across her body. She felt chilled. Nowhere was her father pinned to the board and preserved in a picture.

From the cupboard she took a backpack and began to unpin the photos and put them in it. She took some extra clothes and a few of her favourite dog-training books. She ran her fingers across the fuzz of her felted pony club ribbons and closed her eyes again.

When she opened them, he was standing at the door.

'What are you doing up here? Come to clean me out?'

'Dad.'

God. What could she say to him? She looked into his eyes. What *should* she say to him? Perhaps in that moment he would welcome her back. She stood before him.

'Get out of my house.'

The words hit her like a slap in the face.

'Dad?'

'Don't think you can just walk back in here after you cleared out like that. Don't think you can just come back in here after a year away playing cowgirl. After all you've done.'

'I wasn't . . . I was just . . .'

'You were just getting the hell out of my house.' He waved an arm in the direction of the stairway and stepped towards her. She could see from his eyes he was drunk. He leaned towards her and said through wine-stained teeth, 'The nerve of you and your mother to turn up at this house on the same day.'

'What've I –'

'Shut your face. It's all about "I"s with you. "I can", "I will", "I am". You never respected me. Never. You've always challenged everything I say. Well you're not getting your way. Mick and Trudy are moving in here and they're going to make a go of it with me. Trudy's a good girl. She'll stick by her husband. She'll stick inside the house. She'll bring in the money from teaching. She'll take the pressure off. Not like you. Not like you and your mother. Nothing *like* you. Now get out. Get out of my house.' He grabbed the bag from her hands, threw it on the floor and shoved her out the doorway.

Hazy with alcohol, Rebecca had no retorts. As she backed away from him down the hallway she looked up into his eyes and said bitterly, 'And I love you too, Daddy.'

PART THREE

CHAPTER 12

The judge raised his red clipboard against the blue sky, then let it fall suddenly. The timekeeper nodded at his signal and blew into the whistle. Dags sat at Rebecca's feet with every muscle shivering in his body as he eyed the sheep. She motioned to him and said quietly, 'Dags, get over.' He cast out clockwise in the yard, belly low to the ground. Trotting steadily, then crouching, slinking towards the stock. The sheep moved away from him and bustled in a group towards Rebecca as she opened the gate.

Sniffing at the air, the lead sheep stood in the entranceway of the next pen. The upstanding wether flinched a little when a breeze lifted the string of red and yellow sponsorship flags. They flapped noisily on the fenceline. The crowd 'ahhed' at the unfortunate timing of the breeze. Baulking at the flags, the wether turned and walked out of the entranceway, taking the mob with him. Rebecca kept her cool as Dags instinctively darted around to block and cover the mob. She was racing against the clock, and knew if she wasted time at the start of the trial, she'd run out of time at the end of the course.

'Walk up, Dags.'

The dog edged towards the sheep. The lead wether stamped its front foot at him. Dags swallowed but kept creeping towards the defiant sheep, his eyes fixed, trying to stare the wether down. The wether stamped again but turned away and soon the mob seemed to fold around itself as the sheep moved into the yard. Rebecca closed the gate. A light applause sprinkled through the crowd. She had made it through the first obstacle, but she still had the race, the loading ramp, the draft and the 'put away' to go and time was ticking away.

Her hands fumbled on the gate's chain, but she at last released the catch and swung the gate open. She sucked in a breath. Now came the hard part. Dags sometimes was too bullish on stock for trial work so Rebecca made an effort to keep her voice tones calm.

'Steady, Dags. Hop up.'

In the narrow race Dags trotted along the backs of the sheep to the front of the mob, then dropped down to the ground. Within the race, buried beneath sheep, he pressed his body against the weldmesh sides of the race and ran back towards Rebecca. His mere presence, without even a bark, sent the sheep forward in leaping movements. When he emerged again, Rebecca sent him to the front of the race again over the backs of the sheep to clear a space so she could open the gate at the far end.

This time when she opened the little race gate Rebecca's hands were steadier with the chain. Dags was giving her confidence and she was beginning to enjoy the sort of work he was offering. She'd thought the rough work at the station might have ruined his chances as a competitive trial dog, but today he was steady and willing to fall to his belly the moment she whistled, 'Stop.'

At the loading ramp she sent Dags over the backs of the wethers again.

'Speak,' she said, and he barked. The wethers leapt up the ramp and once Rebecca opened a gate, Dags barked again, making the sheep clatter steadily down the other side.

She was making good time, and from what she could tell, they'd made few errors. The judge had barely put his pen to his clipboard and she knew that she would've retained most of the hundred points she'd started with when the bell rang.

At the draft, Dags waited for her signal as she counted off the first five sheep through the narrow metal entrance. Then Rebecca swung the gate across the nose of the next ten sheep. One of them propped and stood, breathing heavily, looking up at Rebecca. She knew that if she touched the sheep the judge would dock points.

'Come up,' she said. Dags instantly leapt along the backs of the bottleneck of sheep, but the leader failed to move.

'Get hold of 'im,' she said. Dags knew what to do. He quickly bit at the topknot of wool between the sheep's ears. It didn't hurt the sheep but startled it enough to move it forward through the drafting gate.

'That'll do, Dags. Good dog.' Rebecca knew judges docked points for dogs that bit sheep, but she knew some approved of topknotting because it was a rare skill that made a working dog extra special in the yards. Hopefully this judge would approve.

She swung the drafting gate across and the final five sheep clattered through the race and trotted towards the first five sheep which stood huddled in the gathering yard. Rebecca sighed with relief. All she had to do was put her sheep away and she was finished for the day's competition.

She cast Dags out again and he gently moved the sheep towards the put-away pen. The sheep knew they were headed towards the safety of their mates in the larger mob so they complied willingly and trotted past Rebecca and through the gate.

As she stooped to fasten the silvery chain around the gate, a smattering of applause broke out in the crowd. Someone called out, 'Well done.'

The judge, marking the score sheet in his clipboard, walked slowly towards the timekeeper.

'That was the last run of the day,' said the timekeeper into the microphone. 'Just give us a few moments to tally the score to find out who our winners are.'

Rebecca glanced at her watch. She was supposed to be in the ram shed in the next half-hour for the judging of the fine-wool class.

At last the timekeeper switched on the mike with a

loud clunk and read out the winners' names for the open and improver classes. The winners came forward to accept their ribbons and lug away their bags of dog food.

'And winner of the novice competition, by just one point, is Rebecca Saunders with her dog, Dags, on a score of ninety-four. Well done Rebecca.'

Someone slapped her on the back as she stepped forward to take the ribbon and a glinting gold plastic trophy.

Ribbon tucked in her pocket, trophy under her arm, she carried the heavy biscuits towards the ram truck with Dags following at her heels. At the truck she ran her index finger over the engraved inscription on the trophy. '42nd Maranaga Show Utility Dog Trials – Novice Champion.' Dags stood by her boots.

'You done good, Dags,' she said softly, stooping to stroke his ear. He looked up at her with his brown eyes and the end of his tail flickered. 'Never one to show too much emotion, are you, boy?'

Since she'd been on the show circuit with the rams this year, Rebecca hadn't managed to win a trophy in the yard dog trialling . . . until today. She'd had a few good scores, but never a win, or even a place. As she leaned against the truck, she thought of her grandad. If he were here, he'd take her by the shoulders, stoop to look into her eyes and say, 'Good on you, girl.' He'd wink and then return to his serious upright posture and move away again.

As she opened the creaking truck door and reached

up to lay the trophy on its dash, she heard a voice behind her.

'You winner!'

She turned.

'Basil! Charlie Lewis!'

'You remember me!' said the tall boy. He stood there, his green eyes squinting in the sun. His sleeves rolled up, shirt untucked, tanned skin, lean and luscious.

'Well you did make a bit of an impression. It's not every day I meet nude men with buckets on their heads.' Bec's eyes roamed down to the crotch of his jeans and Charlie felt her gaze. He moved to lean against the truck and smiled at her, looking slightly embarrassed.

'Yes. Well. Sorry about that. I was having a bit of a blow-out at the B&S. We'd been harvesting at home for weeks and I hadn't been out to play for a while . . .'

'Oh, don't apologise!' Bec cut in. 'It was a great way to meet you, I can assure you.'

Charlie laughed a little and kicked the dirt with the toe of his boot, but he wouldn't meet her eye.

Oh my God, thought Bec, he's shy. He's actually shy! Take the alcohol out of him and he's a babe.

'So. What did you win?' He nodded towards the trophy in the truck.

'Oh, that! Um, just a novice in the dog trials. With my mate Dags.' She held up the trophy. 'It'll make a good dunny-roll holder.'

'Good on you! Good on you, Dags,' and Charlie bent to cup the dog's head in his big brown hands, scratching behind Dags's ears. Dags relished the attention and promptly leaned his body against Charlie's leg, wagging his tail.

'He likes you. He only does that to people he trusts,' said Bec.

Charlie looked into Dags's eyes, 'Pity I didn't get to see you in action, fella.' Then he looked back at Bec. 'We've only just got here. We were passing through town and Dad thought he'd call in to talk grain with a few of the sheep cockies. What are you up to with yourself? You're miles away from Blue Plains. Are you still working there?'

Bec felt a wave of pleasure wash over her. She hadn't ever told him where she was working, so he must've been asking after her.

'Yep. They put me in charge of the ram shed. I'm supposed to be in the pens now getting ready for the next judging class. I've been on the show-road for the past four months. It's a bit of a pain in the sphincter – some of the people can be so crusty – but I'm seeing loads of country and meeting lots of nice people. Plus I keep getting distracted by these dog trials, but my boss says it's all good publicity for the company.'

She cringed as the image of the cute eighteen-year-old boy flashed into her head. Curly dark hair, slim limbs and a tiny, muscular backside. His name was Jeremy and she'd seduced him after he won the junior judging competition at the western region show. It had been a running joke around the show circuit that Rebecca had rolled in the hay with a toy boy. She could still see his dark puppy dog eyes as they lay together in the rich, clean-smelling straw of the ram truck, his blue ribbon draped across Rebecca's naked body. Both of them giggling in fits. It had been one of the more vibrant memories of her months on the show trail.

Rebecca's days as a groom were sometimes long and monotonous. Feeding the rams, changing the bedding in their pens, washing out their water troughs, driving the truck for hours to the showgrounds which were mostly filled with stuffy old men with sheep. She spent entire days washing the faces of the rams and trimming them up with hand shears, then standing holding them for a crusty judge to look at. She also lugged water in heavy black drench drums from the truck to the rams. It was water from Blue Plains. Bob insisted the rams have the water they were used to. In some towns the rams turned their noses up at the strange smell and taste of the water, so she lugged drums daily.

The team of rams, ten in all, were strong contenders at the shows and she'd become attached to their different personalities. She loved Alf most of all, not just because he was the most productive ram, both to look at and on paper, but because he was a complete sook. Each morning as the sun lifted above the horizon Alf would call out to Rebecca when she entered the truck. Alf was her pride and joy.

She spent hours talking bloodlines and genetics with the men in the sheep pens. It often frustrated her that they were reluctant to take on the new sciences to measure the impact of genetics. She'd become part of the new generation of young merino breeders who were colliding with the old notions at shows. They used technology as a basis for their breeding, while the old generation clung to the traditions of the past hundred years. Some were also clinging to 'old money' and snobbery. It grated on Rebecca, but she tried to be every inch the diplomat for her company – to a point. Once she hit the bars after the shows, Rebecca really let her hair down and company diplomacy went out the window. It had been in a bar in a large town that, through a haze of rum, Rebecca had begun to notice the glint in the eye of the dark-haired eighteen-year-old, Jeremy. In the crush of the male crowd, the stock agents and farmers leered and cheered the budding romance on. The 'romance' turned out to be one night, but it brought a smile to Rebecca's lips every time she saw another junior judging line-up of young boys in baggy moleskins.

The thought of Jeremy, while standing here with Charlie Lewis looking raw and hunky, sparked a desire in Rebecca. She noticed the way the corner of Charlie's mouth turned up slightly on one side in a gentle smile as he listened to her. He tilted his head to the side too, and ran his hand over the back of his neck as if massaging it. There were tiny laugh lines around his eyes and Rebecca wanted to reach out and touch them. She gazed into Charlie's eyes so that she could give him the Look. She and Sally had practised it so many times in her bedroom mirror during school holidays at Waters

Meeting. For hours they had talked about boys and strategies, developing plan As and plan Bs as they rode their horses beneath gum trees and across the mountains. By the time they were seventeen they believed they had truly mastered the art of seduction.

'Well, I'd better be going,' said Charlie.

The Look fell from Bec's face. 'Oh,' she said and almost laughed out loud at her obvious failure to deliver any kind of flirtatious message.

'Dad's over there. I can see him looking over. If I don't go now, he'll start whistling for me to come, just like you'd whistle Dags to you!'

Bec looked over to see a big man talking in a group with his arms folded across his chest. He was looking in their direction now.

'Yep. I'd better get back to the rams. I've stuffed around long enough with my dogs. I'll catch up with you.'

'Yep. Seeya. Maybe next time I'll have my clothes off again.' Charlie gave a slight wave and a big cheeky grin as he walked away.

'I hope so,' said Rebecca with an equally cheeky grin. As she watched him walk away, Bec's mouth fell open and her eyes widened. Oh Lordy mamma! He was wearing Wranglers.

'God take me to heaven now,' she whispered as she watched his neat backside, clad in dark denim, move away. In an instant Charlie spun around and Bec had to suddenly compose herself, closing her gaping mouth shut.

He called to her, 'I might be going up to Springton

next year with some machinery for Dad. We could be contracting out up that way during winter. Will you be about? We could go pubbing.'

'We could. But I won't be around. I'll have left Blue Plains by February – I'm starting ag college at Tablelands Uni. Going to be a nerdy student for a few years. I've already delayed it for a year to muck around with sheep and dogs, so it's about time I knuckled down.'

'Oh.' The disappointment showed in his voice and Bec was suddenly filled with excitement. He had the hots for her, she was sure.

'Well, good luck.' He paused. 'We'll catch you later.'

She raised a hand to him and turned away. As she lobbed the heavy bag of biscuits into the truck her desire melted into disappointment and longing. She wished he could stay. She wished he'd come to the bar after the show and they could sit and drink and talk. Just talk. Make time to become friends before she ended up in a truck with him or in a swag somewhere. A huge sense of loneliness overcame her. She could have as many men as she liked, but still she felt a longing. Was it for her home? Or was it for a man like Charlie? Rebecca slammed the door of the truck. She didn't have time for self-pity; glancing at her watch she saw how late it was.

'No time to lust after boys, Dags!' She clipped the dog to a chain under the truck, pushed his water bowl to him, then ran towards the shed. She was late for the finals of the fine-wool section.

She didn't see Charlie Lewis, leaning his tanned elbow out of his father's grain truck, as he watched her, hair flying, jogging into the pavilion. He captured the vision in his mind. It sent a tingle down his spine. Then the smile from his face and eyes faded and he turned back to look grimly through the windscreen as he sat beside his father.

In the sheep show pavilion Bec couldn't shake off the image of Charlie's shining green eyes, the gentle creases around them as he laughed. Absentmindedly, she stroked the soft white face of the ram which she held gently under the jowls. Goosebumps rose up her arms, even though the day was hot. She stood in the line-up of sheep as the judge in the super-white moleskins with clip-stud pockets looked over the sheep like a monkey looking for fleas.

Bec shifted her weight to relieve her tired aching feet. She had been running up and down on concrete since five a.m. The green fake-grass surface of the indoor show ring offered little relief. All of a sudden Bec was just so sick of wandering. So sick of stud show people. She pictured Charlie's Wrangler-clad butt again.

I'm in *lerv*, came a sighing thought. Her conscience jumped in and sternly said, Keep your mind on the job, you slack tart.

She felt herself standing straighter and taller and willing the young ram to stand tall too. The next thing she knew she was in the front of the line-up and a man in a tweed coat was walking towards her with a blue ribbon. People were clapping. Rebecca knew they were now in reach of the championship.

'Good on you, Alf,' she said to the ram.

CHAPTER 13

Peter Maybury rubbed his itching eye with the back of his hand, leaving a smudge of flour on his cheek. His dog, Henbury, swivelled on the kitchen tiles on his fluffy bottom, looking up desperately to his owner's face, pleading for Peter to throw him some food.

'Go away Henners, the gnocchi's for Frankie. You've had your dinner.' The dog licked his lips and whined. Frankie sat with her feet up on the couch, wine glass in one hand, letter in another, thin gold-rimmed glasses pushed to the end of her nose.

'Just *listen* to this, Peter.' She paraphrased another passage of Tom's letter.

'Trudy's commissioned a landscape gardener *and* a builder for a 'make-over' of the homestead!'

Frankie sighed and shook her head.

'The farm must be doing well,' said Peter.

'It's not being paid for by the farm! It's Trudy's father. He's the one pouring the money in.'

'Yes, I read somewhere he's got the go-ahead from council to do an apartment development at Port Side. Things must be going well for him.'

'Mmm, I saw that in the paper. Another waterfront highrise,' said Frankie bitterly. 'Shame about the sewerage killing the marine wildlife in the bay . . . but at least it's funding his daughter's happiness and her need for renovations.'

Peter heard the edge in her voice. 'More wine?' he asked brightly.

Frankie shook her head and continued, 'There must be so many benefits being an only child. Trudy's a very spoilt girl. It makes me wonder why I bothered to have three children and didn't just stop at one. It would've saved so much trouble with Harry's plans for the farm!'

'Now, now, Frankie. Don't be so cynical,' said Peter gently. 'Your children would be very hurt to hear you say that.'

'It's reality.'

Peter looked at her blandly. He knew she had a hard streak. It was a practical, clinical and scientific approach to life, not the best prerequisites for being a mother. He suspected she berated herself constantly for leaving her children and for not being there for them now. He smiled sadly at her. In the months that they had been together, they had come to realise they really needed one another. Frankie needed to be softened and healed by Peter, and Peter, a dreamer, needed Frankie to steer him along in life. He'd been so lost since his marriage fell apart. Now, he decided, he had never been happier.

Frankie looked up at him and saw the adoration in his eyes. She smiled at him and began to relax a little. 'I'm sorry, Peter. It's just, all these things Trudy is getting for nothing, after all the struggle the boys have gone through, barely getting a basic salary out of Harry. She just swans in and lives a luxurious life. *How* can she get away with such extravagance? Harry wouldn't even let me paint the kitchen, even if I paid for it with my own money! I battled for years to get the extra sunroom put on, just so we could have a little light. I know I'm not the best homemaker, but I often think if I'd just been given a little bit more independence with the house the marriage could've worked. The place was so dark and depressing. No wonder Harry's mother died an early death! Lack of vitamin D. If only I'd been able to feel like the house belonged to me.'

Peter looked at her doubtfully. He knew she lived for her science and, house or no house, that meant the marriage was always doomed.

Frankie sensed what Peter was thinking.

'I'm sorry, you're right. I think it's just a case of pure jealousy.'

'It's understandable.' They fell silent as Peter continued cooking in the kitchen and Frankie read on.

Minutes later she groaned.

'What?' asked Peter as he stood up stiffly after peering into the tiny fridge.

'Tom's moved his gear out into the shearers' quarters so Trudy can get on with her renovating and he doesn't feel like he's in the way.'

Peter wrinkled his nose.

'Those quarters are a mess!' said Frankie. 'Poor Tom.'

'Maybe it's a semi-permanent arrangement until the building is done,' offered the flour-coated Peter.

'Yes. Yes, I suppose so, but I worry so much about Tom. Kicked out of his own home.'

'He's an adult, Frankie. It must've been his decision. He'll know what he's doing.'

'It's all so, so . . . difficult. How on earth can Trudy stand living in the same house as her father-in-law has got me baffled! It drove me nuts when I was a newly-wed and had to share the house with Harry's dad, and I might add,' said Frankie waving a glass in Peter's direction, 'Harry's father was a . . . softer man. More considerate.'

'It *is* a big house.'

'Peter,' said Frankie firmly and peered at him from across the top of her glasses, 'that's not the point.'

'Now come on, Frankie, you've chosen to leave all those worries behind you.'

'Yes. Yes I know, but it's just . . . it's just Tom. He must feel so alone. I wish I could phone him more often, but he's *never* there. I only ever get Trudy or Harry and I can't get a word out of Harry and I can't get Trudy to shut up.' Frankie sighed and continued to read the letter while Peter kneaded the floury lump in a large enamel bowl and swigged on his fingerprinted wineglass.

'He says here the river's in flood and they lost a few

head of cattle on the river flats. The dogs are well and the horses are fat.'

She fell silent as her eyes scanned over Tom's letter.

'Huh! Typical!'

'What?' said Peter as he ran his palms back and forth over the roll of dough.

'He says his father won't change his mind about Tom's idea to get a centre pivot irrigator and put a dam in the hills. Bloody typical.' Frankie continued. 'He's had a letter from Rebecca. She's won a novice dog trial and took out a supreme championship ribbon with a Blue Plains ram at the wool expo.' She looked up at Peter to explain. 'That's a big deal in sheep circles.'

Peter peered under the lid of a steaming saucepan. 'She must be doing well in her new job, then.'

'Yes. I think she likes it and it's made her settle down a bit and take on a bit of responsibility. She'll have to get the hang of the self-discipline thing when she gets to uni.'

'She'll be okay.' Peter said gently. 'Don't worry so much about her. She'll be fine.'

'I hope so,' Frankie said to Peter. 'I hope so,' she repeated to herself and they both fell silent except for the rattle of the saucepan lid and the swoon of Neil Diamond singing softly on the stereo.

'Oh bugger *off*, Henbury!' said Peter suddenly. 'He's doing pooeys *again*.'

Frankie hadn't been used to a man calling farts 'pooeys', but she smiled as she put down Tom's letter and sipped again on her wine. The cold flat wasn't so cold now Peter was here each evening to warm it up with his kindness and muddle-headed cooking ability. She'd got used to the fact he kicked her out of the kitchen and bustled about in it with 'delights' and 'delicacies'. She hadn't been used to someone rubbing her feet tenderly or pushing her hair back out of her eyes. She was soaking up his sensitivity, his gentleness. At first it made her feel coarse and tough. She decided she'd had too many years as an on-farm vet, dagging around in overalls. Too many years suppressing her softness so she could stand strong against the backdrop of Harry and his mountains at Waters Meeting. The comfortable landscape of the city had allowed her to soften, to forget how hard it had been. Some nights, before Peter, she'd felt she missed the brash manliness of her husband, but now as she melted into the soft warmth of Peter she knew she was wrong to want the past again. She felt as though she had started to heal and that she was becoming herself again after all those wasted years. She felt love for Peter beginning to flow. But at night she still dreamed of the river. The river and her daughter. And Peter's arms about her couldn't stop the guilt and the fear she held for leaving her children behind.

CHAPTER 14

Rebecca placed another trophy on the dusty windowsill of her bedroom and flicked away a dead blowfly.

'Not another one!' Dave stood in the doorway wearing Bundaberg Rum boxer shorts with polar bears all over them.

'Moss. She won a novice trial.'

'How'd Stubby go?'

'She was all over the place – trialling's not her thing. Dags is still my hero – we've now qualified for an open. Big show-off that he is.'

'Takes after his owner,' said Dave.

Rebecca raised her middle finger at him. Dave responded by pushing his tongue down between his teeth and bottom lip and widening his eyes at her. She hurled a sandshoe at him. He ducked and ran down the hallway to the kitchen. From her pocket she pulled out an envelope and took three crisp $20 notes from it. She reached under her bed for a large Milo tin, then dropped the notes inside. The pile of colourful cash in there was mounting up. It was her college fund. Most of the money had come from the sale of pups, but after her successes at the trials she'd made good cash from service bookings for Dags. She was relieved when Moss at last came on heat. She had so many orders for pups she couldn't keep up with supply. She joined Moss to Dags last week and was hopeful she'd have a large litter.

Rebecca clamped the tin's lid down and pushed it back under her bed. Then she stretched and wandered from her room into the kitchen. She tried to calculate what date the pups would be born.

'Bugger,' she said.

'What?' said Dave, as he stooped to light the gas grill.

She stood flicking through the calendar on the wall. It was one of Dave's booby-girl calendars. A thick black cross in texta marked the day when Rebecca started university. On the calendar, the blonde girl with breast implants pouted in her too-small bikini, as if sulking. It was as though the days were taking too long to pass and the booby-girl resented it.

'Mossy's pups are due smack bang in the first week I start college. I'll have to write to the uni and ask if there's some kind of arrangement we can come to so I can keep my dogs on campus.'

'Don't be barmy. You won't be needing them for three years! Just shoot 'em.'

'Dave, I hope you're joking,' said Bec as she looked

169

up from the calendar. 'Because if you're not I'm going to have to ring Annabelle and tell her about her cat.'

'What about her cat?'

'About how you ran over it. Deliberately.'

'Was not deliberate. I didn't know the stupid thing was sleeping under my tyre.'

'Yes, well, deliberate or not, you could've at least *told her* so she could bury it. She's still out there every night calling its name. And we all know it's been chucked in the creek.' Bec cupped her hands to her mouth and in a high-pitched voice sung, 'Minteeeeee! Here puss puss . . . MINTEEE!'

'Shut up.' Dave threw a mutton chop at Bec. It hit her in the face with a meaty splat and landed on the floor.

'You dirtbag!' She lunged for the chop. Chair legs squawked on lino as she pushed around the table and ran at Dave. Armed with a glass of water, he fended her off as she began to smear the chop in his hair. Their laughter and screams rang throughout the quarters. Floorboards vibrated and thumped on the wooden stumps of the house as they chased each other around the room.

Puffing hard, Rebecca eventually yelled, 'Stop!' and they fell silent. She looked up at Dave, smeared in fat and dripping wet. She'd missed him since she'd been on the show circuit and now she was back she knew she'd miss his gawky presence in her life when she moved on to college. She'd miss these quarters and the paddocks, people and horses she'd come to know and love. The day when she had to leave was racing towards her. She would have to pack up her life into boxes and load them on the ute. She'd have to pat the stockhorses goodbye. And kiss the cheeks of the ever-oily machinery men – she was dreading kissing Jimbo – and hug Bob and his wife Marg.

The year had rushed by in a blur of blade trimming, chaff mixing and horn polishing. What had seemed like forever on the road in the midst of a sheep show season had come to an abrupt halt after the big win in the west. They had ceremoniously pinned the supreme champion ribbon in a glass cabinet in the ram shed and packed off the gold and garish trophy to the city, where it now had prime position in the entrance to the AR Company headquarters.

Just then the UHF sitting on the fridge crackled to life and the room was filled with Bob's voice.

'Rebecca, are you on channel?'

'Ooops!' said Bec as she picked up the handpiece. 'Yes Bob.'

'The company PR lady's flying in any minute now for the photo shoot. Have you got Alf all groomed for his champion photo?'

'Yep. He's ready to roll.'

'And how are you looking?'

'Why?' she asked cautiously.

'The board of directors want you in the shot too, so you'd better meet her at the air strip. You can take my vehicle. Bring her here to my place when you get her.'

'Err right,' said Rebecca as she looked down at her chop-smeared front and wet T-shirt.

Dave laughed as she ran for the shower.

On the red dusty airstrip a breeze cooled her neck as it blew through her damp hair. Rebecca looked up to the sky and watched the tiny AR plane fly past and then bank in a sweeping circle to the right. The pilot was going to land from the southern end. Rebecca had driven along the length of the strip to make sure no stray cattle were about and tooted the horn at the large brush turkeys which strutted about in the long yellow grass.

The plane pulled up beside the four-wheel drive and Murray, the pilot, shut down the engine.

'G'day Bec,' he called as he undid the door and let the steps down.

'Hey Muzz. Good flight?'

'Yeah, not bad.' He walked down from the step and said something to the woman inside before going to the back of the aircraft to get her baggage.

Rebecca watched as the tall thin woman stepped from the aircraft, her thick black high heels landing solidly on the dusty airstrip. She held a black leather briefcase in her hand and squinted around distastefully at the flat barren airstrip, then she marched to the Landcruiser.

'Ellen Tinker,' said the woman, and offered Bec a wet-fish handshake.

'Rebecca Saunders. Nice to meet you. Welcome to Blue Plains.'

The woman said thank you with a cat's bum mouth and turned away to fix her hair in the vehicle's side mirror. On the way back to the cluster of houses and sheds, Bec concentrated on driving through every dusty pothole on the road she could find, and enjoyed seeing Ellen Tinker's bouffed hair react with a bounce to each bump. When they neared the green oasis of the homestead she braked suddenly, the tyres spitting gravel, and came to a halt beneath a leafy jacaranda tree. Ellen Tinker cast her a cool look as Rebecca led her to the back doorstep. Tiger, the resident Jack Russell, dropped a woolly lamb leg which still had the hoof attached from his mouth, and ran to scratch at the woman's shapely gym legs.

'Git out of it, Tiger,' came a voice from the doorway. It was Marg.

'Hello, Miss Tinker,' said Marg, wiping her hands on a tea towel.

'Ms,' Ellen Tinker corrected.

In the cool of the kitchen, under a humming ceiling fan, Ellen Tinker spread out her documents, took up a neat notebook and poised a polished timber pen.

'I'm to compile the annual report. I've been instructed to interview you about the winning ram for a brief article.'

Rebecca sighed a little and spun a teaspoon around in her hands before she began. She wanted to tell her the truth about showing sheep. She wanted to say, while she loved doing it, some of it was a wank. So outdated. Run by outdated notions from outdated people in the wool industry, clinging onto tradition. Terrified of change. She wanted to say that visual assessment of sheep should be backed by science, and that the marketing advantages for the company did not cover the cost of sending her around with a team of well-groomed, overfed rams. But she knew that most of the company bigwigs knew this and shows were exactly that . . . put on for show.

Instead she gave what Ellen Tinker wanted. She talked about Alf and his superb characteristics as a sire and how, here on Blue Plains, performance of his off-spring would be recorded in their very own progeny-testing program in conjunction with the CSIRO. The words flowed from her and even impressed Ellen Tinker, whose cat's bum mouth relaxed just a bit as she scribbled notes with her flashy pen. On the periphery of the interview, Marg worked about the kitchen, putting biscuits on plates and pushing a jug of milk and a tin of sugar towards Ellen. Ellen sipped at her black coffee, narrowed her eyes a little from the heat of it and nodded, urging Rebecca to expand on the purpose of the ram trial.

What Rebecca really wanted to say to Ellen Tinker was, 'I saw this cute guy who'd won the junior judging – Jeremy – with eyes to die for. We both got completely maggotted-drunk at the sheep bar . . . that always sounds funny, don't you think? Sheep baaa . . . sheep bar . . . get it? Anyway, then we kissed outside the back of the showground toilets and ended up bonking in hay in the AR ram truck. He was short, like me, and skinny, but so cute. Oh. *And* I saw Charlie Lewis at Marananga Show, and he's absolutely gorgeous and I think I lerve him. And I think he's got the hots for me.'

But instead she told Ellen Tinker she'd had a wonderful two years with Blue Plains and her time as a jillaroo and stud ram manager had given her a fantastic grounding in agriculture which was her chosen career path.

After the not-so-probing interview, Ellen Tinker-the-Stinker took her camera and her cat's bum mouth out into the afternoon sunlight to take a photo of Rebecca and Alf against the golden-green backdrop of a sleepy peppertree.

Sunlight mingled with Rebecca's freshly washed hair and draped itself, golden and thick, across the soft wrinkled face of Alf's broad nose.

Even Ellen Tinker whispered, 'Lovely', as she looked at the pretty young woman and the handsome ram through the camera's viewfinder. She pressed the shutter button down and Rebecca the jillaroo and Alf the ram were captured forever wrapped in Blue Plains sunshine.

CHAPTER 15

In the darkness of the cluttered office Harry slammed down the receiver of the telephone.

'Bloody bank managers.' He clenched his fist and punched at the filing cabinet, then stood looking across the sprawl of papers on the desk. In his mind Harry again counted the months until the wool cheque arrived. Sinking down into the office chair, he calculated in his head the number of fattened steers he could sell and guestimated what the prime lambs could make. Hay sales would be minimal because he wanted to keep enough on hand should the winter be a tough one. He added it up over and over, figures spinning and tallying, until he was sure the amount was too small. It would barely satisfy the big-bellied bank manager. He thought of Rebecca and the words she had flung at him.

'You're going to lose the lot.'

He rubbed his forehead on the scratchy woollen sleeve of his jumper. Sighing, he stood and walked down the hallway to the kitchen. He poured boiling water into the teapot which had been left sitting on the edge of the stove from breakfast, and reached for a mug. He was about to go into the sunroom when Trudy burst through the kitchen door. In her arms she held an express parcel which she had just picked up from the mailbox.

'Oh! Hello, Harry! I thought you'd be out on the farm. There's a stack of bills here for you.' She tossed them on the table in front of him and then reached for some scissors in the drawer. She hastily cut open the parcel and pulled out a large packet of neatly plastic-wrapped curtains.

'At last!' she said in a shrill voice. 'Look!' She held up the folded flowery package.

'Curtains for the spare room! I ordered them by catalogue. I just love shopping by catalogue . . . It's a new phenomenon for me! It's a benefit of living in the bush. And I got $100 off the price. They'll look fabulous after the painters have been in. I've chosen the softest yellow, so it can double as a nursery later on.' She giggled at the thought of the possibility of a baby in her very new marriage.

'Trudy,' said Harry in a voice he knew was too stern. She put down the curtains suddenly and looked wide-eyed at her father-in-law. He made an effort to soften his voice, 'Has Mick talked to you about money?' In one fluid motion she slumped onto a kitchen chair and began to pout slightly.

'I don't mind you spending your teacher's salary on

things you like, but you don't have to spend your money on this house. It's in good enough shape.'

'Pah! It's positively crumbling! Besides Mum and Dad have paid for the curtains. They have an account at the store. They don't mind a bit. Mum said, "Whatever makes you happy". And what I buy isn't just to please me! It's for Michael and you, too. Besides, it makes my parents feel good, helping me out with paying for the renovations.'

Harry set down the teapot and cup as if preparing to speak. Trudy looked at him.

'I've been keeping a surprise for you,' Trudy said, 'but I suppose I'll have to tell you now.'

She paused.

'I've ordered a *computer* for your birthday. For the farm. For your book work. It's got email and internet connections and even a photo scanner. There's loads of games on it that you can –'

'Trudy!' exploded Harry. 'Do you think this is a bloody game? This . . . all this.' His arm swept about the kitchen and pointed out the window. 'This bloody farming is no game. We don't have money to spend on landscaping and redecoration or extensions and . . .'

'But . . .' Harry held a hand up to silence Trudy. 'I certainly don't want your parents' money creeping in and buying my house out from under my nose. It's not their place to spend money on a home that doesn't belong to them. I won't have it.'

He stopped himself and fell silent, trying to gauge the reaction he might get. He expected tears. The clock ticked.

Then it was as if Trudy shed a skin. Harry watched the layer of her public persona peel away. Her pout and her girlish sulks dissolved and her face took on a coldness and harshness that even Harry flinched at. She rose to her feet.

'Now *you* listen,' she said in her most stinging teacher's voice. 'Michael sweats every day on this farm. He gets up at dawn and comes in late every night, so that I *never* see him. He barely gets a weekend off while I slave in here cooking your bloody meals for you. Do you think we're doing all that for *you*? *Do you*?' Her fierce eyes bored into Harry and her mouth twisted with months of built-up resentment.

'Well, we're not. We're not working hard for you. We're working hard for *us*. Michael and *me*. He's slaving so he and I will have a *future*. He's the eldest son. He's entitled to the farm . . . and to the house. And what my parents and I do with our money is none of your bloody business. We've been looking at plans for premade cabins so we can get you into a house of your own down near the river, instead of crowding us out. Dad's already contracted a builder. We're in a new marriage, for godsake, and you don't even realise you're just hanging on and hanging about.

'Michael and I have discussed this and we've decided he should be getting a salary from the farm account until you retire. A salary that reflects his hours and his responsibility, not just the pitiful handouts you give him when you feel like it.'

Harry stood stock-still in front of her as she spoke.

His mouth was hanging open in disbelief. This had never happened to him before. A woman, a girl, had never spoken to him in this way. Even Rebecca and Frankie hadn't crossed the boundaries that Trudy had just marched over. She was so certain. There was a selfishness, a viciousness in her that he hadn't known before. He leaned towards her, across the table and gritted his teeth as he spoke.

'*If* you get this house, Trudy. *If* you get this farm, it'll be over my dead body.'

She glared back at him. 'Fine.' She leaned closer. 'So be it.'

Just then they heard Mick open the back door and kick off his boots.

'I'm back. Put the kettle on!'

Trudy's eyes, locked in a stare with Harry, softened and swelled with tears. She slumped her body down on the chair and began sobbing, her head in her arms, tears falling over the plastic wrap of the new floral curtains.

'How dare you pension me out of my own house and stick me in a log cabin. Ungrateful bitch.'

Harry swiped the teapot and mug from the surface of the table. As they fell with a crash to the floor he strode out the door, violently bumping shoulders with Mick on the way.

CHAPTER 16

The metal nozzle of the drench-gun clunked against Rebecca's teeth and a shot of liquid burned in the back of her throat. She swallowed quickly, her eyes focused on the flamboyant crest of the agricultural college. It was embroidered in tight yellow stitches on the rugby top of the large man standing in front of her. She wouldn't look up to meet his eye. Roughly he grabbed her face again and gave her another drench for good measure. Head back, eyes shut tight, she swallowed the vile tasting liquid and felt it burn as it slid into her stomach. She looked across at another first year girl who whispered to her, 'I've been told it's laxatives in vinegar!'

'Bummer,' said Rebecca.

'You're not wrong,' said the dark-haired girl who managed to flash an unsure smile.

They huddled in two lines, males paired off with females in the student carparking area, while stockwhips and utes revved around them. A band of second year boys, the biggest and thickest of the rugby players, tied the legs of the first-year students together with bale twine.

Throughout the new students' orientation week, rumour had spread on campus that the second and third year students were gearing up for a wild initiation ceremony. Word had buzzed around about what might be done to them. Based on previous years, it could be rough. Today was the day Rebecca and her peers would find out.

That morning, when car horns sounded, men shouted and stockwhips cracked outside their dorm windows, Bec felt a wave of excitement and anticipation run through the first-year students. New to each other and new to the college, the students were half dreading, half looking forward to the event as tales from previous years became more and more stretched.

'Feels like we're being herded to the gas chamber,' Rebecca said to the tall man standing next to her.

'It's probably the start of a drinking game . . . you know, like a boat race.' He was trying to reassure her and himself that the ceremony would be fun.

A square-jawed student with eyebrows that ran across the top of his eyes in a thick dark line shoved Bec next to the man she'd just spoken to. He bent and tied their legs together with orange bale twine.

She looked down at her brown leg next to the bloke's long skinny white leg. He was wearing a pair of faded Can't-Tear-'Em shorts with a tear in them and the bristles of his hairy legs scratched against her skin.

'Seeing as I'm tied to you, we'd better introduce ourselves,' Bec said, looking up at him.

'I'm Richard, but most people call me Dick. Dirt-track Dick.'

'Hi Dick, I'm Rebecca but you can call me Bucket.' They shook hands.

'Where do you hail from Dick?'

'The Territory.'

'Oh!' said Bec, widening her eyes as she thought of red dust and wide spaces.

'Yeah,' he continued, 'the Australian Capital Territory,' and then he laughed.

'You mean *Canberra*?'

'Mmm. Not the coolest place to come from when you're an ag student.' He was about to ask her where she was from but the square-jawed student shoved them roughly forwards.

The first years lolloped in a row, legs tied to their random partners, towards the college tennis courts. Some sung 'Jake the peg diddle liddle liddle lum' while others put arms around their partner's waist and counted so their legs moved in time and the bale twine rubbed less. Others mooed like cows or let out long mournful 'baaaas' in response to the stockwhips and the heckling second- and third-year students.

Locked in the high mesh of the tennis court, Bec watched a ute roar up to the fence. A boy with a shock of blond hair pulled the cord of the pump unit on the ute's flat tray so the motor grumbled into life. Water spluttered out of the hose nozzle in a high-powered jet. It hit Rebecca in cold stinging blasts. When she looked about at the huddling group she saw they were all splattered and speckled in red dye.

A small girl with straight blonde hair tied in a navy bow cried out, 'Oh! This is my good shirt!' She held out the front of her floral blouse and shook her ribboned ponytail.

'Get over it,' said a boy from the centre of the huddle.

The sun-bleached ends of Bec's wavy hair soaked up the dye in an instant and her hair turned a pinky red.

As the rabble of second and third year students unlocked the gates, the crowd of first years collectively sighed with relief.

'That wasn't too bad,' said Dick. 'Suppose it's time to go to the bar.'

'The laxatives were a bit rough,' said Bec.

But as they emerged from the tennis courts, they found the ceremony was far from over.

'This is like frigging *Lord of the Flies*,' said Bec, as they were herded onto the football oval and made to sit in a group on the short, damp grass.

Before them stood a bathful of stinking, slopping pig manure, and the man with the dark eyebrow yelled the rules of the obstacle course.

The course had been built from black plastic and hay bales and inside the tunnel, on the warm plastic surface, lay a smeared scattering of sheep's offal, collected that morning from the abattoir.

The dark-haired girl leaned towards Rebecca and whispered, 'I heard they've pissed and crapped in that.'

'Gross,' Rebecca said.

They dragged each pair, one at a time, and took them to the start of the course. Rebecca and Dick were fourth in line. After they were dunked in the bath of pig manure, they were dragged to the entrance of the black plastic tunnel. A boy pushed them down to the ground. On all fours, crawling in pairs, they squelched their way through the stinking offal. Some girls retched, others cried.

Rebecca thought back to the times she'd done a kill on Blue Plains and dragged the heavy offal into the bucket. She pictured Miss Oink and held her breath. This was all part of ag college, Bec tried to reassure herself.

As she emerged from the other end of the tunnel she looked back towards the group of first years. A handful of the boys were trying to wrestle away from their captors. They were quickly swamped by second- and third-year boys and roughly tied with thick ropes to the circular fence of the oval. Then they were smeared with thick watery flour.

Stockwhips continued to crack around them. The chants, badgering and bullying, spiralled upwards as each pair were systematically force-fed pies filled with cat food and warm beers mixed with dog food.

'This is ridiculous,' whispered the girl with the short

dark hair to Bec. Both stood covered in the gritty green slime of pig manure, shivering a little, trying to lay low. Trying not to stand out so they wouldn't get picked on.

'Out of control,' said Bec.

Dirt-track Dick repeatedly asked, 'Are you all right?' and Rebecca repeatedly answered, 'Sure,' but wondered if she was.

The faces of her young peers swum around her. She could tell some of the girls weren't standing up to the ceremony at all well and a few were crying uncontrollably.

'I'd heard college was rough. But this is way off the scale,' she said to Dick. She shook her head. 'I've had enough of this.'

She stooped to undo the twine with cold and shaking hands.

'What are you doing?' asked Dick nervously. 'Don't attract attention. Who knows what they'll do to us.'

'Stuff this for a joke.' She undid the twine and stood upright and proud. She began to walk towards the college dorms on the hillside. A tall young man wearing a college jumper stepped in front of her.

'Just where do you think you're going, big tits?'

'Piss off,' she said. He grabbed her arms and shoved her back towards the group. 'The ceremony hasn't finished yet.'

'Get your hands off me.' Rebecca wrenched herself free of his grip.

'Oooo! We've got a tough one here,' he said to the other students who began to gather round.

'Get out of my way.'

'You're not going anywhere, big tits,' the tall boy said, standing over her and folding his arms across his chest. In one quick movement she kneed him hard in the crotch and he doubled over. Agony twisted his face.

She pushed past him and strode off towards the dorms.

The crowd of shocked and cold first years cheered loudly as they watched Rebecca walk away. Their cheers were drowned out with cracking whips as the second and third years sought control.

But Rebecca had shifted the power slightly. Silently the first year students began to stoop and untie the twine around their ankles. They ignored the rough yells and bustles of their captors and silently, en masse, freed themselves and walked away.

In the row of shower bays, Rebecca stood shivering in her filthy clothes with her hand under the stream of water.

'They've turned the hot water off!' Her words echoed around the large, empty bathroom.

Bec peeled the stinking clothes from her reddened skin and threw them into the rubbish bin. She gasped as she stepped under the blast of cold water. Bits of grime ran down her skin and into the gurgling plug hole. She scrubbed her body with soap as hard and as fast as she could but found the water unbearably cold. She stood away from the jet of water and tried to shampoo her hair. She was surprised she didn't feel like crying. She just felt an anger settle in her. An anger towards the ringleaders of the group. An anger towards the men.

As she tugged at her hair, the girls' bathroom began to fill with the chatter of the female students as they filed in from the oval. They recounted their ordeal and swore at the coldness of the running water. The smell of pig poo mingled with the perfume of soaps and shampoos.

On cool red tiles, Rebecca stood shivering in her towel and combed her still gritty hair in the mirror.

The dark-haired girl came out of the shower bay, wrapped in a blue towel. Her square-set shoulders were white and slim.

'Ahh, the revolution leader!' she said when she saw Rebecca. 'We all walked away after you left. Thanks for that.'

'Well, stuffed if I was taking any more of that bullcrap.'

'Don't you mean pigcrap?'

Rebecca laughed as the girl muttered on, 'Pack of mongrels. There's a group of girls going to the principal to complain. Apparently it's the worst initiation cere-mony ever. Heads will roll over this one.'

'Other things will roll too . . . I wonder when the laxatives will kick in,' said Bec.

'Did you know we've got a bus tour to a piggery in the morning?' said the girl. 'Can you believe that!'

Bec laughed and held her arm up to her nose. 'I can still smell pig poo in the pores of my skin.'

'Better flush it out with rum then! Come on, let's get dressed and get going to the bar. They're having $2 rums and I think we'd better get schlammered so we can get over the trauma of it all!'

She turned and walked to the door of the bathroom. 'I'm Gabs by the way. Short for Gabrielle. But most people call me Scabs.'

They smiled into each other's eyes and shook hands.

'Rebecca. Bucket. I'll meet you in the common room in half an hour.'

On the bus the next day with a pounding head and a gurgling stomach, Rebecca sat in a daze. She barely remembered the night before. She had never been so drunk, nor so terribly hungover. She remembered swinging Dirt-track Dick around by the arm with Gabs on the dance floor. And she vaguely recalled trying to steal one of the college buses with a large pretty-faced girl called Emma so they wouldn't have to go on the tour. But there they all were on the bus now. Emma was sitting, pale-faced, her forehead pressed against the cool window of the bus, staring out to the paddocks whirring past. Dick was up the back with some new-found mates still carrying on as if they were drunk. The mood of the first years was forced though. They were trying to put the memory of yesterday's bullying behind them.

Despite this morning's shower before the tour,

Rebecca could still smell pig manure, and her stomach burned. Gabs hung her elbows over the back of Rebecca's seat and continued her husky monologue. She'd strained her voice last night from singing loudly to every song which came on the jukebox.

'They're having a full inquiry this week. They'll be hauling us all into the principal's office to identify the ringleaders from photos in last year's yearbook. And they're going to expel the main bullies from the uni. Serves them bloody right. Karen, you know that short fat girl from block D, she was carted off to hospital last night. She's really crook from the pig poo. And there's a couple of girls who've packed up and left the course for good. It even made the local news. The staff are crapped off to the max.'

'Speaking of crap . . .' said Rebecca, clinging to her stomach.

'Stop the bus again!' called out Gabs to the lecturer driving the bus.

'Yes!' called Emma suddenly. 'Can we stop the bus again?'

As the driver shifted down a gear, making the bus sway, Gabs rubbed Rebecca on the top of the head. Rebecca looked up at her and they smiled at one another. After a hellish day and their first night out together on the Bundy, they'd bonded. Friends.

Ag college can't get any worse than this, Rebecca thought as she grabbed for the roll of toilet paper in her rucksack and made her way off the bus.

CHAPTER 17

'There's an email message here for you,' called Charlotte from the reception desk as she chewed on the end of a pen. Frankie walked briskly down the corridor.

'For me?' She frowned. She never got emails.

'Looks like it's from your son.'

'My son?'

'Tom.'

Charlotte stood and offered her the chair. The text flashed up on the screen. Frankie smiled when she saw it and she began to read:

Hi Mum! Tom here. Guess what!??? Waters Meeting has made it to the modern world and we now have a computer with access to the internet and email. Of course telecommunications still can't conquer these mountains so the line does drop out a lot and it's still fairly costly and slow. (You'd better close your mouth, because I know your jaw would've dropped by now.) Of course Dad didn't pay for the computer. It's a Turdy-funded project, at least it's funded by her parents. But it's great. It means I can converse with the wild child who is currently educating herself at ag college. She's got email there too, so I've included her address at the top. (She'll get this message as well.) You should drop her a line before she drops out. I think the grog monster is eating up a lot of her study time. (She'll love reading that!)

I'm still living in the quarters. It's not so cold now we're heading into spring. But it's still colder than ever inside the homestead. There's a very frosty war going on in there between Dad and Mick and Turdy. I think it all started over some curtains. Turdy's parents have installed a prefabricated log cabin amongst the gums in the horse paddock – they say it's for them when they come to stay, but Turdy let it slip that it's the retirement village for old farts like Dad. Needless to say the ripples have turned into tidalwaves. I often go in for a surf by saying stuff like, 'I'll move into the cabin!' Stony silence and glares are the usual replies. Don't mind me. I'm just the log, jammed in the river with all the water rushing past. Shearers' quarters are fine for me. It's just not very private at shearing time. Oh well. Enough of my woes. Email us back soon . . . By the way . . . this is a shared address . . . so keep it clean. Don't want to upset Turdy-girl.

Lots of love, Tom

PS Bess and Stinky say hello, as does Hank.

PPS I've been sneaking over here during my sleepless nights and have been putting all the financial records onto a great agricultural business program. Dad hasn't got a clue. I even sneak Bess in and she lies on my feet to keep them warm. No doubt Turdy will notice dog hairs any day now. Needless to say the books do not look any better, even on a computer screen!

PPPS This message will self-destruct in 30 seconds.

Frankie read the message again and smiled.

'Good news?' asked Charlotte as she hung a handful of new cat collars on silver hooks.

'Not really. I'm just so glad to hear from him in this way. Glad he's using a computer.'

'Email's great, isn't it?' Charlotte reached into the box for some more collars.

'Tom's such a clever lad,' said Frankie, staring at the words on the screen. 'He's never had a computer lesson in his life, and here he is mastering it in a matter of weeks.'

'A shame he's never got off the farm much to come and see you in the city,' said Charlotte, as she thought of the day he'd sauntered in here looking for his mother. All shy and farmerish. Blond and gorgeous.

'Mmmm,' said Frankie and she felt herself stiffen. Was it her fault her son was trapped? Too afraid of life outside the comfort of the mountains? Too afraid to tell his father he was leaving? Frankie couldn't help but blame herself. She knew Tom had an artistic brilliance that was untapped. It seemed to brew beneath the surface of his quiet character. It bubbled there, a frustration that never came out. She was sure that's what brought on his moods. Lord knows where the artistic talent came from. The teachers at school had recognised it, and urged Frankie to encourage her son. But it had all got too hard. It was so hard juggling the job and the kids and Harry's silent yet somehow violent moods.

She remembered the day she'd suggested sending Tom in on the bus to after-hours art classes. Harry had looked at her as if she were half mad. He'd muttered, 'Stupid bloody woman,' and stomped off. Frankie knew Harry wasn't going to let his sons chase their dreams. Harry had himself been forbidden a life of dream-chasing away from the farm. He was damned if he would let his boys have the chance.

Charlotte's voice jolted Frankie to the present. 'Why hasn't he ever left the farm?'

'Not sure, Charlotte. Not sure . . .'

She really didn't want to answer Charlotte's question. Then she cursed herself for not facing the truth. What could she say? That her son was so dominated by his father that he was too afraid to leave? That Harry had never paid Tom much of a wage for his work so he always used the excuse that he never had any money? Frankie felt a vast distance from Tom. A distance so great that she barely knew him – her own son. All she knew was that he was the child she had hurt the most when she drove away from the homestead, putting her job first, her career in front of her kids, escaping her husband and the difficult life of domesticity in that huge, dark, isolated house. She sighed and looked at her watch.

'What time was that cat coming in for its stitch removal?'

Charlotte looked up from where she squatted on the reception floor. 'Three. There's still time for you to type back a quick message and send it. I'll show you how.'

'That'd be great, Charlotte. Thank you.'

As Charlotte leaned across her and took over the mouse, Frankie tried to picture the computer in the dark office at Waters Meeting. It would be jammed in between the piles of old newspapers and phone books. She imagined Harry circling it suspiciously and growling at it like an aggressive dog. She found herself smiling at the image.

When Charlotte moved away from the screen Frankie straightened her back and began to type, 'To my darling son, Tom. I've been so worried about you.' She sat. Looked at the words she had written, then reached for the mouse and wiped the screen blank. Instead she typed, 'Hi Tom, Mum here. Cat coming in now, will write again soon. Mum XXX.'

Frankie hit 'send' and walked out of the reception area into the surgery. Feeling cold, she pulled her white coat around her and shivered a little. The steel of the surgical instruments were ice on her fingertips and it made her feel even colder. She longed for the phone to ring. For Peter's warm voice to melt the coldness that had settled around her heart. She heard the door of the surgery open and a cat meow. Her next appointment had arrived.

CHAPTER 18

As she stood behind the leggy Holstein cow, Rebecca felt the wave of its muscle contractions move tightly along her arm until a waft of methane and cow manure escaped and bubbled close to her ear.

'I hate being short sometimes,' she said to the lecturer. The quiet Holstein cow hung her head in the crush and braced herself against Rebecca's arm as she felt along the warm slimy wall of the cow's bowel. The cow flicked her tail so that it made high-pitched 'tings' against the metal of the crush.

'Now can you feel along the base of the bowel wall until you find a firm area?' asked Ross Harman as he leaned on the crush. 'What you're feeling through the bowel is the reproductive tract. Do you think you've located the cervix?'

Rebecca's fingertips ran over the firm rippled surface of the cervix. 'Yes. I think so.'

'If you slide your hand to the left and right you can

feel the horns of the uterus. This is how we can determine if the cow is pregnant. Feel it.'

Rebecca bit her bottom lip as she concentrated on what her fingertips felt inside the cow.

The crowd of students watched from the fence with long rubber gloves in hand, waiting for their turn.

'I think I've found both.'

'Good. Now scoop the cervix up gently with your hand and have a practice with the AI gun.'

Gabs was standing by with the dummy-straws of semen and she loaded the slim silver gun as they'd learned in the lecture hall. She handed it to Rebecca who inserted its tip into the vagina of the cow.

'Now slide it along the vaginal cavity parallel to your arm. You'll feel it hit the cervix. A bit of pressure and you can insert it halfway into the cervix. Now gently and slowly inject the semen.'

Rebecca rolled her eyes at the gathering of boys on the fence who whispered, laughed, smirked and punched one another.

'Are we all watching?' Ross said sternly. 'Some of you . . .' he turned to glare at the disruptive students, 'may one day need to apply the techniques learned today to other areas of your lives, so I'd be paying attention if I were you.'

The boys sniggered as Paddy Finnigan made jokes about finding the right hole. Ross calmly ignored them.

'There. Well done, Rebecca. You seem to have the technique right and you were nice and gentle with your stock. Now if you could let her go and we'll have the next practice cow up.

'Finnighan and Faulkner-Jones. You two are next. Get your gloves on and your smiles off your faces and get down off the fence.'

Pulling the glove from her hand and throwing it in the bin, Bec turned to Gabs.

'I could think of more romantic ways of getting up the duff.'

'Yeah. Cold steel and a shot of semen. Not as nice as a big bully-boy with dangly balls,' laughed Gabs. Both girls climbed onto the cattle-yard rails with the other students to watch the rest of the group go through the motions of artificial insemination.

From up on the fence Rebecca could enjoy a sunny view of the college farm. For the moment she was relishing the outdoors. She knew her afternoon would be spent inside a lecture theatre. She had an accountancy lecture, followed by a computer tutorial.

She thought back to Blue Plains. This time last year she would've been riding behind a mob of ewes and lambs, bringing them in for marking. Lambs trotting along bleating for their mothers. Ewes turning their heads back to look at the rider and the horse before letting out a long deep-throated call and sniffing at each lamb running past. Rebecca looked at the yards. They were so small compared to the cattle yards at Blue Plains. The B&S committee had put in a new sand arena for this weekend's rodeo, which was to follow the night of the Wet Sheep Walk-Out, which was the college's annual B&S ball. The university had tried on several occasions to ban the event from campus, but a few diehard lecturers ensured the event stayed on the grounds because it 'taught the organisers some useful lessons in real life'. Sally was actually taking time off from her ag economics studies to come down for it and, to Rebecca's surprise, Tom had emailed her to say he was thinking of coming too.

'Right,' came the voice of Ross, 'another two students please. Emma and Richard . . . ahh, I mean Dick.' Rebecca watched another practice cow walk slowly into the race. She felt sorry for them.

'What a job!' she said to Gabs and nodded at the cow.

'You're not wrong! I'd hate to have Dick's big arms shoved up my arse like that.'

'You're a shocker,' said Bec.

Rebecca smiled to herself. By the time she finished the course, she would be accredited to preg-test and inseminate her own cattle on Waters Meeting. She imagined she and Tom picking out progeny-test semen from canisters and injecting into the finest herd of glossy black Angus cows. But marching into her daydream came Mick and Trudy and her father. She knew her qualifications after the course could lead her anywhere, even a lofty position up in the AR management chain, but she knew her heart wasn't in that. Each time she discovered more knowledge of what was achievable in farm business she burst with enthusiasm and energy, directing her grand dreams and plans into the sheltered valley of Waters Meeting.

She looked across from the college yards to the dog pens. It had taken half a day and $80 to fix them up. They weren't ideal and they were too far from her room in the dorms, but at least the college had allowed her to keep her dogs on campus, and thankfully the pens were lockable, so that drunken boys couldn't let her dogs out after on-campus bar nights. From where she sat she could see the squiggling mass of Moss's pups romping, rolling and growling in play, while Stubby, Dags and Moss sat upright, motionless, their eyes fixed on her.

'Look at them watching you,' said Penelope Stirling as she adjusted her floral print Alice band. 'Those dogs are obsessed with you. If only you could get a man to look at you like that.'

Someone should tell her Alice bands are out of fashion and look downright wallyish, thought Bec, but instead she said, 'Would you like to buy a pup, Penny? They're dirt cheap at $400.'

Rebecca knew Penelope hated being called Penny and wouldn't know how to train and work a dog, let alone be interested in learning. She was an acre-chaser. A hectare-hunter. A real gold-digger. She was out to marry a private-school boy with vast tracks of land. Already in first semester she and Hamish Faulkner-Jones had teamed up. Penelope knew how to throw Bec looks that stung like needles when she talked dogs with Hamish.

At first, after Rebecca had set up the kennels, she'd walk into the dining hall and some of the boys had woofed and panted at her. The doggy-style jokes ran thick and fast and, when the kitchen staff served up greasy chops for tea, Bec found her plate being piled high with bones.

After a while, though, the boys came round. They began to ask advice and started to buy a pup or two. And a few of them got together now and then to travel to a dog trial. The day Hamish brought his collie dog on campus for Bec to assess, Penelope seethed.

Penelope was seething now as Gabs forced out a loud fart and quickly turned to say, 'Awww Penny. *That's disgusting.*' Gabs waved her hand in front of her nose as the students around her laughed. Ross struggled with a straight face as he called Penelope down from the fence and handed her a glove. She took it with distaste.

Bec spent most of the following accountancy lecture doodling on her notebook, sketching gum trees, dogs and high-stepping horses. By the time the lecturer had assigned the reading and closed his books, Rebecca's head felt fuzzy. She was glad to get out of the room. She hugged her books to her chest as she walked along the pathway past the library and entered the computer room. Like the lecture theatre, it smelt stuffy. The lecturer, Michelle Rogers, tugged on her blue pastel suit-jacket and began writing on the whiteboard. Her gold bracelets jangled as she wrote the heading 'Farm Software'.

Rebecca slumped down at a terminal next to Gabs and watched with a blank face as a short Nick Dunroan sauntered in wearing scuffed cowboy boots. By his side, towering above him, was the tubby Brendon McKenzie, a college jumper stretched over his belly, making its thick stripes bend in half-circles.

'Here's trouble,' Rebecca said to Gabs when the two boys sat behind them.

Not long afterwards Helen Thompson walked into the room. She hadn't made many friends at college, so she sat at the front of the class with her brown eyes fixed on her books in front of her. Brendon and Nick looked at her and began to mumble to each other and snigger.

'What are those dickheads on about?' asked Rebecca.

'They're bagging out Helen,' Gabs said. 'Apparently Nick picked Helen up on Wednesday at the fancy dress night. Nick's just spreading the word that when she took her clothes off she had hairy nipples.'

'Thrilling,' said Rebecca flatly.

Helen tossed her black hair over her shoulder and crossed her thick legs. From behind them Nick and Brendon began making walrus noises. Rebecca looked away from the spreadsheet on the monitor and over her shoulder.

'Huh! What now?'

'The latest is Brendon listened outside Helen's door after she'd picked up Warren Beacroft on Saturday.'

'Not Wozza!' whispered Bec with her eyes wide.

'She was really pissed. Anyway, Brendon was listening to them outside the door and apparently she sounded *just* like a walrus.'

As the walrus noises from Brendon and Nick grew louder, Rebecca swivelled around in her chair. 'Come on, guys.'

The boys fell silent and waved to her.

She turned to Gabs. 'Intellectual giants.'

She looked back to her computer screen and began filling in the spreadsheet as Michelle had instructed them to.

After an hour Rebecca heard Michelle say loudly, 'Right! We'll finish class early today. We've covered enough ground. Some of you can stay on if you like and work a little more; those of you who aren't committed to your education can go home and grow up.'

Michelle watched Brendon and Nick coolly from behind her glasses while leaning against a desk, her long elegant legs crossed at the ankles. The rowdy boys made their way banging and laughing towards the door.

'Just before you go,' yelled Michelle, 'don't forget your case study proposals are due in next Wednesday. You have to pair up with a fellow student and outline your selected property, giving a brief description of how you can overhaul the business. The details are on your course outline. No excuses either, Nick or Brendon. Thank you. That'll be all.'

On the screen Rebecca watched as the messages in her mailbox downloaded from the server. There was one from Sal and one from Tom.

'Aw cool,' she said to herself as she opened Tom's letter and read through it.

'Gabs!' Rebecca said, still staring at the words on the screen.

Gabrielle looked up from behind the smudgy lenses of her glasses. 'What?'

'It seems brother Tom has hatched a cunning plan to rescue my river and Waters Meeting.'

'He has?'

'Yep, it says here he's put all the farm records on computer. He's going to email them to me and we're all going to come up with a saviour strategy.'

'He is?'

'Yep. He says Dad knows nothing about it. Neither does Dick and Turdy.'

'Hey!' Gab's eyes lit up. 'Your place would be *perfect* for us to do our case study on.'

'I don't know.' Rebecca sighed. 'It would be too painful to go there. I'd thought of that, but it would be throwing energy into a lost cause. I can't shift Dad's view of me, even if I could show him we could make a mint off the place . . . he'd still hate my guts and not let me back.'

'Oh come on, Bucket,' said Gabs, swivelling her chair to face Rebecca. 'Don't let him defeat you like that. With Tom as your mole it'd be perfect. Besides, can you come up with a better idea for a case study? Why don't you get your friend Sal to help us. She's the economics guru. This assignment is a biggy – if we fail this, we fail the lot. Come on, trooper.' She punched Bec lightly on the upper arm.

Rebecca looked back at the screen for a while. Her

mind raced back to her days with Tom at Waters Meeting and the hours they'd spent talking through dreams and plans. Dreams that never seemed possible. At least now they could *start* to put something on paper. Suddenly goosebumps ran over Bec's skin.

'You know, you could be right, Scabs, you ol' dog. The first thing we need to do is to set Tom up with a Hotmail address so that we can email him without Turdy seeing it. I'll try and catch him on the phone this Sunday, but he's *never* inside the house while Turdy's there.'

Rebecca frowned and looked back at the computer screen and read the rest of Tom's email.

'No! Wait.' She grabbed Gab's forearm. 'He says he's *definitely* coming up for the Wet Sheep Walk Out and rodeo this weekend! Oooley Dooley!'

'Great! Is he cute?'

'As cute as . . . except business comes first. You're not allowed to snog him until we work the assignment out!'

'But we'll be too smished-pisched to do any study.'

'When aren't we drunk, Gabs?'

'True. We'll work it out. Good. Well, now that's sorted, let's go and find Emma in the library. She owes us a bottle of Passion Pop.'

'Okay. I'll be with you in a minute. I'll just check Sal's message.' Rebecca scanned the text and said to Gabs, 'Sally's coming to the B&S and the rodeo too. It's a bloody miracle she'll take time out from her studies and her new boyfriend! The only thing is Scabs, if Sal rocks up here, you won't stand a chance with my brother.'

'But you just said she had a new boyfriend,' Gabs protested.

'I did. But as if *that* would stand in Sal's way. Tom's got it bad for Sally. I think he's been saving himself for her since he hit puberty.'

'Bummer. Looks like good 'ol Scabs has missed out again,' said Gabs as she packed up her books. 'Come on Tart-face. It's been a long day and I need a drink.'

That evening, as Rebecca walked to the dog pens to give her dogs a run and to feed them, she stared at the setting sun and the spread of pink clouds. She stroked each dog lovingly and handled the wiggling pups one at a time. A noise made her look up from her intense concentration on the pups, and in the dusky light she saw two figures on the hill and the glimmer of a shopping trolley. It was Gabs pushing Emma down the hillside over the road towards her. Emma sat with her rounded knees collected up to her ample chest and held her bottle of Passion Pop in her outstretched hand.

'Come and have a drink with us, dogwoman!' she called to Bec. Emma raised the bottle against the skyline. Rebecca smiled at them, whistled her dogs into the pens and trudged up the hill to meet them so that the three of them became silhouettes in the evening sky. Three young women, a shopping trolley and a bottle of Passion Pop.

CHAPTER 19

Charlie Lewis sat slouched at the dinner table as he pushed the potato around in the gravy with his fork.

'Sit up straight, Charlie,' his mother said as she scooped the leftover potatoes onto his plate.

'I don't want any more, Mum.'

'Nonsense.'

He threw down his fork and shoved his plate away. At the end of the table his father looked darkly at him. 'I'm going to bed.' He stood up from the table.

'But Charlie! Dessert.' He left his mother standing there with a tea towel in her hand, holding a dish of golden apple pie.

When he walked into his bedroom and looked around he breathed, 'Bloody oath.'

She'd been in there again. His pyjamas were folded neatly and placed on the foot of the bed, and she'd changed the sheets again. The fresh ones were tucked too tightly into the bed and smelt strongly of lemon washing powder. Angrily he pulled off his work shirt and jeans and threw them on the floor. His arms were dusty up to his elbows and his feet sweaty, but just to annoy his mother he decided not to have a shower. Worn out from a series of too-long, too-hot, mundane days in the tractor cab, he just wanted to sleep. He switched on the bedside light and climbed naked into the cool, too-clean sheets.

Rolling onto his stomach he reached for his bedside drawer. Sliding it open he pulled out a glossy brochure. His fingers ran over the gold embossed lettering, tracing an A and an R in a swirled font. He flipped to page four of the annual report and rolled over onto his back.

He held the image of the girl above his face, arms extended towards the ceiling. His eyes roamed over her and he drank in her beauty. He read the caption. 'AR employee Rebecca Saunders and champion ram Blue Plains Alpha 655.' He looked at her blue eyes. The sun spilled across the blonde waves in her hair and lit up the peppertree so it shone. Her skin was golden and Charlie imagined kissing it. He touched a finger to her smiling face and felt his erection stir under his mother's newly washed floral sheets. He closed his eyes and felt the desire flood into him.

'Charlie, darling!' his mother's voice sang out from behind the door. He slapped the report down on the bed covers. 'Geez,' he sighed and then called out in an annoyed voice, 'What?'

'I'm making your father a hot drink before bed . . . would you like one too?'

'No,' he said gruffly, then lamented, 'thanks anyway, Mum. Goodnight.'

'Night.' He heard her move down the hallway into the kitchen where she continued to chat endlessly to his father who sat staring at the television in the next room.

Flipping to page four again he said goodnight to Rebecca's photo before putting the booklet back into the drawer. He could feel it coming on again . . . that urge. The urge to blast off in his ute away from the stifling judgement of his mother and father. The urge to become once again 'Basil, B&S legend', to be hailed by his mates as the king of party animals and wild stunts. Not some frustrated little mummy's boy who was too afraid of getting the sheets dirty. Charlie banged his head against the pillow in frustration. He'd tell his father tomorrow. He'd tell him he wouldn't be available next year on the farm.

Charlie Lewis said to himself, 'I'm on a mission,' and he closed his eyes and fantasised about a girl with blonde hair, the bluest of eyes and a cheeky grin. And then Charlie Lewis switched off the light, rolled onto his side and laughed at himself for wanting to wank over a girl with a sheep in an annual AR report.

CHAPTER 20

The gate swung open with a loud clang and a rocking Garth Brooks song blared out from the speakers. The bell hanging under the bull's brisket clattered with tinny-sounding rings as it bucked, spun and snorted. The rider threw one hand in the air and spurred his legs along the tree-trunk girth of the bull. Spinning violently, the bull whiplashed his giant body so that the young man was flung into the air, hand still bound in the bull's rigging. His slim body hung from the bucking brindle bull.

'Wow! Hung up!' cried Rebecca from the crowd.

In the small arena the rodeo clowns danced close to the beast. Amidst a flurry of sand and hooves, they undid the tight strap from around the bull's flank. Its release seemed to settle the bull a little so the rider was able to unhitch his hand. Hitting the sandy surface of the ring, the cowboy rolled on his back, jumped to his boot-clad, spur-jangling feet and stooped for his hat.

He held it up to the crowd, while the commentator read out the score of seventy-nine points with a nasal twang. Rebecca watched the rider's Wrangler-wrapped butt saunter away towards the chutes. The fringed leather chaps were wrapped over his thighs and held by a strap across the base of his backside. The chaps seemed to highlight his small, pert behind and tiny waist.

'Are you looking at what I'm looking at?' Bec said to Sal, Emma and Gabs who sat beside her on a hay bale.

'Mmmm. I just lerve Wrangler butt,' said Gabs.

Sally followed their gaze. 'Well I have to say the chaps do set the butt-cheeks off rather well. But girls, I'm sorry to say, I'm evolving.'

'*Evolving*?' asked Gabs and Bec at once.

'Yes. I'm sorry. I have to admit, I've been falling for men in suits lately.'

'Look out corporate world!' cried Bec.

The three of them looked up as Tom weaved towards them in the crowd of hungover and still drunk B&S revellers. The sunlight caught in his hair and he beamed a friendly smile at the girls as he held up the cluster of drinks he was carrying. Sally's eyes glanced over his rumpled shirt, the opening at the top revealing a bare brown chest. Then the other girls' eyes followed. Emma and Gabs, when they first saw Tom, had crooned to Rebecca that her brother was 'soooo cute!' While the girls thought Tom was gorgeous, Rebecca couldn't help but notice the slight circles that had formed beneath his eyes since she last saw him and the fact that the end of his plaited leather belt was looped around itself like a snake above his loose-fitting jeans. He had lost weight.

'What was that about suits?' asked Tom as he handed around the plastic cups of rum before sitting down with Bec.

'Oh nothing, bro. Just girl talk.' Bec looked at him almost sadly and put a sisterly arm around his shoulders. 'Here's to pissed idiots, B&Ss and rodeo recoveries.'

Poor Tom, thought Bec. It had taken him many hours of nail biting and many glasses of rum last night at the B&S to work up the courage to ask Sally to dance. When he did, she led him by the hand to the dance floor and proceeded to dance dorky chicken dances and the good old waggle-your-knees-and-move-your-hands-back-and-forth dance. After she started walking like an Egyptian Tom gave up and came back over to where Bec was standing with a group of first years.

'Tom-arse,' Bec'd yelled at him above the music, 'I don't think she's picked up on the vibes you've been sending her.' They watched Sally dance off into the crowd in her sequined dress which looked so elegant and sophisticated next to all the ag college girls in their 'battle dresses'.

'Have you said anything to her?' Tom had asked.

'No. Do you want me to?'

'No. No thanks, sis.'

Rebecca had found him later in the night in her ute,

212

which was parked in the college student carpark. He'd unrolled his swag and was curled up inside it. Drunkenly she looked down at him. He was sleeping with a frown on his face beneath a chilly moon at four a.m. She tried to drag him inside.

'You can sleep in my dorm room, you dork, it's just inside.' In her drunken state she raised her index finger and said enthusiastically, 'Don't worry, bro, I'll carry you there.' Grabbing the swag she tried to pull it over the tailgate of the ute. Losing her grip she fell backwards onto the ground.

'Wait. Wait. I'll drive you to the doorway.' She fumbled with the door of her ute.

'Don't be an idiot, Bec,' he muttered. 'I'm staying here.'

'Well, I'll get in with you then,' she said, trying to lift her leg over the side of the ute.

'Don't be a knucklehead, Bec. The boys will stir the crap out of you in the morning if they find you in the back of the ute after a B&S with your brother. They'll call you an inbred mountain woman.'

As Bec considered this, they heard voices and the sound of footsteps coming up the road from the B&S site. Across the gleam of cars in the moonlight they saw Paddy, Brendon and Nick in their white shirts and black dinner-suit trousers. Nick's sleeves were ripped off so his pale upper arms shone in the blue-white light. Paddy jumped on to the bonnet of Helen Thompson's blue Corona sedan and pulled down his trousers. Frowning and peering at him Bec called out, 'Oi!

213

Paddy, what on earth are you doing?' At the sound of her voice Nick sauntered forward with his finger to his lips.

'Shhhhhhh! We're leaving a mystery poo!'

'Tom,' she had said, and slapped a hand on his shoulder, 'the dorm room is smelling pretty good right now.'

Tom had slept on Bec's swag on the floor. From her narrow college bed, just before Rebecca faded off to sleep, she'd mumbled, 'Look on the bright side, bro, you can do some more spade work on Sally Farter in the morning at the rodeo.' Tom hadn't answered and had pulled the doona up over his head.

This morning they had awoken to screams and laughter in the corridors as someone yelled out, 'Mystery poo! Mystery poo! Someone's done a mystery poo in Natalie Ashcroft's riding boot!'

By the time they'd drunk their breakfast beers and got dressed for the rodeo, it was clear Tom was forcing a good mood. He was trying to join in with the conversation now as he sat amidst the group of girls beside the rodeo ring.

Sally was chattering and full of rum, bubbling with the excitement of the day. She was completely oblivious to Tom's dark aura, solemn stares and sad eyes.

Bec shook her head gently as her best friend blabbed on to Gabs and Emma about her conquests at her city university.

'He was a *law student*,' groaned Sal, 'the *sleaziest* breed – and once he told me he used his vibrating

214

mobile phone for unsavoury purposes, that was it. I mean that *was it*. Finito.'

'Sal. The drink is lubricating your lips fairly well,' said Bec, hoping she'd take a hint.

'He'd rather caress a leather BMW seat than my inner thighs, so pooey to him.'

'Sal. You're dribbling now,' cautioned Rebecca.

'Scabs,' Sal said, turning to Gabrielle, 'tell Miss-High-and-Mighty-High-Country to go get a root. She needs to loosen up.'

Gabs turned to Bec. 'Bucket. Farter here told you to get a root.' Gabs then squinted at Sal. 'Is that better, Farter?'

'Yip,' said Sal, nodding an already noddy head. She sculled her drink down in one gulp.

Deciding to ignore her friends, Rebecca watched the college boys canter around the arena on their horses. They were ushering a bareback bronc out of the ring. The mare carried her tail and her head high, propping at the rails and skimming up sand with high-stepping hooves. Rebecca wished she was out there on Ink Jet. With her system soaked in alcohol, Rebecca felt a longing settle inside her. Every time she spotted a Wrangler butt she was reminded of Charlie Lewis.

Gabs elbowed Bec in the ribs. 'Hey, dreamer.' Gabs turned to Sally. 'She's probably dreaming about The Brick. That's the one and only fling she's had since she came to this fine academy.'

'Do tell!' said Sally.

Leaning forward Emma continued the story for Gabs who was swearing and wiping rum from her shirt.

'He was a rugby clone through and through. Lots of brawn and no brains. A complete brick wall in the forward line, so hence, The Brick.'

Gabs went on. 'It was one night after a fancy-dress party and she went to the bar as a rollerblader in a crop-top and pigtails. She virtually rolled into his arms and then into his college bed. Apparently they couldn't get the rollerblades off.'

The girls dissolved into snickers and spluttery giggles and Tom sipped slowly on his rum.

Gabs and Sally leaned their heads together and Gabs said in a whisper which wafted of rum, 'He's sitting in front of us . . . that's him there.' She pointed to a large lad who was watching and whooping at the bareback rider with clenched, brick-like fists. His broad square neck held up a blocky head. He had cropped fair hair.

Bec looked at him. She pictured biting him on the neck and running her hands across his impossibly broad shoulders.

'She was mightily disappointed,' Gabs said shaking her head, 'when she found out her one and only one-night sleaze turned out to have a tiny excuse for a wanger. Reckoned the condom looked like a wind sock. Flap, flap, flap!' Gabs waved her hand about in the air to highlight her point.

'Ouch!' said Gabs as Rebecca punched her in the arm.

'But the size of his fingers don't reflect that,' said Sally, puzzled.

'Blows that theory out of the water, doesn't it?' said Gabs, nodding and rubbing her upper arm.

'For godsake you two, shut up!' said Rebecca.

The next round of rums topped Bec right up. She rested her chin in her hands. The second consecutive day of drinking was halfway over and Bec had hit the wall of sadness. She always hit it when she got this drunk. Longing for love. Longing for her home. Longing to see Charlie Lewis again. Tom sat silently beside her and she felt comforted by his nearness but chilled by his sadness, which seemed so complete.

She thought he'd be buoyant after Sally agreed enthusiastically to help them with the business plan for Waters Meeting, but instead she felt him withdraw into his own world. Every time she asked him about Harry, Tom fell silent. He wouldn't be drawn on what future their father might have laid out for them and the farm. Rebecca couldn't help feel Tom's depression was linked to her departure from Waters Meeting. She urged him to enrol in ag college for the following semester, but Tom kicked at the ground with his scuffed riding boots and shook his head.

'I've thought about it Bec, and if I'm going to leave the farm for any course, I'd leave to do fine arts . . . not agricultural business.'

Rebecca blurted out, 'What's stopping you?'

Tom threw back his drink, shook his head and clenched his mouth shut. Then he slung his arm about his sister and rested his head on her shoulder. It must've been the grog opening Tom up, Bec thought. He rarely mentioned his love for art. Bec knew he'd sometimes sketch things and then hide them from the family – from Harry mostly, she suspected.

She remembered the day she found a bundle of pages – beautiful pencil drawings, mostly, of her dogs and of horses and cattle. She'd found them in Tom's cupboard. When she mentioned them to him and told him how brilliant they were, Tom had flown into a rage and torn them up in front of her, then stormed out of the house. Stunned by his sudden anger, she had sat on the floor crying, trying to piece the pages back together. The very thought of Tom's dark side scared her so much sometimes. She sat in the rodeo stand with her troubled brother sitting right there by her side, and the world swam on around her. She stared ahead and shut her mind down. It was all too hard to understand.

After the rodeo buckles were presented to the winners, Bec, Sal, Gabs, Emma and Tom clambered into one of the taxis which lined the college road. The drivers had waited for the students, in bright afternoon sunlight, to drive them to town and into the darkness of the pub. Fares were hard to get at this time of the afternoon on a Sunday.

At the pub the bar staff were battening down the hatches, preparing for the onslaught of over a hundred and fifty drunken agricultural students.

In the smoky bar Bec felt a lariat fall over her shoulders and pull tight. On the end of the rope was

Paddy. He towed her around in the crush of drunken noisy people. Together they clambered on the table and Paddy began to auction her.

She was bought by a third-year student and spent the rest of the night hiding from him under the pool table. By three a.m. she was in the twenty-four-hour Coles carpark in a shopping trolley being pushed by Gabs. By four a.m. she found herself sitting in the gutter, vomiting an interesting mix of Country Mints and hot dogs. After that, Tom bundled them all in a taxi.

Bricked in her tiny college room Rebecca held the vision, just before passing out on her bed, of Tom lying fully clothed next to a very comatose Sally. His eyes were wide. Huge silent tears fell from them as he tenderly stroked Sally's hair and face.

CHAPTER 21

The sausage roll was still cold in the middle, but Rebecca didn't care as she shoved the last of it into her mouth. The woman from the college canteen folded her arms across her sagging bosom and said kindly, 'Bit crook, love?'

'Hangover from hell,' mumbled Bec with pastry crumbs falling over her T-shirt. She wiped her mouth with the back of her hand. It was worse than the hangover she'd had a few months ago after the rodeo. She'd thrown up all day after that weekend and missed a string of lecutures.

'Can I have a chockie milk too, please? That should make me feel better. Oh, and a packet of barbecue chips.' She fished around in the pockets of her shorts for some money.

Hamish Faulkner-Jones sauntered up behind Bec and poked her in the ribs. 'Bit seedy, ol girl?'

'Mmm.'

'Well, lucky you. My last exam isn't until this afternoon. You guys were so noisy last night, if I bomb out it's your fault for causing me sleep deprivation.'

'You won't fail, you nerdy swat,' said Bec to his boots as she leaned her head on the orange laminex counter.

'I'll just be glad when it's all over and we can head out to the pub.'

'Does that mean I have to do a repeat performance *again* tonight?' groaned Bec.

'Did anyone ever tell you that you drink too much?'

'Mmm. Me and the rest of the college population. You included.'

'You're a special case, Bucket-mouth. You've got issues.' He bought a cup of coffee and sesame seed health bar and wandered back towards the library, leaving Bec standing there wondering, What issues?, even though she knew she had plenty.

It was the end of her first year at college. She spent more time hungover or drunk than studying. The exams had been tight. She wasn't even sure she'd get through to next year.

She sauntered over to the student-mail pigeonholes, dragging her heavy backpack of books behind her. In the S box there was a fat yellow envelope waiting for her. It was a scrawled note from Tom and a budle of photos.

Hi Bucket

Are you still drinking too much? I bet you're hungover as you read this. Enclosed are photos of the farm for your

221

assignment. You'll notice what a brilliant photographer I am. I've included a special one for your desk (not that you're at it much) and Mick volunteered to pose for a picture for Scabs.

Hope you kick arse with the business plan assignment.

Lots of love, Bro (Tom-arse)

PS World War III continues at Waters Meeting to the point where either he goes or they go. Turdy's father has offered Mick a job in his rural property division in the big smoke. He'll probably end up taking it because I don't think he can take being caught between Dad and Turdy any more!

PPS Turdy is up the duff.

Pregnant! Trudy was having a kid! In an instant Bec forgot that her head was pounding, and her nausea suddenly disappeared.

Mick move to the city! she thought. No way! The scribbled words in Tom's note had shocked her. Tom had been emailing her often with thoughts for the assignment on Waters Meeting and with budgeting ideas, but he'd been short on information about home.

With the envelope in one hand, chocolate milk and chip packet in the other, and bag hanging heavily from the crook of her arm, she wandered out into the bright sunlight and sat on the cold brick steps which led up to the library.

She shuffled through the photographs. Pictures of

home. Snapshots of the river flats looking tired and reedy with daggy-bum sheep grazing on them. A band of healthy regal rivergums swept along the paddocks' edge and dropped away to the unseen Rebecca River. The sight of the place took Rebecca's breath away. She looked around at the red-brick campus. It was going to be a hot day here. There was nowhere to swim. Nowhere cool. She sighed and looked back at the photographs. There were shots of the outbuildings and of the homestead. Tears welled up in her eyes when she saw that, to the left of the house, her doglogs were gone. Trudy must've made Mick move them.

Rebecca swiped away the tears and sharply told herself to get it together. It was then she flicked to the next photograph. It was a close-up headshot of Ink Jet. The afternoon sun brought out black and silver contours of the mare's glossy midnight coat. Her ears were pricked forward and light fell on her black eyelashes which framed her deep brown eyes. Rebecca's tears fell fast and hot now. Big fat tears splashed on her legs.

I'm always crying, she thought angrily, and put her hand across her face. She breathed in deeply, sobbed slightly and then flicked to the next photo. It was Mick. At least part of Mick. His white bum cheeks mooned the camera and his grin could be seen as he swivelled his head towards the lens.

'Mmm. That's one for the family album,' came Gab's voice from behind Bec's shoulder. Rebecca quickly wiped the tears away and composed herself.

'Actually it's a snapshot for you. Tom sent it to you.'

'Nice one!' laughed Gabs. 'Is that your older brother?'

'Yep.'

'Cute arse. In a kind of exposed way.'

'He's married . . . and from this note, is about to be a dad.'

'Errk.'

Bec offered Gabs some chips. She took a handful and crunched as she talked. 'I hope all the photos for the assignment don't include your brother's butt.'

'No – thank God. They're not bad actually. We'll be heading for a good mark on this one.'

'Well I'm glad I found you. I've been looking for you everywhere. I've been banging on the door of your room for the past fifteen minutes. I thought you'd passed out in there. Drowned in your own vomit.'

'No such luck. I did wake up with my rubbish tin next to my bed and an empty packet of barbecue shapes. My mouth was as dry as a nun's nasty. It's not been a good morning. Don't know why I'm eating these whooers – I sure as hell don't need any more salt.' She swigged on the milk bottle.

'Has anyone ever told you, you drink too much?'

Bec turned to look at Gabs. 'What? Milk?' She held up the bottle and then sighed. 'Don't you start.' Gabs looked at her friend's eyes.

'Hey! You've been crying. Are you okay?' She put a skinny arm across Bec's shoulders.

'Just mooching over my horse and pictures of home.' She held up the picture of Stinky.

'Ink Jet?'

Bec nodded.

'She's beautiful. No wonder you're teary about leaving her behind. Come on. We'll feel better after we've handed in this project. Let's be nerdy and go to the library.'

'Yes, Mum.' And Gabs helped pull Rebecca to her feet and gave her a big warm hug which made Bec cry again.

The library was warm and, Rebecca thought, smelt of dirty socks. The librarian, known to the students as the 'creature from the depths', waddled past them pushing a trolley of returns. The obese librarian had provided the college boys with endless hours of entertainment speculating on her love life. Well over a hundred kilos, the boys made jokes like, 'How do you find her fanny? Roll her in flour and see where it sticks.'

The taunts and jokes made Rebecca angry. She liked the librarian. She had helped her order in some new dog-training books and she'd often discuss the latest bestseller she was reading.

'Hi,' Rebecca smiled at her.

'Hi girls.' And she disappeared into a cave of books.

Gabs and Rebecca walked past the rows of heads which were bent intently over books for this afternoon's exam, the final one for the year. Hamish looked up, waved and then made vomiting gestures to Bec.

'I think he likes you,' whispered Gabs.

'Penelope-ploppy-bottom thinks that too! So don't you start.'

Rebecca shot Hamish a wry smile and kept walking towards the activity room where large low-slung couches lined the walls. The students laughed at its name, 'activity room'. It was rumoured Paddy Finnighan had once bonked a horse management student in there on the couch. The rough cloth on the couches were often inspected by students, but no evidence of semen could ever be found.

Gabs shut the door behind them. 'I wonder which couch he did it on,' she said.

'Yirk! I'm going to sit on the floor.'

Bec tipped notebooks, a hole punch, pens, glue and scissors from her bag and scattered them on the low table, while Gabs carefully took out the almost finished assignment. It was neatly printed out with gaps where the photographs were to be stuck. As Bec flicked through the weighty document, she felt a tingle of excitement. The assignment included the existing enterprises which, when added up, never made a profit. Then came the proposal for upgrading the property.

'Sally's done a terrific job in the loan submission to the hypothetical bank manager,' said Gabs, staring at the text. Sal was in her final year of economics and had been doing part-time work with one of the state's best rural financial counsellors.

Gabs flicked over the page and inspected the colourful farm maps which showed how the paddocks could be developed to produce high-quality lucerne. The map also showed the proposed dam site, where the pivot irrigator would run, and the next page listed all the costings. Soil test and meteorological figures, which Tom had organised, proved that the conditions were ideal. He'd also developed a way in which existing plant and equipment and sheds could be converted to meet quality hay production standards.

Gabs flicked over to the marketing section. There were local racing stables in the region, plus markets in Hong Kong and Japan. The return on capital was realistic and debt could be repaid in five years. Where the project was weakest was the short paragraph on succession planning. They would lose marks there.

'It's looking pretty good, apart from the family bit about the future ownership of the business,' said Gabs. Rebecca ignored her quip about the family.

'It bloody well should be good. We've worked hard enough on it.'

'Let's get sticking.' Gabs picked up the glue stick and held it up to Bec, rolling its sticky tube in and out suggestively and swivelling her tongue around her lips.

They selected the best of the photos and pasted them carefully on the pages.

'Get your tits off the table,' said Gabs, nodding at Rebecca, who was so intent on the task of gluing the pictures on straight she hadn't noticed her breasts were resting on the surface of the table.

'Where else am I supposed to put them, Scabs?' She tried sitting them under the table, but it just wasn't comfortable.

'I suppose I'm just jealous,' said Gabs, pushing up her own small breasts and trying to sit them on the table. It was at that moment that Paddy put his head around the door.

'What on earth are you two up to?'

Gabs's cheeks flushed a bright pink.

'Just trying to glue our tits to the table,' said Bec, holding up a glue stick, completely unfazed.

'You two are weirdos.'

'Takes one to know one,' Bec retorted. 'Besides, this *is* the activity room and all sorts of activities go on in here. As you know, Paddy. Aren't you supposed to be studying?'

'Yeah, yeah. I was just having a break. Just came to see when you were heading off for Christmas. Are you both going home?'

'I'm headed to the coast with the olds,' said Gabs. 'Leaving this arvo if I can unstick my tits.' They all laughed.

'Me? I'm headed back up to Blue Plains where I used to work. I've got a job there again over the summer till uni starts again.'

'Not going home to your place?' Paddy asked.

'No.'

Paddy knew from her voice not to ask any more questions. 'Well, have a happy pissmas, girls.'

'Good luck in your last exam,' Gabs said. They watched Paddy shut the door and then Gabs threw a book at Bec. 'What was that gluing tits to the desk bit? That rumour's going to supersede the one about Paddy and the horsy girl on the couch!'

'No it won't! Everyone's leaving and they'll have forgotten about it by next year.'

On their way out the librarian called, 'Happy holidays and Merry Christmas,' so that her chins wobbled.

As Gabs and Bec walked to the assignment boxes to reverently place their Waters Meeting project in the box, Hamish ran up to them and placed his arms around their shoulders.

'What's this I hear about you girls getting your tops off, smearing glue all over your breasts and then rubbing yourself over the tabletop in the activity room?'

'Bec, I'm going to kill you,' muttered Gabs.

CHAPTER 22

Across the valley Harry listened to the truck engine changing down a gear as it laboured up a steep cutting on the side of the mountain. He paced up and down in the shearing shed, rubbing his hand on the back of his neck and nervously glancing out the door. His breath caught between his clenched teeth until he let it out, like the hiss of an angry cat. A gleaming red truck pulled into sight, with neat lettering painted on the side. 'Moffet Removals.' It drove past the shearing shed and up towards the homestead. Trudy skipped down the steps and motioned to the truck to come in the side gate of the garden and not over the grid.

Harry looked up to the sky and again held his breath in a hopeless bid to ease the pain in his stomach. As he exhaled he looked across to the mountains. There, on the side of the ridge, he could just make out Tom riding Hank on the long-spur track. He was heading for the cattlemen's hut. The sight of the lonely speck moving slowly across the face of the massive mountain brought tears to Harry's eyes. He pictured the shattered look on Tom's face this morning during the fight.

Tom had sat in the corner of the kitchen throughout the whole raging, roaring argument. His strong compact body rigid on the chair, tears rolling down his cheeks, as Trudy spat hateful words at Harry. For months, in soft girlish whispers in the newlyweds' bedroom, she'd fed the ammunition of jealousy and anger into Mick's heart about the situation at Waters Meeting. Mick began to simmer and then to rage against his father. In the kitchen, Harry raged back. Veins popped up on his neck. Hot spit lay on his lips. Hard words sizzled in the air. With Trudy backing him, Mick stood taller and twice as heavy as his now-stooping father.

'It's over, Dad. We're leaving. You've crapped in your own nest. We won't take your bull any more. No more working our guts out for nothing. Trudy's dad has lined up a house for us. Why should I put up with your crap when I can get sixty grand a year working for him. That's more than I'd get in a lifetime here.'

Trudy moved closer to Mick and stood slightly behind him. In a cold voice she said matter-of-factly, 'The removalists are coming at ten. We're taking what's rightfully ours. No question.'

'Over my dead body,' spat Harry.

'It bloody well *will* be over your dead body you stupid bastard.' Mick scruffed Harry's collar and shoved him backwards into the kitchen bench.

The shock of being pushed by his own son left

Harry with an open mouth and white knuckles as he grasped the bench. Trudy took Mick gently by the upper arm and led him out of the kitchen and down the hallway to the front of the house. They slammed the huge heavy front door shut and it echoed through the house like a shotgun blast.

In the silent house, Harry moved forward across the kitchen towards Tom, who remained sitting on the chair. He bent down, his face close to Tom's and yelled, 'Do something, you useless bastard. Say something!' he screamed. 'Don't just sit there crying like the baby that you are!'

Harry swung his open hand into the air and hit Tom hard across the face. Tom's bottom jaw shot out to the side and a pain ran up over his skull and down his spine. His head jerked. His face contorted with grief and shock.

Tom stood. He moved past his father like a walking dead man, eyes empty, skin grey. He walked out of the house and to the quarters where, in a daze, he rolled his swag and filled a billy can with matches, sugar and tea. With cold shaking hands he packed his saddlebag with packets of two-minute beef noodles and a roll of toilet paper. He jogged to the shed to gather up his saddle and bridle. Hank, seeing Tom, ambled on his long chestnut legs to the gate and waited to be let into the yard. Strapping his gear to the saddle, Tom mounted Hank and rode out, down towards the river.

In the garden shed Mick and Trudy were packing up the last of her spring bulbs. They looked up from the boxes and watched Tom cross the bridge over the river and head towards the hut track which would take him to the top of Devil's Crag.

From where Harry stood now, Tom and Hank could barely be seen through the gums. Up at the house the overall-clad removalist men were lugging the heavy lounge suite across the lawn. It was the floral one Trudy's parents had bought her for a wedding present. Mick sidestepped with the brass bedheads in his outstretched arms. Trudy followed him, carrying the floral curtains from the spare room which she put neatly in the back seat of her car. Harry sank back into the shed and wouldn't allow himself to watch as the truck and Trudy's little red car drove past the shed and away. He slumped on a wool bale, put his head in his hands and listened to the sound of the truck driving out of the valley.

A while later, slowly, with stiff legs and aching knees, he stood and walked up to the house. He wobbled a bit and had to steady himself against the wall. He went into the chilly dining room and bent to unlock the antique cabinet. From its musty interior he pulled out a bottle of whiskey and a bottle of port. He walked into the kitchen and sat down at the head of the table. Over his shoulder there was a dusty space on the mantlepiece where the clock had been, but Harry could still hear the tick inside his head.

He sat for a long time. Just sat. And it was dark by the time he emptied the last of the whiskey into the teacup and reached hazily for the port bottle. He wasn't aware when he fell drunkenly from the chair and slumped to the floor, hitting his head with a loud crack on the table's corner.

But in the early morning light he felt the pain behind his eyes like a stabbing knife. As the world around him became clearer, he realised that the soft white skin that covered his inner thighs stung from urine which had seeped into the fabric of his work trousers during the night. He began to wretch again when he realised one side of his face was lying in a pool of vomit. The cat, which had been meowing for hours to be let out, sat with huge frightened eyes on the dresser, disgusted at itself for having to crap in the corner.

Outside the window, on top of a dark pine, a crow sat. It called out. Harry lay and listened to its lonely horrific cry echoing out across an empty valley.

CHAPTER 23

'You can't use hay bales for a couch, you dork!' Rebecca put her hands on her hips and looked at Paddy as he moved the bale into the corner of the room, traipsing dirt on the already patchy, penis-pink carpet.

'Well you've been using shopping trolleys to hang your clothes on and keep your food in, so I don't see how hay bales will ruin the decor,' a red-faced and sweating Paddy said as he dropped the bale and hitched up his jeans.

'I should've known that sharing a house with you this year would be a bad move. We're not even going to last a semester! I could barely live with you when you were a block away on campus. Besides, how prickly is that hay going to be on your tubby little arse!'

'Prickly! I'll have you know this is *quality* pasture hay . . . and my arse is *not* tubby.'

'Well, go feed your *quality* hay to your stinking

goats – we'll go to St Vinnies and get a real couch for half the price if it's such bloody good hay.'

Both stood looking sternly at one another, their smiles barely hidden behind mock angry faces. Rebecca and Paddy turned their heads to the doorway as they heard the front door bang shut. Gabs appeared, her face flushed from the summer heat and the bustle of carting supermarket bags from her hot Datsun.

'Hey, you planning to set up a feedlot in here?' she nodded towards the bales.

'That, according to Paddy, is "the couch".'

'Cool,' said Gabs. '. . . I think.' She stood looking at the bales and shook her head. Then she remembered the bags in her hands. 'Hey guys! Look what I got! Chokoes were on special. You could get a whole bag for $2.' She proudly held up the bag.

'Chokoes?' echoed Bec.

'What are they?' asked Paddy

'They're disgusting,' said Bec, peering into the bag at the green vegetables.

'Hey! But for $2! It's a bargain!' argued Gabs.

'What's in the other bags?' asked Bec.

'Just some mince for spag bog and some nibbles for the keg party tonight.'

'Speaking of kegs, I'd better go and pick them up,' said Paddy, reaching for his ute keys in his pocket. Gabs bustled off to the kitchen with her shopping bags.

Rebecca stood in the room and looked at its drab grey walls. It was the only rental property the real estate agent would let them have. Ag college students were bad enough, but a student with three dogs was a definite headache. Rebecca had put on her best skirt, brushed back her mop of blonde hair into a ponytail and used her firmest voice when she'd said, 'I can get references regarding my dogs from the AR Company, of which I have been an employee for two years.'

The real estate lady with boofed-up hair and deep lines around her eyes had looked disdainfully back at her. Despite the heat of the day outside, the big old house had been chilly. It had chilled Rebecca even more when the real estate agent had said, 'Of course it was a doctor's surgery for years until it was converted into a mortuary. Hence the wide double doors.'

'They mustn't have been very good doctors,' Rebecca had joked; but the stick-insect lady reeking of stale cigarettes and perfume had simply wafted past her to show her the kitchen. The backyard was a jungle, but it was huge and there was a saggy looking shed where her dogs could be chained.

Because Rebecca had found the house on behalf of Paddy and Gabs, she'd earned the right to choose her bedroom. She'd picked the front room so she could enjoy the sun in the morning; and despite its tatty wallpaper, the room had lovely large windows and an old marble fireplace. Surely they hadn't wheeled the stiffs into this room, she thought.

Over the weekend she'd bought a second-hand double-bed mattress and placed it on the floor in the corner on bricks. She'd made a desk out of apple crates and chipboard and covered it with cloth, and at the bargain store she'd splurged on a chair. By her bed she placed candles. She'd have to buy a lamp later. Besides, she thought, candles were more romantic. She imagined meeting a newly arrived first-year student and undressing him slowly on the low bed.

Bec looked about at the small gathering of boys at the party that evening as she and Gabs lay on their stomachs in the long green grass in the yard. No talent yet, just the same old bunch of hard-drinking yobbo boys from last year.

'So, you ol' tart,' said Gabs, interrupting her thoughts, 'did you get any in the holidays?'

'Na,' said Bec, 'I was so flat out. Alastair had put on a new jackeroo, bloody gorgeous, but he was only a pup. Just eighteen.'

'That's never stopped you before.'

Rebecca screwed up her nose and sipped on the cool froth of her beer, which was the result of Paddy's efforts at keg-tapping.

'How 'bout you?'

'God, I'd do anything for a bit of action. My summer holiday was dry-as,' said Gabs, finishing her beer and motioning for Bec's cup. 'Let's see if Paddy's finally got this keg right.'

It was one of those long summer evenings, with sunshine that stretched on and on. The heat lingered into the darkness of the night and insects buzzed at the bare bulbs of the outdoor spotlights.

The air was thick with excitement as the students from last year saw each other again, and the new first-years sauntered into the backyard, keen for the reputed college party action. After last year, initiation ceremonies had been banned, so keg parties had become the latest way to meet and greet the first-years.

'God. Here comes another batch of "what-school-did-*you*-go-to?" gals,' said Bec, nodding to the group who had just walked into the backyard. They wore Liberty-print shirts ironed neatly with the collars up, and antique jewellery hung heavily around their wrists and necks.

'They'll get over themselves by mid-semester,' said Gabs dryly. 'With the likes of those boys, they'll be pulled down to earth real soon.' Gabs and Bec looked towards the circle of boys who stood around the keg with their pants around their ankles, shooting beer directly into their mouths with the keg gun.

Bec had been drinking beer since lunchtime and the second batch of rough-cut chops and spitting fat sausages were being cremated on the barbecue. Hungry and drunk she and Gabs tore at the half-raw chops like lionesses.

'Lucky it's dark. These taste awful so I'd bet they look awful,' said Bec. A smear of grease lined their mouths and shone under the spotlight.

The neat-as-a-pin first-year girls were now feeling the affects of the beer and one of them said a rosy-cheeked hello to Bec and Gabs as she nibbled on a piece of bread. With chop-greased fingers, Bec shook hands with her and the rest of the group as they nervously moved closer. In between chews, Bec said, 'First years?', knowing full well they were.

'Yes,' said one with a big nose.

'You'll enjoy it. You get to do animal production. My favourite subject.'

'Mine too,' said Gabs. 'We got to study penises.'

'Pardon?' said one with a model-slim body.

'Penises!' said Gabs in a loud voice. 'Part of the animal production unit.'

'Yes. That's right,' said Bec. 'Fascinating. Did you know that a pig's penis is like a corkscrew . . . sort of curly.' She waggled her finger in small circles.

'And a bull's penis is an s-bend and erects with a reflector muscle,' said Gabs, thrusting her hips backwards and forwards.

'Yes. You paid attention in lectures, Scabs! And,' Rebecca continued, 'a ram's penis has a little flicky thing on the end called a flagellum-thingo.'

'I know cats have barbs on theirs,' said the girl with the big nose.

'Yes, they do too!' said Bec, who was pleased the girls were starting to mix in.

'According to our lecturer, Ross – you'll meet him this week – a stallion's penis is most like a man's in that it's engorged with blood when aroused.'

A male voice came from behind Bec's shoulder. 'Does anyone know what a rooster's penis looks like?'

As the girls, including Gabs, looked blank and shrugged, Bec spun around. Her eyes widened.

'Charlie Lewis! What the flock are you doing here?'

'Why, Miss Rebecca.' He smiled with his eyes and leaned forward to kiss her on the cheek.

240

'Mmmm,' he said licking his lips, 'nice chop fat!'

The other girls stood around looking puzzled.

'What *does* a rooster's penis look like?' said Gabs.

Everyone shrugged while Rebecca continued to stare with an amazed smile into Charlie's face.

By midnight warm drops of plump summer rain had begun to fall, landing in sizzles on the cooling barbecue. The second keg was blowing froth and the boys were getting rowdy. Bec, Charlie, Emma and Gabs had been dancing to Garth Brooks songs which blared from the speakers of Paddy's ute. When Charlie casually slung his arm around her waist, Rebecca felt a bolt of desire instantly run through her. The slow, intermittent raindrops fell hot on her face as she looked up to the sky. For some reason her drunken desire was to take Charlie by the hand and introduce him to her dogs. If Dags reacted the same way as last time to him, she knew he was a good person, and in this drunken moment she'd give her whole soul to him.

She looked to where her dogs had been chained all day. They had lain on the ends of their chains and watched the day-long party and Rebecca's every move. Now they had retreated into the shed and were curled up with their noses in their tails.

Paddy was hanging upside down from the Hills hoist with Hamish, and both were doing 'bat-sculls'. They urged the first-year boys to try them too, and the clothes line's metal frame creaked and sagged as two more bat-scullers hung by the crooks of their legs. Their shirts fell about their chins and their bellies shone white and rain-wet in the spotlight. They put plastic cups to their upside-down mouths and drank their beer until it ran from their nose. Someone started spinning the clothes line until it cracked like a dry stick and the boys fell to the ground in a heap, spluttering and laughing in the rain.

Then the party flowed inside.

'This is our dead room,' said Rebecca to Charlie, sweeping her hand across the room.

'Dead room?'

'As opposed to our *living* room. Apparently this is where they used to keep the stiffs when it was a morgue.' She looked up at his face, and in the brighter lights he took her breath away. He was better looking than she'd ever imagined in all those replayed images of that kiss in the river. Dark stubble grew on his square jaw and his green eyes were the same colour as the gum leaves which had waved outside her bedroom windows at Waters Meeting.

In her mind she ran her fingertips over his face and onto the brown, soft skin of his neck. As he kept his focus on her, his strong look, his handsome face, made her suddenly shy. She probably had chop fat all over her face and a massive pimple on her chin. Her hair had long since escaped from its ponytail and was sticking out wildly, and blades of grass and raindrops were caught in her curls.

'Nice couch,' Charlie said, motioning to the hay bales.

'Yes, very handy in drought emergencies.'

The crowded room exploded with cheers as Paddy and a first-year called Bill staggered in with a cardboard box filled with rum and coke. Everyone had thrown bruise-coloured $5 notes into Bill's big Queensland hat and their mission to the bottleshop had been a success.

Bec took the distraction as a chance to duck out of the room.

'Bugger,' was all she could say when she saw the reflection of herself in the bathroom mirror. Her chop fat theory had been correct, and her eyes were red-rimmed.

'Grog monster,' she berated her reflection. She ran a hot washer over her face and brushed the grass from her hair. Her T-shirt was splattered with tomato sauce and ripped under one arm so that her grey-looking bra could be seen.

'Bugger,' she said again.

She dashed down the hall to her bedroom, skirting around the couple who were pressed up against the wall kissing. In her room she pulled off her shorts and T-shirt, found her matching underwear, pulled on her blue jeans and rummaged for her tight-fitting black top. The top accentuated the blondness of her hair and ran neatly over the curves of her breasts. She knew when she wore it that she turned men's heads. That's why she never wore it. Dave had stirred her so much the first night she'd put it on at Blue Plains that she'd changed just before they left for the pub. But this was an emergency situation. She wanted Charlie Lewis. Big time.

As she walked back into the hub of the party she saw Charlie's face light up. He moved through the crowd with two cups of rum and coke in his large farmer's hands which were ingrained with machinery oil.

'You've changed!' He handed her a drink.

'Yep. Got a bit wet outside and I thought the girls might get keen to go to the nightclub later.' She hoped he'd buy her excuse and not think her vain. In her head she wanted to say, 'I'm trying to show off my tits so that you'll be overcome with sexual desire and take me to bed for some serious mattress-dancing.'

By the time the last bottle of rum was finished she again didn't care what she looked like. She'd fallen into an easy drunken conversation with Charlie, so that the party revolved around them as if they were in a fish bowl together, while the world went by outside. They sat together on a large beanbag, which Emma had bought from an op shop as a house-warming present.

'Tell me if I'm jibbering,' she said.

'No. No.' He held up his hand. 'Tell me if *I'm* jib-bering,' he jibbered.

They'd covered cropping, machinery, dogs, families – that part of the conversation had continued on for hours – they'd talked about politics, the state of rural Australia and even period pain. It was slurred, drunken talk that flowed comfortably. Every now and then the conversation was interrupted with splashes of rum thrown from cups and by people landing on top of them.

'How come you're only doing the two-year associate diploma and not the full three-year degree?' asked Bec.

'I chose it so I'd finish the same year as you,' said Charlie.

Rebecca's mouth fell open and a puzzled look came across her face as her muddled drunken brain tried to work out his words. Her face changed as his meaning became clear.

'But you hardly know me!'

'I know. But I know I haven't stopped thinking about you since the day I met you. It's weird, you know, here I am supposed to be "Basil Lewis, B&S king and party animal", but I'm stuck, Rebecca. Really stuck. I've been stuck on a picture of you in my head. A picture of you in a river. And . . . in an AR annual report.' He ran his fingers through his short dark hair and said to his rum, 'Now this *is* sounding like jibber. You'll think I'm a weirdo. Some sort of sick stalker.'

'No! No,' she said gently and was about to reach for his hand and tell him she felt the same way when a biscuit of fresh-smelling hay was thrown on top of them. Next, the zip on the beanbag was undone and they were rolling and laughing on a sea of white beans and golden-green shreds of hay. Chokoes smashed in pale green pieces against the wall and bottles shattered against the steel of a shopping trolley. The party had hit overdrive and it wasn't long until the police were at the door, stepping over the crumpled body of a drunken first-year and a pool of fresh warm vomit on the carpet.

Rebecca saw Gabs take on her look of responsibility –

a rare look for Gabs – as she walked up to speak to the policemen. The music stopped, the yelling stopped, the smashing stopped. The party spilled out onto the street and quietly took itself off to the pub, with the policemen calmly and sternly watching them go.

'Do you want to go to the pub?' said Bec as she stood ankle-deep in hay and beanbag beans, cups and bottles.

'No.' Charlie looked into her eyes.

'Well, come on then, I'll show you my train set.' She took his hand in hers.

'Your train set?'

'Yes, I keep it in my bedroom.' She looked at him with wicked eyes. Then she led him into the room, shut the door and lit the candles.

'There's no train set, is there?' he said, smiling and pulling her close.

'No,' she said as she raised her mouth to his.

It was only nine o'clock but already the heat in the room was unbearable as the morning sun tapped on the tin roof and crept through the windows. Rebecca rolled over, frowning as she felt the hangover and heat sweep over her. Then she felt the smooth skin of Charlie Lewis who lay next to her. She smiled with her eyes closed, savouring the touch.

'Good morning.' His deep gentle voice washed over her and goosebumps rose on her skin.

This is too good to be true, she thought as she opened her eyes to see his face. He was propped up on his elbow looking at her, running a strand of her hair through his fingertips.

'Hi,' she said in a croaky voice. 'Are you feeling as seedy as me?'

'Crook as a dog,' he said. 'Do you remember last night?'

Rebecca smiled. 'Yes.'

He pulled her to him so her naked breasts pressed warm onto his chest. The defined muscles in his arms stood out and she felt like sinking her teeth into them. There was something about farmers' arms.

'I just didn't want to . . . you know . . . go all the way with you until we were both sober.' He kissed her then pulled back to look in her eyes. 'So we could both remember it as special . . . Does that sound dorky? You must think I'm weird by now! We were both so hammered, I just thought it best.'

'It's certainly an unusual decision. You're at ag college now, Charlie. You're supposed to "use and abuse"! But it's really sweet of you just the same.' She paused and shot him a flirty look. 'I didn't think it was a case of Fosters Flop.'

'It certainly wasn't,' Charlie said, with a glint in his eye.

Rebecca began to run her fingertips over his back, 'Am I sober enough for you now, Charlie Lewis?'

He looked into her smiling blue eyes, and buried his head into the smooth skin of her neck.

'I want you,' she whispered as she touched her lips on his shoulders.

He drew her body closer so she felt the hardness of his penis against her thigh. She looked up at him meekly and asked, 'Do you have protection?' and immediately cringed at her cliched question.

Charlie was just reaching for his jeans, which lay on the floor by the mattress, when the door flew open and the dogs came hurtling in, panting, tails wagging, whining with excitement.

Gabs put her head around the door and said, 'Thought you guys might like to do it doggy style.' She slammed the door shut and laughed her way back down the hay-strewn hall.

'Mossy!' squealed Bec as the dogs leapt on the bed. 'What are you all doing inside?'

Charlie sat up with a big grin on his face.

'Hello Dags ol' buddy!' He pulled the dog to him and patted him with big, firm bloke-strokes. Stubby play-bounced and barked on the bed in search of feet under sheets.

'This is the crew,' said Bec to Charlie. 'I hope you like them!'

'They're doozies! Hey, I know! Now that we've been so rudely interrupted and now that it's so bloody hot in here, let's grab some grease to fix the hangovers and take the dogs out to the river. I know a great swimming hole. Mum and Dad used to stop there for us on our way out west after we'd been to the city.'

'Sounds good,' said Bec, but began to wonder . . . was Charlie trying to hide something in the bedroom department? She pushed the thought aside and decided to enjoy his company for the day, thrilled he wanted to spend it with her.

'Come on Dags. Shift your black butt, we're getting up now.'

Charlie looked at Bec as he went to fling the sheet aside, 'Don't look.'

'You've got to be kidding – I've seen it all before, Charlie Lewis.'

'I love that.'

'Love what?' asked Bec.

'I love it when you say my name.'

'Don't go all mushy on me,' she teased. 'You can grab the towel on the back of the door. The shower's second on the right.'

Wrapped in the sheet, she leant against the doorway and watched his muscled back as he walked down the hall. A still-drunk Gabs sprung from her room laughing and pulling at his towel while the dogs danced and barked around him. Rebecca was tempted to join him in the shower, but decided against it and waited in her room until he came in to get dressed.

'You can borrow a clean shirt if you like,' said Bec. 'I've probably pinched a couple from my brothers . . . Have a rummage around in the drawer. There's some boxer shorts in there too. Help yourself.'

As she left for the bathroom Charlie felt a wave of pleasure from the intimacy of looking through Rebecca Saunders' cupboards. Judging by her clothes, this girl was cool. No flowery bullshit like the girls his mother liked. Charlie held up a T-shirt and laughed. In red writing on the back it read, 'Drink till he's cute.'

Fresh from her shower, her hair falling in wet ringlets, Rebecca found Charlie in the dead room in the midst of party aftermath, a garbage bag in hand. Gabs leant on a rake chatting to him.

'Feeling better?' he asked.

'Much.'

Gabs nodded to the door. 'Your dogs were good at cleaning up Donger's spew!'

'Gross!' said Bec before she ordered the dogs outside.

With the floor now clear, the house looked slightly more ordered, but chunks of chokoes still lay in spatters along the windowsill.

'Bugger this,' said Gabs. 'I'm going for another spew, then I'm going back to bed. We can finish cleaning up tonight.'

In the ute the warm breeze whipped the hair around Rebecca's brown shoulders. She felt so excited to be driving Charlie Lewis through the traffic lights and out of town. He looked so right. So right in her life. Sitting with his elbow propped along the doorframe, fiddling with the radio in search of good songs. He found the golden oldies channel and they sang along laughingly and loudly to Elvis.

The river he led her to was stunning. A shimmering trail of silver, running through red and brown craggy rocks. It had been a fairly long walk down a rough gravel track. The heat of the screaming bush brought Bec out in a sweat. Alcohol oozed from her pores and she longed for the cool rush of the river. Her palms sweated as she carried the cooked chook and bread in a shopping bag. Charlie carried the drinks, fizzy cold lemonade and a big bottle of water. In Bec's rucksack he carried two towels and a box of condoms.

The dogs trotted out ahead of them on the track. They could smell the river and there was excitement and anticipation in their eyes. Every now and then Stubby turned to look back at them and let out little barks, as if to say, 'Hurry up!'

At the river's edge, the crags of red rock towered above them. Shallow-rooted trees clung to the sides of the riverbank and leant over as if looking for their reflection in the slow-moving water. It was dark water, dark and cool. The ripples from Charlie and Rebecca's naked bodies quickly dissolved the reflections and their whoops and splashes echoed up in the gorge as they swam side by side upstream. Mossy, Dags and Stubby swam in circles about them and unseen wallabies watched. Birds cried out. Charlie found an underwater rock and sat while Rebecca touched his fingertips. He clasped her hands and pulled her through the water towards him. She sat on his underwater lap. He looked at her beauty. She felt his warm mouth on hers. Wet fingers on wet young skin.

'This is like the first time I kissed you,' he said.

With his eyes fixed on hers, he led her downstream. Back to their towels and the bag. Back to the grassy bank. Beads of water lay on Rebecca's skin with tiny reflections of the gorge contained within them. As she lay down on a towel, the perfect silver beads were broken and smeared as Charlie moved his body over hers. He kissed the wetness away and drank in Rebecca by the river. She ran her hands over his brown skin and felt for his tight muscled buttocks. His weight on top of her on the grassy bank was so satisfying. So comforting. So right.

As he pushed into her, Rebecca looked past his hair which smelt of sweet river water and up to the bluest of summer skies. She felt her soul up there. Up there next to the silent eagle which hovered on warm clear thermals. They shuddered together and then lay looking into each other's eyes as the river quietly slipped on by.

CHAPTER 24

Each day in the cool of dawn, before the sun stretched itself across the mountain, Tom and Hank would ride slowly away from the hut, their breath passing as white mist from their nostrils and mouths in the cool mountain air. From the track Tom looked out across the valley and followed the ribbon of gums that lined the river. The farm had once looked so pretty from up here. Now, in the dry, it looked barren and heartless. Even the beauty of morning sunlight couldn't lift Tom's heart. The dark body of water, which was once the proud and plentiful Rebecca River, had slowed to a thin stretch of silver through a winding path of grey boulders.

His father never saw him ride into the yards on Hank, with Bessie trotting at his heels. His father was now always in bed until at least nine when he would slink down to the kitchen table in stinking work clothes. He wouldn't emerge outside until eleven, moving about slowly with a blank face and cold eyes. Tom recognised his father's depression. He understood it. He knew what it was like to sink into that cold abyss. Dark walls all about, with no way to climb back out.

It was his father's depression that had at first made Tom decide to stay at Waters Meeting. For the first few weeks Tom had made plans in his head to leave. He pictured himself packing up the work ute with his swag, bags and Bessie. Travelling north to find work or heading to the city to enrol in an art course. But as the days wore on, Tom found himself frozen with fear, a deep fear of the outside world. It overshadowed the fear he had for himself and the fear he had for his father. As the days passed he watched the depression settle over his father like a black cloud. It drew his father's mouth and shoulders downwards and shrouded out the light in his eyes. When his father began to drink each day and order in cartons of whiskey from Dirty's pub, Tom felt he could no longer go anywhere. His world had slipped beyond something real. His world was black. And so Tom stayed – down there in the abyss with his father.

Dutifully, Tom fed the chickens and collected the eggs. He'd sit half of them in a metal bucket at the back door and wrap the rest carefully and place them in his saddlebag. He fed the last remaining straggly bales of hay to the horses and the steers and carted water in buckets from a muddied pool in the river to the troughs. Tom had opened all the gates to the mountain run so the breeding cows could find feed in the gullies. The grass was hanging on well there, but they needed rain desperately or the mountain springs would run dry.

The merino sheep had all been sold and the silos were now empty of grain. As Tom watched some of the weaker ewes stagger and fall in the mud surrounding the waterholes, his heart sank further. It dragged on and on. Day after day of dryness.

On some days, when Tom couldn't face the starving stock any longer, he'd hide away in the darkness of the machinery shed and busy himself with jobs – like changing the oil in a vehicle or fixing the hydraulics again on the bale-feeder. But he hated the darkness and the smell of the shed. It reminded him of Mick.

Every Tuesday and Friday, Tom cranked over the ignition of the old farm ute and drove the ten kilometres to the mailbox over the dusty road and up the other side of the valley to pick up the grocery order and mail.

He'd leave the groceries at the back doorstep of the homestead, feed the cat, fill his saddlebag with fruit or potatoes and top up his quart-pot with milk.

Sometimes he'd knife a skinny killer and hang it dressed and quartered in the shed for his father. He'd take most of the chops because there was no oven to roast a leg or a shoulder at the hut. Tom cooked on an outdoor fire which smouldered and sulked all day while he was away working on the lowlands. Occasionally he passed his father in the yard without a word. In the shed once, as Tom was coming and Harry was going, their shoulders almost touched, but they could not look at one another.

On nights when the moon was full, hanging high

and huge in the sky, Hank and Tom descended through the ghostly white of the mountain gums. Tom would sneak into the house and tiptoe along the hall to the office. In the bedroom above his head, his father lay in a drunken stupor between grimy sheets.

The cool blue light of the computer shone on Tom's face as he checked the books once more. They could hang on for a year. Just a year. He paid the bills on-line and wrote another email to the bank manager. He couldn't bring himself to write to Rebecca. Her life was a whole world away from here. Her message to him flashed in the inbox. He clicked on it.

Hi Tom

Have been dog-sick worried about you. Are you still in your hut hideaway? What's the go with the farm? How's Mick's new job/life/Turdy pregnancy going? How's the old bast . . . I mean Dad? Write to me! I'm worried sick. Has Turdy taken the computer and that's why you're not writing? Please get in touch.

Love sis

PS We snaffled a high distinction for our assignment on the farm. You should email Sal and thank her. Thanks for your help on that. Can't wait to put it into reality and get Waters Meeting back on track with you some day.

PPS I've teamed up with the loveliest bloke . . . His name's Charlie Lewis. You'd love him.

Tom closed his eyes. Then he switched the computer off and the room was suddenly dark.

It was two a.m. by the time he reached the hut and the moon had sunk beneath the line of snowgums. Still clothed, he kicked off his boots and fell into the icy sheets beneath the canvas of his swag. He reached under the thin grimy pillow and pulled out a sagging worn teddy bear. He hugged it to him before falling into the blackest sleep.

CHAPTER 25

He asked Frankie over a steaming dish of roasted lamb on a bed of rosemary, drizzled with a rich garlic sauce. Peter put the plate down in front of her, poured a tinkling stream of red wine into a crystal glass and knelt down next to where she sat.

'I hadn't planned on doing this so soon and it's an impulse thing, so I won't be offended by your reaction, but . . . Dr Frances Saunders, will you marry me?'

While Frankie looked at Peter's frowning and almost pleading face, Henbury waddled up to where Peter knelt. The dog sniffed at the dinner table and then sniffed at Peter's crotch.

Frowning, Peter elbowed Henbury. 'Go away Henners. You always interrupt at crucial moments!'

Peter's eyes crinkled in a smile as he reached for Frankie's hand and looked up into her eyes. A breath caught in her throat. She was stunned. Feelings of joy and panic came all at once. She laughed and breathlessly said, 'Peter!'

She reached out to hug him and laughed again. 'This is such a surprise. I don't know what to say!'

'Yes! Say yes!'

'I want to say yes. I'd be delighted to say yes . . . Oh!' She placed a hand over her mouth. Her future life flashed before her. She saw them, growing old together. Getting a proper house with a garden, not just this tiny flat. The two of them, tying up tomatoes, podding peas and pottering. Lazy weekends reading thick weekend newspapers in the sun. Evenings filled with their easy chatter about science, her vet work and his students. A life filled with his warmth, his gentleness. But as the images flicked through her mind, Frankie felt the guilt kick in. Any time she felt joy for herself, her subconscious stole it away. She was the woman who had left her children – unforgivable. Would they see this as her final desertion? Peter watched as Frankie's joyful expression fell from her face. He held her hands tighter. 'If it's too soon, and you need time to think . . . you can have all the time in the world, Frankie.'

'Oh, Peter, it's not that. I love you. I truly do . . . It's just . . . oh, I don't know . . .'

'Well while you think about it, I might get up – my knees won't take much more of this,' he said, trying to bring a little light to the situation. But there was hurt in his voice. Frankie heard it and more guilt flowed into her being. He moved to get up, leaning heavily on one knee and straining stiffly, holding his back as he rose.

'Don't know why you'd want a clapped-out old fella like me anyway,' he joked.

'Peter,' she said gently and placed a hand on his arm, 'sit down here next to me.' She pulled out the straight-backed dining chair. Then she kissed him lovingly on the lips and held both his hands in hers.

'First, let me explain how I feel,' she said gently.

'Yes. Go ahead.' he said.

'Yes, I would love to marry you, but I can't help feeling there's a but.'

Peter nodded. 'Your children?'

'Yes,' she said, looking down.

'They'll be fine.'

'I know! They're all adults, I know, but I can't help feeling that this will be so final. That they'll feel like I've left them for good.'

'Frankie,' he said, 'you'll always be their mother, whether you're married to me or not.'

'Yes, but what sort of mother? I've been terrible. It's this . . . this *guilt*.'

'No. Don't say things like that. You can't carry guilt around with you like that, it's useless. It's not good for you.' She felt his love for her flow into her. Tears welled in her eyes.

'Look,' Peter continued, 'your children will be fine about it. I know it. They're off making their own lives. They'll probably react the same way as my children will. They'll be shocked at first but they'll grow used to the idea. Besides, if we don't take this chance, we could both grow old all alone, and I don't want that for either of us.'

Frankie nodded and swallowed back her emotion as Peter continued to reassure her.

'We'll both get time off. We'll arrange to go on a trip. We can drive up to Waters Meeting to break the news to Tom. We can even go as far as Rebecca's college ... Frankie, they'll be fine about it. I promise. They might even like the idea.'

His eyes pleaded with her. She reached out and pulled him to her. He smelt so good. Of soap and the rich smells of cooking. She felt so safe with his arms about her. She drew back and looked at him.

'Oh, Peter,' she sighed, 'I'm a sucker for your eyes and for your hugs.' He laughed and they hugged again.

A knock on the apartment door broke their embrace.

'Who could that be? Were we expecting anyone?' Peter frowned as Frankie walked to the door.

'Frankieee! Hi,' Trudy's high-pitched voice rolled into the flat and the quiet atmosphere was shattered.

She bustled in kissing Peter and Frankie on both their cheeks, Mick following quietly behind with a cylindrical container tucked under his arm. Henbury shuffled out from under the dining table, whined a greeting and waved his feathery tail about.

'What a lovely surprise!' Frankie beamed when she saw how healthy her son looked. She put her hands on his upper arms and squeezed them. 'Good to see you! And Trudy, you're looking so well.'

Trudy put her hands to her swollen belly. 'Not long to go now. I hope we're not interrupting dinner,' Trudy eyed the plate of food on the table, 'but we're so excited! We've just picked up the plans for the new house. Daddy's architect friend is building it on his Whispering Pines housing estate. It's perfect!'

'Wonderful,' said Frankie cautiously, looking for a reaction from Mick. But, as Mick excitedly swept away the newspapers and magazines from the coffee table and unrolled the house plans, Frankie realised he was just as happy and proud of their new life in the city suburbs. His fingers, no longer stained with oil and callused from fencing, ran over the clean lines of the house plans, explaining to Peter the benefits of the design and proudly showing his mother which room the baby would have.

'We were just soooo excited,' Trudy sung again, looking at the plans from over Mick's shoulder. 'We know we haven't seen you much since we moved back from the bush, but we were driving past and I . . . *we* . . . thought what a good idea it would be to drop in!'

Frankie placed a hand on Trudy's forearm and looked into her shining brown eyes. 'We're so glad you did. There's more dinner in the oven. Peter always cooks enough for an army. Would you like to stay?'

'Great,' Michael said.

Trudy clapped her hands.

'In that case, we'll be needing this.' She began to rummage in her bag. From it she pulled a brown paper bag and held it in the air, 'Champagne!' They all cheered.

'Of course *I'll* only have a *little* sip!' said Trudy patting her belly.

'Perfect!' said Frankie. She looked across to Peter and smiled excitedly.

'Peter and I were about to start a celebration of our own.' She dared herself to say it. To test the water.

'He's just asked me to marry him.'

It was like dropping a stone from a high cliff. Frankie waited for the smash as the stone hit the ground. The silence seemed forever. Then Trudy let out a squeal.

'Ooooh! That's terrific for you. Wonderful!' She clapped her hands again and bounced her pregnant self up and down on the spot.

Frankie twisted her fingers together, waiting for Mick's reaction. Relief swept through her as a smile came to his face and he stood to offer a hand to Peter.

'Congratulations.' He moved over to his mother and kissed her on the cheek. 'Good on you, Mum.'

'Hang on! I haven't really said yes yet!'

They all laughed.

'Judging from our reaction Mum, I really think you should,' Mick said, as he put his arm around her.

'Yes. Then, yes!' And Peter moved over to hug her.

As they sipped their champagne and toasted the new house, new baby and the new engagement, Frankie watched her son. Their move away from Waters Meeting seemed to have lifted a cloud from him. He seemed less defensive, less arrogant. Trudy was happier too. She seemed more . . . likeable now.

'How's the new real estate job going, Mick? Are you missing the farm?' Frankie asked.

She let his answer unfold, listening with interest, her head tilted on the side, glass held still in the air as she leaned an elbow on the table.

Later, as the laughter around the table mingled with the clatter of knives and forks on plates, Frankie realised that, yes, their choices had been right.

During the night Frankie woke with a dry mouth from too much wine and champagne. In the bathroom as she drank thirstily from the glass she remembered the water. The water in her dream, raging fast in the riverbed. Further downstream in a quiet eddy which seethed underneath, her son Tom lay face down, naked, with sticks and leaves clustering against his white skin. She shook the dream from her head and went back to bed to snuggle against the warmth of Peter's back.

PART FOUR

CHAPTER 26

From the window of Charlie's old Holden ute Rebecca squinted at the trees and red rooftop in the distance. The house and sheds were surrounded by a swathe of green wheat fields running next to neat rows of cotton bushes which stretched to the far horizon. No fences divided the crops, only straight lines of barren, cracking dirt or the hump of an irrigation channel bank.

'You said your house was on a hill!' said Rebecca. 'You call that a hill?'

'Of course it's a hill . . . can't you tell?' said Charlie as he drove the ute over the grid without slowing and muttered, 'Just because you're from goat country.'

Bec punched him lightly on his thigh. He slung an arm about her neck and kissed her firmly on her head. He was excited to be taking her home. He had delayed it long enough. Rebecca had wanted him to show her the family farm during the term, but he'd managed to put her off until the end of the university year.

When he looked towards his parents' house in the distance Charlie felt tension rise in his shoulders. He already knew what his mother would think of the girl sitting beside him in the ute. He looked across at Bec now. She was brown as a berry. The tan ran along her lean, strong arms and over her shoulders. She was wearing a soft blue singlet, which matched her eyes and faded blue jeans, a chunky leather belt and her old faithful cowboy boots. Her hair had been blown about by the hot wind through the window and had escaped from her ponytail. Sexy, thought Charlie. But Charlie knew his mother expected him to marry a girl who would take care of not just him, but his washing, his meals, his garden and his children. Not a girl like Bec who was independent and 'couldn't be fussed with frills', as she had put it when she'd got dressed this morning.

Frills, thought Charlie. Frills. So often he had been dragged to church on Sunday by his mother and thrust at young girls wearing florals and frills. 'Nice girls', Mrs Lewis would call them. They were always daughters of her churchgoing friends. They would stand there in long skirts and cardigans and stare up at Charlie's handsome face with wide eyes and hope in their hearts. Sometimes Charlie wondered why the girls didn't just stamp the words 'marry me and breed with me' on their foreheads. He once thought about saying this to his mother. Instead he just put up with her matchmaking efforts and humoured her enough to keep her from nagging.

'Mrs Conningham's Alice is a pretty girl, don't you think?' Mrs Lewis would say as she sipped milky tea from a chipped cup in the church hall.

'She's about your age, Charlie. Perhaps you'd like to ask her over for lunch one Sunday after the service.'

Charlie would inwardly groan but tell his mother he was busy on the farm with a breakdown on Sunday. 'The part's arriving this week and Sunday's the only day I can fit it,' he'd lie.

To his surprise, his mother always believed him. She didn't have a clue about the day-to-day management of the crops and machinery on the farm. She didn't even know the paddock names on the property. It was like that at their place. The house was her domain and she ruled it like a queen bee. But the farm, that was the male territory and she only dared venture onto it if asked, which was not very often. Mr Lewis liked it that way. To him, women belonged in the kitchen and the garden, but not in the paddocks. Children also had to be quiet and obedient. They had to respect their elders and be loyal to their parents. These things were never expressed in words, but in daily goings-on that was just the way it was in the Lewis household.

They perceived themselves as good churchgoing people following what the Bible said – women serving husbands, children respecting parents. It had always been that way. That was until Charlie had insisted he have time off to go to ag college. His father had yelled red-faced at him that he was 'disobeying his wishes'.

They'd had the same argument a few years ago when Charlie, a fresh-faced school leaver, packed his bags and headed north to work on a cattle station for a year. His mother had cried and his father had raved the day he drove away. The same scene had been played out when Charlie drove off to the Tablelands University.

They were about to get another rude shock, Charlie thought, when he turned up with Rebecca. He again glanced at her and smiled. She had her feet up on the dashboard and was singing along to a Green Day song, biting her nails at the same time.

Bec was nervous. She should've worn something tidier, she thought anxiously. She shouldn't have tried to play 'tough girl' to Charlie. She'd known it would make him nervous when it came to meeting his parents, so she had done it half to tease him and half out of a growing resentment of the Lewises' far-reaching control over their son. All year she'd pieced together enough of Charlie's words to know that his father hadn't yet forgiven him for leaving the farm to study. Despite his wild side at parties, Rebecca knew Charlie was repressed in so many ways. Bec had painted a picture of his parents in her mind. She thought she knew their types – traditional, conservative mother with dominating, controlling dad, made worse by the isolated upbringing on the farm. But Bec so desperately wanted to see where he lived. When Charlie discovered alcohol and a bunch of wild mates in the district, the foundations of their rock-solid family must have rumbled a little, but Charlie still remained tied not only to his family but also to the community church.

Bec knew the Lewises were strict churchgoers, the sort who helped with Sunday school barbecues or baked pikelets for the church fair. Their religiosity made Bec even more nervous about the visit. It was so far away from her world. She rarely went to church, especially after the forced services she'd endured each day at boarding school. She remembered going through her hymn book and underlining all the masculine words in red ink. Him. He. His. After leaving school she didn't like the idea of worshipping a male God in a man-made church. Her religion belonged to the land, her river, the mountains. A female God. A mother nature Goddess. A cyclical God made of earth and air and water. Not one made of man-made rules, one run with money.

In the ute she looked across to Charlie. She wondered if she should ask him if she would have to go to church with the Lewises. To start with, she hadn't brought anything to wear.

As they drove closer to the house Rebecca stared at the tidy square hedge which surrounded the freshly painted white weatherboard house.

'Shoebox' was all that came to Rebecca's mind. Pink flowers in rows lined the pathway. She thought they were primulas, but she wasn't certain. A sprinkler swirled in a circle of droplets on a mown lawn. From the shade of the porch a tiny lady walked out into the bright sun, wiping her hands on a floral pinafore which fell over a flat bosom.

Bec sighed, stretched a little and wiped her hands on her jeans as the ute rolled to a stop.

'She won't bite,' said Charlie as he opened the ute door. Rebecca stepped out onto the red dusty drive and smiled at the lady who had a halo of neat grey hair.

'My boy!' Mrs Lewis said with her hands outstretched. Charlie gave her a quick kiss on the cheek. 'Hello, Mum.'

He stepped back and proudly stretched his arm out in the hot dry air. 'This is Rebecca.'

'Hello, Mrs Lewis.' Rebecca moved forward and held out her hand, expecting her to reply with, 'Call me Joan.' But instead Mrs Lewis took her hand lightly and said, 'Rebecca. Let's go inside. It's frightfully hot out here.'

In the small dark kitchen Bec sat at the table and laid her hands flat on the cool laminex surface. Some of the pattern had faded away after years of wiping. Charlie pulled out a chrome chair and sat next to Bec. As he sat she felt him grab her firmly on her thigh with his big strong hand.

Rebecca bowed her head and stifled a smile as Mrs Lewis said, 'Cup of tea, dear?' In front of her, Mrs Lewis placed a plate of peppermint slice and a basket of steaming scones.

'Yes. Tea would be lovely, thank you, Mrs Lewis,' said Rebecca. Beneath the table Charlie's hand slid further up her thigh. Rebecca pulled a 'stop it!' face at Charlie.

'You may want to wash up first. Charlie will show you where the bathroom is.'

Along the narrow hallway gold-framed pictures of studio family shots lined the walls.

'Ahh! Little brother Glen, I presume!' said Bec, pointing to the smiling skinny boy who sat next to a younger looking Charlie.

'He's not so little now . . . between year eleven and year twelve he's shot up at least a foot. Must be Dad's genetics, because it sure couldn't be boarding school food.' Bec looked at the big tall man in the photos who, no matter which way the photographer arranged him, looked out of place. She remembered the man's face from the day she saw Charlie at the sheep show. It was a face that gave little away.

Charlie followed her gaze. 'He's still not officially talking to me,' he said. 'Still mad at me for clearing out to college.'

'I would've thought it was a good thing for the farm,' said Bec.

'Not for my old man. You'll see.' Charlie ushered her into the bathroom. 'Soap. Towel,' he said as he picked up each item from the white benchtop. Then he wrapped his arms around her.

Bec let herself fall back against the cool bathroom wall and tilted her head up towards him. She shut her eyes and concentrated on feeling the warmth and pleasure of his wet mouth and tongue. She pushed her breasts against his chest and felt the hardness of his erection under his jeans as he pressed against her.

Suddenly the image of Mrs Lewis in her pinny and the now cooling scones flashed into Rebecca's mind and she pushed Charlie away, laughing, 'Your mum will be waiting for us, Charlie! The scones!'

He looked into her eyes, bit her playfully on the neck and then promptly left, pulling his shirt out of his jeans and over the bulge in his crotch.

Closing the bathroom door, Bec turned and looked at her face in the mirror and exhaled a deep breath.

'Yikes,' she whispered, as she felt the blood still rushing deep within. She shut her eyes before splashing cold water on her face. Instantly she could smell sulphur and was reminded of green rotting eggs.

'Yikes,' she said again, this time flatly. 'Bloody bore water.'

By her third piece of peppermint slice, fourth scone and second cup of tea, Rebecca had managed to avoid answering Mrs Lewis's tricky questions about her family farm. She had only once mentioned her dad and the word 'divorce' had not entered the conversation. It was a word which didn't seem to fit in this tidy, functional family house.

Charlie sat on the kitchen bench grinning and gazing at Bec, to the point where she could no longer look at him and concentrated instead on staring at the cover of *Woman's Day* as she spoke. One glance at him, Bec thought, and she would burst out laughing and splutter scone all over the laminex.

Throughout the conversation Mrs Lewis never once sat at the table. Instead she moved around the kitchen as if on autopilot, preparing what looked like the evening meal.

'Are you sure I can't help with anything?' Rebecca asked again.

'No! No dear. It's fine, thank you.'

To Rebecca's relief Charlie jumped down from the bench and said, 'We might go find Dad now . . . and I'll show Bec around the farm.'

'She mightn't want to see the farm, Charlie. She may want to rest up a bit. It's been a long drive.'

'No! No. The farm is good. Seeing the farm is good,' said Rebecca, jumping up almost too quickly from the chair, its legs scraping on linoleum.

In the ute they drove through the yard, past huge skillion sheds which moaned in the wind, and towering silver silos. She looked around the homestead area.

'Where are your dogs?'

'Dad won't have them. We used to run a few sheep, but he sold out of them and pulled the fences up. The shearing shed's now lined with tin and used for grain storage.'

'No horses?'

Charlie shook his head.

By the time she'd asked, 'Where are the trees?' and 'Do you have a river anywhere to swim?', the excitement on Charlie's face had dropped away and silence filled the cab of the ute. She knew she'd hurt his feelings, so she made an effort to lift his dwindling spirits.

'The sky's so lovely and huge out here,' she said,

ducking her head and looking up out of the windscreen at the vastness of blue. He looked across at her and smiled a disappointed smile.

Ahead of them a large Deutz tractor with a wide boom spray unit lumbered up and down the rows and rows of cotton.

'I take it that'll be your dad.'

'You take it right,' was all Charlie said.

When the tractor at last lumbered to a stop, Mr Lewis opened the cab and stepped slowly down to the ground. He hitched his pants up beneath his rotund belly and stood with his arms folded across his wide chest. He looked at Charlie and nodded.

'Son.'

'Hi, Dad,' said Charlie.

Then Mr Lewis's eyes roamed over Rebecca. His face gave away nothing. He stood. He waited.

'Um. Dad,' Charlie's voice filled up the silence. 'This is my . . . friend . . . Rebecca.'

Rebecca smiled, took a step forward and held out her hand.

'Hi,' she said brightly.

Mr Lewis shook her hand, but Rebecca was sure she could see a glimmer of distaste roam over his red, round face.

At dinner Mr Lewis barely said a thing to Rebecca, and spent more time swearing at the politicians who appeared on the '7.30 Report'. He said even less to Charlie. Rebecca sat and chased peas around her plate, feeling uncomfortable.

'Another glass of water?' Mrs Lewis asked with a smile.

'Thank you. Yes.'

Rebecca was relieved when the meal was over and she could leave the room to carry the plates into the kitchen.

As Rebecca and Charlie washed up side by side at the sink, he whispered, 'You okay?'

Bec smiled kindly and kissed the air between them, as if to say, 'I love you anyway, even though your parents are completely off the dial.'

When Mrs Lewis ushered Rebecca into the spare room and told her she could pick either one of the two single beds, Bec's cordial smile faded altogether. She and Charlie had been virtually living together for the whole year at college. Surely Mrs Lewis knew that. So why separate rooms?

Grumpily Bec dragged from her bag her only pair of pyjamas, which she *never* wore, and pulled them on like a sulky child. In the bed the sheets scratched Bec's skin. Too much washing powder, she thought, then mentally slapped herself around the face for being so critical. Switching off the light and lying in the strangeness of the dark room, she tried to close her eyes and sleep, but she craved Charlie and his naked warmth. She knew his bedroom was down the hall, through the kitchen and in a room on the other side of the house. But could she navigate her way in the dark without Mr and Mrs Lewis hearing her? Pulling back the sheets, she swung her legs out of bed and stood up. She was damn well going to try . . .

CHAPTER 27

'Congratulations, Mrs Maybury!' Tom raised his glass unsteadily and sloshed champagne on his shirt. He took a slurp from the glass and then kissed his mother's cheek. His kiss left a wet patch on the light dusting of make-up which covered her face. He then moved over to the trestle table under the shade of a large gum and tipped the remaining champagne from the fat green bottles into his glass.

From the small cluster of wedding guests in the city park, Bec watched him. She saw how his shoulders sloped downwards and his clothes hung from his skinny frame. His hair had grown long and stuck up in a shock of waves. Dark brown stubble grew across his angular jawline. His skin was an odd pale tan colour and yellow circles ringed his eyes. On his brow a frown line slashed his young skin vertically between his eyebrows.

Bec watched as Sally bounded up to him by the bar

and kissed him warmly on the cheek. Tom looked right through her as if she wasn't there at all.

His eyes left Bec cold. Instinctively, she moved closer to Charlie and slipped her hand into his as he stood and laughed with Peter who was fidgeting nervously with a length of golden ribbon.

At the end of the ribbon sat Henbury, who had busily been licking the feathery place where his balls once were. The dog had sat like that all the way through Peter and Frankie's short wedding ceremony, despite the occasional subtle kick from the toe of Peter's shoe.

'You did a top job as pageboy, didn't you, Henners,' said Charlie as he stooped and patted the dog, letting go of Rebecca's hand for a moment.

As Peter and Charlie continued to chat, Bec scanned the crowd and saw, in the midst of the guests, a skinny Trudy holding onto a fat baby boy.

Her high-pitched monologue floated above the conversations of the crowd and the people she talked to smiled and nodded at her with glazed expressions on their faces.

'Of course Daddy's given Mike a *lot* of time off work which is *great* because Danny's been *such* a handful, haven't you, my big boofie boy? But the new house is just perfect, we couldn't have coped with anything less modern and spacious, especially when we have number two, although, not yet! Not yet! I don't think I could handle two just yet. Of course Mum does come over to help a lot. She's been *great*. I *can't* imagine how I'd have coped if we'd still been living out in the bush.'

As she eavesdropped, Rebecca felt someone tug on her hair. She turned to see a suit-clad Mick with tidy short-cropped hair.

'How's the final-year college girl? Feeling important now you've almost got a piece of paper?'

'It's been great . . . just a shame I haven't been able to put it into practice anywhere.'

'Ah, from what I hear, young Charlie's not short of an acre or two. You could take that on. No point worrying about Waters Meeting – Dad and the drought have buggered that. Won't be long till it gets cashed in.'

'Don't talk like that!'

'Ah come on, Bec. Getting away from that place has done me a power of good . . . I've actually got my own money in the bank. I would've thought it'd done you good too, made you realise those dreams of yours and Tom's are just that. Dad's not letting go till he drops off the perch. The old prick.'

'Drunken old prick,' said Tom as he ambled up behind them, holding his glass at an angle so champagne spilled onto the grass.

'How are things going there?' Bec asked gently.

'What would you care?' Tom said, glaring at her.

'Three months, Tom. Three months and I'll be done. Finished with the course, graduated and out. Then I'll be home and we can do what we planned to do!'

'Like hell. Have you been there lately?' He swung his arms about his body wildly. 'No! None of you buggers have been there lately. Waters Bloody Meeting, my

280

arse! The waters haven't met in over a year – both rivers have run dry! There's no stock left, 'scept for Hank and your lonely old horse, and Dad's shot all the dogs. Didn't even bury the bastards. Just left them on the end of the chain to rot. Don't give me all this college "I'll save the farm crap"!'

The bitterness in Tom's voice cut short the wedding chitchat. Guests fell silent and turned to stare at the three of them. Charlie turned to stand behind Bec and put a hand on her arm. Frankie looked up nervously from where she was serving the wedding cake. Amidst the silence, Trudy set her mouth in a grim line. She handed the baby to her mother and walked over to Tom. On his arm she gently placed a slim manicured hand but her fingertips dug into his muscle.

Between clenched teeth she quietly said, 'Settle down, Tom. You're drunk. Don't spoil your mother's wedding, now come with me and we'll get some cake.'

'Stuff the cake you, controlling witch!' He shook off her grip and staggered backwards.

Mick flew towards him, scruffing his shirtfront. 'Don't you talk to her like that.'

Tom took a swing and missed, stumbling onto the grass. From where he crouched he looked up at them. 'None of you will face it! Piss off, the lot of you.'

Frankie stepped forward, her cheeks flushed red. 'Tom! Stop it!'

'What would you care? When have you *ever* cared? *Mum*?' he added sarcastically.

Frankie froze. She stared in horror at her son's

twisted, angry face. He looked into her eyes, then his face contorted with pain. Tears ran fast and a strangled sob came from deep in his throat.

'Deserting bitch!' Tom grabbed a champagne from Rebecca's hands and sloshed it into his mother's face. He turned and ran towards his ute parked in the street. Everyone watched, silent and still, as he drove away into the traffic and towards the freeway which ran out of the city.

'Charlie, we've got to go after him!' cried Bec.

'I think I've had too many to drive, Bec,' he said quietly as he waved his glass about.

'If you won't go, I will.' She turned to leave but Mick stood in front of her.

'Bec. He'll be right. He's driven pissed that many times before. He'll be fine. You'll get yourself in trouble if you drive. We've all had too much.'

Rebecca turned to her mother. 'Mum?'

Frankie stood as Peter placed a hand on her shoulder.

'Mum. For Chrissakes do something! For once in your frigging life, do something for him!' The anguish in her voice stretched out around the silent wedding guests. 'Why don't you face it, Mum. It's *you* he needs help from. I can't mother him any more. It's you!'

Someone had handed Frankie a paper serviette and she stood in a daze dabbing at the dripping champagne which pooled in dark patches on her silk jacket. Frankie's lip began to quiver. She turned and buried her face in Peter's chest. He put his arms around her protectively.

282

'It's not your mother you should be blaming, Rebecca,' Peter said quietly. Then he ushered her away.

As Rebecca stood in the city park with a cold fear running through her, Trudy walked towards her. 'Wedding cake?' she asked, holding the plate in front of her.

CHAPTER 28

Harry Saunders' gut ached with a stabbing pain, but he still felt the need to eat something. In the kitchen he looked into the tins with jagged edges which cluttered the tabletop. Green fluffy tufts of mould sprouted around red smears of baked bean sauce. Angrily he pushed the tins from the table with one sweep of his arm. The clatter of cans on the slate floor no longer sent the ginger cat flying for the door. The cat had long ago retreated to the safety of the wood heap and lived there on a lean diet of skinks, mice and birds.

'Where's that bloody Tom?' Harry threw open the window and screamed through it. 'Where the hell are you, boy?' His voice echoed around the hills.

Harry staggered to the kitchen bench and poured another shot of whiskey into a coffee cup.

'Lazy bugger,' he mumbled.

On the porch by the laundry, Harry looked for the bucket of eggs or some sheep meat wrapped in cloth or a box of groceries. There was still nothing there. Nothing. Harry looked up towards the mountain and squinted before shutting the door and going back inside the kitchen.

At the hut, Tom fed Bessie a hunk of mutton neck which she took gently from his hands.

'Good girl, Bess,' he said, and watched her trot over to chew on it under the old tank stand. From a hessian bag he tipped some oats into the old tyre with a plough share base, which served as Hank's feed bin. Hank whickered and walked up to the bin.

Inside the hut Tom neatly stacked splintery hunks of split wood by the fire. He shook out his swag sheet and then rolled it up tightly in the canvas and left it on the sagging camp bed. Then he took up the old broken-handled broom and swept the floor clean. A large hand-felled tree trunk stood in the middle of the room as a main support post. Carved in its smooth wood in old-fashioned lettering were the initials of his great-great-grandfather and the year he had carved his name there – ALS 1901. Archibald Lewis Saunders. Beneath that in a deeper cut were carved his grandfather's initials – DJS 1945. Douglas John Saunders. Tom ran his fingertips across the letters and said their names aloud. Nowhere on the post could he find his father's initials.

From his leather pouch he took out his knife and carved his own initials below those of his grandfather.

TJS. Thomas John Saunders. Then he carved the year. He sat back and looked at the initials, trying to picture the dead men moving about the hut.

When Tom at last stepped outside onto the verandah, a thick mist was rolling in. A chilly wind blew the damp cloud wailing through the cracks in the hut. The loose tin on the roof which covered the old shingles banged angrily. Perhaps, he thought, the front might bring rain to the low country. Something to break the drought.

He saddled Hank and called Bess to the heels of his horse. In the mist they descended from the mountain. During the long ride down, he could see nothing of the valley below, the mist was so thick.

Harry came to the back door again at dusk. This time he found Bessie. She sat beating her tail against the concrete step and whining. Harry looked out across the yellow and brown dusty ground. At the trough where the tap leaked, Hank was tearing at the short tufts of green grass with his teeth. Bessie trotted down the path and leapt over the gate, disappearing into the garage. Without bothering to put on his boots Harry shuffled along the cracking concrete path in his socks to the gate. He trod over the dusty ground. Burrs stuck to his socks.

At the garage entrance Bessie sat and barked once at him. Harry's car was parked in there. On the dusty bonnet sat a box of groceries. A stick of celery sprouted from between Black and Gold pasta, white sugar and Dalgety's tea bags. An old saucepan full of eggs and a hessian bag with a leg of lamb were placed beside the box. Harry was about to gather up the groceries when, in the dimness of the garage, he saw a side of lamb hanging from the beams, wrapped in a dark cloth.

'What's wrong with using the killing shed, boy?' snorted Harry. 'Lazy bugger,' he slurred.

He moved into the garage and was about to cut the sheep down when he realised the cloth was an oilskin coat. Sticking out from the coat were two legs. Tom's boots, swinging in midair. From the cuffs of the coat white hands hung limply. Dirt under fingernails, dead white. Harry stepped backwards, almost falling against the car. He turned his head up to the beams, his mouth hanging open in a silent scream.

Tom's head was bowed down. Tom's face, blue with bulging eyes, staring. His expression was still. So still. His lips, thin blue lines. When Harry backed away from the body he saw lettering scrawled in red raddle on the roof of the car.

'Will this make you see, Dad?' The lettering screamed.

As Harry ran back towards the house, guttural sounds came hurtling from his throat and echoed in the hills. He slammed the door and shut out the world.

In the stillness of the evening Bessie trotted inside the garage and looked up at Tom. She sniffed at the air nervously then backed away a little and sat beneath

Tom's feet. She sighed and began to lick at a grass seed which was caught in her flank.

By the trough Hank shook away a fly with the twitch of his skin and ambled to the garage to nibble and pull at the celery top which stuck out from the box. He rested his back hoof and dozed there. Near Tom.

CHAPTER 29

Rebecca was sitting her agricultural economics exam. She had a pen behind her ear and was frowning as she tapped at her calculator, trying to work out wool futures earnings. The supervisor walked between the rows of desks and bent to whisper in her ear. He asked her to put down her calculator and pen and step outside. She looked up at him in disbelief. At first she thought they were accusing her of cheating, but the sympathetic look in his eyes told her something was horribly wrong. A few students glanced up at her as she slipped quietly through the door. Others kept writing.

Outside Ross put an arm in the small of her back and ushered her towards the college principal. Grey curls framed his red face. He was frowning. Charlie stood a little way off on the brick pathway. He edged closer to the principal. Rebecca looked from the principal to Charlie.

'Rebecca, I've got some bad news for you,' the

principal said gently. He reached out a pink hand and gripped her shoulder softly.

'It's your brother, Tom.'

Before the principal could say the words, Bec knew Tom was dead. She knew. All the breath, all the life, was hit out of her. As her body crumpled, she cried out. It wasn't a scream, just a moan, an agonised moan.

Charlie stepped in front of the principal and gathered Rebecca up into a hug. The sound of her grief nearly crushed him. He knew it would. When the principal had rung to ask for his help and told him the news, Charlie's first reaction had been anguish for Bec. How could he protect her from something like this?

In Charlie's arms Bec's mind raced. Then a panic rushed in. Her knees felt as though they would give away under her and she thought she was going to be sick.

'Why? How? Oh my god . . .'

Charlie whispered the details to her, the words stinging. 'Killed himself.' 'Suicide'. 'Yesterday.' Words pieced together to shape a horrific new reality in Bec's mind. As she absorbed the news, she felt hate and anger towards her father rush in. She gritted her teeth and wailed through them, her eyes clenched tight.

Charlie put his hand on her head and held her to his chest as he half-carried her away. Ross walked with them, his gentle hand on Bec's back. The principal walked slowly behind. His face grim. A piece of paper clenched tightly between his fingers.

———

In Rebecca's bedroom, Charlie made her lie down and pulled the doona up over her shoulders. He drew the curtains and shut out the sun. He lay beside her for a time and stroked her hair. He said he would take care of everything.

Rebecca shook. When the phone rang Charlie kissed her gently on the head and left the room, closing the door behind him.

In the dimness of their bedroom she rolled over and screamed into a pillow until she felt the nausea rise in her. She tried to lie still and quiet and her eyes blurred as she stared at the glowing green digits of the alarm clock. Outside the room she heard Charlie on the phone speaking quickly and quietly. As soon as she heard him say goodbye and hung up, the phone rang again.

When he finally came back to her into the room, she was asleep; asleep in her Tom-less world.

CHAPTER 30

As the mourners slowly moved away from the grave-
side, Harry shuffled along in their silent wake. He
stood in the shadow of the church, on the fringe of the
small crowd. His watery eyes scanned the mourners.
He was looking for Rebecca. First he saw Frankie. Her
auburn hair was blowing wildly in the wind. She
seemed to lean into its chilling force. Harry watched as
Peter put his arm around her and led her away from the
grave towards the parked cars.

In the crowd he saw Mick walking up the hill carrying his son, Danny. Mick lifted the child closer to his
face and pressed his mouth against Danny's soft ruddy
cheek as he walked. Trudy clung to the crook of Mick's
arm with her tiny perfect hands, and dabbed at her eyes
with a tissue.

Beyond the small crowd Harry finally saw Rebecca,
standing, looking out across the dry paddock beyond
the church. He held his breath. A tall young man with

dark hair stood next to her and kept his hand in the small of her back. When she turned and faced the crowd Harry saw her distraught face stained with tears. Twisted in pain.

She was so beautiful, he thought. So much like Tom. In her hand she held tightly onto a kangaroo leather lead. The lead was clipped onto Bess's collar. The dog stood quietly beside her and sometimes leaned on Rebecca's leg and sniffed at the crowd, searching for Tom.

As Harry stood and looked at Rebecca he suddenly felt the crush of what he had done. He had taken his anger out on his family. He had destroyed the weakest of them. Poor Tom. Poor, quiet, caring Tom. Harry felt his mouth twist as the full force of reality hit him. Through tears he stared at his daughter, her strength almost crushed, leaning into the tall, young man.

Harry swallowed. He would make it right, he thought. He decided there, standing in scuffed boots in the dandelions beside crooked old gravestones, that he would pull himself and his property together. He wouldn't punish his children any more. He turned and began to walk away towards town.

In the chilly afternoon light, the mourners turned their backs on the sandstone church and dispersed in the wind. They climbed silently into their cars and utes, stuffing hankies and tissues back into pockets; some feeling glad they were alive and could feel the sting of the wind, some feeling shaken that death was so close, taking a young life. The people in the cars and utes formed a slow-moving line along the winding gravel road towards the pub.

As Charlie opened the door of the pub and ushered Rebecca through, Bessie pulled on the lead.

'Alright. Alright,' Bec said to the dog and unclipped the leash. Bessie sneezed, then trotted to the barstool where Tom had always sat. The dog sunk down alongside the wooden foot rail beneath the bar and lay with her head on her paws. She occasionally raised her muzzle to accept offerings of crusts from sandwiches and pastry from fat sausage rolls.

Rebecca and Frankie stood in silence amidst the crowd holding clattery cups of tea in their hands. Charlie and Peter hovered near and talked to the guests and family members. In the corner of the pub Trudy shushed Danny and held him on her hip as he screamed.

By the time Dirty's wife had cleared away empty sandwich plates and teacups the hushed voices of the funeral-goers had begun returning to normal. Beer flowed through the lines and into pint glasses. People began to chat and warm themselves with alcohol. The chill of death, especially suicide, was too much to endure for long. They tried to shrug it off by lifting glasses of beer to the air and toasting the life of Tom.

Outside the pub, on the verandah, Harry sat on a rough-carved log listening to the rising voices inside.

When Dirty's wife tried to whisk his empty teacup away, he held onto it with both hands. She folded her arms across her bosom and looked down at him with pursed lips. 'Not drinking today, Harry?'

She snorted air quickly from her nostrils. 'I'll get you another cup of tea.'

His eyes followed her gratefully.

Inside at the bar, the rum and coke warmed Rebecca. She sat on Tom's stool and felt the sadness of him run through her. She could feel him in her soul and realised all of a sudden that he was with her, and would always be. Dirty put another full glass down in front of her and she smiled at him softly and looked to the end of the bar where Charlie and Mick leaned, with elbows bent on the bar top, talking. From behind her she felt a hand on her shoulder. It was Peter.

'We're going upstairs to our room. Your mother needs to lie down.'

'Thanks,' she said to him. Bec slipped off the stool to hug her mother. When she felt Frankie's arms about her, emotion welled up in her throat again and tears rolled from her eyes.

'Was it our fault?' Bec said into Frankie's soft, sweet smelling hair.

'I don't know,' Frankie said and began to cry again. Peter led her away as she sobbed, the drinkers stepping out of their way and sadly watching the mother of the dead boy being ushered from the room.

Bec pushed through the crowd and walked out onto the verandah. In the cool air she was shocked to find it was dusk and the sun was now only just managing to light up the tops of the mountains above the river. The wind had died down and the world was now still. Cockatoos swung on the powerlines and called out in wild screeches. She wrapped her arm around the smooth worn verandah post and leaned her head against it.

'Hello, Bec.' She heard the voice and knew it was him. Spinning around she saw her father, sitting still in the dark shadow of the verandah. He was hunched over, his hair now a shock of grey. His skin seemed to hang from him. Hollows in his cheeks, bags under his eyes. Weepy eyes, like an old dog. Clothes too big for his body. Rebecca could barely recognise the man she knew as her father. She hadn't seen him in the crowd at the funeral. He looked like an old-timer who spent the final days of his life sitting on pub benches. He was trying hard to look into her eyes.

He stood up, walked towards her and put his arms around her. They stood, like that, in silence for a time. Rebecca was rigid with hate. She stood coldly in his arms. Then Harry began to shake. His body shivering. He stepped back and wiped his red eyes with his thumb and forefinger.

'I blame myself,' he said, and then walked away into the blue dusk to the far end of the parked cars.

'So you should,' Rebecca said coldly as she watched his headlights beam across gums. Her eyes followed the lights until they disappeared around the bend in the road.

When Charlie found Rebecca she was sitting in the dark down by the river bend near the pub. She was cradling her knees in her arms, rocking back and forwards and crying, almost wailing.

He used the sleeve of his shirt to wipe away the tears and spittle from her face and held her in his arms. 'Shhhh. Shhhh. Shhhh,' he said.

CHAPTER 31

In the motel room Charlie handed Rebecca a bowl of Weetbix and she took it without looking up at him. From the cloud over the weather map on the TV, almost the whole east coast was awash with rain. She unfolded her legs on the bed, stood up and carried the cereal bowl over to the window. She stood there watching the rain fall in heavy sheets. Water clunked noisily in a down pipe outside and cars sprayed up roaring gushes of water as they drove past the motel.

Charlie came over to her.

'Eat up. It's going to be a big day, and a big night.'

'Tom's sent us some rain. The river will be flooding at home. I hope Inky and Hank aren't trapped in the river flat paddocks.'

Charlie frowned at her then took the bowl from her hand and placed it on the breakfast tray. He put his arms about her and pulled her close. He talked in whispers above her head.

'Come on, Bec. It's our graduation day. Don't be sad. Tom will be with you. Let's just have fun today. See all our mates, have a drink. I'm not saying let go of your grief. I'm just saying put it aside. Just for today. Then you might feel like getting on with it.'

She pulled away from him. 'Getting on with what?' she asked angrily, then she dashed into the bathroom and shut the door hard. She stood under the shower and let hot jets of water sting her reddened skin. She had counted the days, weeks and then months as they moved away from Tom's last day on this earth. She had tried to piece together his thoughts, his moods. She pictured him there in the hut alone, and she cried every time she thought of Hank and Ink Jet at Waters Meeting with no Tom there to love them.

In the shower Rebecca thought back over the last two months. They were a blur. She could barely remember what had filled up her days. All she could remember was the grief . . . the unbearable pain of grief. She recalled sitting the last of her exams with her peers, despite Ross's offer to postpone them. She sat at the desk, writing her answers, with a lump in her throat, on the verge of tears. She couldn't remember what subjects she sat for, nor the answers she had scrawled in the booklets before the supervisor had said, 'Time's up.'

After her last exam, she packed her books in boxes and sold her furniture to a second-year student. She hugged Gabs, Emma, Dick and Paddy goodbye, tied all her dogs onto the back of the ute, this time adding a chain for Bessie. Then she kissed Charlie.

'I've just got to go for a while, just until gradua-tion.' She couldn't bear to see the hurt in Charlie's eyes, so she drove away quickly without looking back.

She had driven north again. Back to the quarters on Blue Plains, back to see Bob and Marg. To find comfort in some sort of home. But things up there had changed. She had changed. The grief had aged her. She had grown wiser, deeper and more solemn as she carried Tom's death with her. Her dogs felt it too and they thrust wet noses into her palms as an offer of comfort. After a month, she knew she had to leave Blue Plains. Tom's death was just as real there. It was too soon to try to go back to the life she'd known before. So Rebecca had just kept on driving.

In the motel room Rebecca turned off the shower. She knew she should be grateful for Charlie's love and kindness. She wrapped the tiny scratchy towel around her body and stepped out into the bedroom. She gave Charlie the slightest smile and he was over to her, wrapping her up in his big arms, kissing the water away and loving her. Rebecca thirsted to feel the life of him, so she kissed him back hard. So glad to be with him again.

In their hired mortarboards and black flapping gowns the college graduates tucked their certificates under their clothes and ran from the building. They laughed as they ran in the heavy rain. Rebecca and Charlie ran with them. Like black crows they flew across the silvery wet road, down the street until they burst into the quiet warmth of the pub.

'Hey Dave,' shouted Gabs, 'can we put our gear in your back room?'

'Sure! No worries!' said the barman as he looked up from the fridge.

The students pulled their musty smelling rain-sodden gowns from their shoulders and stacked them high in Gabs' arms. Some balanced stacks of mortarboards on their heads and walked up the creaking stairs as if learning deportment. Helen gathered everyone's certificates, diplomas and degrees and laid them safely in a pile in the back rooms of the old hotel.

At the bar alongside proud parents, the graduates began to drink. Rebecca raised her glass and chinked her rum and coke against the glasses of Gab's parents. She smiled when she drank, but beneath the smile she felt a bitterness. A bitterness towards her mother who had told her she was too busy to come.

By six o'clock Rebecca was on the dance floor with sweat running from her scalp and down her cheeks. She and Gabs swung each other around in the midst of the other students. When Charlie came to her she grabbed onto him and jumped up and down on the spot. Then she yelled in his face, 'Thank God your parents didn't come, we'd be having dinner in some cheap restaurant by now and missing out on all the fun.'

He walked away from her and went back to sit at the bar.

———

301

The rain had eased to a fine mist which shone underneath the streetlights. Rebecca sat on the edge of the kerb and let the rain soak through her clothes. She shivered a little. To warm herself she tipped back her head and poured Stones Green Ginger Wine from the bottle into her mouth.

Behind her Charlie came out from the pub and stood above her.

'For godsakes, Rebecca, just stop it!' He tried to pull the plump green bottle from her hand, but she clung to it.

'You've had enough. Come on, get up. We're going back to the motel.' She hugged the bottle to her and shook her head.

'Rebecca. You don't need to drink that much.'

'Huh! Look who's talking, Mr Basil Lewis. Whatever happened to your party animal nature? Was it just an act? To cover up the fact that you're just a mummy's boy deep down.'

'Bec. You're drunk. You're baiting me. I'm not going to get into an argument with you just because you're hurting over Tom.'

Charlie felt her flinch when he said Tom's name. He softened his tones. 'Destroying yourself with drink isn't going to bring him back, Bec. And it's not going to solve things at home. Just let it go. Let it go.'

'What would you know?' she screamed at him. 'You've been brought up in perfect family-land . . .'

He tore the bottle from her hand and pulled her to him as she began to cry. 'I don't know anything, Bec.

All I know is that you're a very lost woman at the moment. And I love you.'

Rebecca let herself be drawn into him and buried her face against his woollen jumper. He was warm and dry and smelt of cigarette smoke from the pub.

After a while as they sat in the rain he said, 'Come home with me, Bec.'

She pulled away and looked at his face.

'Come home. We can fix the cottage up and move in there . . . away from Mum and Dad. There's plenty of places you'll find work. We can get a float and bring Ink Jet and Hank home . . . and I'll build you some kennels for your dogs. We'll get some sheep again.'

In the misty rain she heard herself saying, 'Yes.'

'Okay. Yes Charlie, yes.'

She hugged him tightly and spoke into the warmth of his neck, 'I love you so much.' Then she stood up unsteadily and dragged Charlie back inside the pub.

Still drunk and wet through with rum and rain, Rebecca found herself with Gabs. They were watching the sun come up behind the clouds which hung low over the rooftops in the town. The rain had stopped and everything shone in a grey hue. Charlie had given up trying to coax her from the pub. He had walked back to their motel in the quiet wet darkness just before dawn.

She and Gabs sat in the centre of a roundabout amidst circles of neat flowers and bushes. Both girls had daisies tucked behind their ears and were raising their pub glasses to the taxis and delivery trucks which circled and drove on by.

'I laaaaarve him!' Rebecca said to the dull sun. 'I laaa-ha-ha-harve him!'

'I know you love him, you dork,' said Gabs as she picked at her nose. 'But you're gonna hate it out there with his mum. And besides, there's no mountains . . . and no sheep.'

Before Bec could argue, both girls spotted a police car approaching.

'Yikes!' said Gabs. They ducked and stifled their giggles in the forest of green flower stems in the garden bed as the police car pulled to a halt.

'We're standing out like dog's balls,' gasped Gabs.

'Shhh!' was all Bec could manage as they both dissolved into peels of laughter.

The policemen tried not to smile when both girls offered them a flower each.

'Come on, girls. We'll take you home,' said the young one.

'Home,' said Rebecca, getting unsteadily to her feet. 'Now there's a tricky thing.'

CHAPTER 32

In the tiny cottage Rebecca looked up at the ceiling fan as it made steady high-pitched grating noises. The fan stirred the air around her shoulders and she felt goose-bumps rise on her flesh. She was so sick of staring at it, she scrunched up a piece of paper and threw it into the blades. The ball of paper flew to the wall and fell onto the floor.

'Four runs,' Bec said to the fan.

She had waited and waited for Charlie's crackly voice to come through on the UHF. She'd tried gardening until the sun stung too hot on the back of her neck. Then she'd come inside and slumped on the couch and waited.

She got up and began to fill the water cooler. His call came through at last. Charlie's robotic sounding voice and radio static filled the kitchen.

'Ready for another pick-up, Bec?' She pressed the button on the handpiece.

'Roger, I'm on my way.'

'Who's this Roger bloke?' came Charlie's teasing reply.

She smiled at the radio. 'I'm leaving now.'

On the verandah she pulled on her boots, put on her hat and carried the cooler to the truck. As she drove past the homestead entrance she saw Mrs Lewis waving to her to stop.

'Bugger,' said Bec as she looked at Mrs Lewis in her long flowery summer dress and yellow apron. Bec ground the gears a little and backed the truck up to the gateway. She jumped down from the cab and walked towards Mrs Lewis who was wiping her clean, dry hands on her apron.

'I heard you just then on the radio, that you're off to help Charlie. I've baked him some scones – they'll be two minutes. Come inside.'

Scones, thought Rebecca, in this heat? She followed Mrs Lewis inside after kicking off her boots.

'I'm making a casserole for tonight. Would you like me to prepare some extra for you and Charlie?'

'No, we'll be fine, thanks Mrs Lewis.'

'Oh no. I insist. He's got you running about so much this harvest, you must be pressed for time to prepare decent meals.'

'It's been busy, but that's okay. I like busy.'

'Any word yet about the office administration job at the grain traders?'

'No, not yet.'

'I'm sure you'll be the successful applicant. You present yourself so . . . confidently. I'm off to town to do some shopping next week. Would you like to come? You'll need some office clothes.'

'Yes. Yes. Good idea.' Rebecca tugged at her torn denim shorts and smoothed down her oil-stained singlet as Mrs Lewis bent to lift the tray of scones from the oven. She carried them over to the table and they tumbled from the tray onto the cooling rack.

'Mmm. They look good,' said Rebecca. Just then Charlie's voice blared on the radio.

'Rebecca are you on channel?'

'Yep.'

'Have you left yet?'

'Nope.'

'Good. Could you grab some oil before you come out. It's in that yellow drum in the big skillion . . . near the Honda.'

'No worries. See you soon.'

'Look forward to it, babe.' Charlie's flirtatious voice crackled across the kitchen and Mrs Lewis stiffened and her face hardened.

'They're very public things, radios. A lot of others in the area are on the same channel.'

Rebecca looked down at the holes in her socks. She felt guilty for being so negative about Charlie's mother. Over the past few months Mrs Lewis had been so kind. She'd given Rebecca space to grieve and looked after her as much as Rebecca would allow. But there was always a distance . . . and that silent sense of disapproval. Mr Lewis had it too. Rebecca noted how he looked her up and down from head to toe each morning. At first she'd turned up, in her work clothes, every morning at seven in the machinery shed. Reporting to work like an eager young soldier keen to go into battle. But after a few weeks, as Mr Lewis continued to refuse to give her a job, Rebecca just gave in and took to sitting with Charlie for hours on the machinery, or handing him shifters or screwdrivers in the shed.

'For Chrissakes, Charlie,' she had screamed one morning, 'he might as well tell me to my face that he thinks I belong in the kitchen or in the garden! He's worse than my dad!'

Charlie tried so hard. He comforted Rebecca's tears over Tom which came to her in the dark of night. He stood patient and calm between his mother's fussing and tugging and Rebecca's defiance. But as always he bent to his father's will. If Mr Lewis ordered Charlie to do a job, one that Rebecca could easily do, Charlie never challenged him.

Charlie continued to promise to set aside a weekend to pick up Hank and Ink Jet from Waters Meeting, but the weekend never came. Rebecca loved Charlie, she knew it, but the resentment began to rise and sometimes she'd find herself making love to him not just with passion but with a kind of anger. Anger for all that had happened in her life and for what wasn't happening in her life. She felt out of control. Lost. It was as though she was watching another girl. This other girl living in a cottage, throwing cushions at the wall, rocking back and forth, trying to picture her life before, with Tom and her dogs on Waters Meeting. Trying to work out what life would be like without Charlie – whether she could stand life alone, with no home.

When harvest arrived and the district began to buzz with activity, the Lewises found they had to rely on Rebecca more. She had a truck licence after all. At first Mr Lewis only let her drive the truck on the property, but as the urgency rose to get the grain to the silos before rain swept across the huge sky, she found herself boring down the road away from the property towards town. A touch of freedom in a truck.

Today, as Rebecca drove with the bundle of Mrs Lewis's fresh-baked scones on the passenger seat, she stifled a yawn. The harvesting days were long, and Rebecca and Charlie's days were separated by the vast-ness of the crops. They were always travelling in the opposite direction, Charlie in the header, she in the grain truck. They would meet in the paddock when the bins were full and he would wave to her as she set the grain auger up to fill her truck and take it to the silo. There was no time to stop. It was harvest time and the sun was shining. After the last front had passed through, the weather bureau had forecast that there'd be no rain for weeks. No excuse to stop. After the grain harvest, there was hay to be made. Then there'd be soil to prepare for the seeds to be sown and it would begin all over again. The years repeated ahead of her end-lessly in this strange flat place she didn't belong to.

There were times, however, when being with Charlie made it all worthwhile. When the harvest had first begun there'd been excitement in the air and

Rebecca had started to have fun. She and Charlie had begun skylarking on the radio together.

'Roger-dodger, Ranger One, this is Smokey Bandit Jail Bait reading you loud and clear.' Flirtiness and fun flew between them on the airways. But Mrs Lewis had just put a stop to that, Rebecca thought.

She looked at Dags who sat on the floor of the truck salivating at the smell of the scones. 'Well, life is pretty dam serious after all,' she said to him. 'There's not too many jokes in the Good Book, if you know what I mean.'

Dags put his paws on the dashboard and peered out the windscreen, looking for nonexistent sheep amidst the yellow wheat stubble. Bec ran her hand along his smooth firm back.

'Sorry Dags. We'll get you some sheep one day soon.'

On the single strip of bitumen road she waved to Mr Lewis as he bumbled by in the cotton harvester. He was headed for the neighbouring place on a contracting job. Bec steered the truck back onto the centre of the road after he had passed.

'Old mongrel,' she said. Dags looked up at her and stopped panting for a moment. 'Not you!' Rebecca laughed.

She thought about Mr Lewis. She recognised her own father in him. When he spoke so condescendingly to Charlie, she felt her anger rise. It was bad enough that Mr Lewis virtually ignored her, but when he cut Charlie short every time, it made Rebecca so angry.

Charlie's shoulders seemed to slump when his father entered the room and a silence settled on him like a cloud. Charlie had so many brilliant ideas for the farm, which he shared with Rebecca. He was bursting with passion for farming, yet he had no room to move.

'Minimum till is the way to go with soil like this,' he'd said one day. 'Conservation farming. It would boost yields out of sight, and we'd use less water on the irrigation country . . . It would be great all round.'

Rebecca had discussed his ideas with him and then, with unbridled enthusiasm, pushed him to mention them to his father. Part of her eagerness for change came from her frustration that she could do nothing with Waters Meeting. With Bec's strength and encouragement behind him, Charlie had begun to speak his mind. But then the arguments between Charlie and his father had started. Shouting in the machinery shed. Bikes and utes revving away from each other. Angry silent gaps at the dinner table. Mrs Lewis casting glances loaded with blame on Rebecca. Mr Lewis's disapproving sighs at the thought of his son 'shacked up' with a girl.

Rebecca would've packed up and left one hundred times, if it weren't for Charlie's sake. A terrible fear lay in the pit of her stomach that if she left, like she had left Tom, the worst could happen. A lovely, lonely farm boy. Isolated. Shut out.

Dags pushed a wet nose under her hand and Bec smiled at his sensitivity. She brushed her depressing thoughts aside, pulled down the radio handpiece and pressed the button, putting on her cheeriest voice.

'Where are you now, Charlie?' During the pause before he answered, she imagined his brown hunky hands reaching up for the radio.

'On the eastern side.'

Eastern. Eastern? She had trouble out here in all this flat country knowing which way was where, but she soon spotted him. She changed down a gear as she swung the truck into the crop. She leapt out, calling Dags, and stood with her hands on her hips in the heat, watching the machine roar to a stop. Dags sniffed the air, wagged his tail at the sight of Charlie, then lay in the shade of the truck to snap at flies.

Charlie jumped down from the cab and walked towards her. He was wearing shorts and she could see his leg muscles flex with every step.

'Hello, schpunky,' she said, reaching up to kiss him.

'Time for a break,' he said and he popped the top of the cooler and drank deeply from the opening.

'I thought that thing was airconditioned,' Bec said, nodding towards the header.

'It is. Come on, I'll show you my air vents.' He led her by the hand and she followed him with a smirk on her face.

'Oh, hang on. Your mum's scones.'

In the squash of the header cab amidst gears, gadgets and dials Charlie bounced up and down on the well-sprung seat.

'Good suspension,' he said.

'Here, let me try it.'

Bec straddled his lap and locked her fingers around

the back of his neck. She began to kiss him there, on his neck, and then moved her lips down to his chest. He smelt of wheat dust and oil. Unbuttoning his shirt she kissed his skin lightly down to his belt buckle. At this point she stopped and turned her blue eyes up to him with the Look, which he now recognised.

'This will give a whole new meaning to the term header,' she said, as she roughly tugged at his belt buckle.

Charlie's sighs could be heard amidst the hiss of the chair's suspension as it rocked up and down. Charlie gripped tightly on her shoulders and shuddered when he came.

The scones lay cooling in a tea towel on the floor of the header.

CHAPTER 33

Harry watched the last of the beer boxes smouldering in the incinerator and turned back towards the porch where he tipped dried cat food into the bowl and sung out, 'Puss Puss.' There was still no sign of the cat, but the food was being eaten during the night. It was possibly a good sign, thought Harry.

He shut the laundry door and swept the porch with three quick sweeps, then lent the broom against a cobweb-covered wall.

Walking to the yard he sung out, 'G'up, g'up, g'up.'

Hank raised his head with hay still protruding from his mouth and Ink Jet began to stroll over from the trough, her head hanging low to the ground but her ears pricked forward.

Walking towards the black mare Harry said softly, 'Whey girl. Whey Stinky.' He ran his hand over her neck and dust rose from her coat.

Hanging the reins over her neck he pulled the bit

into her mouth and looped the bridle over her neat black ears which flickered nervously. It had been almost a year since she'd been handled. She flinched slightly when Harry threw the crusty, stiff stock saddle on her back, but she stood when he tightened the girth.

He sat heavily in the saddle as he rode towards the river, feeling the quick step of the mare. He felt his muscles and his heart ache. It had been years since he'd been on a horse. It had been years since he'd allowed any feeling at all – since before Frankie left . . . since the day his father died. Harry felt the ghosts of his family members all about him. They breathed down his shirt collar in the draughty hallway and they banged things in the machinery shed when his back was turned. Sometimes in the still of the morning he thought they were all dead. Not just Tom. All of them. Mick, Frankie, Rebecca, all gone to dust. It took him months to shake the madness of his son's death from his head. But during the cold winter, once the alcohol had dissipated from his system, he had begun to stand a little taller. To put his life back on some sort of slow steady track. Somehow he thought he would make it up to Tom.

He crossed the flowing river. Winter snowmelt further up in the mountain range had brought it to life. Rain had brought a luminous green tinge to the valley, but there hadn't been follow-up showers. The grass seed and clover burr had shot out green hopeful stems, but bitter frosts and winds were beginning to kill off the hopes of spring.

Along the track, ducking below recently cracked and sagging branches, Harry rode, trying to get the feeling of his son. He looked for some sign of Tom, who had travelled this track months before. Perhaps the faded wrapper of something dropped accidentally from his horse as he rode. He saw nothing but a scattering of leaves in the dry understory of rain-starved bush. On the slopes the trees thickened and grew taller, leafier. On the rise they thinned out and the landscape became twisted with chilled, windblown snowgums.

Harry looked about for red hides and listened for the crack of sticks in the bush. Since Tom had turned them out in the bush, hoping they'd survive the drought, the breeding cows would've wandered far into the gullies in search of food. They could even have already taken themselves up to the high country run in search of the fresh green pick that would be emerging from beneath the melting snow. The cows were the only herd left on the property since the drought. It would be a hard job to find them and even harder to gather them without a dog. Harry sighed. After Tom's funeral Rebecca had taken Bessie, the only dog left on the place.

Rightly so, thought Harry. Rightly so. He recalled with shame the day he'd taken the gun in a drunken rage and shot all the dogs on their chains. He shook from his head the hideous memory of Mardy lying bleeding in the dust. He had to be strong and make amends. He tried to concentrate on where the cattle might be. They wouldn't be on this side of the ridge, not after such a severe drought. His father had told him that. The old man's voice filled his head now.

'In a good season, you'll find them on the north-facing slope if anywhere. But if it's been dry, head down into the gullies towards Heaven's Leap. You'll find them there.'

'Don't question me, boy,' his father had always said. Harry thought back to when he was a young child. Trying hard not to cry when his father had sat him high on a huge cob horse. His father had laughed.

'Can't see much cattleman in you, boy.' His father had been hard. So hard. Sometimes Harry felt a lump rise to his throat when he thought that his father loved his old dog and horses more than his only child. As a young man Harry had battled the cocktail of emotions for his father – admiration, love, hatred and despair all rolled into one confused mess. With agonising guilt Harry realised he had repeated the pattern with his children. No wonder Tom had been crushed. If only his father had taught him how to love. Harry spat and rode on.

He planned to camp the night in the hut and then get an early start on the plain. It could take him weeks to find the cattle. Harry stretched in the saddle and felt the muscles tingle along his spine and his hips crack with pain. He now wished he had packed a flask of whiskey. But he knew he had to dry out. Had to keep things going.

He thought of his children as he rode. They normally gathered the run. Tom and Rebecca. They were the stockmen, so much like his dad, thought Harry. His dad, the old bastard.

Half a kilometre before Harry reached the hut, fat drops of rain plopped onto his hat brim and soaked into Ink Jet's coat, forming tiny rivers which trickled down her legs to her fetlocks. Through a sheet of rain he saw the hut. He could see smoke from the chimney. Tom had lit the fire.

When he rode closer he saw it wasn't smoke at all. Just mountain mist.

After she was unsaddled, Ink Jet backed her tail into the wall of the shed and let the rain fall on her. She held her ears back as the rain landed on the dry patch where the saddle had been.

Harry threw down the saddle onto the verandah and took off his hat and coat, hanging them on a nail. The door was neatly latched with a chain and piece of wire. Tom had looped it securely. Harry's wet, reddened hands trembled as he struggled with the wire. His breath came in short gasps.

As he entered the hut it was so dark he couldn't see much at first. Then he noticed something hanging from the low beams in the corner. A dark shape. His heart skipped a beat and he clung to the door.

It was just an old sack. An old hessian bag with some salt for the cattle. It hung on a wire hook. Tom must've hung it there.

So dark were the rain clouds outside, Harry lit a

candle and sat it on top of the black, cold potbelly stove.

'Good boy,' he said as he noticed the neatly piled kindling, wood and newspaper.

'You were such a good boy.' Harry put his hand over his eyes as he remembered how much Tom had done to try to please him. How much he had tried to fit in as the farmer's son. How much he had given up . . . that gift of art. The gift passed down from Harry's mother. Suffering silently. Both of them. If only Harry had said he loved him. If only he'd said it once to his child.

Squatting at the already set fire, Harry felt tempted not to light it. Tom's hands had placed the sticks there, just like that. But a chill ran down his spine and he flicked the match so it fizzed and burned. The stove woke, sighed and began to murmur and then to roar.

In the corner of the room was Tom's swag, rolled neat and covered with a fine layer of dust. Harry ran his fingers along the straps, then quickly undid the buckles and rolled it out. Stripping down to his underwear, Harry flipped back the canvas and climbed into the swag. He pulled the cold dirty sheets and grey gritty blanket over his shoulders. He was arranging the crumpled pillow when he felt something beneath his hand. He pulled out a threadbare, furless teddy bear. Its glass eyes caught the flicker from the candle which stood on an old tea-chest by the bed. Shocked, Harry put the bear back inside the pillowcase.

As he lay his head there and breathed in the smells

of Tom, an aching belly wail came from his open mouth. He shut his eyes and saw the little boy, running towards him in the sheep yards, dragging the teddy in the dust. Harry's shuddering wails crept up through the shingles and through the tin and merged with the mountain wind which whipped the trees and moaned through the night.

In the morning, barely comforted by the cool light, Harry stooped to put on his boots and grabbed the post to steady himself. His fingertips dipped into the grooves of newly carved wood. Peering at the post in the dimness of the hut he saw the last marks Tom had left in this life. The last marks, except for the angry red slashes on the roof of the car. Through a fresh welling of tears Harry stared at the initials until finally he saw what he needed to do.

He went out in the dawn and set about saddling the horse to muster the cattle so he could bring them to the lowlands for drenching before he sent them back to the plains with a bull.

Behind him the hut seemed to sigh over his shoulder. It should have been Harry who had died next in this line of cattlemen. Not Tom. History was out of whack.

CHAPTER 34

Rebecca was in Mrs Lewis's kitchen handing her the mail when the call came through.

'Bec! Dad! Fire! The header's sparked a fire!'

The panic in Charlie's voice scared her. In an instant she grabbed the radio handpiece. Mrs Lewis rushed forward and stood by her side.

'Got you, Charlie, I'll call the brigade.'

'Hurry,' was all he said.

She switched channels and put the handpiece to her mouth. 'Yarella base. Yarella base, are you on channel?'

'Receiving,' came the voice of Mrs Chapel.

'This is Parkside base. We've got a fire in the crop on the eastern road. We need trucks urgently.'

'Just a sec, I think Bill's in the machinery shed.'

Bec gritted her teeth and impatiently said off the airwaves, 'Hell.'

Mrs Lewis folded her arms across her chest. Within

seconds Bill Chapel was on channel, talking from the two-way in his ute.

'Rebecca, I got all that . . . We'll be with you as soon as possible.'

'Roger that. Switching to channel nine now,' Rebecca said, hooking up the handpiece and turning the channel dial. She glanced at Mrs Lewis. 'Charlie's got a water tank on the ute and three spray packs. We'd better get going and help him. He'll need a driver.'

'Oh,' said Mrs Lewis backing away, 'I don't normally go to fires. Someone needs to stay by the phone.'

'But Mr Lewis is away on the contracting job! Charlie'll need us! They can reach us by radio.'

In her kitchen, Mrs Lewis stood her ground.

'Fine, let the crops burn. Just make sure you've packed the sandwiches,' said Rebecca quietly before running from the house. She pulled on her boots and roared away in the Toyota.

On the horizon she could see a huge, black, billowing cloud rising up in a column into a blue sky. As she neared the paddock, orange flames spread out in a dancing line beneath a curtain of black and grey smoke. There was Charlie, hopelessly spraying at the flames with a backpack. The stubble crackled and roared as wind fanned the flames towards the unharvested crop. She parked the ute where she thought it would be safe and ran towards Charlie's vehicle with the spray unit. She felt the hot wind gust around her face, blowing her hair across her eyes.

'Oh my God!' she said when she realised the huge

heading machine that had started the fire could burn if the wind swung round.

'The header!' she screamed at Charlie and ran over the rough-surfaced paddock as fast as she could. In the cab she lifted the comb before driving the machine quickly over the paddock. Once she'd parked it next to the ute, she again ran towards Charlie's vehicle which had the water tank and pump on the back.

'I'll drive!' she yelled as she ran. Charlie followed. He dumped the heavy plastic backpack onto the tray of the ute and ripped at the pump's starter cord. Leaping on the tray he banged on the roof as a signal for Bec to drive to the edge of the fire's front. Holding the nozzle firmly he sprayed a jet of water onto the fire, where the flames instantly died down to reveal a swathe of blackened, scorched ground.

They edged their way along the front but Bec could see they were losing the battle. The fire was spreading to the north and racing to the east. By the time two of the brigade trucks rolled in, a lot of the crop was burning. But as several more trucks arrived, Rebecca was flooded with relief. The radio in the cab was alive with urgent voices.

'There's a bore five hundred metres from the gate to the east. You can refill there,' came one voice.

'We've just arrived, Charlie. Where do you need us?' came another voice. Rebecca grabbed for the handpiece.

'We need a truck on that northern side,' said Bec into the radio. 'There's a track there. We can stop it there.'

Men in orange overalls clambered over the backs of

the trucks and started jets of water from hoses. Others drove up in farm utes and began to bash at the fringes of the fire with wet bags.

When the water ran out in the tank on Charlie's ute a man volunteered to drive it to the bore to refill it. Gratefully, Bec jumped from the ute and she and Charlie slung on the heavy water backpacks. They worked side by side, squirting water at the line of crackling flame that danced forward frighteningly fast with every gust of wind. Flame licked at the yellow stubble, burned it orange and then left a wake of smouldering blackness. Willy-willys spun madly across where the fire had been and picked up fine slivers of black grass which disintegrated and smeared on their sweating faces. Charlie looked at Bec. She knew he was about to ask if she was okay.

'This is the hottest date I've ever been on,' she joked, trying to allay any concerns he may have for her. Charlie's face relaxed a little and a smile came to his lips. They felt they were winning a little now help was here.

Suddenly the warm breeze swung around and, before Bec and Charlie could run, smoke swamped them. Bec felt tears streaming down her face. Both of them ran, trying to find air. Clean air somewhere. All around was a haze. They made their way through the smoke towards a red truck.

'Need a lift?' said a cheeky voice and Rebecca and Charlie gratefully leapt on board.

'You alright, love?' asked a tubby man with an upturned nose.

'Yep,' said Bec. 'Fine.' She pressed her fingertips into her stinging eyes.

The truck moved steadily along the front as the tubby man pointed a blast of water at the snaking line of flames. As Bec clung to a rail on the truck's side, she could see that at least eight trucks were all battling at the fringes of the fire.

'Thank God. I think the wind's dropping,' said Charlie as he watched. It was now swinging back across the flames which settled the fire to a slow trickle across the stubble. In the distance, a tractor from the Chapels' property was hurtling down the road with a cultivator hitched to the back. Bec watched it coming. As it drove into the crop the driver of the big Deutz tractor dropped a few revs before lowering the cultivator to the ground. It drove ahead of the flames, turning the red earth into a broad firebreak.

With the wind changing and then finally falling still, the panic amidst the men lulled. The flames died down and trucks lumbered around, mopping up spots which still smoked.

As the haze began to clear the trucks eventually congregated on the fringes of the blackened earth. The firefighters, some sitting on the edge of flat tray utes, others leaning from the backs of the fire trucks, gathered to take stock of how much had burned and who had turned out to fight the blaze. With the panic over, the gathering evolved from an emergency into a social event. Charlie, still shocked by the suddenness of the fire, was taking in the moment. 'It could've been a lot worse,' the men told him. He was enjoying the taunts and the rough comfort offered by the men.

But his demeanour changed when Mr Lewis drove into the paddock and along the stretch of blackened earth.

''Bout time you showed up,' joked Mr Chapel.

Mr Lewis stepped from the vehicle looking red-faced and worried. 'How much crop did we lose?' he asked Charlie.

'I'd say a couple of hundred hectares.'

'Stop panicking,' said Mr Chapel, 'it could've been worse.' Mr Chapel slapped a hand on top of Charlie's shoulder.

'These two young 'uns did good for you, mate. No need for you to come rushing home.'

'No need, was there, Bill?' said Mr Lewis with a smile as he turned towards his vehicle. He pulled a slab of beer across the bench seat.

'Well, you old devil,' said Bill Chapel happily.

Mr Lewis tore at the beer box and pulled out the plastic-wrapped six packs. He handed each man a cold brown stubby. When he handed Rebecca a beer he kept his face straight. Not even a smile. She felt the sting – she was not supposed to be here. Charlie noticed his father's disapproval. He moved closer to her and wiped at the smudges of soot which covered her face.

'Thanks for moving the header, Bec,' he said so his father could hear. 'If you hadn't, we would've lost it and much more of the crop.'

She smiled back and sipped the froth away from the lip of the bottle.

Rebecca was swigging on her second beer when a car tossed up dust along the strip of red road. In the passenger seat, sunk down low like a child, sat Mrs Lewis, while Marjorie Chapel drove. When the car stopped, the women got out and, without a word, pulled thermoses and a basketful of sandwiches from the car boot. The two ladies trod carefully through the unburned wheat stubble and handed around the sandwiches.

Rebecca was sitting on the edge of the ute dangling her legs and talking dogs to one of the men when Mrs Lewis offered her a sandwich. She wiped some beer from the corner of her mouth with the back of her hand, took the white bread between black fingers and said, 'Oh! Thank you very much.'

Mrs Lewis's silence and dark look said it all. Rebecca pushed back her cap and ran her fingers through her smoky smelling hair.

Stuff it, she thought.

In the shower that night, as Charlie rubbed a face washer roughly over the back of Rebecca's neck, she said, 'This . . . me . . . being here. At your place. It just isn't working, is it?'

Charlie's stopped scrubbing. When she turned to look at his face and saw the hurt in his eyes, all she could do was hold him.

CHAPTER 35

From inside the carport Charlie watched. He liked the way she smoothed her strong tanned hands and fingers over the ears and faces of each dog. A tinge of jealousy perhaps. She would never leave her dogs, thought Charlie bitterly.

Wheat dust scratched on his neck and he ran his fingertips against his sweat-gritty skin under the collar of his shirt. It was hot. Even in the shade, it was stifling. He felt the panic rise again.

He saw her stoop to unclip each dog from their chains. The steel supports of the skillion shed served as tethering posts and the corrugated-iron roof provided shade. It wasn't ideal kennelling and she pouted over it like a spoiled child. Charlie had promised, after harvest, to build her a proper run. But there just hadn't been time. The crops and the machines came first. Endless.

In the sunlight the dogs danced in circles around

her in the dust. She pointed towards the long red road which led to the front gate and they bounded away. She walked slowly after them, whistling a stop command every now and then and raising a hand for them to sit. Charlie's eyes followed her as she grew smaller, walking towards the shimmer of heat. She was walking to the dam. In search of water to swim in.

He turned his back to her shimmering shape and went inside the house, picking up the local paper from the kitchen table and continuing on into the darkness of his old bedroom. He had a vague sense his mother was standing near the stove, but he didn't look up to say hello. He just shut the bedroom door. His parents' house and his room seemed so different since Rebecca had moved into the cottage. It no longer seemed like it was his house at all. Nor his room. The ebb and flow of seasons, of harvests, ploughings, plantings and sprayings had been disrupted. The pattern of mother and father and two boys had shifted entirely since Rebecca had come. No one said a thing. But everyone now questioned where they would stand in the family's new shape.

When she had first arrived and moved into the cottage, he had felt his parents' prickly silence when, after dinner, he stood up from the table and said goodnight to them. He knew they sat and listened to the click of the gauze door as he made his way outside to sleep in her arms in the cottage. His mother had long since given up the pretence of each morning going into his room to make his bed. He had given up sneaking into

329

the house before dawn and climbing in between the tight sheets. He liked the softness of Rebecca's bed. Naked limbs entwined in soft crumpled sheets which smelt of her. It was too hard to leave her there in that tangled bed. It was too hard to keep up the pretence for the sake of his churchgoing straight-backed mother.

Now here he sat on the edge of his stark boyhood bed, feeling so much like a boy. He looked at the ad he had just circled and the black ink which read, '150 CFA ewes'. He wanted to buy them for her, then re-fence the killer paddock, so she could at least work her dogs a bit. But first he'd have to ask his dad. He'd need his father's signature on the cheque. He let out a frustrated sigh and crumpled up the newspaper. In his head he'd phrased and rephrased the question . . . the question of how to ask his old man for the money to buy her a ring. He threw the paper on the floor and rolled onto his stomach on the bed. He buried his face in the gap left by his folded arms. He could feel the panic again. He was going to lose her. She didn't fit here.

When they first arrived after graduation and he carried her bags to the cottage, she had sworn and raged in the tiny living room when he'd told her he would still live with his parents for a little while.

She'd thrown down the boxes and slammed the door, screaming through it, 'Mummy's boy! Frigging old-fashioned, hypocritical God-squadders!'

She was right. He was a mummy's boy. He hated that. So many of the local girls who had seen him at B&Ss were stunned by his party persona. They would say to him as they ran their eyes over him, 'If only your mother could see you now, Charlie Lewis.'

The soft voice of his mother still sizzled on his brain like a brand. She had put down the wheelbarrow and slowly pulled off her gardening gloves. Not looking at him.

'Of course you're not assuming you can move into the cottage too? At least not until an official engagement.'

He was too gutless to go against the flow of the family. He hated himself for it. Bec had shown him how free a spirit could be. He longed to be like her. To be able to turn his back on his family and walk away. But it was here, on this land that he'd always pictured himself, that he belonged. Even as a little boy he could see himself as an old man, driving up and down endlessly on a tractor. Turning the soil. It was his home. They were his parents. He'd been taught to obey. He'd tried so hard to please them all but Rebecca just kept challenging all of that. He didn't know where he was going any more.

Charlie reached out, opened the drawer beside his bed and pulled from it the glossy AR brochure. It fell open at Rebecca's photo. The girl who was now walking along his family's dusty drive had turned out to be so much better in real life than the dream. Better than the fantasy. Better than the photo. The real-life Rebecca was so not like his mother. He just loved that. He just loved her.

That night as he lay next to her warm sleepy-girl body, he could hear her breathing alter. She murmured in her sleep and rolled over. He pulled her closer to him and spooned her body so he felt her rounded backside next to his groin.

'You okay, Bec?'

'Mmmm?'

'You all right?'

He could almost hear the river's rush. She was dreaming again. Of her river. He wondered if she'd tell him about it in the morning. He cupped his hand under her breast and kissed her gently on the shoulder. He wanted to marry this girl, but not because of his mother, or because of the rules of his mother's God. He just wanted her. In the darkness he stared at the curve of her shoulder and sighed. She was not the marrying type. Not to a flat-soil farmer anyway.

CHAPTER 36

In the sunroom a large fly beat itself against the window, distracting Harry from his newspaper for a moment. He cautiously sipped again on his too-hot tea and scanned the advertisements in the paper. One caught his eye. It was the symbol of the Landcare organisation. Two cupped hands meeting at the fingertips carefully formed the shape of Australia. He squinted at the print. They were advertising grants for riverside weed control and revegetation programs.

On the muster yesterday, as he ambled behind the slow-moving Herefords, Harry had noticed the dark green spread of blackberries along the edge of the water. Tangling outwards from the dark clumps were bright green leaves of young willows. He'd lost track of how long the boys had been gone, but the spread of weeds choking his beloved river tore at the last of his pride. Rebecca's words had come to him, 'You're going to lose the lot.' He'd said it again out loud and realised he'd already lost it all. His wife, his kids. Tom now gone. The river and its tangle of weeds didn't seem to matter so much any more. Even though he still had his land for the moment and his mountains and sky, he had nothing. Nothing at all.

Ink Jet had splashed across the river in the wake of the ribby dull-coated cows. From her back Harry had looked up towards the homestead. It had been as though he were seeing the place for the first time in years. As if he shared the eyes of his father and his father's father, riding up towards the sheds and yards. In the gentle afternoon breeze they'd come back from the dead, down from the plains, to see how their fortunes had crumbled into rotted wood and rusted tin. Because of him. All because of him.

As he'd unsaddled Ink Jet and hung the saddle up in the shed his fingers had lingered on the leather surcingle. How easy it would be to hang. To hang from the beams with leather around your throat. Harry had been about to pull the strap through the slits of the saddle when he'd felt the cat rub against his leg. He'd looked down and the cat had looked up.

'Reow-wow,' the cat said to him.

It had made him smile.

Today in the dozy sunroom Harry tore at the newspaper, around the edge of the advertisment. As he did the cat stalked into the kitchen, rubbed slowly against the solid wooden table legs and greeted him.

It then lay in a patch of sun watching Harry. It watched through narrowed eyes. Slowly Harry stood

334

up, each muscle aching from yesterday's ride. He cut some devon from a fat roll and threw it to the cat. Then he shuffled over to the phone.

The first call was to the neighbours in search of hay for the cattle. The weather was still too cold to risk droving cows in such poor condition up on the high plains. He had to buy some hay to buy some time – enough time perhaps for the river flats to recover. A steady rain from the east had brought on some pasture growth, but it was so patchy with weeds that fertiliser and resowing would be needed, together with follow-up rains. God knows how he'd pay for pasture renovation. God knows how he'd get the breeder cows in condition for joining. He didn't even have a bull.

The voice of his neighbor, Gary Tate, came down the line and Harry found it hard to begin. He cleared his throat, and for the first time in his life Harry Saunders begged. Gary at first was shocked to hear from Harry, then he began to lap it up. He didn't have much time for the man, so he was enjoying the call.

'It'll cost, I'm afraid,' said Gary through a small thin mouth. 'Although we've got the irrigation, we still need some bales on hand for our own stock and, as you know, hay's in short supply . . . It's getting dearer and dearer by the day. Not enough rain.'

Harry bit his bottom lip and agreed with what Gary was saying. He held his breath when Gary told him the price. When he hung up the phone Harry almost turned to stalk down the hallway to the dining room and the dark, dusty cabinet which contained old decanters of bitter-tasting sherry. But instead he picked up the phone again and ran his finger along the 1800 number printed in the Landcare ad. A smooth-voiced lady switched his call through to the local Department of Ag office.

'I was after the Landcare fella,' he said to another female voice on switchboard.

'I'll just put you through . . .'

He heard a click and listened to the hold music – Vivaldi, he seemed to think. He watched the cat in the sun lick its back leg.

'Hello . . .'

Momentarily confused by the youthful female voice, Harry stuttered. 'Ahh. Yes . . . I was ringing about your river revegetation program . . . um . . .'

Sensing Harry's confusion, the light and cheery voice on the end of the line helped out. 'Yes, you've got the right person . . . I'm the new Landcare facilitator and rural counsellor for your region. Who is it who needs help?'

'It's Harry Saunders here. From Waters Meeting.'

There was a pause.

'Well, I'll be. It's Sally here, Mr Saunders. Sally Carter.'

The name at first didn't register. The voice tried again. 'Rebecca's friend.'

Harry stood stock-still. It was the first time he'd heard his daughter's name voiced out loud for nearly a year. Sally sensed his apprehension and immediately stepped in. 'If you're free tomorrow I can be out there by ten a.m. We can discuss some options.'

'Ahh . . .'

'Fine. I know my way. See you then.' She hung up the phone quickly.

Harry stood in the kitchen for a while. Thoughts of Sally flooded back into his head. He pictured the skinny well-spoken doctor's daughter as she splashed and swam in the river with his daughter. Harry smiled, moved over to the sink and then turned on the tap. It was time he did the washing up.

In her office in town Sally sat back in her chair and stared at the phone. He wasn't backing out of that one, no sir-ee, she thought. She was less than two hours drive from where Harry stood in his socks in his kitchen. She'd have to reschedule some of her on-farm appointments, but she wasn't letting this chance go.

She stared at the fish which swam about on her computer screen. Then swallowed and sighed. 'Rebecca's friend.' She didn't feel like Bec's friend. They'd barely been in touch since Tom's funeral. Sally couldn't help the guilt over his death. She hadn't even contacted Bec to tell her about her new regional job. It sounded so flippant now, that she'd given up chasing suits and city living. It was Tom's death which had sparked the change in her.

So many times she'd started a letter to Rebecca. Her words becoming more and more dramatic and emotional. She would write a page, read it, then crunch it between her slim hands. She'd start the letter again, tears in her eyes. Then she'd give up. Now she knew Harry's call was giving her a chance. A chance to save her friendship with Rebecca and a chance to somehow make it up to Tom.

In blue ink she scribbled in her diary, 'Waters Meeting, ten a.m.' Thoughts of the business plan flooded back. Where had she put her copy? She thought of the box of university books sitting in her bedroom at home. She'd reread it tonight.

She reached for her address book and looked for Bec's details. There was a series of numbers scribbled in and crossed out. The last one was Rebecca's share house at Tablelands Uni. Sally had heard Bec had moved out to her boyfriend's farm. She scratched her head with her pen. What was Basil's real name? Charlie? Charlie . . . Lewis.

A monotone voice at directory assistance asked, 'Homestead or Cottage One?'

In an instant Sal said, 'Cottage One.' It could be the workman's house, but Sally guessed there was no way Rebecca Saunders would shack up with her boyfriend's parents. She dialled the number, and when she heard Rebecca's familiar voice say, 'Hello,' on the end of a crackly line, goosebumps ran over her flesh.

'You'll never guess what,' Sally said excitedly into the phone.

CHAPTER 37

Charlie's veins bulged in his neck and his face flushed red as he yelled at Rebecca. He paced up and down in front of her in the tiny cottage and ran his fingers roughly through his short black hair. The anger and fear in him was so strong. The look in his eyes terrified her.

When he grabbed her on both arms and searched her face for a reaction, she cracked.

'I can't take any more of this,' she screamed. She shook off his grip and ran out of the cottage, slamming the door.

In the shed she fired up the four-wheeler bike and rode it away from the homestead area, past the vast paddocks of yellow crackling stubble. The wind blew her tears along the side of her face so they spread and itched in her scalp.

'Where is there to run in this country?' she said to herself. Her words, spoken through gritted teeth, were whisked away instantly by the wind that ran through the wheat stubble surrounding her. She wanted the closed-in feeling brought on by thousands of trees, all living, all breathing around her. She wanted the weight of the mountains, millions of tonnes of rock, all cracking, expanding and contracting with the touch of the sun and the frost. She rode towards the only rise she could see. An irrigation bank. Weeds grew up its red surface. Strange melons on prickly vines reached out across the dirt.

She switched off the bike so that all she could hear was the wind in the stiff stalks of the beheaded wheat. She ran up the bank and sat on the edge facing the water. Deep and brown, it swirled past her. She found no comfort in it. It seemed sinister. Man-made and sinister. Rushing past too fast, water stolen from rivers. Water that would bring more salinity to the land. She looked along the stretch of it and then stared at the scuffed toes of her boots, wishing she'd brought a dog with her so she could cry into its fur.

It was Sally's call that had sparked the fight. After she'd hung up the phone Charlie had looked at her, waiting for the news. She sat cross-legged on the couch and he brought her a stubby. As they drank she recounted Sally's conversation.

'She's got a rural financial counsellor job in the region, and she's doubling as a Landcare facilitator for the moment until they find an extra person. Dad called her about river revegetation funding, not knowing it would be her. Sally's got an appointment there at ten a.m. tomorrow.'

Charlie took in the news and nodded, trying to be positive, but alarm bells rang in his head. As she talked excitedly about the possibility of returning to Waters Meeting, Charlie's fear grew.

'Now that he's asked for help outside, there's a chance, don't you see? He's realised. He's seen he can't do it on his own. If Sally can open the door just a little, just a gap, he'll realise he needs me back there.'

'But Bec, do you really think your father deserves you to help him out? What about all the pain he's caused you . . . He's treated you like crap. And what about Tom? Have you forgotten what happened to Tom?'

When Charlie said Tom's name out loud, it hung in the air between them.

'How dare you! You just want me here to be the perfect farmer's wife, like your bloody mother! Look at me! I'm lost here and you know it. And how dare you bring Tom into this! If I don't go back there, Tom has died for nothing! Don't you see? Where do I fit here, with your mother crowding us and your father controlling our future? You change, Charlie Lewis, when you're on this place. It's not you, it's not the Charlie I kissed in that river. You lose your strength. You lose yourself.'

'Huh! You're a fine one to talk about losing yourself! You would've drunk yourself into a hole by now, Rebecca . . . like your father has. Don't you get stuck into me about my family issues. I've put up with yours long enough.'

The emotions in Charlie had come unstuck and the years of repression had hurtled out. He didn't want Rebecca to go. She heard the panic in his voice. She had clamped her fists to her temples and begun to cry as he yelled at her.

And now here she sat on the irrigation bank. A tiny dot on a huge patchwork of massive squares divided by straight lines of swirling water. Rebecca in this landscape with no river.

She heard the ute before she saw it. Charlie drove towards her steadily, then parked it by the bike. As he stepped out of the vehicle she stood up. He climbed the bank and without saying anything took her in his arms and held her. He just held her. She held him back and felt the life in him, felt the goodness of his soul. She loved every cell, every inch, every part of him.

'I'm sorry,' he said.

Eventually he took her by the hand. 'Come on,' he said, 'I'll cook you fish fingers for tea.'

CHAPTER 38

Harry surprised himself when he uttered the words to the tall, well-dressed girl.

'So how is Rebecca getting along?' The words came out jerkily and he couldn't bring himself to look at Sally. She sat on the bench seat of the ute looking straight ahead as they bumped over the track in the river flat paddocks.

Sally smiled gently, took her gaze away from what was left of the lucerne paddock after drought and overgrazing. 'She's fine. Just fine. And Charlie's well, too.'

She thought back to her phone call yesterday. Her heart had raced when she first heard Rebecca's voice. She wasn't sure how Rebecca would react to her after she'd dropped out of her life so suddenly. But instantly Sally could hear the smile in her friend's voice. Rebecca had been truly joyful to hear from her. After Sally had discussed the possibility of swaying Harry into taking

Rebecca back onto the farm, their conversation had turned to Tom.

'I know I haven't been around for you like I should've,' said Sally quietly. She expected Rebecca to stir her along with a teasing remark but instead she said, 'I can understand why. I know you felt partly responsible for Tom's death, Sal . . .'

Sally wasn't sure how to react so she remained silent.

'But it truly wasn't your fault. It wasn't anyone's fault. Tom had to pin his dreams onto something, and that something happened to be you.'

'If I could turn back the clock . . .'

'Don't be ridiculous,' Rebecca had cut in. 'You would never have suited Tom and we both know it, so don't even think things like that.'

Suddenly Harry's voice snapped Sally back to the here and now.

'Has she got a job?' Harry asked.

'She hasn't been looking too hard. She's doing great things on Charlie's place . . . His family can't get enough of her farming skills,' she lied.

Sally wasn't going to give away too much. She'd play him along a bit. See where he stood when it came to his daughter's future.

Despite everything, she couldn't help but feel sorry for Harry. She had been shocked when she drove up to the house. It had been the house she'd dreamed of when she was a child. Even though she'd spend weekends on her family's hobby farm, her father's brand-new brick homestead-style house never had much heart or soul. But Waters Meeting, the house, the land, the sky above, was crowded with ancient energies. Teeming with ghosts of people and animals gone by. History could be felt in the wood, in the tin, in the wilderness. As children, Sally and Rebecca had found the richness of the past everywhere – tiny fragments of pottery in the soil, a rusted nail in the daffodil patch, an old horn from a house cow long dead, the rusted chain of a dog none of them had ever known.

She had envied Rebecca, growing up in the rambling homestead, nestled amidst the trees and paddocks of the picture-postcard valley farm. Her school holidays spent here were now golden memories of endless sunny days, riding ponies bareback, splashing in the warmth of the summer river. Of Frankie turning up with tiny orphan piglets, calves or lambs. Of bounding puppies and thick white bread and homemade raspberry jam. There was a chaos to it all but at the same time a peacefulness. As children they could find so much joy in all the living things around and find so much intrigue from the lives that had once walked the land.

Now the house seemed dark. The souls quiet. The valley empty. As Sally had walked along the path to the front door she'd heard the wind wailing in the shadowy pines and she'd shivered a little. She'd thought of Tom. Did he hang himself from a smooth grey branch? She wasn't sure where. Or how. She couldn't help but look for ropes or marks on horizontal tree limbs. She'd shivered again and reached for the old cow bell at the back door which hung above a spidery nest of old boots. As the bell clanged, the black spiders inside it panicked and crouched further into their webs.

When Harry opened the door, Sally refused to come in for a cup of tea. Instead she said in a voice that was too light, 'Let's get straight into it. Go take a look at the river. We can talk while we drive.'

Harry was relieved. Even though he'd tidied the kitchen and swept it clean, he was not keen on fumbling around to make tea using slightly off milk. He was fearful of sitting in uncomfortable silence without even the tick of the clock.

In the ute now the engine revved over their silence and bumps, rattles and jolts filling up large gaps in their conversation.

Sally kept her questions simple and on target. She was there as a Landcare representative, not in her normal role as counsellor. She asked about weed control programs, the size of areas, previous revegetation work. She jotted his answers in her notebook in staggering writing as they jolted along the track.

Relieved and somewhat impressed by her serious professionalism, Harry began to open up and quiz her about financial counselling.

'Got many takers for the counselling side of the job?' he asked.

'Yes. We can't keep up at the moment . . . particularly since the drought. Most farmers find they can't do without one,' she said. 'And because the service is part government funded, and part funded by the banks and private industry, it doesn't cost the farmer anything.' She knew from the look on his face that she was winning him over.

Under a gnarled old rivergum, Harry stopped the ute. 'This is the worst area. And there's a bit of wash-up here in the creek.'

Sally looked over the area. 'If you're prepared to fence that, we can get you back at least half of your fencing cost through an erosion control program. When the weather's right, some of those blackberries further up the gully there could be burned and sprayed.'

'Sounds good,' Harry said.

After he waved her goodbye from the gate and watched the car wind its way up the steep valley, Harry suddenly felt very much alone. The cat was nowhere in sight. He'd wanted to ask more questions about Rebecca, but something had stopped him.

He walked to the machinery shed, making sure he didn't look at the garage. The tractor fired up easily and he was surprised at its steady, healthy sounding rumble. He drove the tractor to the side of the shed and backed it up to the three-point linkage of the fence-post digger.

It had been over a year since it had been moved from the spot and long yellow grass tangled around its metal frame. Harry secured the pins and linked up the power take-off of the tractor. Adjusting the revs and pulling a lever, Harry made sure the digger still worked. The large spiralling borer spun around easily. He drove

347

it back to the shed and flicked the tractor's off switch. On the ute he threw some steel droppers, a roll of hinge-joint wire, a roll of plain wire and the box of fencing gear. Tomorrow morning he would begin. He would stop the erosion that was eating away his land.

CHAPTER 39

At first Peter thought it was Henbury whimpering which woke him in the darkest part of the night. It was not uncommon for the dog, who was getting quite old, to ask to go outside at irregular hours of the night. Peter leaned up on one elbow and looked at the black blob which lay curled up in the basket at the foot of the bed. Only little grumbling snores came from the shape. Then Peter realised it was Frankie who'd woken him. She lay with her back to him, shaking and crying silently.

'Hey,' he said gently and rolled over, taking her in his arms and brushing back the wet hair from her face.

She tried to roll away from him, turn her back on him, so she could be left alone in her own private world of grief. Peter held on tight.

'No you don't, Frankie.' She relaxed a little in his arms. He knew not to coax the words out of her. Despite what he'd learned in the student counselling seminars, talking about it was not always best. Especially in Frankie's case.

She bore the pain of her son's death in a private, silent kind of hell. By day she put on her autopilot smile with her clients, and during evening meals in the flat she smiled at Peter and patted him lovingly on his hand or knee. Nothing was ever said about the fact that Tom was dead. The fact that it was suicide. She wore the guilt as only a mother could, and it was beginning to drag the sides of her mouth down permanently and bring streaks of grey to her auburn hair.

Nights were the worst. The darkness lay heavily on her. Each night she lay awake listening to Henbury and Peter snoring in an odd kind of rhythmic song.

Tonight the insomnia interspersed with dreams of Tom and the river were too much to bear. She buried her face into Peter's chest and felt the fuzziness of his flannel pyjamas on her cheek. She breathed in his smell. The guilt rose in her again, this time for the way she shut Peter out. She'd left him out there in the cold. His new bride running away with grief before they'd even had time to settle into their married lives together. As she forced herself to speak, Peter forced himself to be silent.

'It's like he's still there. It's like it never happened. I wake up each morning and in my head I think, Mick and Trudy . . . in the city with baby, Bec and Charlie . . . farming cotton and wheat, Tom . . . at home on the farm. But he's not home. He's not there. And the dreams. They're so vivid. So real. He's looking at me and his face is so white. The river is always rushing and roaring so loudly. Oh God, Peter! I should never have left them. Never. I should never have left him there with that man.'

Peter took the words in. Some hurt him. Some angered him, but he kept silent, rubbing his hand up and down her back. Then she said what he'd been waiting to hear.

'I have to go back there. To Waters Meeting. I have to see for myself that Tom's not there. I have to be in the places where he last walked.'

Peter nodded understandingly. It was just what they'd said in the counselling seminar about confronting demons. He was about to say he'd take a sickie and they could leave first thing in the morning when they heard movement in Henbury's basket and a loud yawn.

Frankie rolled over. 'For chrissakes, Henbury.' She swung her legs out of bed and fumbled in the dark for her robe.

'It's alright, Frankie, I'll take him outside.'

'No, it's fine. I'll go.' She was relieved to have an excuse to get out of the flat and away from the hellish feeling of not being able to sleep.

As she stood in the doorway of the units and waited for Henbury to shuffle out of the tiny garden, Frankie looked up. It was the first time in a long time that she missed seeing stars overhead.

CHAPTER 40

Harry was so keen to get the fencing underway, he rose before dawn and lit the stove to put the old kettle on. The sun was just stretching up behind the dark mountain when he stepped from the house and began to drive the ute to the erosion site. He parked in the shade of a gum and stood with his hands on his hips trying to work out how long the job might take him on his own. He had to walk back to the sheds to pick up the tractor. It would take him a good half an hour, he thought. Normally he'd curse at having to walk, but watching the sun come up in a shimmering flame-red and golden ball above the mountain seemed to calm him. Insects skimmed on the surface of the river and fish jumped, making a sudden splash. For a time, the sadness in Harry's heart lifted. He decided then, as he watched the river pass silently by, that he would find out from Sally where his daughter was. He would ask Rebecca if she felt she could come home.

The spiral blade of the post-hole digger slipped easily through the rich black river soil. Harry had the first four holes dug in no time but, as he backed the tractor onto the rocky ridge, he knew the next fence-post hole would be tough to dig. He set the tractor on high revs and lowered the post-hole digger onto the surface of the soil where it spun, tossing up soil, severing blades of grass and stirring small stones from the earth.

Metal hit rock and the machine laboured as a large stone was spewed up amidst the soil. The stone lay next to the rotating blade and scraped against it as the digger turned. Harry reached forward to grab at the stone. In an instant the whirring noise took on a different tone as shirt sleeve, then skin, then flesh, then bone grated against metal. The machine laboured as Harry screamed. With his free arm he reached up. His fingertips touched on the lever. He sunk to his knees, his weight bringing the lever down. The spinning digger stopped. Harry hung his head. Sweat beaded on his brow. His skin grew pale. Blood seeped into soil. When he opened his eyes he could see what was left of his arm, twisted into the machine. His hand, white, waved back at him from the other side of the borer. In horror he pulled back but realised his arm wasn't completely severed. He was stuck there in the machine. His screams rang out around the hills and sent the black cockatoos screeching towards the mountaintops.

CHAPTER 41

The day was so still and the air so clear. Trees hung limp beneath a haze of chilly blue. The winding road hugged the curves of the mountainside, and leaves and fern fronds flickered and waved slightly in the short blast of wind from the car as it drove past. Frankie and Peter sat in a comfortable silence. Henbury stood on his tartan rug in the back, leaning hard against the door with his nose upturned to the gap in the window. By mid-morning, they had passed the Dingo Trapper Hotel without stopping.

'No need to book a room for tonight,' said Frankie as she smiled at Peter. 'Hardly anyone ever stays there . . . I'm sure there'll be a room when we come back later.'

They fell back into silence and drove on.

Frankie felt a tinge of excitement mixed with dread as they passed the Twelve Mile stockyards . . . They were getting nearer to Waters Meeting, nearer to facing Harry and the place Tom died. As she sat staring out of the car window, Frankie waited for the sudden expansive view which often shocked travellers as they rounded the hairpin bend on the long spur. She loved that sight. They hadn't made this journey since Mick and Trudy's wedding, and back then the valley had shone yellow from the dry. Now the paddocks were green, but Frankie could still recognise the damage the drought had done. There were long-running scars across paddocks where hay and grain had been fed out to stock. The animals were now nowhere to be seen. On stock camps on hillsides and in the corners of paddocks, weeds sprouted. The remaining pasture was patchy and short. But despite this, the valley from up here looked stunning. A luminous swathe of green, flanked by the deeper green-brown of the surrounding bushland.

'Wow,' said Peter as he saw the view for the second time in his life.

Frankie looked at the silver river, edged with leafy gums. It snaked its way through the black soil river flats. A clump of green pines, silver birch, oaks and well-watered gums shaded the house from view but Frankie could just make out the machinery shed and the old barn and stable. The road wound down towards the river valley's base and the view was gone, just as suddenly as it had arrived.

She remembered the first time she had driven along this road. Fresh out of college. A graduate vet with the world at her feet. Ambitious, flirtatious and attractive, even in overalls. She'd driven into the property, peering through the trees at the two-storey house.

'Wow,' she had said as she'd driven past the house. It had loomed up high above the river flats. It was tall and proud. Roses flowered madly along the fence and lavender bushes scented the air heavily on the edges of its wide verandahs. Geraniums in boxes flowered from the upstairs verandah. Stunned by the beauty of the house and garden, the young vet drove on down to the yards.

It was early morning and a golden light had crept over the mountains and shone on the wooden yard railings. It was then that Frankie saw him. Her mountain cattleman dream. Harry in a worn hat, handling a prancing young colt which quivered with nervous excitement. He smiled at her as the horse pranced about. A wicked smile, crinkling the corners of his eyes, 'You must be the vet,' he grinned.

It was then that Frankie felt the sexual rush run through her. A desire that was so strong it sent a rosy flush to her cheeks. As she shook hands with Harry, she felt a charge run through her again.

The colt was her first gelding operation since she'd graduated. The operation didn't go terribly well, but Harry didn't seem to mind. He spent most of the time leaning near her, breathing in the smell of her as she bowed her head to thread a curved needle with shaking hands.

She didn't sense any anger in the tone of his voice when Harry phoned a few days later to ask her to come back to treat an infection in the colt. As she swabbed away the pus, disinfected the wound and needled the horse, she felt the nearness of Harry again as he held onto the halter rope with his strong hands. She could smell him. A sweet male smell. They had made love there and then in the stable, in a flurry of desire amidst dank straw and the tangy smell of horse manure.

Frankie could still see the shocked look on Harry's father's face as he entered the dim, musty stable. He turned his back on them and walked out, muttering he'd like a word with Harry. It was assumed from that day on that Harry would court then marry this woman, the vet. That was how it was out there then, in those days. That was just how it was and Frankie went along with it. It was her city girl dream. Harry was her stock-solid farming man and Waters Meeting her glorious country home.

The first year of marriage had been exciting. The buzz of romance as they rose at dawn and saddled horses to ride to the hut on the plains. The sunny days spent in the garden with Harry's gentle but insipid mother. But after a year or so, reality hit. Frankie was learning that the country manor house came with a price. Inside its walls, she had to mould herself around Harry's silent father and mouse-like mother. She found herself wanting more. More from Harry. More to fill her head. The isolation, too, was beginning to tell on her. Too many days at home. Stretches of days that contained little more than farming and domestics. Too many days without something to challenge her mind. Conversations that were too one-sided began to wear her down, and Harry's hardness at times scared her. Despite his pouts and silence she took on part-time vet work. Part-time work she desperately pursued.

Eventually, at night, Harry and Frankie had run out of things to say to each other. It was Frankie who had one day decided that children would be the answer. They would make Harry happy again. They would make him open up to her and fill the void she felt in her soul. Children would make it work.

In the car, as she and Peter drove along, Frankie felt the emotion rise up in her when she thought of Tom, Rebecca and Mick. She had tried to ring Harry this morning before she and Peter left. Horrified to hear Tom's voice still on the answering machine, she had cursed Harry and put her hand to her mouth to stop herself wailing.

After the machine's beep Frankie had sucked in a breath and said icily, 'For godsakes, Harry, change that message.' She'd paused as she'd sought control. 'I'm just ringing to say that Peter and I will be arriving tomorrow at lunchtime. I just have to see . . .' Frankie's voice had faltered and wavered for a moment. '. . . see where he . . . died.' She'd hung up the phone quickly.

In the car Frankie put a hand to her mouth again and fought back tears. She looked out the window and let the bush blur by. Peter laid a gentle hand on her thigh and said, 'You okay?'

'Sure,' she said.

When they reached the front gate, she got out to open it, dragging it across the dusty road. Just then she heard the 'whump whump whump' of a helicopter overhead. Treetops stirred in the stillness.

Shutting the gate and looking skyward, Frankie said, 'Strange.'

From the front gate there were still ten kilometres of winding road to travel. When the homestead and yard at last came into view, Frankie was shocked by the flurry of activity.

The chopper, blades spinning and motor running, was in the grassy yard, stirring the still air into a crazy rush of wind. Emergency workers in orange SES uniforms and medics in white ran here and there between an ambulance, its lights flashing, and the chopper. Further away along the river's tight bend, fire trucks and forestry vehicles lumbered up and down, hosing a grass fire which was edging towards the scrub-covered hills. The smoke in the still air cast a haze over the scene.

'What on earth is going on?' asked Peter.

Frankie shook her head, a look of fear on her face. Henbury, spotting the strange orange overalls, began to bark loudly.

'Quiet, Henners,' said Peter.

As they drove into the yards, the chopper lifted from the ground and flew south in the direction of the city from which it had come. The emergency workers looked skyward and watched it fly up and over the mountain until it was out of sight.

Frankie moved about the Waters Meeting kitchen and was shocked at her familiarity with it after all the years away. She reached for cups, opened canisters and spooned crumbling mounds of tea-leaves into a large pot. She stoked the fire. There were no biscuits. She was shocked at the state of the pantry – instant noodles and tins of plain label baked beans was about all she could find. At least there was some sugar.

She glanced up. It was so odd to see Peter sitting at the Waters Meeting table. He looked so . . . so city and out of place. Around him the local volunteers chatted about the accident and the fire and glanced nervously at Frankie. They hadn't seen her in the area for years. The ambulance officers sat in the sunroom waiting for the kettle to again boil for coffee.

Amidst the chatter, Frankie tuned in on the dry voice of Harry's neighbour, Gary Tate, as he recounted his story. Peter sat across the table from Gary and watched the man's weathered face as he spoke.

'He ordered some hay last week, so I came down to deliver it. When I got to the yard I couldn't see anyone about, so I stopped me truck and came into the house yard to knock on the door and sing out a bit. Wasn't sure where to unload it, you see, and there wasn't a tractor about with forks on, so I couldn't do it on me own. Thanks love.' He took the cup of steaming tea from Frankie and slowly poured a dribble of thin powdered milk into the cup. He then spooned some sugar into the brown steaming liquid.

Frankie and Peter leaned forward waiting for him

to continue. Gary seemed to savour the moment. As he began to speak, the fire and emergency volunteers gradually stopped chatting and fell silent to again listen to the story.

'Well I was just at the garden gate when I saw smoke. Ah! I think he's over there burning off a bit. I thought to meself, It's too far to walk, I'm not taking the truck along that track, so I look in the shed and see a motorbike. I thought old Harry wouldn't mind. So I check the fuel and off I go. He'd left all the gates open so I got to the tractor pretty quick. The thing was though . . . what I thought was strange was that the fire had burnt away from the tractor and up the paddock. It wasn't in the gully at all where you'd expect to burn off. It was just creeping along, over green grass, sort of jumping from sag bush to tussock. Smoking a lot. Not doing much 'cause there was no wind.'

Peter shifted in his seat and sighed. Gary took this as a hint to get on with story and his voice moved on faster.

'That's when I saw his boots at the back end of the tractor. He was sort of half hanging, half lying with his arm stuck in the digger. He was out to it by the time I got to him. Bloody white as sheet. Thought he was dead. But when I shook his face I knew he wasn't.'

Gary paused here as he replayed the grisly discovery in his mind. He again felt the rush of nausea, and the smell of blood and smoke came back to him. He swallowed. He hoped he wasn't going to vomit again.

'Anyway, I just hot-tailed it on the bike back to

the house and phoned triple 0. They sent the lot – fire, air ambos and you guys.' He waved his cup in the direction of the ambulance drivers. Then he turned to look Frankie in the eye. Her face was pale and she was holding onto the back of a chair, unable to move.

'Bloody lucky he was, the chopper blokes said. The machine had wrapped his shirt round his arm and into his muscle so tight it had slowed the bleeding. Would've bled to death otherwise. And it was also bloody lucky he had a lighter on him, or I'd never have spotted him.'

The people in the kitchen sat in silence. Frankie, without knowing it, pulled the chair away from the table and plonked down on the hard seat.

Just then, in the silence, the door opened. A young emergency volunteer popped his head around the door.

'Hey Gaz, I've just driven the tractor back to the shed. Do ya reckon I should hose the post-hole digger down before we take it off.'

'Yeah, mate. Good idea,' said Gary, feeling important that he was considered by the younger men to be in charge of mop-up operations.

'And while you're at it, could you put the forks on the front. Then I can unload the hay. Oh, wait a minute, mate.' Gary turned to the ambulance officers. 'Do ya reckon he'll pull through . . . I mean . . .' He shifted in his seat. 'Will he be needing the hay?'

Frankie spoke sharply and almost too loudly. 'I'll write you a cheque.' The room fell silent again except for the hiss of the kettle. The young man at the door retreated outside. Frankie looked across at Peter.

He was pale and she was sure he was about to faint.

When they had waved away the last of the rescue workers, Frankie and Peter stood with their backs to the large empty house and looked out across the river flats. Henbury snuffled about at their feet, sniffing at tufts of grass and lifting his leg on fence posts. The sun was setting and painting the top of the mountains in an orange-red. It was a beautiful sight but, in the corner of her vision, Frankie could see the garage. She could sense it. Suddenly her knees felt weak. She reached out for Peter's arm to steady herself.

'Do you want to head back to the pub for the night?' Peter asked.

Frankie looked up into his eyes. 'Um . . . I'm not sure.'

They stood looking at the river flats for a time before she spoke again.

'Would you mind, Peter, if we stay the night . . . here?'

Peter smiled a thin smile. Of course he minded. He didn't want to stay in the big old house in the middle of nowhere – her ex-husband's house.

'Of course I don't mind,' he said. 'We can stay as long as you like.'

Frankie laid a grateful hand on his arm. 'Thanks. I'm sure there are some animals that will need feeding now that Harry's . . . not here.' She looked back out across the valley again. There below she could see Hank and Ink Jet grazing side by side.

'Peter?' she said cautiously.

'Mmm?'

'Can you ride a horse?'

Peter looked at her suspiciously.

'Why?'

'It's just . . . tomorrow . . . I'd love it if we could ride up to the plains. Spend a night in the hut . . . where Tom was.'

Peter swallowed and pulled an 'I don't know' face.

'Please,' she urged. 'It's something I have to do.'

'I suppose I could try.'

Frankie laughed a little as she kissed him lightly on the cheek.

'I love you, Peter Maybury.'

She ushered him inside, with Henbury following them. It was time to light the fire.

Later that night, Frankie left Peter lying in the sagging bed of the spare room and gently tiptoed around the house. Even in the dark she still knew her way. Her hand reached automatically for doorknobs. Knobs that opened the doors to her boys' rooms. She touched her fingertips on the gleaming plastic football trophies in Mick's room. In Tom's room, she stroked the pillow on Tom's bed and she opened a cupboard and held an old work jumper to her breast. Tears fell silently on the rough woollen fabric. Her fingers ran through the yarn where the elbow had worn. I must mend that for him one day, she thought.

Like a ghost in the shadows, Frankie retraced the steps of her past about the house. When she went into Harry's room, the smell hit her like a slap. The smell of him. She took a few steps towards the bed that they once shared, peering at the unmade, rumpled sheets and blankets. It was as if he was still sleeping in there. She reached out a hand and felt the coldness of the bed-spread. Then she turned her back, shutting the door and the past behind her.

Outside, still clutching Tom's jumper, she looked up at the masses of stars that crowded the night sky. The cold air sent goosebumps shivering along her skin. She walked over the cool concrete of the pathway in bare feet, then across the dewy grass and into the blackness of the garage. She crouched down amidst the dust, dead leaves and white crusty swallow droppings and she began to sob. She sobbed into the fabric of Tom's jumper. Frankie crouched there crying, with the image of her son swinging above her head.

CHAPTER 42

Charlie insisted he come too and threw his bag into the back of Rebecca's Subaru. The four dogs sniffed at the bag from their short chains and wagged their tails as he jumped into the passenger seat. Rebecca said nothing. She just started the ute and drove quickly away from the cottage. Charlie's mother came out of the house, stood by the hedge and waved slowly, watching them go. In her hand was a tin of biscuits she had hoped to give them before they made the long trip to the city.

Rebecca sped over the grid. She thought back to when she got the call from Sally.

'Bec, word's out around the office that your dad had an accident yesterday. Has anyone called you?'

Rebecca's mind raced. An accident? Was he dead?

'No. No one's called,' she said quickly.

'All I know is that he was flown to the Royal last night. I only just found out. Do you want me to go down there . . . to see how he is?'

Rebecca, pale-faced and short of breath, sat down for a minute.

'Yes. Sal. Yes, I'll leave now. I'll drive down now. And I'll meet you there this afternoon.' After she hung up the phone she ran to the toilet. She was going to be sick.

In the car now Rebecca tried to sum up her reaction to the news. Initially she was filled with concern for her father. What had happened? Would he be all right? Was he dying? Now she'd had time to think, she was not so sure how she felt. Sally hadn't given her any details, and when she'd phoned the hospital, the nurse had just said he was stable. She wasn't sure why she felt so compelled to go to him after all that had passed between them. She'd tried to phone Mick and Trudy, but all she got was their answering machine with Trudy's recorded singsong voice. In between packing her bags and refuelling the ute, Rebecca also tried to ring Frankie. There was no answer in the flat so she just left a message.

At the vet surgery Charlotte answered the phone. 'No, sorry Rebecca, your mum's not here,' she said. 'She's taken a week off and has gone away with Peter . . . for a drive somewhere.'

Rebecca had slammed down the phone.

'Bloody typical,' Bec said to the road ahead as she thought of her mother.

'What?' asked Charlie.

'Mum. She hardly ever rings me, and when she takes off on holiday, she doesn't even let me know where she's going. Now I'm supposed to deal with this Dad thing on my own. Like frigging usual.'

Charlie looked over to Bec and pushed a wisp of hair back behind her ears. 'It'll be okay, Bec,' he said gently. 'And besides, you're not dealing with it on your own. I'm here for you.'

'Oh, I don't know, Charlie,' she said, not hearing him, 'I used to think Mum was superwoman, putting up with Dad and all her work, plus us kids . . . but now . . . now, after Tom, it's changed. It's like she's never really been there for us at all. I don't think she must've ever been there for Dad . . . not with her heart and soul. She was always running away.'

'Sounds like someone I know,' said Charlie blandly. Rebecca flashed him a look.

'I used to blame it all on Dad, you know. It was always Dad's fault. But now . . . now I think I'm starting to see.'

'It takes two to tango,' said Charlie.

Rebecca fell silent and thought of her mother and father and the days they had all lived under one roof. Maybe she was remembering it wrong. A tension ran through every part of her body. She didn't slow when a truck passed them on the single strip of bitumen. The two wheels of the Subaru threw up dust and fine gravel as they veered off to one side of the road to let the truck pass.

'I think I should drive,' Charlie said gently. 'You're too upset.'

'Don't you patronise me, Charlie Lewis.'

'Don't you confuse patronising for caring, Rebecca Saunders,' said Charlie smoothly, and eventually she smiled at him.

When they stopped for fuel in the first town they swapped seats. As they drove out of town Bec touched Charlie gently on his neck and smiled at him. He smiled back. Then she leaned her head on the seat, shut her eyes and held in the tears. She was scared about what she'd find at the hospital.

Charlie and Rebecca stepped sideways as a man in a pale blue uniform wheeled a trolley past them. The smell of the hospital made Rebecca wince. It was as if she breathed too deeply she too would become ill and be trapped within the cold walls of the hospital with the sick, aged and dying. A woman in a tired-looking dressing gown wandered along the corridor in front of them, wheeling a saline drip. Her face was sullen and grey. She glared at Rebecca, as if reading her thoughts.

'I hate hospitals,' Bec whispered to Charlie.

The corridor opened up into a large reception area and waiting room. In the corner on a plump chair was Sally. She was sitting near the receptionist's desk next to a statue of the Virgin Mary. Mary's head was bowed downwards under a veil, as if gazing solemnly at Sally. When Sally stood, Rebecca noticed how thin she'd become and how pale her face was, but her eyes shone with warmth to see her friend again. They hugged.

'Charlie,' Sally said warmly and hugged him too.

'Sorry we're a bit late – traffic,' he said.

'It's okay. Me and the Virgin Mary here have been yarning away.' She leaned towards them and whispered, 'Bit of a bore really – we don't have that much in common.'

'I wouldn't imagine you would,' smiled Bec. 'You should've gone in to see Dad instead of waiting for us and yakking to the Virgin.'

'Nah! I hate going to see people in hospitals. Thought I'd wait for you guys. Besides, when I asked where he was they said only close family could go in to see him.'

'As if I'm classed as "close",' said Rebecca sarcastically. 'You're coming too, Sal, you're his counsellor, remember?' Rebecca tweaked Sally on her sleeve.

'His rural *financial* counsellor, not his post-op counsellor.' She looked at Rebecca's face, then conceded. 'Oh all right then. He's on the third floor,' she nodded towards the lifts.

The three walked over in silence, all frightened at what they might find up there in the ward. Inside the lift's stainless-steel interior Bec could barely breathe. She reached for Charlie's hand. He held it tightly. As the doors slid open Sally said, 'You go in and see him first. I'll wait outside.'

'No. No, Sal. Come in with us. I'll need both of you.' Rebecca's blue eyes pleaded with her.

At first, in the large ward, Rebecca's eyes scanned past the old man who slept, propped up on pillows in the too-narrow bed. Then her eyes roamed back to him and with shock she recognised the old man to be her father.

She looked up at Charlie and indicated the bed. His eyes followed her gentle gesture and came to rest on Harry. All of them looked at the place where his right arm should have been. A rounded stump beneath a swathe of bandages rested on the pillow.

When Rebecca stood by his bedside and touched him on his left arm he woke with a start.

'Oh! G'day,' he said in a crackling soft voice. He pulled up the sheets as if trying to cover his embarrassment. Rebecca was shocked at how weak he seemed.

She tried to avert her eyes from the bruise which began as black from beneath the bandaged stump and then faded to strange mottled yellow and purple hues across his bare chest and neck.

'How are you, Dad?'

'Could be better.' His voice was barely a whisper through dry, crusty lips. The whites of his eyes had yellowed. He looked at the foot of the bed as he spoke. He couldn't look at his daughter. There was silence in the room except for the snoring of another patient and the chatter of a television mounted high in the corner.

'I don't think you've met Charlie properly yet, Dad. Charlie Lewis.' Rebecca nodded towards Charlie who stood beside her. Harry looked at him and said weakly, 'I'd shake hands but . . .' his voice trailed off.

Charlie, not sure if he should laugh at Harry's attempt at a joke, waved a hand in the air and said, 'Nice to meet you, Mr Saunders.'

'And you know Sal.'

Harry nodded in her direction.

Silence again. Charlie and Harry turned their eyes to the television and watched the news clips of a golf tournament. Sally rummaged in her bag and produced an assortment of Landcare and farming magazines.

'I brought you these.' She placed them on the cabinet beside his bed. As he nodded in thanks, Rebecca's heart raced. She could feel the pulse in her neck thumping beneath her skin. She looked at her father's profile and suddenly wanted to scream at him. She wanted to hit, bash and claw him, heap all her rage over Tom onto him. Hate him. Mock him. Spit on him.

But he turned to look at her and said, 'Bec. I'm sorry. I didn't expect you to come.' Tears started to run over the red rims of his eyes and he began to shudder and sob. He awkwardly put his left hand up to his eyes and wiped a big smear of tears across his face. Charlie watched the golf. Sally straightened the magazines and Bec stood numbly by the bed, not knowing what to say as Harry's shoulders hunched and shook and he wiped snot and saliva away with the back of his hand.

'I'm sorry. You'd better go. I'm sorry.' What he said was barely audible. He tried to get the words out again, but they came out in deep moaning sobs. The other patients looked over at him. Charlie and Sally looked at each other and then left the room. Rebecca, tears now rolling from her eyes, reached for a box of tissues by his bed. She pulled out one for herself, then sat the box next to him. She drew the blue curtain around her father and left him there in the bed. She walked away down the corridor quickly, trying not to listen to the sobbing man behind her.

Outside a shock of sunlight and the roar of traffic beyond the hospital's garden hit Rebecca's senses with a jolt. Bec, Charlie and Sally squinted in the brightness, not knowing what to do or say.

'Shall we sit over there for a while?' Sally suggested, pointing to a seat beneath a shady oak tree.

On the seat Charlie put his arm around Bec and she rested her head on his shoulder. With a clenched fist she held the sodden tissue in her hand. Sal kicked at the pile of cigarette butts which lay on woodchips beneath the seat.

At last Sally said, 'Do you want to hear my theory on life?'

'Sure,' said Bec.

'Don't laugh.'

'Okay.'

She spoke with her jaw jutting out. 'I believe people get sick or have accidents for a reason. Your dad's sabotaged himself because he wants you back. It's his way of punishing himself over everything that's happened. It's why he's lost his arm.'

Rebecca sat up and looked at her friend. A deep frown line furrowed her brow. Sally shifted a little and softened her voice.

'I know you might think this is none of my business and it's hard to hear the meaning of life from a drunken, boy-chasing friend like me who broke your brother's heart, but if you want to be happy, Bec, you're going to have to sort this out. Your dad is the sort of bloke who won't ask for help. He won't, or at least can't, ask you to come home. He can't tell you he loves you. He can't say he's sorry. It's just him. So life, the universe and everything has construed to bring this accident upon him, so that you can forgive him.'

'Forgive him!' exploded Bec. 'How dare you tell me I should forgive that bastard! He virtually killed my brother!'

'Bec.' Charlie pleaded. 'Hear her out. You've got to deal with this.'

She looked deep into his eyes. Sally put her hand on Rebecca's arm. Sally was crying now.

'Do you think I want to tell you this? I've virtually gutted myself over Tom's death. I led him on. In my own little selfish way, I led him on. I liked the attention . . . and the fact a bloke was bonkers over me. If only I'd been truthful with myself and him, he mightn't've . . . left us . . .'

'Shhh!' said Rebecca. 'It's okay Sal. It's okay.'

The two girls hugged and each wiped tears from their faces. Charlie sat alone on the end of the bench. Staring. Swallowing. He knew what would come next.

'Go back in and see him, Bec,' Sally urged. 'It's your chance with Waters Meeting. Do it. It's your chance.'

Bec looked at her friend and drew in a deep breath. She stood suddenly and jogged away from Charlie and Sally towards the heavy glass doors of the hospital. Charlie watched her disappear into the massive building.

When Bec slipped in through the gap in the curtain, Harry was staring at the two lumps that were his feet beneath the white cotton bedspread.

'Dad?'

He looked up, startled again. Then he patted the bed for her to sit. It was a strange action coming from Harry. She propped herself awkwardly on the edge of the bed.

'Dad,' she said, not knowing what to say next. The silence between them was painful and awkward. Instead Harry spoke for her. Through his pale thin lips he talked gently.

'Rebecca, I want you to come home. I want you to take on the place. I need you.'

For a moment Rebecca felt a rush of warmth run through her. How often had she dreamt of her father saying those words? But the joy was short-lived. The anger came again.

'You need me? You're saying you need me? Huh! That's obvious,' she pointed at his stump. 'You used Tom on the farm. Now he's gone, you want to use me... What's changed, Dad? Is a young woman more useful than an old man with one arm?'

She could see the stab of pain in his eyes from her hurtful words.

'Bec,' he said quietly, 'I can understand your anger,

but just this time, give me a chance. I decided before this,' Harry inclined his head towards the freshly bandaged stump. 'I decided before this happened. I was going to call you. I was going to ask if you'd come home. I promise. I was.'

Rebecca looked into his eyes and she believed him. Her father might have been a hard, silent man, but he certainly wasn't a liar.

He continued, a pleading look stretched across his face. 'If you want to come home, it's there. I'm sorry it's taken so much for me to realise.'

Rebecca knew he was referring to Tom, but saying his name was still too painful for Harry.

'What do you say?' Harry reached out his hand across his body and placed it lightly on Rebecca's hand.

'I don't know what to say,' she said with tears in her eyes as she felt the unfamiliar gentleness of his touch.

'Don't say anything yet,' said Harry. 'Just come here and give me a hug.'

Cautiously, Rebecca leaned towards her father as he awkwardly put his hand around her head and pulled her to his chest. He smelt of soap. She thought she might cry, but instead she stayed rigid, not trusting the moment. She drew away from him after a short while.

'I'm sorry I've never been much of a hugger,' Harry said. 'If I had been, your mother might have stuck around longer.'

Rebecca shook her head sadly and then the tears

began to fall. That's when she found herself being cradled by her dad. Cradled in his one strong arm. Her hair being stroked by his one strong hand. She felt him kiss her on the crown of her head as he shushed her. Then he said it. He said, 'I love you.' And he began to cry too.

CHAPTER 43

In the stifling heat of the grain truck's cab, Rebecca had played the images over and over in her head as she drove along the straight line of bitumen during harvest. She had pictured taking Charlie there, to Waters Meeting. The two of them swimming naked in the cool river. Lying on damp green clover beneath dappled shade. Making love in her big airy bedroom with the verandah doors open, curtains blowing softly and gum trees casting shadows on their skin. But when she drove her Subaru into the yard at Waters Meeting the images dissolved. For one thing, Charlie wasn't in the vehicle with her, so they hadn't been together to share the spectacular view when they drove into the valley. Instead he was following behind in his ute.

They had fought about the journey in the tiny cottage at the Lewises' farm. Charlie had insisted he needed his vehicle in case he had to rush home to the farm for work. His father had insisted too.

On the drive into her home district, Rebecca had wanted Charlie by her side, so she could tell him everything about the country and the farms they drove past. About the time when they drove Mick's old Morris into the dam just past Dirty's pub. Or the night Rebecca rode Ink Jet all the way home from the pub after her eighteenth birthday, so drunk she remembered waking up at the front gate and finding wattle flowers in her pocket and her saddlebags rattling with empty cans of Dark and Stormy.

Today's trip from Charlie's flat land to the valley had felt extra long. The distance that stretched between the two farms put a feeling of desperation into Rebecca's heart. When they swung their vehicles into service stations along the way for fuel and food, the mood between them was tense. A few words, a quick kiss, and they were back on the road again. Each alone in their vehicles with a monologue of uncertain thoughts running through their heads. Rebecca didn't even stop at the Fur Trapper. She drove straight on by. In her dream she had taken Charlie there for a beer and a back slap from Dirty before driving him on to Waters Meeting.

Now that she was here, standing on the weedy gravel drive, Rebecca's heart sank further. The farm had changed so much. She'd noticed it right from the front gate. Potholes in the road, thistles and ferns overrunning what was once improved pasture. Fences lying on the ground as if they'd just given up. What was the point anyway, there was no stock to keep in or out.

The house, instead of looking like her charming

childhood home set amidst greenery, looked shabby and old, like a beautiful woman who no longer cared. Everything had given up. Grey branches from the big pines had cracked and fallen across the once-sentinel garden fence. The branches stuck up into the air at angry angles like broken shards of bones. The sheds looked rough and tumble. Boards slipped from their sides and tin flapped and banged steadily in the wind.

When she stopped the ute near the side gate of the garden, Rebecca remembered her dogs that were clipped on the back. Dags, Mossy, Bessie and Stubby were dancing with excitement to be let off, especially Tom's dog, Bessie. They knew they were home. Bec suspected Bessie would go looking for Tom straightaway, even as far as the hut.

'Settle down,' Bec growled at them. She unclipped them all except for Bessie. 'Sorry, girl.' She stroked her. 'In a little while.'

Charlie parked next to her vehicle, got out of his ute and stretched, looking around and up at the massive mountains which shot up suddenly from the grassy flats.

'Phew!' he said. 'Real goat country.'

The comment stung her. She grabbed her dusty bags from the back and walked towards the house, swearing as she struggled with the gate's chain.

'Calm down,' Charlie said as he helped her with it.

It was obvious Ink Jet and Hank had found their way into the garden earlier that morning. They had left trails of fresh manure across the pathways and eaten some of the garden-bed plants down to thick green stalks.

From the front gate Bec looked for the horses. Her eyes searched for a black dot and a chestnut dot dozing beneath a tree on the river flat, tails swishing away an occasional fly. But instead the river flats were bare.

'I wonder where Hank and Stinky are,' she said, more to herself than Charlie. Charlie followed her gaze.

'They'll be about,' he said.

She'd imagined coming home to the horses and calling out to them. In her mind they had come cantering and whickering towards her. But there was no sign of them. Another piece of her dream slipped away.

On the porch, flies buzzed in the shade. Cobwebs spun across the openings of cracked leather boots had caught soft fuzzy seeds of dandelions and sharp slivers of grass seeds. From out of the laundry the wormy ginger cat trotted, greeting them with a high-pitched friendly meow. Bec felt his ribby side rub against her leg. She picked him up.

'Helloooo,' she said softly and was appalled to see the fleas and weeping sores spread over his body.

'Don't worry, puss. I'm home now.' She put the purring cat down. 'We'll feed you up in no time.'

As she searched for the key in the boot box, Charlie kept his hands in his pockets and his mouth shut.

It was dark inside. All the curtains had been drawn. The deep interior of the house was silent except for the buzz of a large blowfly which flew past their heads as they stood, waiting for their eyes to grow used to the dimness of the hallway.

381

Light from the sunroom made a square on the carpet in the hall. Rebecca moved towards it and entered the kitchen. The room smelt of Pinoclean.

'I reckon Dirty's wife's been here to clean up after Dad's accident,' Bec said aloud to herself.

She began to open the cupboards and look in the fridge.

'Strange,' she said. 'Whoever it was who cleaned up has also stocked the pantry and fridge.' She picked up the box of Pistachio Café Selection biscuits.

'It doesn't look like it was anyone from town . . . especially not Dirty's wife.' She picked up the packet of half-eaten camembert cheese.

'Definitely not Dirty's wife . . .'

'What?' said Charlie, walking into the kitchen.

'I said, someone has been here since the accident.'

'This place is huge!' he said, ignoring her and looking up at the old ceilings, stunned by the size of the house.

'And empty,' said Bec.

As she stood there in the kitchen Bec wasn't sure what to do. Where to start. She felt like calling out for Tom. He'd be along the hall somewhere, in the office, or his room upstairs. She stood for a moment choking back tears. Charlie put his arms around her from behind and kissed her neck.

'Cup of tea?' she said in a voice that almost cracked. Then she broke away from him and moved to the kettle, wondering why it felt as if she were entertaining a stranger.

'I'll get the milk and other stuff out of the car,' said Charlie.

As the electric kettle boiled in the kitchen, Rebecca ran from room to room, roughly tugging back curtains and sending the blinds whipping up in a noisy flurry. She wanted light and life in the house again. In the office the red light flashed angrily and urgently on the message machine. Bec knew it would be clogged with calls from the bank manager, stock agencies wanting payments, messages about Harry's accident. She decided to listen to them later.

From the damp darkness of the dining room Bec knelt on an old sofa and peered out the window. Through the dull light of the pines she saw the garage. It looked sinister. She imagined Tom hanging there and shuddered.

'Helllooooo?' Charlie was wandering down the hall looking into the rooms, trying to like the musty smell of the old house. Trying to feel comfortable in it, for Bec's sake.

'I think I've solved the mystery of the restocked cupboards,' he said with a grin. 'I just had a poke about the sheds, and your mum's car is parked in one.'

'Mum?' said Rebecca with surprise. 'What's she doing here?'

'I sung out, but there's definitely no one about,' said Charlie.

'Ahh. That explains Inky and Hank. They must've gone for a ride on them.'

Rebecca fell silent, trying to absorb the strangeness

of what was happening. The strangeness of being back at Waters Meeting. Of her mother being here, somewhere.

Charlie stood in the doorway, trying to read her mood. 'The kettle's boiled,' he said.

Rebecca turned her back to the view of the garage and ran to him. She sucked in a breath and looked at him. Leaning there on the doorframe in his jeans and blue shirt. Sleeves rolled up, green eyes shining. She felt a wave of desire run through her.

'Come on,' she said, holding out her hand. 'We'll have a cuppa later. I'll show you upstairs . . . and my bedroom.' She waggled her eyebrows and grinned. 'Before Mum and Peter get back . . .' All of a sudden she wanted to feel alive. Wanted the warmth and comfort of Charlie's smooth skin against her, to shut out the coldness, shut out death and the decay of the house and farm.

She took him by the hand and led him up the creaking stairs. He ran his hand over the smooth wood of the banister and followed her up.

She planned to throw him down on the bed and love him so hard he would never leave for the flat country again. And then tomorrow she planned to take him for a mountain horse ride so he could lose himself in the wildness of her landscape. She played it over in her head. But instead when she threw open the door of her room the thick smell of death choked in her throat. She looked to the brown patch on the ceiling and fresh fat squirming maggots on the cover of her bedspread.

'Bloody possums,' she said and sighed.

———

The last of the day had turned grey, and misty clouds clung to the sides of the mountains. Mossy was sniffing about the garden when she let out a sudden bark. The other dogs pricked their ears and barked too, following Mossy's stare towards the river crossing. Rebecca looked up and was relieved to see Frankie and Peter splashing across the shining stones riding Ink Jet and Hank. A footsore Henbury waddled some distance behind. A smile came to Rebecca's face.

'Charlie!' she called over her shoulder. 'They're back . . . They won't get caught in the rain after all.'

Charlie emerged from the side of the house, wiping his hands together having just tossed the dead possum on a wood heap. He rinsed his hands under a tap and stood watching the black mare and chestnut gelding walking fast over the paddocks towards them. Frankie rode a little way ahead on Ink Jet while Hank ambled quickly behind with his ears pricked up. Soon they'd be taking off the saddles, saddlebags and sleeping rolls and the horses would be set free to trot away together and sniff and paw at the ground, preparing to roll on the grass with grunts of pleasure.

Rebecca laughed a little when she saw Peter on Hank. He sat with rounded shoulders, clearly uncomfortable with Hank's quickened homecoming gait. Peter's smile of greeting when he saw Rebecca and Charlie on the rise was more like a grimace.

'Poor Peter!' Bec said. 'Looks like we better run him a hot bath.'

Rebecca jogged towards them, Charlie following a

little way behind. The dogs scouted out ahead, their tails and their whole bodies wagging joyfully at the sight of Hank and Ink Jet. The horses tossed their heads in greeting to the dogs and whickered. Bec opened the gate and waited for them there.

'Mum! Peter! Hi!' She walked up to Ink Jet and put her arms about her wide neck and pressed her cheek to the mare's warm coat. Then she ran a hand along Hank's long smooth neck.

'Hello, you two,' she said gently to the horses, then she turned her face up to her mother and smiled. 'Fancy seeing you here.'

In the kitchen, with the stove roaring and the saucepans rattling, the house seemed almost normal. Rebecca took comfort in the scene. Her mother, putting out plates for the dinner. Peter, fresh from the bath, sitting by the stove in a whicker chair rubbing his bruised calf muscles. And Charlie chopping up apples for the fruit salad.

Peter looked up at Charlie. 'Can you ride a horse? For your sake, I hope so . . . If you're going to hang around these girls, you'll need to learn. And believe me, it's not as easy as it seems.'

Charlie laughed a little. 'I can ride a bit.'

'A bit!' Rebecca interrupted. 'Charlie worked on a station up north for a year when he first left school. He was thrown straight into the saddle, and from what I hear, he was a natural. He came home a cowboy . . . although he hides it well.'

386

'It's been a while since I was on a horse. The closest thing to horses I've been on lately are shopping trolleys . . . sometimes just as fickle and pigheaded.'

Rebecca smiled at him. 'How about tomorrow? We could take a ride about the place and try to work out what's left of the stock. Did you see any on your ride, Mum?'

'No. Not a single beast, apart from the cows on the flats.'

Frankie had been quiet this evening. She was still reeling from the night she had spent in the hut, lying in the tiny camp bed where Tom had slept. Peter, being the gentleman, had lain on the sleeping mat on the uneven floor by the bed. She had listened to his breathing as he slept and had tried to pretend it was Tom lying there breathing next to her. In and out. The breath of Tom. She'd not slept a wink and had listened to every noise the hut gave to her. The creak of tin, the tap of the door blowing in the breeze, the dull murmurs of the stove as it burned slowly.

Coming back to Waters Meeting had been harder than Frankie had ever imagined. Now that she had been to the hut, she felt an overwhelming urge to leave. The house, the memories . . . it had all become too much to bear. She wanted to escape back to her comfortable life with Peter and leave the ghosts of her past life behind. She looked up guiltily at Rebecca.

'Peter and I have decided to head off in the morning. You don't mind, do you? We had planned to spend a few nights on the coast before we headed back to work.'

'No! You go on. Charlie and I will be fine. You have a break.' Rebecca tried to make her voice sound light, but a tinge of resentment crept in and gave her voice an edge, an edge her mother recognised.

'Come on Bec,' Frankie said. 'There's a little while before dinner. I'll help you put fresh sheets on your bed.' Reluctantly, Rebecca stood up and followed her mother out of the kitchen.

In the bedroom Rebecca was silent as Frankie bustled and chatted, smoothing the sheets down on the mattress, trying to cover the tension in her voice.

'There,' she said, putting her hands on her hips, 'all nice for you and Charlie.' She looked at her daughter. 'How long is he staying?'

Rebecca sat heavily on the end of the bed and said flatly, 'I don't know.' She sighed.

Her mother came to sit next to her.

'Rebecca. Do you really think it's a good idea, coming back here? I mean, aren't you better off with Charlie on his place . . . at least it's a farm that's up and running . . . and without sounding like a cliched mother, he's a nice boy. A really lovely man and I can see he adores you.'

Rebecca felt a redness flush into her cheeks. 'Don't you think it's a little late to be giving mother–daughter lectures to me in my bedroom? And how can you say that? How can you say that I should give all this up just because it'll be easier? You've never understood, have you? Never. You've never belonged here and you've always resented the fact that I do. You've always run away. You've never been there for us! Never.'

'That's not true and you know it! What about all the times I picked up the pieces for you when you were at school in the city . . . all the times I protected you from your father? Don't you try and dump that on me, Rebecca Saunders. You're old enough and brave enough to understand. Sometimes marriages just don't work out – and that's it. Your father and I weren't meant to be together. I stuck at it for as long as I could for your sakes. I stayed for as long as I could. I gave you as much as I could at the time. I'm sorry, Rebecca, if that wasn't good enough for you. But don't you dump any more guilt on me. Do you think I don't carry enough around with me now . . . especially after . . . Tom.' Tears came to Frankie's eyes and Rebecca looked at her mother as she began to sob.

'I'm sorry,' she said quietly and placed a hand on Frankie's arm. 'It's just, it was you who taught me to go out and get what I want. You always wanted your own practice, and now look at you – there's room to expand and buy another. If you'd hung around here because everyone else said you should, you would never have reached your dream. You left . . . and did what your heart really wanted. And this is what my heart really wants. This place here. So don't you tell me, Mum, to just give it all away.'

Rebecca had always blamed her mother's departure squarely on her father. She had held Frankie up on a pedestal for so long that it was almost a relief to discover the truth about her. That she was human, with all the faults and fears of a human, the same as her father.

389

When she thought of her father she felt a tension in her spine and a rush of fear for the future of Waters Meeting and for her future with Charlie. Her face crumpled with anxiety, and she tried to swallow the emotions back down.

'Oh, Mum. It's so hard.'

Her mother stroked her hair as she cried. 'I know. But remember I love you, darling. And I'll support you in any decision you make ... and ... I'm proud of you.' Frankie put an arm around Rebecca's shoulders and pulled her daughter near. They sat there for a time.

'Thanks Mum,' Rebecca said at last, straightening herself up and blowing her nose on a tissue. She took a deep breath. 'I reckon the spuds will be cooked now.'

In the darkness Rebecca and Charlie made love in her bedroom. There was a sadness to it all. A tenderness that touched Rebecca so much she cried silent tears as she felt Charlie's smooth warm skin on hers. She kissed him on his face and eyelids and along the curve of his neck.

'I love you,' she said to the dark shadow of him.

'I love you too,' he said.

Standing naked in the soft morning light, Charlie opened the French doors of Rebecca's bedroom and a cool breeze blew in, stirring the curtains. Rebecca rolled over and looked at the naked beauty of him. His skin golden. The gumleaves outside the verandah moved in the breeze, framing him. Magpies sung a wavering tune. For a moment Rebecca's dream was alive in the room. He walked over to her and stood before her. He took her hand.

'Morning, beautiful,' he said with a smile and he kissed her gently on the head. She could hear the pipes clunking in the house and knew Frankie or Peter were in the shower. There was time to pull Charlie back into the warmth of the bed for a few more minutes before they went downstairs to breakfast. She took both his hands and drew him towards her. Then the phone rang downstairs.

'I bet that's Mum,' said Charlie. 'I'll get it.'

She rolled her eyes as he let go of her hands. He slipped on his jeans, hurried out of the room and dashed downstairs. Wrapped in a sheet, she sat at the top of the stairs and listened to his voice echo up the stairwell. It seemed to change when he spoke to his mother.

Later that morning, when Rebecca and Charlie entered the kitchen, Frankie had already made a pot of tea. The smell of warm toast filled the room. She had stoked up the fire so the room was pleasantly warm. She stood behind Peter, massaging his shoulders. The cat slept curled up on his lap.

'Morning,' Frankie smiled.

'Hi,' said Bec, reaching for a slice of toast.

'We thought we'd get an early start,' said Peter, 'Well, your *mother* thought we'd get an early start. She kicked me out of bed and called me a lazy city slicker.' He pulled a face as she squeezed too hard. 'Ouch!'

Rebecca smiled at their antics, desperately wishing they would stay longer, but too proud to ask.

After breakfast Rebecca and Charlie helped carry their bags to the car.

'Now, I've left all of the food for you in the fridge,' Frankie said. 'We'll be back at the flat in a couple of days, so give me a ring if you need anything. I'll come up one weekend soon and help you clean up the garden and the house, so you can have more time to concentrate on sorting out what you're going to do with the farm.'

'Thanks Mum. We'll be fine,' Rebecca said as she hugged her mother and kissed Peter on the cheek. Charlie was just kissing Frankie goodbye when they heard the phone ring from inside the house.

'I'll go,' said Charlie as he jogged inside the house.

'It'll be his mum,' Rebecca said dryly.

Frankie smiled, 'Bloody mums, eh?'

'Yeah,' said Rebecca as she rolled her eyes in mock disgust. Another quick hug and Frankie and Peter were gone, the sound of their car engine buzzing through the bushland.

Rebecca held one hand in the air, waving to them as they passed along a clearing; her other hand stroked Dags's ear as he sat beside her.

'You stay near the house,' she said to the dogs. When she disappeared inside they settled down on the lawn to doze in the sun. The ginger cat walked slowly up to Mossy and rubbed itself against her, flopping down next to her in the morning sunshine.

In the office Rebecca stood behind Charlie, looking at his broad shoulders as he spoke. She folded her arms across her chest. She knew what would come after he hung up the phone.

'That was Mum again,' he said when he turned to her. Rebecca clenched her jaw.

'Dad's got a big contracting job – sowing for the Cotton Co. They need me back to run the farm. Glen's back from boarding school, but he's not up to it on his own yet.' Charlie stooped a little to look directly into Rebecca's eyes. 'But it's okay, they don't really need me just yet. I can leave tomorrow.'

'Tomorrow! Great,' said Rebecca flatly as she stomped down the hall away from him.

'What? What can I do about it? I didn't know he'd get the contract,' Charlie said, following her with outstretched hands.

She stopped at the kitchen door and stared at him, the hurt and anger rising in her blood. 'Nothing. No, that's great. A whole three days here is great. For chrissakes Charlie, you haven't had a break from that place since you got home from college – no weekends, nothing . . . They could at least give you –'

'Oh come on, Bec, do you really think staying here for a week will be a break for me? We haven't even seen the rest of the farm, but the yard and sheds are a mess . . . and as for this house, what can I do here for you in a week? It'll take a lifetime to fix this mess.'

'Oh! A bit of support would be nice!'

'Support! Ever since we've been going out I've given you support – through your family dramas, tiptoeing around your moods, dealing with Tom's death.'

The words opened up a silence between them as thoughts flew around Rebecca's head. Suddenly she was ranting in a voice that was seemed to belong to someone else.

'Oh! So *that's* how it's been! I've been a burden for you. Tom, the whole deal . . . You've just been playing the role of supportive boyfriend, and all along you've been resenting me! Can't you see how hard it's been for me? It's not just this,' she gestured wildly, indicating the house and farm, 'but trying to fit in with your family! They never once acknowledged the work I did, let alone paid me. They never once let me really get involved. I'm not good enough for their firstborn. Nowhere near. They can't wait to see the back of me!'

'That's not true!'

'Bull, Charlie! They want you to have a wife who gardens and cooks and has a nice little off-farm income like teaching or nursing. Or volunteer stuff, like making sandwiches for tennis days! Well I'm not going to sit back and watch you do all the work. I can't. I want to work alongside you. You're just a slave to your father. And a mummy's boy to boot. I've landed right back in the situation I was when I lived here!'

'Oh that's nice. Really nice.' He clenched his jaw and a small muscle moved under his skin. Anger pumped blood into his cheeks. 'What do you expect me to do? Drop everything I have at home and come here to help you drag this place out of debt?'

'Drop everything at home? What do you mean by that? Charlie, you don't have *anything* at home. Your dad controls it all and your mum controls you!'

'Don't you start giving me lectures about family – at least mine sticks together. With a family like yours, you're not in a position to give advice! And as if I'm in a position to step into this mess!' He turned his back and walked into the kitchen. Rebecca followed him to where he stood at the sink looking out the window at the pines.

'Charlie. We've got to sort this out! You have to talk it through with me.'

'Sort it out! Talk it through? How can we sort it out? We've been through it before. It never changes.' He turned to her and held both her arms. There were tears in his eyes. It shocked her.

'I've been wanting to ask you to marry me . . . I love you Bec . . .'

The words washed over her and for a moment filled her with joy. But Charlie continued speaking in low tones.

'I know you hate it at home and you feel like you don't fit in with my family . . .' He began to sound urgent and spoke quickly, pleadingly. 'I know you don't like the flat cropping country but we can work it out. We'll get some stock. You can run the sheep. We'll bring your horses home with us. We don't have to live in the cottage near Mum and Dad's. We can build another house further away.'

Rebecca tried to picture this new world, this new future with Charlie.

'No.' she said too suddenly. She began to back away from him. 'No. I've just got back here. I'm not leaving now. Not ever again.'

'But there's nothing here for you! Besides, what can you do with this place on your own?'

'What do you mean, on my own? You don't think a female's capable of doing this! You're starting to sound as sexist as our fathers.'

'Don't be stupid, Bec.'

'Stupid! You're just like all the other bastards! You think I don't have a right to work the land, but because you're a man, you do! You're entitled to your bit of flat, chemical-and-salt-infected dirt, but I'm not entitled to my rundown, destocked bit of mountain country. Don't you stand there and tell me there's nothing here for me. I've got a chance to fight for this place . . . I'm entitled to it!'

'Fine,' said Charlie, as he spun around and walked out of the room. He ran up the stairs and began to throw his clothes into his bag.

'Charlie!' There was hysteria in her voice as she entered the room and saw what he was doing. He shook off her hands which clung to his shirt.

'Leave me alone!' Angrily he zipped up his bag and marched loudly down the stairs, along the hallway and out the door. The dogs rose to their feet as the door slammed and looked anxiously from Bec to Charlie. They knew something was wrong so they hovered near Rebecca.

'Where are you going?' She jogged after him.

He yelled as he walked down the path, 'It's your choice, Bec! You've chosen this place and your father over me! Fine. I'll leave you to it! Have fun.'

He opened the door of the ute and got in.

'Charlie,' said Bec, her voice rising in panic. 'Charlie! Don't leave yet.'

He looked at her with tears spilling from his green eyes. 'Leave *yet*? You've got no intention of coming home with me. You've never thought it was enough just to be with me in life. You're too bloody selfish. Like your father.'

He was trying with every muscle in his body to hold back the tears. He clenched his jaw and started the engine.

Rebecca grabbed at the handle to open the door but he roughly pulled it shut. Her face red, tears falling, she screamed at him, 'No Charlie, don't go! Don't leave me!' He took one last look at her and drove quickly away. She sunk onto the dirt and sobbed.

The rage came out in throaty screams as she tugged on her hair. Years of anger poured out. She sobbed until she was curled in a ball in the dust. Her dogs came to lick at her tear-stained face. Mossy sat a little way off and began to howl with Bec's screams.

When she opened her eyes she saw a sideways view of the farm. The sound of a gentle breeze ran through the tin and timber of the sheds. At the corner of her view were the dark pines and the garage. She rose to her feet and ran to the machinery shed, rolling back the heavy wooden doors so light spilled into its cluttered, oil-stained interior. She gritted her teeth as she moved about the shed like a madwoman, throwing bits and pieces into the back of the farm ute. She threw in a tin of fuel, earmuffs, gloves, chains and hefted the largest chainsaw onto the flat tray. Tears stung her skin. The dogs, sensing her mood, slunk away and sat at the back door looking fearful.

Rebecca drove the ute near to the garage and, bending down over the chainsaw, she ripped at the pull cord. It wouldn't start. Furious, she tried again, making angry noises through her teeth as she pulled again and again on the starter cord. At last the chainsaw spluttered to life.

Uncut, the gnarled base of the pine didn't seem like wood. It was an eerie smooth grey colour like dead man's flesh and it made her feel nauseous. When the metal chain of the saw hit the surface the thickness of the wood surprised her. Then the outer bark gave way to softer wood as sawdust flew from the neat line cut by the chainsaw. The tree's limbs shook as she made two cuts on one side and then began to chainsaw the other. She hoped she'd made the cuts in the right place.

She could feel the tree about to give way and stepped backwards. When it fell the echo of its crash slammed through her whole body. The garage on which it fell seemed to splinter into hundreds of pieces and the corrugated iron crumpled and tore like tinsel. She stood for a moment, puffing and watching until the branches no longer moved, as though she was waiting for a giant beast to die. Then she began on the next tree.

By the time a blackness had settled across the valley, Rebecca had cut down all the massive pines and had dragged them over to two piles using a chain on the largest John Deere tractor. Dead branches, pinecones and needles were scattered all over the yard and in the house garden. It was like a battlefield. Dragging dead weights over dirt and piling them up for a mass burning. She knew green pine burnt well. She lugged the drum of diesel from the back of the ute and took a box of matches from the glove box.

The pine fizzed with sap and squealed and oozed. The dry timber of the garage crackled and blackened amidst licking orange flames. Outside the ring of heat the night was cold and wintry. She pulled her shirt about her and hugged herself. It was a black night. She continued to watch the garage burn until long after the red glow of the hot corrugated iron had died down to nothing.

Inside, she slept on Tom's bed and held his football which she'd tucked into his footy jumper. She rolled up in a ball. Every muscle in her body ached and her bloodied hands curled like chicken's claws. They were raw and sore and bled from scratches and blisters, despite the gloves.

At last, when she woke, the house was ablaze with golden morning sunlight. From every window she could see the mountains. She ran to each room and saw the light shine in. She felt better, for a moment. And then she thought of Charlie and she began to cry again.

C H A P T E R 4 4

'Wow!' said Sally as she put her hands on her hips and looked at the decimated pile of pines and giant stumps which still bled sap.

'When you get upset, you *really do* get upset!' She turned to her friend. 'You could've killed yourself doing that, you *dickhead*.'

Rebecca hung her head and folded her arms across her chest. Sally swung a gentle punch, hitting Bec on the upper arm, and hugged her quickly.

'Come on. Inside. We've got work to do.'

In the kitchen Sally dumped her heavy briefcase onto the table and flicked open the clasps. From it she pulled the thick bound copy of Gabs' and Rebecca's farm business assignment, a pad of paper and pens. Next, she pulled out a bottle of Bundy.

'Thought we could use this to help lubricate the mental faculties.' She sat the bottle of rum on the table. 'Grab some cups and open her up.'

Rebecca shuffled over to the cupboard and awkwardly tried to pull at the door handle. Her hands were cramped and curled up. Blood had sealed the cuts shut, so that when she stretched her fingers they tore and bled again. She winced as she tried to pick up the cups. Sally, busy shuffling through documents, looked up.

'Oh, Bec! What have you done to yourself?' She took her hands and looked at them closely.

'God! They're a mess! You *dickhead*! You must've really lost it yesterday during the great pine-tree massacre!'

'I did go a bit feral.' Rebecca sank into the chair and watched Sally mix the rum with spitting, fizzing coke.

'I think I knew all along Charlie wouldn't stay. But I thought . . . I thought he'd at least give it a go . . . just for a little while. He tried to act pleased when I told him Dad was going to let me take the farm on, but I knew . . . I knew he was gutted. Oh, Sal! What do I do?'

Sally handed her a drink. 'There's only one thing to do . . .'

Bec looked at her while she sipped at her drink, squinting her eyes above the spray of fizz which landed on her nose and cheeks.

'You've got to follow your dreams . . . Now is your dream Charlie or is it this place?'

'Both. They're both my dreams! Sal, why is everything so complicated? Should I call him? I could go back there . . . and . . . put a manager on here or something, once it's up and running again.'

'Would that make you happy?'

'No,' said Bec quietly as she looked down miserably into her now empty glass.

'Well?' There was silence between them as Sally poured another glass of rum and coke. Then, Bec spoke.

'Bugger Charlie Lewis, he's just a mummy's boy. Let's get this show on the road! *This* is my dream!' She swung her glass over the table and toasted the view from the window. With the pine trees gone, the window now framed a sweeping view of the valley upstream from the house. The sun was piercing through soft grey and golden clouds. In the sky, streams of white light fanned out onto the wildness of the mountain bushland below.

'Here's to your dream then!' said Sally as she raised her glass and chinked it with Bec's.

As Rebecca drank, a sadness settled in her heart and stayed there. She would have to learn to live like that. Learn to live without him.

Warmed by rum and comforted by the rumbling kitchen woodstove, the pair sat at the table, not realising that two hours had slipped by as they worked on plans for Waters Meeting.

'My stomach's complaining,' said Sally, and she went to the fridge.

'Stir-fry?' she asked, holding up a green capsicum.

As Sally sliced the vegetables Rebecca looked at the job lists written in Sally's tidy writing. The lists looked daunting, but the overall big picture of the business plan excited her. It made her want to jump up right now and start doing everything all at once. Phoning, faxing, searching the net, tidying the house and sheds, ploughing, planting, everything. The excitement of it all swirled in her head as she visualised the future of her place.

After they stacked the dishes on the sink, Sally poured them a 'roadie' for their journey along the long hallway to the office.

Rebecca clunked the old light switch down. A naked bulb hanging from a long black cable cast a bright, exposing light around the farm office. Papers, magazines, envelopes, books, ear tags, tail tags, toy trucks and dusty old books clustered in old wooden pigeonholes and spread out across the desktop. The only clear space in the room was the chair and the area of desk where the computer sat. The walls were covered in fading black and white family photos of the glory days of the farm and old posters from rural newspapers of champion show sheep and cattle. Calendars from *Hoofs and Horns*, stock and station agents and local produce stores hung on the same nail in a vertical stack with curling yellow edges. Year after year moving by until no more would fit on the nail.

'Holy cow,' said Bec looking around the room. 'Where the flock do we start in here?'

'You do the clean-out and I'll search the computer and go through the mail to see where we're at with debtors and creditors.'

Sally pressed the button of the computer and it came

to life, humming gently in the room. She settled herself in the chair as if about to fly a plane. She rubbed her hands together before grabbing the mouse and muttered, 'Righto, Tom. What have you got for us here?'

Rebecca looked at the glowing blue screen and pictured Tom sitting there. She walked out of the room to get garbage bags and boxes.

Despite the pain in her hands, Rebecca worked in a frenzy, clearing shelves, stacking papers, dusting off surfaces, and throwing out inkless pens, old business cards and newsletters. When she pulled down the calendars, disturbing a spindly spider, she noticed the square of darkened wood beneath them. The timber walls had faded with age. She was surprised Trudy hadn't got to the office. The rest of the house had her touches, but not in here. This cold place, once darkened by the pines outside, had been the men's domain.

Rebecca crumpled papers noisily and rustled garbage bags, and Sally muttered to the computer as she took in the information stored there.

'He's been very methodical,' she said. 'It's pretty much all here, all we have to do is upgrade it, print it out and it's ready for the bank manager. I think we can make an appointment with him for the end of the week. Too soon for you?'

'Not soon enough,' said Bec.

Sally fell quiet for a moment.

'Bec. You'd better come and look at this.'

Rebecca looked at the file which appeared on the screen. She began to read it. Her heart leapt when she realised it was written by Tom.

> Dear Bec, If you ever find this file, it'll mean you've found a way towards making Waters Meeting a great property again. You've probably extracted Charlie from that crappy cropping country and married him and are setting up shop on this place. I hope so, but as I write this I don't have much hope for anything. Only hope for you. You're the strong one out of you and me. I can see a vision for this place, but stuffed if I can make that journey. I'm all messed up Bec. The way things are now, I don't think you will ever find this file, but if you do, good on you sis.

Tears clouded Rebecca's vision. She swiped them away and scrolled down the screen. She read on.

> This file contains a list of like-minded farmers in this region who are keen on getting some sort of cooperative together . . . some were keen on the enterprises we've looked into. There was a meeting at the pub and I got a list of names and numbers. Things went quiet after the meeting, so nothing's got off the ground. They just need someone to stir the possum. Someone like you, Bec. So go on . . . just do it. But don't do it alone. Don't be alone like me, ever. Remember I love you. Tom.

Bec scrolled down further, scanning through a list of names and telephone numbers. She was searching for more of Tom's words in the machine. None came.

In the bed that night her limbs slid around the sheets, seeking the touch of Charlie's warm skin. She wanted to breathe in his musky male smell. But the bed was cold. Rebecca hugged herself and let the tears fall quietly.

In the morning the shrill ring of the phone woke her. She sprang from her bed and thudded down the stairs. She was sure it was Charlie.

'Hello,' Rebecca said, trying to sound extra bright and awake.

'Got you out of bed, did I?' It was Harry.

'No,' said Rebecca defensively, unsure how to react to her father. The tone of his voice settled her. It was the same as it had been in hospital. Without conflict, without arrogance, just a humble quiet string of awkward words.

'I . . . um . . . They said I'm right to come home in the next couple of days and, well, I wanted to see if you were coming down to the city, and if so could you give me a lift home?'

'Sure Dad,' said Rebecca a little too gently so she added, 'There are conditions though.'

'I see,' he said cautiously, 'holding your crippled father to ransom.'

'You bet! It's no drama, Dad, it's just that Sal and I have worked out some figures for the place . . . a business plan and marketing strategy. To get the farm rolling again.'

'That was quick! How long have you been back there? What, a week? Talk about a miracle cure! Can you fix missing limbs too?'

Rebecca slid her back down the wall and sat on the floor. 'No Dad,' she said tiredly, 'you don't understand. We've all worked on this for the past few years . . . It's a business plan. I compiled it for uni. Sally and Tom helped.'

'I see,' Harry said quietly.

'If we have your backing we'll have more sway with the bank manager . . . and we'll need to sort things out with the lawyers.'

'Lawyers?'

'Don't panic, Dad, just a bit of succession planning . . . You know full well it's long overdue. You agreed to it in the hospital. Remember?'

'Must've been the drugs they were pumping into me,' said Harry.

'Dad,' Rebecca urged.

'Yes, yes. I hear you,' he said, sounding tired and defeated. 'Just let me know when you're coming down.'

'Okay. I'll give you a ring after I've made all the appointments. Bye then.'

'Bye.'

Rebecca was about to put down the phone when she heard her father.

'Bec! Wait.'

'Yep? What?'

'You'd better get that log cabin fixed up for me.'

'What?'

'I'm sick of that big old house. Log cabin would suit me better.'

'Right,' she said.

The line went dead.

'Cool!' she said in the empty hallway and then bounded up the stairs two at a time, calling Sally's name.

Rebecca spread the tablecloth out across the pine table, smoothed down the edges with her fingertips and stood back.

'There! What do you think.' She took a step back and looked around the cabin.

'Very homely,' said Sally as she peeled off pink rubber gloves and sat on the arm of the chair. 'Your dad will love it.'

They had worked nonstop on the cabin all morning. Washing windows, sweeping cobwebs away from corners, putting clean sheets on the bed and arranging recent newspapers and magazines. Bec tried hard to ignore the pain from her cut and cramped hands as she worked.

'Ouch!' she said, shaking her hands vigorously in the air and pulling a face.

'What?' came Sally's voice from the bathroom.

'Mr Sheen does not feel good on raw wounds.'

'You'll get over it, psycho woman,' teased Sally as she scrubbed at the shower's tiled wall. Bec shook her head and kept wiping the low-slung coffee table, before making her way into the bedroom. On the bedside table, she placed a small photograph in a silver frame. It was a picture of Tom, Mick and Bec as kids, all three kneeling on the grass in the garden with a poddy lamb. Mick was holding a bottle with a teat and Tom and Bec hugged the lamb. They had camera smiles on their faces. Rows of white teeth and scrunched-up eyes. She sat it beside what would now be her father's bed.

As they stood looking at the clean cabin with the newly positioned furniture, Rebecca sighed. 'It's going to be so weird, Sal. Just him and me here.'

'Give it time,' Sally said. 'At least you'll be living in separate houses.' They pulled the door of the cabin shut behind them and Rebecca bent to straighten the door-mat that Mossy had been lying on.

'I'll get the brushcutter later and cut that grass away. It'll be sweet,' she said.

The cabin was set a fair way from the house amidst some old gnarled rivergums that grew on a small rise above the river. It didn't share the same spectacular mountain views as the house, but the position Trudy and her parents had chosen was a good one. The river wound around at the front of the cabin past its small deck. The trees sheltered it from the views of the house and outbuildings. It had a private, secluded feel to it.

'Could've moved in there myself,' said Bec. 'Would save me rattling around the big house.'

'You'll be right,' said Sally. 'I plan on visiting you lots . . . and inviting all your old college mates for wild cocktail or murder parties!'

Rebecca smiled and turned to Sally. 'Thanks for everything. Taking time off work . . . for everything, thank you.' She hugged her friend.

'No worries,' said Sal, waving her pink rubber gloves, 'I'll send you the bill.'

And then the two trudged up the hill towards the house, both smiling when they saw the sunlight shine onto the verandahs of the homestead.

'Looks great without those big old trees,' said Sally with a smile.

'Sure does,' said Bec, and she raised her eyebrows and nodded. Things were starting to feel okay again. Mossy trotted at Bec's side as they walked up to the house.

CHAPTER 45

In the car Rebecca and Sally sang along to the Dixie Chicks in twanging tones and laughed at one another. Sally turned the car into the wide entrance of the housing estate and Rebecca made gagging motions as she indicated the large tacky sign saying, 'Whispering Pines Estate – The Peaceful Way of Life'. They drove along the new bitumen road and turned left into Radiata Drive. Sally stopped the car outside number 12 and Rebecca exhaled a low whistle as she looked at the house from the window of the car.

'Now that's a *glorious* new home,' Rebecca said with a nasally voice as she and Sally looked at the carpet-like lawn, brick pillar mailbox and long low stretch of red brick house. White paint reflected the morning sun from the eaves.

'Mmm. Suburban paradise,' said Bec.

'Don't be so sarcastic,' said Sally. She swivelled round to Harry who was sitting in the back seat of the car.

411

'I don't know where she gets it from. Do you?'

Harry smiled at Sally and shook his head. 'It's got me beat.' For the entire journey from the hospital Harry had sat in silence, disfigured, looking like a returned soldier, his sleeve pinned up neatly by the nurses. Rebecca knew he was nervous about the family meeting. She was too. Best to get it out of the way as soon as possible, she thought, as she opened the car door.

She looked up to see the large front door of the house swing open. Trudy appeared in a floral dress. The basketball-shape of her unborn baby made her dress stick out like a shop awning. Danny toddled to the door on stumpy legs and, clinging to Trudy's dress with a podgy little hand, peered at Sally's car. In his other hand he held a big yellow plastic truck.

'Ahh! It's mini-Mick!' said Rebecca. 'Jeez. He's been in a good paddock too!' She eyed the toddler's bulging tummy which stretched the Bananas in Pyjamas into very elongated shapes.

'Bec, behave,' growled Sally.

Trudy motioned for them to park in the driveway, a wide stretch of grey concrete lined with neatly edged lawn. Before they could open the back door of the car to help Harry out, Trudy was there, bustling and fuss-ing. She undid Harry's seatbelt and manoeuvred him from the car, keeping up a constant banter all the while.

'How are you all? So lovely to see you. Danny, say hello to Auntie Becky and her friend Sally.' She pushed

Danny forward gently and Bec stooped to look into the little boy's eyes.

'Hey groover,' she said as he looked back at her shyly.

'Let's get you all inside,' Trudy said. 'Danny, you grab Grandpa's walking stick, honey, and hold it up for him. Mick's just in the office, he'll be out shortly. Did you have a good drive down?'

When she had them on the verandah she gave them all a hug and a kiss.

'Ooops!' she said as she bumped Harry with her stomach.

'Not long to go,' said Harry, nodding at her belly.

'Waiting, waiting,' said Trudy, patting her stomach. She ushered them into a vast parquet-tiled foyer which echoed with their footsteps and voices.

'Rrrrrrr!' Danny said as he pushed his yellow truck down the echoing hallway. They followed him into a large kitchen–dining area.

Trudy motioned to the couch. 'Sit down! I'll put the kettle on.'

Harry pulled out a straight-backed chair from the table and sat down, grimacing a bit as he bent.

'That'd be great, thanks,' Rebecca said, looking up at the clock on the dresser. She was shocked to find it there. It was the clock from the Waters Meeting kitchen. The tick sounded different in here. An old thing in a new home.

'What time are Mum and Peter getting here?'

From behind her new kitchen bench Trudy stood smiling. 'Any minute now,' she said. 'Tea or coffee?'

Rebecca was about to answer when the doorbell rang.

'There they are now,' said Trudy. 'Spot on time. I'll go.'

As she walked down the hall Mick came in from another door, smiling as he entered.

'Mick! How you going?' said Bec brightly, glad to see him. He sauntered over and gave Bec a big bear hug. He'd put on weight.

'Hey Sal,' he said with a wave.

'How you doing, Mick?'

'Great!' he said, patting his tummy. 'I'm in seventh heaven. But you've been keeping me busy lately with your succession planning meeting . . . I've set up the whiteboard and everything in the dining room for you. That okay? I even pinched a few new textas from work so these business plan diagrams you're going to draw for us will look flash!'

'Good on you. That's great,' said Sal. 'We should get started soon, though, because we've got an appointment this afternoon.'

'Yes ma'am,' he said, saluting her. Mick looked beyond Sally and saw his father sitting uncomfortably in the chair.

'Dad,' he said and walked over and put his hand on his shoulder. 'Good to see you. Glad they let you out. You're looking just fine.'

The chatter along the hallway signalled the arrival of Frankie and Peter. Danny roared about their legs with his truck as they stood in the kitchen greeting one another with kisses, handshakes and awkward hugs. Frankie looked flushed and nervous. When she saw Harry leaning unsteadily against the table she sucked in a breath. Her anger towards him eased a little to a feeling of pity when she saw the sleeve pinned over his stump. Harry looked at her blankly, taking in her city clothes and tidy hair. He nodded at her and mumbled a greeting. It was Trudy who smoothed the situation, offering biscuits, making hot drinks and saying all the right things. That was until she let out a screech.

'Ohhhhh! Michael!' All of them looked up. Danny held in his little fat fists two textas and was making wild slashes of red across the walls of the hall.

'I told you to keep the door *closed*!'

'It's okay, Puffin. It'll wipe off,' Mick said to his wife as he picked Danny up in a sweeping motion and tucked the yelling child under his arm. 'I think it's time we got the meeting underway. I'll just go and put this one on the street to play in the traffic.'

Sally sucked a breath in. It was her cue to take over. She gathered up her briefcase.

'Show me the way.'

In Trudy's dining room Sally stood facing the Saunders family as they sat around the glossy wooden table. She held in her hand the proposal she, Tom, Gabs and Rebecca had compiled. On the whiteboard she drew an outline of the proposed enterprises, which included export hay production, prime lamb production, direct sales of high country labelled domestic beef, forward contracts of export beef and a producer cooperative. As she talked she listed the costs. The income. The return on investments. She talked casually, yet formally. She had been the mediator at many farming family meetings, so she was cool and well practised. But this time she found it hard to stop her hands from shaking and her voice sounding thin from nerves. A lot was riding on this meeting for Sally. It wasn't just her childhood connection with the place, it was Tom, it was Rebecca. She even felt a pang of concern about Harry's future in it all. She swallowed down her nerves and talked on, tapping her index finger on the tabletop to indicate just how strong the business proposal was. How it all made sense.

Even though Rebecca knew her friend so well, she didn't detect Sally's nerves. She sat in the straight-backed chair and marvelled at how fantastic Sally was at putting forward their project to the toughest of audiences. Rebecca looked around at her family as they sat in the plush, almost plastic-feeling dining room. At one end of the replica antique table sat Harry. Next to him was Mick. Next to Mick sat Frankie and Peter. Trudy seemed to come and go with cakes and biscuits and fresh pots of coffee and tea. She was content with her house and safe in the financial care of her family. It seemed the farm was something she had left in her past. She hovered on the periphery of it all, happy to stay out of it. Trudy came into the room now and sat down, elegantly crossing her legs, listening out for Danny in the hallway. Rebecca smiled at her and she smiled sweetly back.

For Rebecca it felt so strange to have them all here

in the one room. Everyone's eyes were focused on Sally, as if looking at one another was too hard a thing to do. Rebecca resisted the temptation to throw in comments when Sally went through the plans to revamp the farm. Instead she scribbled incessantly on a piece of paper, drawing flowers, stars, horses' heads, lightning bolts and gum trees. She was too nervous to consider the outcome. What if her family said no to the plans? She longed for Charlie to be by her side and for Dags to be sitting at her feet. She was out of her comfort zone in this strange, clean, plush-carpeted new home. Her palms sweated and her mouth was dry.

'Now you can see from this,' said Sally indicating the diagram on the whiteboard, 'that Tom and Rebecca really did their homework well. I'm not saying you have to accept this. It is, after all, only a proposal, but the gathering here today is not just about keeping Waters Meeting in the family, it's about keeping the family together through open communications. Now I think I've said enough, it's your turn.'

She swiped the whiteboard clean. 'You've seen what the business plan contains, we now need to find out what each of you want for this family farm.

'What I need each of you to do is to give me a list of goals you have for your future. It doesn't matter whether they're dreams or not. It's what you want to happen in your life in the next ten years.'

Harry squirmed in his seat, pulling a face and muttering. Sally thrust a fist full of coloured textas in front of him.

'Pick a colour,' she said.

'Black,' Harry said.

She offered the pens around, Rebecca took red, Mick and Trudy green, and Frankie and Peter blue.

'The purple marker is Tom's,' said Sally. The name cut through the uncomfortable air in the room. 'We can't forget him. He's the reason we're all here. He's the reason we have to lay our cards on the table and set a common goal. He's why we have to start talking.'

'Harry,' Sally said, 'we won't start with you. I know this process will be the most difficult for you. Mick, we'll give your father time to think, let's start with you.'

'No, Sally,' Harry said almost too loudly, 'you've said this meeting is about communication, so it's about time I spoke.' His voice wavered a little.

Sally smiled encouragingly at him and pulled off the lid to the black marker, ready to write on the board.

'I'd like to see the proposal go ahead. I've hung onto the reins for too long and we all know what trouble that's caused. I'd like to see Rebecca take on the farm and put the proposal into place . . . that's if the bank will give her the go-ahead. It seems Mick and Trudy have set themselves up here nicely. Mick, you don't seem to miss the farming life.'

Mick shook his head, 'Never been better off, Dad.'

'See,' said Harry. 'It's solved.' He set his hand on the table and spread his large fingers out on the smooth wooden surface. 'Rebecca can take on the farm. She's welcome to it.'

'Hold your horses, Harry,' Sally interjected kindly. 'It's not that simple. We need to hear from each of you what your individual goals are. Every one of you in this room has to have input. Now Harry, it's all very well for you to decide that the future of the farm lies in the hands of Rebecca, but you haven't said where you sit in the next ten years. What are your goals? Rebecca's not part of that question.'

Harry shifted in his seat, uncomfortable again. He put his hand to the back of his head and scratched slowly at his scalp. The room was silent for a time.

'Landcare,' he said suddenly. 'I've always wanted to join Landcare,'

'Good, that's good,' said Sally as she wrote the words neatly under Harry's name on the board.

'And the river, I've always wanted to get the community going downstream about cleaning up the river . . . and of course I'd like to still help on the farm, when I can,' he said, moving his stump forward a little.

The black marker began to fill a corner of the whiteboard with words, linking Harry's future up into a picture. Rebecca could see an excitement in his eyes, something she'd not seen for years.

When Harry finished speaking, Sally began to ask Mick for his goals. He too took some time to speak.

'Well. I'd like to move up in real estate, get up the corporate ladder. Maybe invest in a holiday house on the coast. As far as the farm's concerned, I'd like some share of it financially one day, but not till it's secure and profitable again. But I want to support its recovery mostly as a place to take my boys on holidays so I can teach them fishing, how to shoot . . .'

'Excuse me!' interrupted Trudy.

Oh no! thought Rebecca, Trudy was about to unravel the progress of the meeting.

But instead Trudy continued with a smile. 'You said "boys". Boy-ssss,' she said, exaggerating the 's' and rubbing at her stomach. 'You don't *know* this is a boy! *She* might be a *she*, after all! And *she* might want to go fishing and shooting at Waters Meeting just as much as Danny!'

'Good point, Trudy,' said Sally with a smile and the rest of the family laughed.

Mick threw up his hands in mock defeat and continued on with his comments while Sally wrote them up in the green pen. Rebecca felt a wave of relief sweep through her, and for the first time a feeling that Trudy wasn't a bad sort after all.

As each family member talked through their goals the whiteboard became a colourful picture of words which made up a painting of dreams for the future. The atmosphere in the room began to change, with each of them beginning to feel the excitement of what the next few years could bring. Rebecca, in particular, sat on the edge of her seat as she felt the energy of her family swirl about her. It was a new feeling. A good one.

Finally, when the meeting seemed as though it would draw to a close, Sally raised Tom's purple texta.

'Let's see what Tom makes of all this,' Sally said.

She began to circle the words that were the same in every case, and then connecting them altogether with a purple line. Each family member had wanted access to Waters Meeting for their children or for themselves. Frankie and Peter, Mick and Trudy, all of them wanted Waters Meeting to remain a family farm to visit. Not one of them had suggested it be carved up or sold for cash. Rebecca knew it was the river that ran through all their hearts. Even though she was the only one who had the real passion to farm the land, each of them still had that common thread. The Rebecca River. She was the key to holding it all together.

'See the pattern here,' Sally said. 'Tom wanted this. He wanted you all to come and go freely and happily from that place. But,' Sally said sternly, 'it's not all sunshine and cups of tea on the verandah. The property is in terrible debt and unless we can sway the bank manager, it will have to be sold.' Sally's words cut the air and dampened the atmosphere of excitement and reconciliation.

'One meeting isn't going to fix everything,' Sally said. 'We need to draw up a letter now, signed by Harry, in support of the proposal and our push for refinancing. We've got an hour until our appointment with the bank, so we'd better get our skates on.'

Outside the house, with the freshly printed and folded letter safely tucked in Sally's briefcase, the family gathered to wish Sally and Rebecca luck at the bank and to wave them away. Rebecca hugged Trudy and whispered, 'Thanks.'

'Thanks to you too, Becky. I think we're all feeling a lot better, don't you? Like the air is cleared or something,'

'Sure. It's great. Anyway, we'll be back this evening after the bank to pick up Dad. We'll see you later.'

'Are you sure you don't want to stay the night? He seems awfully tired.'

'Might be a good idea. And you never know, if the meeting goes well with the old crusty at the bank, we could have something to celebrate,' she said with a wink.

Rebecca turned to see Harry offering an awkward left to right handshake to Peter who was about to take Frankie back into the city. Frankie smiled at Harry and kissed him lightly on the cheek, then she looked over towards Rebecca.

'Rebecca. Can I talk to you for a minute?' Frankie called out.

'Sure, Mum,' Rebecca said frowning, thinking that all the talking had been done for the day. Her mother stood on the pavement looking a little tired, but still excited by the meeting. They walked a little way down the driveway.

'I want you to have this.' She handed her daughter a piece of paper. When Rebecca unfolded it she gasped. It was a cheque for $350 000.

'Mum! Where the flock did you get that? And why are you giving it to me?'

'Shhh! Put it away before your father sees. It's the

money from the divorce settlement. I've had it sitting in a fund . . . I've never wanted to use it. I never could.'

'But Mum, your surgery . . . You could use it to –'

'Take it, for the farm, put it all back into the farm. I insist. That money came from your grandfather's estate anyway. It belongs with Waters Meeting, not with a Saunders divorcee. You know my parents looked after me financially after the divorce. It was their money which started me off in my surgery. Now it's my turn to help you and this money belongs with you.'

With tears in her eyes Rebecca hugged her mother.

'Thank you. Thank you so much, Mum. You won't regret it, I promise. By this time next year, you won't recognise the place.' Just then Danny ran headlong into Rebecca's legs with his truck.

'Crash, crash, crash,' he screamed as he battered the tip-truck on her shins.

'Jeezus!' said Bec. 'Danny! You're looking for a right hook from your Auntie Bec.' Mick stood back with his arms folded and laughed while Trudy put a hand to her mouth.

'You told him to do that, didn't you,' said Bec to Mick with a growl in her voice and a twinkle in her eye. Rebecca scooped Danny up in her arms and simul-taneously tickled his belly and blew fart noises on his neck as he screamed and thrashed his legs.

As Bec slammed the door and fastened her seatbelt she raised her eyebrows at Sally. 'Phew. Kids,' she said, rubbing her shins. 'Danny seems pretty full on! Give me pups over kids any day!'

Sally dropped the sunglasses down from the top of her head, over her eyes. 'So you're like me – not even close to wanting kids? I don't know, when on earth are we ever going to get clucky, Bec?'

'You've got to get truck'n before you get cluck'n, Sal. Let's face it, you and I are in a drought phase again. El Nuno.'

Sally stopped at a red light and looked over to her friend. 'You know, you're a real feral, Bucket-mouth. How on earth are we going to convince a bank manager to lend *you* a squillion dollars.'

'I know,' said Bec. She began to unbutton her shirt and push her cleavage out. She stuck her tongue out as far as it would go and ran it around her mouth.

'Ew! Stop it!' said Sally, slapping her arms and hands.

The balding driver in the black BMW next to them looked over and kept his look there. He ran his tongue across his top lip.

'Ew! Yikes! Yuck!' said Sally. 'Go green. Quick, go green!'

Rebecca sunk down in the car seat, shaking with laughter as Sally floored the automatic away from the intersection and the man.

'You're back to your old self, Bec . . . and it scares me!'

'I'm just on a high. I know we're going to kick arse today at the bank. Just like you kicked butt in that family meeting.' Suddenly serious she said, 'You were fantastic today, Sal. You really pulled the whole family together. I didn't think it was possible. How can I thank you enough.'

Sally turned to her, pulling her shades down the bridge of her elegant nose and looking her in the eye. 'I'm not just doing this for you. I think Tom had something to do with it. I owed him one.'

Bec smiled at her friend as they merged through the traffic towards the city. 'It's going to work out for us all, Sal, I know it. Look what Mum gave me.' She held up the cheque while Sal tried to read it and drive at the same time.

When she at last worked out the figure she said, 'Holy schnappers! That's just injected a bit of adrenaline into the farm budget!' She grinned and pushed in a cassette tape, turning it up loud.

Despite the pounding tunes of Killing Heidi, Rebecca couldn't help the sadness in her heart. Charlie Lewis. The river kiss.

In the high-rise carpark Rebecca smoothed down her hair and tugged at her skirt. She put the jacket of her suit on.

'How do I look?'

'Like a million dollars,' said Sally.

'Good. That's what we're after.'

She sucked in a breath. She had settled into a quiet nervousness, and her stomach felt queasy. Sally, however, looked as neat and sleek as a cat. She strode towards the lift with her stylish briefcase in hand. When the doors slid open, she walked in and pressed the button, like an attorney in an American movie.

As they were ushered into the plastic-smelling air-conditioned room, the bank manager half stood and indicated the seats, then got confused as to whether to shake their hands, or just nod in greeting to the two young women.

The strength of Rebecca's handshake and the coarseness of her hands surprised him. She was such a pretty little thing, he thought. Rebecca pulled her hand away, sensing the man's thoughts and hoping he hadn't noticed the dried cuts and blisters that covered her palms and fingers.

Sally and Rebecca sat, each crossing their legs the same way, at the same time. Sally's legs, long, pale and elegant. Rebecca's, toned and honey brown. They were both so *young*, the manager thought. Sally Carter had sounded so much older on the phone. The blueness of the eyes of the blonde one stunned him. The unusual freckled brown and green in the eyes of the tall one intrigued him.

'A pleasure to meet you face to face, ladies,' he said in deep, smooth tones. His eyes slipped below their necklines, and as he spoke he was drawn to the large, perfectly rounded breasts of the blonde one. He cleared his throat and smoothed a hand over his grey lacquered hair. His gold wedding band caught a hair, tugged it out and it fell on the lapel of his navy suit. As he spoke, he continuously ran a hand over his red tie which lay on the contours of his stomach.

'I received a copy of your business plan and loan proposal in yesterday's mail.'

He moved the neatly bound documents in front of himself and shuffled forward in his chair, leaning his elbows on the desk.

'I was very impressed with the boldness of it. It's an ambitious plan for two young ladies such as yourselves. I've taken on board your request for a loan, however, there are a few questions we need answers to. Especially in regard to the ownership of the land and in whose name the loan will be drawn.'

Before he could continue, Sally pulled from between the folds of her black case a crisp white envelope. She handed it to him with a charming smile.

'I think this letter should answer all your questions on the loan proposal. It provides full backing from the property owner.' She slid the envelope across the desk.

There was silence in the room while the bank manager opened the letter and read the neat typing, his eyes resting on the scrawl of Harry Saunder's signature at its base.

'Well, with full support from your father, Miss Saunders, the proposal is looking more favorable. Shall we get down to business . . .'

Outside the bank Rebecca bit into her fist and tried hard not to scream. Sally clutched onto Bec's arm and jiggled up and down on the spot.

'We did it!' Bec said. The girls laughed and hugged. They jumped up and down holding hands, looked into each other's tear-filled eyes and screamed . . . just a little. Then they walked quickly away from the building, hoping the bank staff inside hadn't seen their disguise of professional cool slip away.

PART FIVE

CHAPTER 46

The first few weeks at Waters Meeting were an edgy time for Rebecca as she settled into the big house on her own and began work on the farm. Daily calls from Sally and Frankie kept her going, but in the evenings she ached for Charlie and always on the periphery of her thoughts was Harry. She would look out the window at night and through the trees see the lights shining from the cabin. She imagined him watching the news or sipping on sugary cups of milky tea.

She had decided to leave him alone at night, but each morning she would walk down over the paddock, with Mossy or Dags, Bessie or Stubby, always at her heels. She'd knock nervously on the door of his cabin, and she'd hold her breath when she heard him call out, 'Come in.' She had been fearful her father would snap back to his old ways and slowly start to crush her dreams. But instead she mostly found him dozing in his armchair in the morning sun, reading a book or a newspaper, or listening to the ABC on the crackling radio. He seemed content to stay where he was. Rebecca suspected he was still in a great deal of pain, but if he was, he never complained. He always pointed to the kettle and said cheerfully, 'Help yourself to a cuppa.'

'When are you due for your check-up?' she asked one morning as she nodded towards his stump.

'Next week.'

'I'll drive you.'

'No need. I can manage the automatic,' Harry said.

She had watched him one day from the window of her bedroom. He had snuck up to the sheds and got into his old car. He had driven it slowly down the drive, past the shearing shed and then turned in a wide circle in the paddock. Then he had driven it back to the shed again.

Rebecca had at first been puzzled at what he was doing. Then she had realised. He was *practising* driving – practising with one arm. She had felt a sudden sorrow for her father at the realisation of how difficult and frightening it must be to come to terms with his disability.

She looked at him now, sitting in the chair in the patch of sun. His grey hair cropped short, his work clothes clean and neat.

'No, Dad, don't go to town on your own. I'd like to come too, so I might as well drive you to your appointment. And besides, I need you there. There's a herd dispersal sale on Tuesday . . . and I'd like you to come too. See what you reckon. But I have to warn you, they're Angus cows. Not *your* preferred breed of red and whites, but they've got great genetics. All performance recorded, all certified OJD- and HGP-free. Good cows for a foundation herd. Best to get them now while the prices are still lowish.'

Harry's reaction surprised her. 'Sounds good. I'd like to go.'

'Great.' She smiled at him. 'Oh, and Dad, another favour, if you've got time . . .' She dug her hand into her pocket and pulled out a piece of paper. 'Here are the numbers of a few contractors in the region. Would you be able to organise some quotes from them? I'd like to get started on the dam construction as soon as possible. I'd phone them myself, but it's just that I've decided to head up to the hut tonight. The cows up there need salting and I thought I'd check a few fences.'

Harry held up his hand. 'Bec, it's fine. I'd love to help. You know me, I'm great at haggling. I'll get you the best damn dam-building deal yet. And,' he said firmly, but with a friendliness to his tone, 'will you stop pussyfooting round me. Your old man's mellowed in his old age, can't you see that? I'm not going to make the same mistakes twice. You're going to do great things with this place. I trust your good judgement, so you don't have to explain it all to me. I'll help you however I can.'

He gave her a wink. Rebecca felt a warm tingle run through her body. She smiled at him. He continued. 'When you get back down from the hut tomorrow, call in here. I'll cook you a roast.'

'That'd be great, Dad!'

'I want to talk business with you over dinner.'

'Business?'

'Yep. I'd like to buy a pup from you.'

'A pup?'

'Well, if I'm going to be any use to you with one arm, I'd better learn how to work one of your fancy dogs. It's not like I can drive a manual ute any more, or roar round the stock on the bike. I'd be better off doing it the quiet way. Horse and dog. The way it should be done. Could you help me out on that one?'

'Sure Dad,' said Rebecca warmly. 'You can start by reading a great kelpie-training manual I've got, one by Tony Parsons.'

'You're giving me homework already!'

'Do you want to get some new ideas or not, Dad?'

He smiled at her. 'Of course I do. I'm tackling life differently from now on.'

'Who said you couldn't teach an old dog new tricks?' said Rebecca as she turned and walked out the door into the sunshine. Her dogs danced around her as she jogged towards the stable where Inky stood, tied to the rail.

Just for the hell of it, Rebecca let Ink Jet have her head. The mare grunted with effort as she cantered up the steep rocky slope, hooves clunking on stone, shoes chinking on rock, black mane flying. Bec leaned forward in the saddle and urged the mare on. Her saddlebags were weighted down with fencing strainers, pliers and

434

food for her evening meal at the hut. A hessian bag with salt for the cattle was rolled up neatly and strapped to the front of the saddle, resting on Inky's strong neck.

Despite her burden, the strong, stocky mare was enjoying the canter in the mountain air. Bec watched as Inky pricked her ears forward as she reached a plateau. A cold wind lifted Bec's hair off her shoulders and stung her cheeks red. She whistled a release command which sent the dogs scooting ahead on the track. She ducked beneath the contorted white limbs of the snowgums and rounded a curve in the track, which took her onto an open treeless area of the plain. Spring was on its way and the yellow-brown grass emerging from patches of snow was starting to recover and shoot out vibrant new stems of green.

On the edge of the plain, in a fringe of trees, Bec sat back suddenly in the saddle. The cantering mare propped and stopped on a cliff edge. Inky's ears shot forward. Rebecca, her four dogs and mare gazed out across the expanse of dips and ridges. Bush as far as they could see. Heaven's Leap they called it, a name given by the gold miners. It was the spot she'd imagined bringing Charlie to. She'd imagined pointing out towards the gullies, showing him the source of the two rushing creeks. Two creeks, meeting in a rocky gorge and rushing down towards the rich river flats of the property as one. One river, the Rebecca River.

The wind up here was so icy it stung her lips. She drank in the view as she thought back over the past few weeks. The change in her father. The exhilaration of being granted the loan for the new-look farm business. It still made her tingle. She'd felt an inner strength again which, she knew, stemmed from the support and comfort of her family. She smiled at how things were turning out. Yet up here, on the edge of heaven, Rebecca also felt the sadness. Two men in her life. One dead. One gone.

She looked out again across the beautiful expanse of wilderness. Too rugged ever to be tamed. So massive, wild and ancient. She felt the exhilaration of life and had the realisation that she, Tom and Charlie were all part of it. All part of that huge breathing wilderness laid out before her. Then she turned the mare towards the direction of the hut and rode away from the blast of wild air which had rushed over and through millions of gum trees.

Rebecca was surprised at how saggy and old the hut now looked. Low mountain clouds had wrapped everything in dampness and caused wood to rot and tin to rust. She must bring Sally here, she thought. Perhaps Sally would know if Heritage Funding could help keep it upright. It was obvious Tom had done some work on it while he lived up here. Rebecca ran her fingertips over the shining nails which were hammered alongside rusting old ones on the verandah floor.

She unhooked the door and moved inside, into the still air. Wind whistled through the nail holes in the tin and the slits between the handsawn wood, but despite the draftiness of the hut, Rebecca felt comforted in here. Sheltered.

Running her fingers over Tom's initials and those of her grandfather and great-grandfather, she said each name out loud. Then she pulled a pocket knife from the leather pouch on her belt and flipped out the blade. In the wooden post she began to carve her initials deep in the thick timber. And, as she did it, she realised that it was wasted energy to be heartbroken over Charlie. This was where she belonged. This place, she thought, where two rivers meet.

CHAPTER 47

From outside, Rebecca could see her father framed in the window of the log cabin. He was at the sink, washing up. As she rode past on Inky, she called out to him.

'I'm going to get the mail.' He waved a dish mop at her in acknowledgment and watched her ride away with Mossy trotting behind.

Mail came on Tuesdays and Fridays. On Tuesdays Harry drove to get it. On Fridays, when she had time, Rebecca rode. She sometimes checked the stock on the way or rode the fence lines with her pliers and fence strainers in her saddlebag and a loop of wire slung over her shoulder. The rides gave her time to think. She liked Fridays. The past two years had been such a whir. Days rolling by at a frenetic pace. Friday was her time-out day.

Today she was happy just to feel the sun on her face. She put decision-making, business plans and debt out of her head and let the sun warm her right through.

She looked over to the merino ewes and lambs. As the ewes grazed, the lambs lay stretched out in the sun. Little bright white dots on a blanket of green. In the next paddock, sleek, fat Angus cows lifted their heads and watched her ride by, chewing slowly and turning their heads to check on the curious calves which roamed from their mothers' flanks.

After Rebecca opened the first gate on the road, she urged the mare on to a trot up the steady climb of the hill. The rhythmic beat of the horse's hooves echoed up through the trees and into the gullies.

At the mailbox, Rebecca leaned over Ink Jet's sweat-covered shoulder and lifted the heavy canvas mailbag. She undid the big buckle and loosened the leather strap. Her mare shifted her weight, rested one hind leg and dropped her head, preparing for a doze. Mossy lay panting beneath the shade of a wattle in the long grass.

For the first year the mail contained bill after bill. Bills for stock, for fertiliser, for grain, for hay, for machinery parts, power, phone, groceries. It seemed endless. Sometimes Rebecca held fistfuls of the stiff pieces of paper in her hands and sobbed. The debt to the bank felt as though it would crush her. Then she'd pull her shoulders up, wipe her tears away and ride home to phone Sally and they'd work out a plan to manage payments.

On some days a letter from Charlie arrived. Most were written on thin, lined paper, his loneliness spreading out across the page. In other letters his passion was so real Rebecca could feel the touch of his hand on her skin. Sometimes he just wrote about his father's farm and refused to let love into his words. There was still bitterness underlying their long-distance friendship. As Rebecca read his letters, sitting astride her horse, fat tears sometimes fell from her eyes. At other times she would ride home and look out through the bush or along the dusty road, trying to ignore the presence of Charlie, folded, sealed and stamped in her saddlebag.

As the second round of seasons came and went, Charlie's letters slowed to a small trickle and then suddenly stopped. She assumed there was someone else for him now. She stopped writing too.

So much had happened since Charlie. The work had been incredible. Hard and exciting. A new three hundred megalitre dam now filled up one of the gullies, the smooth water stretching along grassy banks, which had become a home for wild ducks. The dam filled Rebecca with a quiet confidence about the future. The water stored in it guaranteed an income from the crops and ensured water for the stock in the driest of times when the river would again be reduced to a trickle. She had already started a rotational grazing program with the stock, altering fence lines and gateways and putting in water troughs. With the improved pastures and the efficient grazing program, it meant they could increase stock numbers without exhausting the land. In this Harry helped her wholeheartedly – the troughs meant they could fence off stock access to the river, which would protect its fragile banks and, in Harry's eyes, that was a huge plus. He'd stand on the edge of the dam, his feet set wide apart, one hand on his hip, his stump sticking out as if the other absent hand also rested on his hip, and he'd shake his head.

'We should've done this years ago,' he'd say, more to the memory of his father than to Rebecca.

The dam was the first stage of the farm's irrigation project, something that would boost returns even more next year. Already the semitrailers had lumbered into the property loaded up with parts for the brand-new pivot irrigator. Harry, being more machinery minded than stock minded, was looking forward to the introduction of irrigated specialist cropping. It would mean scouring the countryside at clearing sales for old machinery that he could do up, weld, modify and fix.

He was getting quite ingenious at coping with only one arm. But Rebecca often worried about him. Sometimes she'd hear him in the machinery shed swearing and raging. There would be a crashing sound as he threw an object, sometimes a shifter, sometimes a screwdriver, against the tin walls in frustration. There were days of dark depression and silence. Days when Tom's death kept Harry locked inside his cabin and curled up in bed.

But most of the time the days rolled on, Rebecca working and her father helping when he could. He still avoided the stock work, but he had stuck to his plan of training up his lively new pup. He'd called her Cloe. She was out of Stubby. Cloe was a little red and tan bitch that had been sired by a Karawarra dog in the district. She danced at Harry's feet and looked willingly up into his eyes. He took her with him everywhere, and on the deck of his cabin he'd made a cosy kennel for her out of an old tea-chest filled with blankets. Every day Harry had worked on her obedience training, as Rebecca had shown him, and he'd been amazed how the early training had paid off when he'd first cast her out around a mob. Rebecca marvelled at how much her father had changed. Harry had at last found a companion and some compassion for working dogs.

She also saw changes in her mother. If she had to find something positive in losing Tom, Rebecca could see it emerging in her parents. Frankie now drove up regularly from the city with Peter. She had become Rebecca's ally in the stock enterprises. During lambing and calving, Rebecca and her mother had tended to the animals night and day. Each creature was so precious. Rebecca had invested most of the money Frankie gave her into restocking with good quality merino ewes for fine wool production, and composite bred ewes for prime lamb production. Every breeding ewe or cow counted so much towards the future. They had to boost numbers fast, so as to boost returns.

In the city, Frankie had at last found a partner to join her in the running of the surgery. It meant she had more time for her daughter. She would drive into Waters Meeting with her car packed full of discounted vaccines and drenches, dog food and stock feed. She even brought with her canisters filled with dry ice, containing straws of semen bought from the best bulls and rams they could find. She helped Rebecca with the breeding program, turning her hand again to embryo transfer and artificial insemination in livestock, an area she'd been fascinated with during her years as a country vet. Frankie again revelled in the work with large animals and she took on the research of stock genetics with a passion, emailing Rebecca each day with new-found statistics or research programs for increased production in stock.

'Every little bit of help counts,' she'd said to Rebecca as she handed her new collars for her dogs and began to unpack the car, revealing Peter sitting beneath an armload of bags.

'Peter!' laughed Rebecca. 'Didn't see you there.'

Peter, too, enjoyed the trips to Waters Meeting. He spent his time on the riverbank flicking his fly rod, or climbing the lower mountainsides looking for fossils. Harry would sometimes venture up to the big house when Frankie and Peter were there and duck his head in the kitchen door to say hello. If there was any bitterness, Harry hid it well as he chatted easily to Peter about rivers and the rock types that the waters slowly carved away each year. He was civil to Frankie, but kept his distance. Rebecca knew he was still hurt by her mother's absence and had times of incredible loneliness. But she also knew there were single older women in the district who saved up their special smile for Harry at Landcare meetings.

'Watch out for the widows,' Rebecca would teasingly call out to him as he drove off towards town for yet another Landcare gathering. He'd pull a terrified face at her and then smile before driving away.

For the past two years, thankfully, rain had come to the mountains at mostly the right times and the valley flats had responded well. It had buoyed the spirits of Rebecca and Harry.

Sometimes, as Rebecca looked at the rain clouds gathering silently above her head, she'd say to Harry, 'Tom is looking after us up there.' She loved the rain. She'd sit on the verandah, Dags lying at her feet, and watch it fall down on the leafy garden. Pounding on tin, forming miniature rivers on the drive. Sheets of water moving silently towards the river. Since she'd been home, the river had flooded twice and soaked the soil on the lowlands with sweet, life-giving water, pressing debris against the wire of fences and trunks of trees. When the water had seeped away, Harry had spent hours on the tractor for Rebecca, sowing new pastures made up of clover, cocksfoot and rye, and sowing down lucerne on the river flats. She'd help him fill the seeder and he'd drive away in the tractor, changing gears with one hand while steering with his knee. The seeds had shot almost instantly in the bed of warm rich soil and the paddocks were now nearly back to full production. The lucerne was growing madly and brought a luminous swathe of green to the river's edge.

Their efforts were at last paying off thought Rebecca, as she tore open an envelope, still sitting astride the mare. In between the bills, now cheques began to arrive in the mail – payment for her produce.

Today was a deposit for a pup and payment for a hundred and fifty early lambs they'd sold at the start of the month.

'Wow!' she said when she saw the cheque. The agent had said the Waters Meeting lambs had made top price at the sale and she knew that, in the industry, prices were on a high. Holding the fat cheque in her hand thrilled her.

After she'd torn open all the envelopes she thought might contain more cheques, Rebecca rebundled the bills and put them in her saddlebag. She again reached for the mailbag. There had been something else at the bottom of it, weighing it down. She reached in and pulled out a copy of *Landscape*, a glossy national magazine.

'Ahhh! Mossy!' she said. 'It's finally come.' The dog opened her eyes, stopped panting for a second and looked at Rebecca with her head cocked to one side.

Rebecca excitedly flipped open the magazine and then laughed when she saw the photographs of herself. She raised a hand to her mouth.

'Oh my God! What a dag!'

Covering both pages was a picture of her sitting up on Ink Jet, with black cattle, fat as mud, grazing on the lucerne. On the next page, set amidst the text of the story, Rebecca sat with her dogs on the small square bales of lucerne hay – their first crop of export-quality hay, destined for Japanese racing stables. Dags was licking her face and Rebecca was screwing up her nose, knowing he'd just been chewing on a rotten sheep's skull.

When she read the first line and saw her age set in type, twenty-seven, she sat back in her saddle. Twenty-seven! She couldn't believe it. It looked so old in print like that. She wondered where the time had gone.

She began to read the article, and the words of the journalist brought goosebumps to her skin. The headline read, MUSTERING A BRIGHT FUTURE IN FARMING.

Rebecca sighed. She could be proud of what she and her family, including Sally, had achieved in such a short space of time. She read about the producer co-operative she and Sally had formed in the region. It had started out as a beef cattle producer group. Now they had a machinery ring and were supplying high-quality lucerne hay to racing stables in Asia. Rebecca's business plan had come to life, and was not only slowly dragging Waters Meeting out of debt, but helping other farm businesses in the region as well. She read the article, amazed at how professional she sounded.

'In just two years we've not only secured payment for our hides, but also forward contracts for our beef. We regularly tour the abattoir to see what our customers in Japan are demanding – at the moment it's black cattle, so we buy in and breed predominantly Angus and finish them here on the river flats.'

Traditionally Hereford country, Rebecca has retained her family's line of cattle and still runs cows on the high country surrounding Waters Meeting.

'There's a demand for organic grass-fed beef, so we sell

our red cattle on domestic markets to specialist butchers who supply city restaurants with specially branded high country beef. We even had a busload of restaurateurs visit the property to see first-hand just how environmentally conscious we are and how much importance we place on being gentle and kind to our stock.

'We have regular meetings on each farm with all the members of our producer group to give each other support. The directions we take in the business are also guided by our Department of Agriculture beef officer, Nick Hammond, and rural financial counsellor, Sally Carter.'

Rebecca smiled seeing Nick's name in print. She recalled the first producer meeting at Dirty's pub. She and Sally had sent invitations to all of the farmers Tom had put on his list. In the pub the farmers sat on chairs, their arms folded sceptically across their stomachs. She, Sally and Nick had looked across a sea of blank faces while they gave their presentation. At the time they'd known Nick just a month. Sally had met him in the Department of Ag head office one morning and had promptly whisked him off to the pub by the time five o'clock came. By eight o'clock she had him in her bed. He was a big, solid, good-looking guy. Not fat but beefy, like a beef officer should be. He wasn't the type to wear suits, and instead ambled about in jeans and boots. Sally panted after him – and his dark hair, healthy cheeks and massive shoulders.

At the meeting, as Rebecca stood between them, fielding curly questions from the stern-looking farmers about the beef scheme, she could feel the sexual tension running between Sally and Nick. She had known then and there, in the squash of the pub's meeting room, that the two of them would become a permanent item. An unlikely item, she thought, but a permanent and happy one.

Rebecca looked at her watch now as she put her letters to be posted in the mailbag, did up the leather strap and sat it back in the mailbox for tonight's collection. Sally and Nick were heading up to Waters Meeting for the weekend. They'd be here soon, she thought. She bundled the magazine into her saddlebag and buckled the straps.

Mossy scratched behind her ear, making her collar jangle, and stood up to go. Inky lifted her head and swished her tail at a fly.

'Come on, girl.' Rebecca shifted her weight in the saddle and they rode off in the direction of the homestead.

Sally, Nick and Rebecca chinked their glasses of rum and coke together around the kitchen table.

'Here's to the new pivot irrigator!' said Nick.

'. . . and the fullness of the dam,' said Sally.

They all drank. As they stood for a moment in silence, Rebecca looked out the window to the pile of silver pipes lying in the paddock, which, when assembled, would become the new irrigator.

'How the flock am I going to put that thing together?'

'We'll give you a hand,' Nick said, waving the assembly booklet at her.

'Plus we mentioned to Dirty on the way through that you had a new fifty-span irrigator. The first of its kind in the district. He's rounding up a few fellas tonight at the pub . . . they'll all be busting their guts to come and have a look at it. They'll give you a hand. It'll be up and running in no time and you'll have crops galore to sow and reap,' said Nick as he reached for a corn chip and crunched it between his teeth.

Rebecca stood at the end of the table and began to slice some tomatoes.

'Thanks guys. So much for you having a weekend off. I always put you to work when you come and stay.'

'It does us office-types good,' said Sally, patting Nick on his backside.

'Oh bugger,' said Rebecca suddenly.

'What?' asked Sal.

'Forgot to feed the dogs.'

Nick put down his glass and stood up. 'I'll go.'

'Thanks.' Bec smiled after him as he went out of the kitchen. She called after him, 'Make sure you feed Dags first . . . top of the pack and all that.'

'Yeah, yeah. I know the drill,' he said, popping his head back around the door.

'And make sure you make them sit and wait before they touch their food.'

'Yes, Miss Dog Psychologist.'

After he shut the door behind him Rebecca said,

'He's a good one that one. I'm so glad you've stuck to him, Sal.'

Sally crunched on some corn chips. 'Love him to bits.' Rebecca felt a stab of sadness. Sally and Nick were so in love. When they skylarked together and kissed each other warmly in front of her, Rebecca couldn't help but feel the loss of Charlie. She wondered if she'd ever find a passion so intense again, or a lover who was so comfortable with her.

Sally sensed her thoughts and moved over to Bec, putting an arm around her.

'And what about you? Still no action on the man front?'

Rebecca shook her head. 'Plenty of creepy offers down at Dirty's pub, and there's been this late-thirties bachelor farmer who dresses in St Vinnies dead-old-men shirts.'

'Ew,' said Sally, wrinkling her nose.

'And he's got copious quantities of dandruff – he's been on my tail whenever I go to the store or a farmer meeting, but other than that, zilch. I've lost interest.'

'Bec! Your virginity will grow back! Seriously. You need a break from this place. Things are looking good on paper and in the paddocks. Now's the perfect time to get away.'

Sally poked her friend in the ribs. 'Just look at you. You're bloody skinny! You're working too hard. How about that trip to Asia? Why don't you come with Nick and I – it'd do you good to meet your racing clients face to face.'

'Come on, Sal! We've got the irrigation coming on, we've got crops to get in and then –'

'Harvest, and shearing, and lamb marking and drenching and mustering the plains . . . I know all that. God. What have I started here? You're going to turn into bush woman and be barren and lonely and baby-less. For godsakes, Bec, at least get yourself a nearby bonk.'

'Did I hear someone say bonk?' Nick came in, bringing with him a waft of fresh air into the warm kitchen.

Sally slung her arms about his neck and kissed him lovingly. 'I was just saying that Bec here needs a bonk.'

'More like she needs a cropping manager so she'd have time to have a bonk,' Nick joked.

Sally chewed on a chip and thought for a moment. 'You know,' she said slowly, 'that's a great idea, Nick!'

'Yeah. As if we could afford that,' said Bec heavily. 'Besides, Dad can help me.'

'Come off it, Bec. You know your old man's not up to it any more. He's happy being headman in the Landcare and Riverwatch groups. He's never been so non-grumpy. Leave the poor old bugger alone. You'll work him to death.'

'Huh!' said Bec in disgust.

Nick reached for the rum bottle and filled up their glasses. 'We all know your strengths lie in livestock management, Bec, but most of the money will come from specialist cropping on this place once the pivot is built. You need someone who's in the know.'

'Don't give me that beef officer rhetoric – you bloody people from the department!' She downed her full glass in a series of gulps and slammed it on the table.

'Don't you start sounding like a cranky old farmer, Rebecca Saunders. You know Nick's got a point here.' Sally put her hands on her hips.

'Don't do that,' said Rebecca warily.

'Do what?'

'Do that. That thing.'

'What thing?'

'That thing you're doing now – with your hands on your hips. I know you, Sally . . . I know that look you get. You're not letting this one go, are you? You're going to hound me until I put on a manager and then you're going to stuff me on a plane to Asia.'

'You're dead right I'm not letting this one go – this is something we should draw up a plan for. A cropping and irrigation manager – it's perfect. Of course I'll have to rearrange the budget.'

'You and that bloody budget, Farter! I'll rearrange you in a minute. I thought the whole point of getting a pivot irrigator, with a bloody expensive computer to drive it, was so the whole thing managed itself.'

'See, I told you she had no idea about cropping,' Nick said to Sally teasingly.

Rebecca hid her head in the fridge for a few moments while Nick and Sally continued their spiel. Eventually she emerged brandishing a bunch of celery.

'Will you two shut up. Or else!'

'Whoah! Settle down, Bec,' said Nick, taking a step back and putting up his hands. 'It's not that serious.'

Rebecca waved the celery closer at them and Sally and Nick stepped back into a corner of the kitchen, clinging fearfully to each other.

'Are you going to shut up?'

'Take it steady,' cautioned Nick. 'Now put the celery down . . . or else someone might get hurt.'

'Or worse,' said Sally in mock horror.

'Well? Are you going to shut up about it?'

Sally and Nick nodded solemnly, glancing nervously at the celery which Bec waved menacingly near their throats.

'Good. Now get me another rum.'

'I'm on the job,' said Nick, who dived under her arm, wrenching the celery from her grasp and throwing it out the window.

CHAPTER 48

Charlie kicked off his boots and sauntered in through the flywire door. He stood in his socks in the kitchen, his black hair sticking out at all angles, his square jawline dark with stubble. His face was tanned, highlighting his green eyes. His shirt was rumpled and jeans grimy with machinery oil and red dust. Glen was at the kitchen table reading a copy of *Machinery Deals*, wearing a neatly ironed work shirt. His mother was in a powder-blue dressing-gown, carefully dishing out eggs onto two bits of toast. It was a sunny Saturday morning. Saturday was the day that Mrs Lewis allowed herself to rise an hour later and to get dressed after breakfast. She shuffled about in pink towelling slides on the lino.

'Would you like some breakfast, dear?' she asked, not looking up. 'I've just made some eggs for your brother.'

'No thanks, Mum,' Charlie said. 'I'm on my way to town. Just called in to see if you needed anything.'

Mrs Lewis's mouth formed a thin line. She knew her son was headed for the pub again, that he wouldn't be back until tomorrow, when he would arrive with smoke and alcohol reeking from his skin. He would then shut himself away in his cottage, to sleep or watch sport, instead of coming with them to church.

'No, thanks dear, I think we're right for milk. I'm doing a big shop on Monday anyway.'

'Righto, see you later then.'

'You're not going to town like that, are you?' Mrs Lewis had her back to Charlie as she ran water into the frypan to soak it. Charlie looked down at his clothes wondering how she knew what he was wearing if she hadn't even looked up at him.

'I'll iron some trousers and a shirt for you.'

'No Mum. I'll be right,' he said almost angrily. She turned, looking hurt. Glen tipped sauce on his eggs and began to chew on his toast.

'You don't want to come too, Glen?' asked Charlie, knowing the answer already.

'No thanks,' Glen said after he'd finished chewing. 'I want to service my bike, then give it a run out the back paddocks.'

'Righto. Have fun. See you.' Charlie turned, almost running into his father who had just come in from his weekly ritual of reading for half an hour on the toilet before his cooked Saturday breakfast.

'Seeya Dad,' Charlie said as he quickly bolted out the door. He scooped up his boots and headed for his ute. He had to get out of there.

With his younger brother, Glen, home from school for good, things had changed a lot for Charlie. His mother now almost ignored him, fussing instead over Glen. It was obvious she was so glad to have one of her boys back in the house that she mostly overlooked Charlie's decline.

After Rebecca had left, Charlie had insisted that he live in the cottage, despite his mother's protests. It gave him time to be alone with his grief, anger and confusion. It also gave him more freedom to come and go. He'd work hard all week for his father, then on weekends wipe himself out at the pub, or the golf club, or a party in the town hall. The next day, still drunk, he'd drive home recklessly, weaving along the single lane of bitumen highway, knocking guideposts sideways and fishtailing on gravel. His party animal persona now emerged every weekend, not just every now and then as it had done in the past.

He spent his Sundays lying on the couch in the cottage beneath the ceiling fan, feeling trashed.

Most weekends he'd pick up a pen and write long letters to Rebecca, but as the months passed Charlie felt a cloud settle over him. A damp, dark cloud that shut out the vision of Rebecca. Eventually the words were too painful to write. Writing her name hurt. The thought of her hurt. Time distanced her from him, so that soon all he clung to were the weekly binges on the grog. Drunken nights with glimpses of euphoria as he sung with his mates and danced on tables. Sometimes his mates called in with more beers and the house came to resemble the roughest of jackeroo quarters, his mother no longer able to bear facing the mess. Occasionally his father said a few things as he walked into the stifling, stale-smelling cottage on Monday mornings when Charlie was too sick to work. His father looking disapprovingly at the empty stubbys and his pale-faced son.

With Glen home, the pressure for Charlie to be the model son had eased. Glen was their golden boy. He didn't like drinking much, he was obsessed with machinery and cropping so had no desire to be any-where else in this world, and what's more, he was going out with one of the churchgoing daughters of Mr and Mrs Lewis's friends. The relationship had blossomed last year after the church fete when Glen and Kathlene had been asked to stack the chairs and fold the trestle tables. He had taken her out for Chinese at the RSL and since then the relationship had slipped easily into the routine lives of both families.

With Glen taking on much of his workload, Charlie felt his passion for the farm slipping away, and with Rebecca gone he simply went through the motions of it all as he tried to convince himself he was happy. Driving tractors, drinking, playing footy, partying hard with his mates, loads of freedom. An ideal life, he told himself.

As he drove along the road towards town he sent the grey galahs flying up to the limbs of thirsty-looking gum trees. They sat with their dusty pink bellies, squawking after the ute that had just revved by.

Charlie drove towards the sixty kilometre speed

sign, not bothering to slow down. He knew Arnie, the potbellied policeman, was helping out with the Kanga cricket clinic in the next town. He was about to pull up outside the pub when he remembered their Eftpos machine was broken. He hazily recalled immersing it in a jug full of beer last week. Rog had stood behind the bar with an angry look on his face, while Charlie threw his bank card at him and said sheepishly, 'I'll pay for it'; then he'd remembered that he needed the machine to get the money out. This fact sent him into convulsions of laughter that doubled him over so that he found himself on the floor of the pub, clutching his stomach. He was sure when Rog came to haul him up off the floor that there was a small hint of a smile in the corner of Rog's mouth. Charlie was, after all, his best customer and, in Rog's words, 'a funny bastard'. Now, a week later, the new Eftpos machine was yet to arrive.

Charlie drove past the pub and pulled up outside the general store. He leapt out of the vehicle and clattered through the screen door, sending the string of bells tinkling. Janine was there behind the counter, reading a magazine.

'Morning, Basil,' she said flirtily, while straightening up, pulling in her stomach and pushing out her breasts.

'Going to the pub today?' she asked, knowing full well he was. She rolled her eyes. 'We don't shut until seven tonight, so I'll be late.'

'Bummer,' said Charlie, quite relieved she wouldn't be shadowing him at the pub today.

'Ahh, can I get a bucket of chips, two dim sims, a potato cake and . . . um . . . that'll do me.'

'Haven't had breakfast yet?' She moved to the counter, clicking her tongs together as she tossed chips into a paper cup. As she put the dim sims and potato cakes into brown paper bags Charlie shoved his hands into his pockets and sauntered over to the magazine and newspaper stand. Most of the magazines curled over, dog-eared, dusty and out of date. The newest arrivals sat at the front of the stand next to the weekend papers. A glossy magazine caught his eye.

He began to flip through it. There were stories on 'beaut utes', bull catching and an organic pig farm.

'There you go,' said Janine, as she sat his bags of greasy food on the counter.

'Can I grab a milkshake too?' asked Charlie.

A vehicle pulled up outside and Charlie looked up at the sound to see a ute with kelpies chained to the back. His heart skipped a beat. They were well-bred, glossy-coated dogs. A red and tan with a broad nose, and two black and tans with finer features. Being a cropping area, only a few people bothered carting dogs about with them, and most of the working dogs were of the Heinz variety – a mix of this and that, accidentally bred, and only half willing to work. It was rare to see such fine creatures in the town. Dogs like Rebecca's.

The tall man got out of the ute, walked into the store and waited for Janine to turn off the noisy machine which frothed Charlie's milkshake. He handed over some notes as he asked for some tobacco and papers. Then he turned, nodded at Charlie and walked out of the shop.

Charlie watched, the magazine still in his hand, as the man drove off down the street, the dogs wagging their tails and turning their noses to the wind. He wondered if the dogs were related to Bec's.

Charlie sighed sadly and turned back to look at the magazine. There on the page was Rebecca. Smiling, sitting up on her horse, her golden hair falling out from under her hat. Charlie's mouth fell open and a shiver ran right through him.

'Is that all?' Janine asked with her head cocked to the side.

Her voice snapped Charlie out of his reverie.

'I'll take this, and a paper and two hundred bucks cash out.' He drummed his fingers impatiently on the counter as she swiped the card.

'I've been running out of cash since you buggered the pub's Eftpos. I can only give you fifty bucks.'

'Fine,' said Charlie. When she had handed him his card and cash back, he tucked the magazine and the newspaper under his arm and, juggling his milkshake and bags, bustled out of the store, barely able to contain his anticipation at reading the article on Rebecca.

He stopped the ute under a peppertree and got out, dumping his food and magazine onto the paint-chipped picnic table. Beside the roadside park the irrigation channel swirled past a rusty crooked sign which said, 'No swimming'. He sat, opened the magazine and drank her in. Reading every word, rereading the article again and again. Staring at her eyes, her smile, her hands. Running his finger over the shape of her. He looked sadly at the photo of Dags. He even missed her dogs.

He scrunched his eyes, ashamed to feel tears coming to them. He shut the magazine. By the time he ate his chips, they were cold. He chewed them slowly as he read the rural newspaper, trying to resist the temptation of again opening the magazine to look at her. When he reached the employment section in the paper his eyes scanned over the ads for jobs. Then he saw it. He read it again. Goosebumps shivered his flesh. He leapt up and ran for his ute.

Mrs Lewis was stunned to see Charlie driving back from town just two hours after he had left. He didn't go to the cottage like normal. Instead he crashed into the kitchen with an excited look in his eye.

'Mum,' he said, 'I need to use the computer.'

'What on earth for?' asked Mrs Lewis, frowning, wiping her hands on a tea towel and following him down the hallway into the farm office.

CHAPTER 49

From the window of Sally's office Rebecca watched the traffic rush by on the street below. Her friend tried again.

'Come on, Bec.'

She turned towards Sally with her blue eyes wide and said again, 'No, no, no. *No!*'

'*Yes!*' said Sally through gritted teeth.

'You said I had to come to town to sign an export contract, not to interview potential employees! You lied to me.'

Sally sighed and spread her hands on her desk. 'Bec, it's for your own good and it's for the good of the business. You can't keep going on like this. If I told you the truth, you wouldn't have agreed to do it. If you weren't such a workaholic, you would've given yourself time to read the papers. You would've seen the job advertised. It pays to be informed in business, you know.'

'And where do you suggest we house a new manager? Especially one with a family?'

'Look, that's just minor details. Your dad suggested we build another cabin, or there's plenty of room in –'

'You spoke to my dad about this!'

'Of course I did. He helped me word the ad. Of course he agrees. He can't keep up with you. You and your dad need a crop and irrigation manager.'

Rebecca sighed and slumped into a chair. 'Fine . . . You're always right, Sally Carter.'

'Bloody headstrong woman,' Sally muttered back.

Rebecca sat in a stormy silence, glowering at the string of contenders who, one by one, entered the room for the job of irrigation and cropping manager. Sometimes she asked impossible questions and at other times she refused to participate and instead stood staring out the window. The same scenario ran through her head. She pictured herself clashing with the new manager. He'd resent being bossed by a young woman, he'd take away her privacy, he'd have a wife and noisy kids. He'd be cruel to animals. He'd be a sleaze or a peeping Tom. She felt as though her world would be invaded. Yet part of Rebecca knew Sally was right. She needed someone not only with brains but with brawn. Already she had hidden the fact that her shoulder permanently ached and her back gave her trouble at night. Physically, emotionally and mentally, the past couple of years at Waters Meeting had been so very hard. Even though her family were supporting her, and Sally was so devoted, she still felt the responsibility weighing down upon her. She missed being carefree and casual. Nights out at parties, dancing till the sun came up at B&Ss. She knew Sally was right, but she was determined to resist the invasion of anyone who wasn't perfect.

After the fourth applicant hitched up his pants over his massive gut and exited the room, Rebecca growled at Sally, 'And if we hired him, where do you plan to put him? With me in the house?'

'I told you, there are options. I've investigated kit homes. They're within budget.'

'Oh, you've got it all sussed – you and your bloody budget! I don't believe you're doing this to me.'

'Put up and shut up! Now are you going out to get the next applicant or am I?'

Sally looked at Rebecca's stormy face and threw her hands in the air. 'Alright! I'll go. Here, take a look at his CV – he's got great qualifications; in fact, I think you'll find he's exactly what you've been looking for.'

She tossed the black folder on Rebecca's lap. Instead of reading it, Bec busied herself with cleaning out her nails with a paperclip. She didn't even look up when the next applicant came in.

'Take a seat,' Rebecca heard Sally's smooth, smiling voice say. Sally stalked around the room on her long elegant legs and took her position behind the desk.

'I'm glad you had a good trip down. Now, we've looked over your CV and your qualifications are wonderful, but can you tell us why you really want a job with this sour-faced grumpy old biddy in the corner there?'

Rebecca look up from her nail cleaning.

'Well,' began the applicant, 'because I love her.'

A tingle ran through Rebecca's whole body when

she saw Charlie sitting in the chair. He flashed her a broad smile and said, 'Hello, Bec.'

'Charlie!' He looked better than in her dreams. His hair was freshly cut, he was wearing a suit. She'd never seen him in a suit and he looked gorgeous. His skin so brown against the white of his shirt. The greens in his tie highlighting his eyes. The jacket falling over his broad shoulders. Hands, big tanned hands, clasped in front of him. Rebecca felt the blush run to her cheeks as she took in the delicious sight of him.

Then they were both suddenly standing, walking towards one another. She put her arms up around his neck and pulled him to her. His smell, the feel of him swamping her as love flooded back into her soul. She lifted her head up towards his face, looked deep into his eyes and they kissed.

She broke away from him for a moment as the situation sunk in. She turned and stared at Sally.

'You knew! You knew! And you put me through all those other interviews! You've known for a week or more!'

Sally just grinned and shrugged. 'You deserved it.'

She turned back to Charlie and felt the tears and the laughter come at once. 'You utter bastards!'

Then she kissed him passionately again, drinking in all of him. Never wanting to let him go ever again. And he drank in her. The warmth of her, the strength of her, that soft golden hair and her strong sensual hands. Rebecca and Charlie kissing again, feeling the river washing over them.

Rebecca pulled back, putting her hands up to touch his face, laughing through tears, then kissing him deeply again and again.

At last Sally cleared her throat. 'Err . . . does this mean he's got the job?'

CHAPTER 50

Droplets from the Rebecca River landed on Hank's chestnut shoulders as the gelding plunged into the water. Charlie, wearing only a faded pair of jeans and a large battered Akubra hat, sat upon him and laughed and leaned forward. With a huge hand he scooped the water into a shimmering series of splashes towards Rebecca.

Ink Jet tossed her head beneath the falling drops and Bec laughed as she felt the cool river water land on her tanned legs. She was wearing denim shorts and a singlet, and riding Ink Jet bareback. She laughed and screamed a little as the horses spun in the water and threw their heads. She was laughing so hard she thought she might slip from Inky's back. Charlie grabbed her arm and threatened to pull her from the horse into the water. She threw him a flirtatious look and urged her horse to a canter out of the water and up the riverbank. Charlie followed on Hank, watching Rebecca's hair fly.

Across the lucerne paddock she cantered, letting out mock screams, looking back over her shoulder until she pulled Inky to an abrupt halt under the giant boom of the pivot irrigator. Rebecca jumped from the mare and Inky dropped her head and began to tear at the sweet soft leaves and purple flowers of the lucerne. Charlie arrived, laughing, a moment later, cantering up on Hank.

'I was just coming to check on your pivot, Miss Boss Lady,' he said in a Texan accent. 'I'd say the crop's lookin' mighty fine to me, ma'am.'

'Why yes, I do believe it is,' she said genteelly, 'Perhaps though, it could do with a little more waterin'.'

Charlie slid from the horse with a twinkle in his eye. 'Allow me, ma'am.'

He strode over to the box which contained the irrigator's computer. He pressed a series of buttons so that soon water sped along the pipes and a fine spray shot out of its nozzles. He wrapped his arms around Rebecca and dragged her into the spray.

In the gentle afternoon sunlight Rebecca and Charlie let the water wash over them as they kissed. She pressed her breasts to his naked torso and looked up into his eyes, smiling. Then Rebecca pulled Charlie down into a soft forest of sweet smelling lucerne that grew at the foot of the mountains. Waters Meeting. Their place.

ACKNOWLEDGEMENTS

This book wouldn't be here without the love and support of my husband, John. In 1999 he took me to outback Queensland for a year so I had some space to begin this book. He convinced me we could survive on love alone – plus lots of station beef. Thanks also to Dougall, my dearest (canine) friend, who was by my side for eight years, but tragically died from snakebite before the last word was typed and before the last sheep was shorn. Thanks to my other dogs, Gippy, Diamond, Alfred, Taxi and Stubby who spent far too long on their chains while I was shut inside the house writing.

Joe Bugden from the Tasmanian Writers' Centre and my writing mentor, Robyn Friend, provided the next step in the novel's development and without their wonderful direction, the first draft may never have been completed.

On the home front, a big 'cheers' to cousin Jamie and Michelle for providing a farm cottage on rental rates that matched my writer's income. And to cousin Doug and Louise for making me realise I wasn't the only person in the valley with vague and strange creative behaviour!

Credit to my friend Margareta for brainstorming outrageous plots as we bombed around Queensland in the Falcon, and to my mates Steph, Sarah, Wooks, Debbie Lee, Mev and the Woodsdale Footy Club girls who have shown me just how far a girl will go to have fun.

Thanks to mum, Jenny, for crying and laughing (in the right places) while reading the first draft and to dad, Val, for help with the serious business bits. To my brother, Miles, who always made time for me and his wife, Dr Kristy – thanks for your medical know-how.

To my in-laws, thank you Doug and Mary for your great response after reading the first draft and for your ongoing encouragement with my writing career despite the fact John and I should've been in Victoria fencing or marking calves for you. Thanks also to Sharon and Rob for your love and support. To sister Anna and Pete, brother Ben and Fiona, Paul and Kate . . . you simply rock!

Truck loads of thanks to the fantastic crew at Penguin including Clare Forster, Rebecca Steinberg, Cathy Larsen and many, many others behind the scenes, including Joe from despatch who gave me a great warehouse tour. My baptism into the publishing world has been a pleasure because of you all. Also thanks to my Queensland editor, Julia Stiles, for her professionalism, humour and inspirational use of the yellow sticky note.

Big hugs to fellow dog-lover and photographer, Bill Bachman, for capturing such a beautiful cover shot and thanks to Sally Bachman for her hard work in the home office. To my good looking mates Chris Stoney, Rachel Parsons, Mahogany the horse and Froggy the dog, thanks for your modelling skills. Thanks also to Lee Kernaghan and Tony Parsons for your generosity and goodwill.

Lastly, this book was written for all the wonderful farming women and men who I have met, lived and partied with over the years. I thank you for your inspiration and your strength. Agriculture rules!

This novel was written with assistance from both the Tasmanian Writers' Centre and the Australia Council; the Federal Government's peak arts funding and advisory body.

Also by Rachael Treasure

The Stockmen

Rosie Highgrove-Jones grows up hating her double-barrelled name. She dreams of riding out over the wide plains of the family property, working on the land. Instead she's stuck writing the social pages of the local paper.

Then a terrible tragedy sparks a series of shocking revelations for Rosie and her family. As she tries to put her life back together, Rosie throws herself into researching the haunting true story of a 19th century Irish stockman who came to Australia and risked his all for a tiny pup and a wild dream. Is it just coincidence when Rosie meets a sexy Irish stockman of her own? And will Jim help her realise her deepest ambitions – or will he break her heart?

The Stockmen moves effortlessly between the present and the past to reveal a simple yet hard-won truth – that both love and the land are timeless . . .

'*I loved this honest and heartfelt tale of life on the land – it captures the very essence of being Australian.*' Tania Kernaghan

The Call of the High Country

TONY PARSONS

In the heart of Australia's rugged high country, three generations of the MacLeod family battle to make a living on the land. As a young married couple, Andrew and Anne work together to make the very best of their property, High Peaks, but at what cost to their happiness? In time the property will pass to their son, David. Handsome and hardworking, he is determined to become the best sheepdog handler in the land. Nothing is going to stand in his way – not even the beautiful Catriona Campbell, daughter of the wealthy grazier next door. An inspiring and heartwarming saga of a family battling through hard times, of a love that defies all odds, and of dreams that won't be broken.

Return to the High Country

TONY PARSONS

In the beginning there had only been High Peaks, the MacLeod family property in the heart of Australia's rugged high country. Andrew and Anne MacLeod struggled on the land to give David, their only son and heir, a better life.

Wracked by grief following his father's death, David is determined to succeed. With the MacLeod love of the land running in his blood, and the beautiful Catriona at his side, he builds an impressive empire of gazing properties for the sons he hopes will follow him.

But grooming a suitable heir proves as challenging and heartbreaking as rural life itself. It is David's passion for his beloved high country, and the support of the women in his life, that keep his dream alive.

Here is a story that will transport you to the heartland of Australia's bush and keep you spellbound till the very last page.